Happy Reading

[signature]

DYNAMIC ENTRY

Fiona Morgan

Artemis Publishing Company,
Tennessee

DYNAMIC ENTRY
Published in the United States of America

By Artemis Publishing Company
P.O. Box 633
Springfield, Tennessee 37172 USA
https://www.artemispublishingco.com
Copyright 2019 by Fiona Morgan

ISBN: 978-2-7339944-3-9

ACKNOWLEDGMENTS

The idea for Dynamic Entry came about during a conversation as I researched 'What's Mine' and it bided its time until it demanded to be written.

I love watching my characters come to life, their own personalities shining through, and this has been the case more so with Sophie and her love of cars and my love of cars. This brings me nicely onto my first thank you, and that is to my dad.

Thank you for helping me pick out the cars in this story as well as giving me my love of cars, teaching me about them, and of course, fixing them for me.

Now to my mum. Thank you for keeping me right on court proceedings and asking my questions to the girls in the Witness Service in Airdrie Sheriff Court, and any of the lawyers you managed to catch. All the information was much appreciated, and any mistakes are my own or have been smudged to fit. Thank you for being my Sunday crossword buddy, now if only we could remember all those answers!

Gary and Eveline, thank you both again. Gary for all the research, letting me ask all my weird questions and answering them so fully, and thankfully with the right answers that I needed.

Eveline, thank you again for letting me use your character, I love her and you.

Jim, thank you for all your answers to my questions, your time and advice was much appreciated.

Ben, thank you for letting me use your name again.

Louise, I used your name, I hope you don't mind, and Niamh and Emma I will get your names in the next one.

Erin and Sian, thank you for letting me use your names for characters and thank you for being as amazing as you both are. Dad and I love you both so much.

Not quite last, and never least, thank you, Liam. You continue to support my dream of writing, helping me visualize things and spell far too many words as well as supporting me when my head is playing up on me, so thank you for everything and I love you always.

To my editor, Diane Gilmore, and to all my readers, thank you, thank you, thank you!

Oh, and before I forget, thank you to all my Twitter Tribes, I love you all!

DEDICATION

To my girls, Erin & Sian.

Thank you for being you.

Love always, Mum

PROLOGUE

3 Years Earlier

Sophie stands in her Chief Superintendent's office on the top floor of the Northumbria Police Headquarters in Tyne and Wear and scrunches her hands into fists, feeling the bite of her fingernails in her palm. The sting reminds her to breathe, keep her eyes trained straight ahead, and to hold her tongue. The summer sun is streaming in through the floor to ceiling window, but it's not the heat from the sun that's starting to make her hot under the collar of her starched to within an inch of its life, crisp white shirt; it's the anger bubbling under her skin that's doing that.

Her boss is talking about how she'd outdone herself on her assignment. An assignment she'd been on for nine months, an assignment that she'd had to go undercover as a private car salesperson, with the premise of being a gun seller and ended up acting as a drug dealer. Where she ended up having to circumvent the self-appointed leader of the gang's unwanted sexual advances towards her by using the 'don't mix business with pleasure' excuse at every turn and always making sure they were in a public place. Jason Hamilton was a tall light brown-haired, brown-eyed, sculpted Adonis of a man, but he knew it and he was arrogant with it. He was also dangerous with little scruples, even fewer morals, and not Sophie's type. Even if he wasn't a criminal being investigated.

Her boss clears his throat bringing Sophie back to the office and her anger back to the forefront of her mind.

"Now, Sophie," He says, with his put-on, privately educated London accent and smarmy smile. "I am under the impression that the information you gathered

1

and provided the team with over the past nine months has been somewhat, invaluable. Now I know I wasn't fully behind the plan to send you in to infiltrate that gang." Her superior puts his hands in the air as if to admit a mistake. "Yes, I thought there were more suitable officers for the job, namely a male officer."

Sophie bristles at his words and digs her fingernails into her palms again, as her boss continues to talk. "But I was somehow convinced or maybe I was overruled, and you got the assignment."

Sophie could feel the dislike her superior had for her palpable in the air around them, and if it was something as simple as a personality clash, she could find some professional respect for the man, but it wasn't. His dislike for her stemmed from his archaic, sexist views of women in the police force, and what made Sophie worse was she is a woman with a brain, working and succeeding at dangerous 'man's' work. She would like to think that his type of attitude had been left in the twentieth century, but apparently not. Some of the dinosaurs made it through. She inwardly berates herself for thinking that way. She feels it's unfair on the actual now extinct dinosaurs, they didn't deserve to be connected to such a horrid human.

"So," he continued, "now that you are finished with the assignment, are you sure you got away clean?"

Sophie opens her mouth to answer but her boss talks over her. "What I mean by that is, was your cover blown? You know, did anybody discover that you were a police officer? That you were infiltrating them?"

Another squeeze of her fists, welcoming the bite of her fingernails, again. "I understand the concept of getting away clean, sir, and yes, I got out clean," Sophie replied. "I told them I had to leave on a business trip for a few months. I explained that I had to do more research and acquire more information on a new client that I was hoping to sign. The bust is going down next month, so there will have been enough time between me leaving and the arrests being made for there to be no suspicion thrown onto me. My squad is clever like that." She smiles sweetly at the old dinosaur while fighting the sarcastic tone in her voice and the roll of her light, silvery blue eyes.

"Yes, I understand the men looking out for you were extremely diligent at keeping you safe."

Another fight with her eyes for them to remain unrolled. "That they did, sir, and a fine job they did, too!"

Her boss gives her a sharp nod. "Now, I have been informed that you wish to make a transfer back up to Scotland, is that correct?"

Sophie takes a deep breath. She is desperate to get back to her home city of Glasgow, back to where the weather was mostly grey and when the sun did shine, people removed their tops even though the temperature hadn't quite made it into double figures (sun is oot, taps is aff!). She loved how the gruffness of a voice could still convey happiness and the unique sense of humour only Glasgow could get away with. A life-size model skeleton climbing up a building with nothing but a hard hat on, how could that not be funny? She pushes aside her memories. "Yes, sir. Well, my work here was due to reassignment, so…"

Her boss mumbles something about him not being involved in that decision then looks up fully at Sophie for the first time since she walked into his office.

"Well Ms. Pearsons, I feel that sometimes your presence in my station has been something of an interference. Some of my other officers have had to take a back seat and have not been able to show off their skills as you have been, shall I say, persuasive in putting your services forward. So for that reason, amongst others, I will personally ensure your reassignment is moved back up to your own kind in Glasgow. Pitt Street is it?"

Sophie manages a nod. Her blood boiled in her veins at the man's words and tone.

He went on. "Then my men can get back to doing what they do best, active policing instead of sitting in the back of cars watching out for someone who can't look out for themselves." Her boss makes a disgusted sound at the back of his throat and Sophie clenches her fists more as she also clenches her teeth. If she didn't get out of this office soon, she is going to break the skin on her palms, break her teeth or break her boss' face with her fists or head, (she is from Glasgow, why not go with the cliché of a Glasgow kiss?)

Her superior looks up from the paperwork again. "Ms. Pearsons, what are you doing still standing in my office? Go and empty any desk you have and your locker and go back to Scotland."

A grin erupts on Sophie's face. "Right away, Sir!" She fights the urge to salute the archaic, sexist excuse for a senior officer. Instead, she thanks her lucky stars and leaves the room. In the locker room, she does a happy dance.

She's going home.

CHAPTER ONE

Present Day

Sitting in the darkest corner of what seems to be the filthiest pub in Glasgow city centre, Sophie and Belle sip their pints of lager and settle in to watch the very drunk ned who is making a show of throwing his money about, telling anyone who was listening and everyone who wasn't, how he made all his hard earned cash by driving a few packages about, and he couldn't believe how easy it all was. "I mean," he snorts at the black-haired goth hanging off his every word, "all I hid to dae was pick up a wee box, well I say a wee box, it wis a boot yon size." The ned motions with his hands to show a space that was about eight inches by eight inches. "And then I dropped it aff at this pure huge hoose."

The ned was on a roll with his story and was ignoring the warning looks he was getting from the barman. He was too busy enjoying the attention from the young goth at his side. "I swear to god, I widnae hiv been surprised if a butler hid opened the door, it was that fancy. But there wisnae a butler, just —"

The barman takes his opportunity to interrupt the ned's tale before he gave away too much information. "Right, you! I think that's enough talk. May I suggest you shut yir trap, finish yir pint, and then git tae fuck!" The ned turns to the barman, amusement dancing in his eyes. "I canny finish my pint if my gub is shut, kin I?"

Dynamic Entry

The goth sitting next to the ned snorts out a laugh then promptly becomes silent when the barman shoots her a look so hard it could set her to stone.

He turns his attention back to the ned. "You need to shut that flappin' smart arse mouth of yours and leave before I do it all for you." Sophie can see the anger building in the barman's stance and hear the warning in his tone. The information hound in her wanted the ned to continue with his story, but the human in her desperately hoped he would shut up before he got himself hurt, or worse, killed.

The ned snorted out a drunken laugh. "Aye, right auld man, you and whit army? You canny hurt me. I work for Ja —" Before the ned could say anything else, two Neanderthal men walk forward and stand closer to the ned than any lover would be and place a crushing hand on each shoulder.

The barman smirks. "I know who you work for, ya wee shite. That's why I'm telling you to shut the fuck up. I was trying to help you, but then you were a cheeky wee bastard to me, so now I just want rid of ye, so, my security officials here are going to see you safely from the premises." The Neanderthals grab an arm each and frog march the ned to the door, depositing him roughly out onto the street. Closing the door behind them, the security officials turn to Sophie and Belle and mumble an apology about the disturbance. Belle assures them there was no problem and the women go back to drinking their pints.

Belle turns to Sophie who has gone very quiet and lost what little colour she had. "You okay? You look like you've seen a ghost."

Sophie drags her eyes to her best friend and work colleague.

"Was he just about to say Jason?" she asks.

Belle squints her eyes at Sophie in confusion "Eh, maybe. He only got J-A out, so I don't know. Do you know a J-A or a Jason?"

Sophie shrugs. "Maybe. Let's finish up here, we're not going to get anything more tonight." Belle agrees and they finish their pints, then slip out the door.

The next morning on shift, Belle corners Sophie in the cafeteria. She sat across from her with a cup of coffee. "You okay Soph? You took off quickly last night."

Sophie plays with her mug of cold tea and gazes over her friend's shoulders. She'd spent the rest of the night after she got home trying to convince herself that there was more than one gun-running drug dealer called Jason in the world, and that the one she knew from her undercover work lived in England, and if other people had done their job properly, he would be in jail down there too since she had given them enough evidence to put him away for a long time.

Belle places her hand on Sophie's, bringing her back to the present day. "Something you need to talk about?" Belle's soft tone and kind eyes make Sophie smile.

"Aye, unfortunately, there is, and to the boss too."

Belle's eyebrows scrunch together. "It's something and nothing, I hope."

Sophie takes a sip of her tea giving herself a moment's peace before giving voice to her fears, then grimaces as the cold liquid hits her taste buds and slides down her throat. "Urgh, that's disgusting!"

Belle gives her friend a look to tell her to hurry up with the explaining.

"Okay, okay," Sophie begins. "The last assignment I was on down South involved a self-appointed 'leader of the gang'. He was a total prick. Arrogant, smarmy, a right Mr. Smooth. Unfortunately, he had the good looks — I mean like Greek god Adonis type of good looks — to back it all up. The female population fell at his feet, and all guys wanted to be him, so he managed to get away with things us mere mortals would be hung for."

Belle is nodding as she listens. "And?"

"And he was a very dangerous man whose name was Jason Hamilton and he didn't get sent down!"

The penny drops with Belle. "Ah, and that ned last night said the start of a name that sounded like Jason," she says. Sophie nods. Her brows crease. "But I thought that group got busted, and wasn't that in England?"

More nodding from Sophie. "Aye, in Northumbria, but the idiots down there botched up the raid and they never pinned anything on him. I'm guessing the case fell apart after that. I was already back up here so they never gave me any of the details." She blows out a stressed breath before talking again. "Now I know the odds that the ned was going to say Jason, and that that Jason would be the same one from down there must be like a zillion to one, but my gut still clenched."

Belle looks thoughtful for a second, then nods. She's learned to listen to Sophie's gut. "You are going tell the boss at the briefing this morning?" she asks.

"Aye, I am, but not in front of everyone. I'll leave the embarrassment of being called paranoid between him and me."

"And me!" Belle nods. She grins and it lifts Sophie from her worry for a second.

"Oh, okay and you." The friends grin at each other, then rise from the table to make their way through to the incident room they are working from.

****

Fiona Morgan

Standing behind the counter in the elegant Saltire Jewelers in the iconic Argyle Arcade, and holding out two diamond engagement rings, Ross paints a smile on his face. Normally he loves selling diamonds in the jewelry store he works in, especially when it involves engagements and lovers. Ross is a romantic at heart, especially if he is serving a couple who are genuinely in love, or the relationship he is in with someone feels like it could be 'the forever one'. Although his best friend, Sean, said that he felt like that with every girl he went with.

Unfortunately, the couple standing in front of him was not genuinely in love. The guy was trying his hardest at impressing his soon to be fiancée by trying to push up the size of the diamond, which means he's pushing up the price at the same time. The female was making a good show of saying she didn't need the flamboyant ring even though her eyes and body language said otherwise. The way she was making eyes at Ross and letting her fingers linger on his as she takes rings from him to try on made Ross think she had no intention of getting married or being faithful if they did make it that far.

"Can I try the square one on?"

Ross nods with a smile as he takes the Brilliant Cut diamond solitaire from her slender finger and brings out the ring that was asked for. "This is a 2.5 carat Princess Cut solitaire. Its colour is E which is colourless and is IF, which means internally flawless on the clarity scale. It's set in claws in a platinum band.

The female oohs and aahhs and the male swallows, hard. "How much is this one?" The female asks as she turns her hand this way and that letting the almost immaculate diamond catch the bright spotlights above them.

"This one comes in at £9999."

Dynamic Entry

The female's eyes sparkle and the male covers up a cough. Ross grins and continues. "And it's a perfect fit for the lady, saving the gentleman money as there will be no sizing involved."

Another sound of panic comes from the guy.

"I love this one! Can I get this one, darling?" The female makes puppy dog eyes at her boyfriend who quickly smiles. His bravado earlier about money being no object had left him at hearing the price.

"If that's the one you that'll make you happy, sweetness," He says tightly, "then that's the one you shall have." She grins again then slips the ring from her finger, pressing it into Ross' hand and squeezes. "Can you wrap it nicely, please? Ribbons and bows and things?"

Ross tries to smile, but it comes out more of a grimace. The female still hasn't let go of his hand and was caressing it, shivers run up his spine as he pulls his hand from hers.

"You have a choice of two boxes." He brings out the two boxes. One is a classic wooden ring box with the initials 'SJ' hand engraved in the lid and the other was an antique looking glass box.

The female makes a face of disgust, neither of them seemed to be up to her standard. "What, no ribbons?"

Ross shakes his head. "No, we prefer simple, classic and beautiful here at Saltire Jewellers." The female picks the glass box and Ross goes to polish up the ring and gets it all boxed. Once everything is packed up, he goes back to the happy couple asking how they would like to pay for their purchase. The answer that comes back has Ross biting the inside of his cheek.

"Eh, over three credit cards if that's okay?"

Ross nods his head and starts the transaction.

Five minutes later the couple, consisting of one happy female and a male now in ten grand worth of debt, have left and Ross is standing in the staff room pulling on his jacket.

"Thank fuck that's over!" he says.

His boss, who is having her lunch looks up from her sandwich. "Hard sale?"

"Well, kinda, but they spent ten grand."

Her eyes widen. "Go you."

He gives her a comical bow. "Why, thank you. It wasn't so much as a hard sale as an expensive break up gift. Either he's going to dump her for getting him into ten grand's worth of debt then cheating, or she's dumping him now she had the ring and moving onto the next stupid sod."

"Awe, it's not like you to be so cynical, but I'll believe you. You have this creepy thing about couples."

Ross laughs. "It's not creepy. They give me vibes and I just know if they'll work out or not. Anyway, it worked with you and yours, did it not?"

His boss smiles and pats her small bump. "Yes, it did and thank you again. Now where you going for lunch, The Pub?" Ross nods.

"Aye, best bar lunch around." He turns to leave when his boss shouts on him.

"Ross, tell me again, why did Sean name his bar The Pub?"

Ross gives a laugh and shrugs. "He couldn't be arsed thinking of a proper name for it." His boss shakes her head then says her goodbyes. Ross leaves the shop thankful for the hour away from the bright lights and the big band music of the jewelry shop.

Getting into The Pub on Mitchell Lane, Ross strides to the bar, saying hello to people as he goes. He perches on the bar stool he always sits at and orders his lunch and drink. His best friend and owner of the bar, Sean, comes out from the kitchen area to welcome his friend.

"All right pal, how's it goin'?" Ross looks up from the newspaper he had borrowed from behind the bar. The men have an easy friendship as they had grown up together from birth.

"Ah, so you're actually doing some work today then?"

Ross grins at his friend as Sean flicks with him a dish towel. "Aye, you cheeky git! I thought I'd better do something for my keep round here." Ross gives his friend a laugh. He knows how hard Sean works to keep his bar running smoothly and popular.

"You working tonight?"

Sean nods his head. "I'm afraid so. Next week is my monthly night off." The friends decide to meet for drinks for the next week and Sean goes back to work, leaving Ross to his newspaper and lunch.

Walking up to the bar Sophie stands next to Ross and orders drinks for her and Belle. At the sound of her voice, Ross turns his head to face her, at the same time his fork takes that moment to try and pierce a burnt chip, causing the chip to snap in two. With perfect comedic timing, one-half of the chip slides from the plate as the other, covered in brown sauce, ricochets from his plate and stabs Sophie's cheek. Her hand flies to her now sauce covered cheek as she turns in the direction of the offending flying object. Her eyes settle on Ross, whose hand is clamped to his mouth, letting his fork clatter to the plate.

"Oh god, I am so sorry." He mumbles through his fingers, his eyes, dancing with humour, locks on to Sophie's. "Wow!" he exclaims. His eyes turn to desire as he realizes he is looking at the most beautiful woman ever.

CHAPTER TWO

"Wow what?" Sophie tries to demand, but it comes out more like a query, as she wipes the brown sauce from her cheek with the napkin she'd snatched from Ross's hand. She's trying to look annoyed but is finding it difficult due to the look of lust in his dark navy-blue eyes. This was unlike her, she was a ball buster, not a weak female who swooned at a handsome face. But the person who had just assaulted her with a chip is extremely handsome looking with his light brown hair which is gelled into a perfect quiff and his slender physique making her think he isn't a gym nut but still likes to look after himself, and she can see the tail ends of a black and grey tattoo peeking out from the cuffs of his white shirt.

"Your eyes. They're amazing!"

Sophie can do nothing but stare at the handsome man, unsure what to do or say to the information she was receiving from him, which again is very unlike her. "Eh... thank you." She blushes and wonders why.

Ross smiles then flicks his eyes to her left hand then back to her face, trying to commit her features to memory. "You come here often?"

Sophie replaces the napkin back into his hand then stares at him slack jawed. "Did you really just ask me that?"

Heat rises in his face, making Ross think the top of his head may explode. Why he was channelling his inner teenager at that moment he wasn't sure.

"Apparently so. I'm sorry about… well, all of that, really."

Sophie nods and lifts her drink.

Ross desperately wants to say something wittier or more intelligent, but all he can do is watch the swish of honey blonde hair and the swing of Sophie's hips as she walks away from him. He snaps his mouth shut and swallows hard. He needs to get to know that woman.

Getting back to the table Sophie hands Belle her drink then takes her seat, making sure she is facing out towards the bar area. This was a habit she had gotten into as she was always on watch, but today it also helped her watch the handsome guy sitting at the bar.

Belle nods her head towards the bar. "What was all that about?"

"His chip went renegade on him and attacked me," Sophie says. "He laughed, and I think he apologised, then he hit me with a pickup line from the eighties." Belle's eyebrows go up in question. Sophie blushes again, and again she wonders why. "He asked if I came here often!" Belle squeals with laughter making Ross turn around in his seat to look over at them. His eyes find Sophie's and he smiles. She gives him a ghost of a smile back before making herself look elsewhere. She is sure he could see her blush. Belle, who can see her blush, looks between them like a person watching a tennis match.

"Wow, what was that?" asks Belle.

Sophie's head snaps to her friend. "What was what? There was nothing."

Belle nods her head knowingly. "Aye right, and I'm Santa Clause! He is sexy. You did notice how sexy he is, didn't you?" Belle eyes her friend again.

"Yes, I did… but, that doesn't matter; we are on an assignment so no time for sexiness. So you can keep your looks and thoughts to yourself."

"That's what you always say. All work and no sexiness make Sophie a boring, grumpy old mare!" Sophie glares at her friend, but Belle ignores the threat in the glare and continues talking.

"Anyway, what happened with the DI, and don't think I didn't notice that I wasn't invited to the confession. You said I could be there to witness the paranoia at work!" She pouts at Sophie then laughs.

The waitress comes to take their order. Once they are alone again Sophie starts to answer Belle's statements and questions.

"I do not always say that I was seeing that guy, what's his name not long ago." Belle rolls her eyes.

"That was over a year ago, but never mind what did the DI say?"

"Plus I am not a boring and grumpy old mare, you cheeky witch! But anyway, it was the boss's idea for you not to be involved... kinda." Belle gives her friend a withering look and a non-committal 'hmm'. "Well, he says I've to keep an eye out. I probably am being paranoid, but just in case to remember my pseudonym."

"You remember it all, it was three years ago." She looks about to make sure no-one was within hearing distance of them and dropped her voice lower just to be on the safe side.

"Aye, I tend to stay close to the truth, makes it easier for me to remember, but if and I mean if anything happens and it is Jason he'll know me as Sophie Peterson and I will refer to you as Ella if we are together."

Belle huffs. "What?"

"I hate being Ella. I dream of the day I can be someone exotic, like a, Mercedes." Sophie snorts out a laugh.

"Mercedes, really? Would you remember that name?" Belle shrugs. "And you know there would be no way in hell you'd be working with me with a name like that!" Belle shakes her head.

"You, my girl, are a car snob!"

"No, I'm not, I just don't do Mercs. I like my Jaguar too much." As the women discuss the rights and wrongs of Sophie's attitude towards cars, their lunch arrives and they tuck in, both of them making oohhs and aahhs at the deliciousness of the food.

Ross watches as Sophie laughs with her friend then watches some more when he sees her reaction to the food in her mouth. He knew the food Sean served in the bar was amazing but seeing the expressions on Sophie's face as she ate was making him hard. Sean took that moment to speak to his friend, making him jolt in his seat.

"See anything you like there, pal?" says Sean, arriving at his side.

Ross shoots his friend a look. "Aye, you know her?"

Sean looks over and shakes his head. "No really, I've seen them in a few times for lunch, but that's about it. She's sexy as hell, don't you think?"

"Aye, she is, and don't you even think about it, I'm planning on doing something about it." He brings his eyes back to Sean. "You're into brunettes! Eyes off the honey blonde."

Sean slaps his friend on the shoulder. "I'm talking about the brunette. Jealous much?" Ross feels his face heat up at the accusation but doesn't give Sean the satisfaction of an answer.

"So you're actually going to ask her out?" Sean continued. "Or are you going to sit there with your semi and wish?"

Ross swipes out at his friend, but Sean manages to sidestep it with a laugh. "Don't be crude about your customers, or me." He moves in his seat trying to find a more comfortable position. "Yes I'm going to ask her out, and I'm going to do it before I go back to work."

Sean lands his hand on Ross' shoulder. "Aye, right! Well, good luck my son. I need to get back to work, let me know if you need me to hold your hand." Ross flips him the middle finger and slides off the bar stool, walking towards the table where Sophie and Belle are sitting.

Sophie puts her fork and spoon down on her plate and groans. "Oh god, that was the best carbonara I have ever had."

Belle rolls her eyes. "It must've been, you never shut the hell up all through eating it. Honest to god I thought you were having an orgasm at one point."

"Ha ha, very funny. It was good, though."

Belle gives her a quick nudge under the table. "Don't look now, but your Mr. Sexy is coming up here. Wipe your chin." Sophie does as she's told whilst mumbling that he wouldn't be coming over to them, and she really believed that right up to the point where he is standing at their table looking straight at her like there was no one else in the entire bar.

"Hi, again. I'm Ross. I wanted to apologise again for what happened. You know, down there, with the, eh, chip." Ross could hear his heart hammering away in his ears, which he thought was a good thing as it drowned out the bumbling crap spewing out of his mouth.

"That's okay, no harm done." Sophie smiles up at him and tries not to look into his dark navy-blue eyes. They were the sort of eyes that were kind and cheeky and she wanted to stare into and get lost, but she didn't dare, she was working, and nothing came between her and her work.

"Thanks." Sophie can see Ross swallow, assuming he is trying to get his now-empty mind to work again. He starts to stammer again proving her thoughts to be correct. "I am, eh, headed back to work and I thought I would come and say hi." Belle watches the conversation between Ross and Sophie.

"Oh god this is embarrassing and just plain hard to watch," says Belle."

"Belle!" Sophie chastises her friend and Ross chuckles. "It probably is. I'm not very good at this." A silence envelops them. Ross clears his throat. "I was wondering if you'd like to get a drink with me, at some point?"

Sophie smiles a sad smile and starts to answer, but Belle interrupts her. "Of course she will. How does tonight sound? In here at, say, seven?" Sophie throws her friend a murderous look.

"Cool." Ross grimaces. Sophie holds back a snigger at his choice of words, realising the whole situation may have turned him back into his teenage self again. "That sounds great, but will you be here to talk for her?"

Belle laughs. "No, she'll manage that all by her own self. It's just the agreeing to have fun part she has difficulty with." Another dirty look is thrown Belle's way, but she just smiles at Sophie. "And I'm going to ignore the dirty looks she is throwing my way as I know she is really just a pussy cat."

Sophie can't help the growl that rises in her throat. "I'm sorry about my friend talking for me." Ross' face falls which sends a flutter through her heart. A feeling she's not used to. All of a sudden, she can't bring herself to say no to the sexy man standing in front of her, his face full of disappointment. There is also a shiver running down her spine telling her to take a chance. "I would love to meet you for a drink tonight."

Both Ross and Belle's eyebrows shoot up in surprise. "You would?" They both ask at the same time making Sophie laugh.

"Aye, I do, I mean I will, yes, so, seven in here?"

Ross nods enthusiastically. "Fantastic! I'll see you later then."

Sophie smiles and her heart gives another flutter at the happiness she sees in Ross' dark navy eyes. She shouldn't be feeling these things, nothing good comes from these feelings, and she is even liking them. They all mumble their goodbyes and Ross walks from The Pub.

****

Getting back to the station in Pitt Street, Belle slides up onto one of the desks in one of the brighter, cleaner investigating rooms and dangles her legs back and forth whilst looking through some of the paperwork about the case they were working on.

"You know, if that wee ned last night was talking about the Jason you know, that would be a huge jump forward in this case." Sophie spins on her heels, turning her back to the information wall she was looking at.

"That's not funny Belle!" Sophie's heart is pumping double time in her chest, she doesn't want to even think about that Jason.

"I'm not trying to be funny, it's the truth." Sophie knew what her friend and work colleague was saying was the truth, but the thought of the two cases being connected made her stomach turn. She hadn't enjoyed her time in Northumbria, and she enjoyed her time undercover working with Jason even less.

Dynamic Entry

He may have looked like a god, all smooth skin and rippling muscles, but that is where his god like similarities ended. He was evil. He had no scruples and even less morals. More than once Sophie had witnessed Jason having one of his customers on their knees with a gun to their head begging for mercy. Promising that they weren't the cops and they understood that if they spoke to anybody about Jason or his business that he would cut out their tongues. Then Jason would pull them to their feet, give them a 'man hug' with back slapping and jovial punching, telling them he believed them and that they must see his point of view. With his line of business, he could never be too careful.

By that time the customer was grateful the gun was away from their head and so was agreeing to anything and everything Jason was saying. It also helped Jason that his customers were desperate for his product of cocaine. There was a rumour that Jason had in fact cut out someone's tongue for talking back to him, but Sophie wouldn't be surprised if he had started the rumour himself. He loved the thought of people fearing him, and he loved boosting his reputation.

She looks up from her paperwork to see Belle staring at her intently.

"What?" Belle starts to swing her legs again.

"Why did you get picked to infiltrate that group? Did it have something to do with your female status?" Sophie's eyes round out.

"No, it was not! The chief down there didn't want me doing it for that particular reason. He was an absolute dinosaur. No, I got picked because of my love of cars. Jason is a big car guy and that was our only way in. We got some info that he was looking to buy some cars, so I put up a 2015 Jaguar XF for sale and he came to see it. He was really interested in the boot size in particular."

Belle cocks her head to the side. "Which is?" She asks.

"540 Litres."

Belle laughs. "I knew you'd know it. You are such a car geek!"

"Wheeshed you! Anyway, he bought the car and I got him talking about other cars, his likes and dislikes. Through this he told me he wanted a muscle car for himself. 'Something flashy, just like him.' His words by the way."

Belle's jaw drops. "You managed to get two crazy expensive cars out of Northumbria police?"

Sophie grins and bobs her head with pride. "Oh aye! It was a tough sale, but I did it. I do think that may have been my finest hour down there, it also may be another reason why the powers above didn't like me so much."

Belle makes a face, sarcasm evident in her features. "No fuckin' wonder. You canny get a new fricken pen up here without three ton of paperwork and your buying and selling muscle cars like sweeties."

Sophie waggles her forefinger at her friend. "It was only one muscle car, a 2015 Porsche 911 Carrera S, and technically Jason paid for the cars."

"Semantics. You know what I mean. Now that gives me an idea, why don't we hit the car sales. You know round Maryhill, see if any of them have sold or even just been asked for anything fancy, or at least more fancy than a 'blue one'."

Sophie shakes her head. "I am not going looking for Jason. I don't think this case is connected to him." She tries to put more belief in her voice than she actually felt. The more she thought about the case, the more similarities popped out at her and the more her gut clenched and told her otherwise. Belle wasn't taking no for an answer as she jumped down from her perch on the desk and grabbed Sophie by the hand.

"We're not looking for him, we're just looking into another area of interest, trying to get a break in this case. Plus it will get you all revved up for your date tonight. See what I did there, revved up, get it?"

Sophie groans as she allows herself to be pulled from the room. "Oh Belle, don't give up your day job, you're a better investigator than you are a comedian. Your jokes are awful!" Sophie groans as she is dragged from the room.

"They're not that bad, now hurry up and I'll even let you drive." The friends leave the station headed towards car dealerships, and hopefully not Jason.

CHAPTER THREE

Getting ready for his date that night was harder than Ross had ever imagined. Normally he threw on a pair of jeans and a top on, or a shirt if he was pushing the boat out, but tonight he was struggling. Looking around his bedroom he laughs out loud. It looks like a young girl had been getting ready to go out and not a 26-year-old man.

There are jeans and dress trousers spewed all over the bed. T-shirts and shirts are hanging out of drawers or lying in a crumpled heap on the floor, left there in disgust as Ross didn't like the way they looked on his body. He really was turning into a teenager, again, he thinks. Taking a deep breath, he grabs his comfy, well-worn black jeans and a black shirt then goes to the bathroom to start to style his hair, pulling on his clothes as he goes.

He feels like a teenager going on his first date, feeling totally self-conscious about every aspect of the date. A thought hits him like a lightning bolt. He somehow managed to get a date with the most beautiful woman he has ever seen, through her friend, but never managed to ask her name. He shakes his head at his stupidity.

The main reason he was feeling so self-conscious was the way his last relationship ended. His then-girlfriend constantly moaned at him for being too skinny, telling him he needed to bulk up and get muscles. She wasn't happy that he wasn't a gym monkey, so went and got herself one, though she omitted to tell him this information until he found them in bed together. Apparently, she was having her cake and eating it for two months before being found out.

Ross liked looking after himself and loved swimming, but he never saw the point of looking like you had no neck. He hadn't thought the break-up had affected him, but now he is dipping his toe back into the dating pond, it seems like it may have. He is wondering if it has given him a trust issue to struggle with too, he didn't like being lied to.

After throwing some microwaved dinner back his throat, Ross phones a taxi. Normally he would get the train from his local station in Shettleston into Glasgow Queen Street, but on this muggy July night, he didn't want to get into a sweaty mess walking down Buchanan Street to Mitchell Lane. Plus there wasn't enough time and he didn't want to be late.

The taxi pulls up at the kerb on Argyle Street and Ross makes the short walk to The Pub. As he turns into the cobbled lane, Ross must stop short as a hulking form walks straight into him, with a phone glued to his ear. Ross throws his hands up and starts to apologise when the man, made of solid muscle, turns his deep brown eyes onto him.

"Fucking watch where you're going, dick!" The growl comes from the hulking figure and Ross side steps out of the way, noting the strange accent as he speaks.

"Aye, okay, whatever." Shaking his head Ross mumbles about people not looking where they're going. The hulking man stares menacingly down at him then walks away. A shiver runs down his spine at the danger he saw in the stranger's eyes, he was glad the sun was still bright. Mitchell Lane is a shadowy place even on the brightest day and he certainly wouldn't want to bump into that mountain in the dark.

Entering The Pub, Ross physically shakes himself to rid himself of the uneasy feeling left over from the encounter outside. He stands at the bar and looks around for the beautiful honey blonde, silvery blue-eyed goddess he is there to meet. He inwardly berates himself again for not asking her name. A schoolboy error he thinks then chuckles to himself, as that was exactly what he'd turned into when he was trying to ask her out and again when he was getting ready. Sean takes that moment to step behind the bar from the kitchen area.

"You're back? And on a school night?"

Ross turns to his friend. "Aye. I managed to ask that girl out and she's meeting me here at seven." Ross checks his watch. "Well, at least I hope." Sean gives his friend a quizzical look. "It was her friend that agreed to the date on her behalf. Then she agreed herself, but the friend looked and sounded as shocked as me."

Sean looks up at the clock above the bar then over to the door as it opens and Sophie walks in, looking about shyly. "Aye, well your lucks in pal, here she's here."

Ross turns on his heels to see Sophie walking towards him. His heart stutters in his chest at the sight of her in her tight blue skinny jeans, white crop top and white strappy sandals. Her honey blonde hair falling completely straightened around her shoulders. She is the epitome of beauty as she smiles at Ross, the light blue of her eyes sparkling, taking his breath away and making his mind go blank.

He takes a step forward instinctively but stops short, reigning in his basic instinct of wanting to take her lips in a kiss there and then.

Dynamic Entry

"You came?" The words are out of his mouth before his brain can engage his man voice, so he sounds like an adolescent.

Sophie looks at him, confusion all over her face. "You thought I would stand you up?" She sounds almost hurt.

"Well, maybe, kinda. I'd hoped not, and I'm glad you're here." Sophie smiles shyly as a blush tinges her cheeks, then frowns.

Ross can see Sophie have what looks like an internal battle wither self herself.

"What would you like to drink?" Ross asks and watches as she takes a deep breath, the internal battle continuing.

"I'd love a pint if that's okay?"

"Aye, I mean why wouldn't it be okay?"

Her shoulders relax at his confusion. Some guys think it's unfeminine or crude for us mere females to drink pints." Another look passes over Ross' face when he hears her concern. He wonders if this is part of the reason she plays her cards so close to her chest.

"Aye, well I'm different, I believe in freedom of choice." He grins and gives Sophie a wink. "You grab a table and I'll bring the drinks over." With her heart hammering in her chest Sophie walks towards the same table she had sat at that afternoon, knowing that it had the best vantage point for keeping an eye on the entire bar.

"Well?" Sean asks with a waggle of his eyebrows.

"Well, what? Two pints of lager by the way." Sean starts pouring the drinks. "Well, do, you even know her name? I never heard you say it and you never introduced me."

Panic flashes over Ross' face. He was planning on asking her when she arrived, but the fact that she did arrive, then seeing how stunning she looked turned his mind to mush. "Shit, no. Why do I keep forgetting to ask the most important question?"

Sean laughs. "Might have something to do with the fact you go all goo-goo eyed when she's about. Now here, take these on me, as long as you get her name."

Ross gives his friend a sarcastic look then leaves with their drinks.

Sitting down across from Sophie, Ross hands over her pint then tries to relax.

"I'm sorry," He starts then takes a deep breath, his pulse ratcheting up in his throat. "I've been really rude. I never asked your name."

Sophie searches her memory bank, wondering if she'd told him her name, she wasn't in the habit of giving her name out to people too quickly, she comes up a blank so guessed she hadn't told him. Another slight blush comes up her cheeks.

"Sorry, it's Sophie."

Ross smiles. "That's beautiful, like you." Both of their eyes widen at his words. "Sorry, that's a bit forward. I'm normally better at this stuff."

Sophie arches an eyebrow at him. "What chatting up women? You do that often do you?"

"Aye, eh, no, eh, oh fuck, oh sorry." He drops his head in despair.

Sophie lets out a laugh at his nerves and inability to make a coherent sentence, both of which she found endearing.

"That's okay. As long as you're telling the truth, I don't mind you calling me beautiful." She smiles as she hears his breath catch in his throat.

"Good, I like telling you you're beautiful." They smile at each other for a second, both of them relaxing into the date more.

The conversation takes on an easier feeling as the couple gets comfortable with each other and their pints go down.

Sophie rises to her feet and lifts the empty glasses.

"My round, same again?" Ross starts to nod his head, then remembers he hadn't paid for the first round. The gentleman in him has him bursting to his feet.

"No, I'll get them." Sophie bristles with annoyance. "I'm not letting you pay for the whole night."

"I know, but I'll get these, you can get the next round."

"You got the last ones." She steps round the table but Ross steps to the side, blocking her path.

She can feel his presence pushing in what she classes as her personal space, and she's unsure how she feels about it. She should want him to take a step back, but part of her wants him to take a step forward, get closer. Taking a breath Ross explains his situation.

"I didn't actually get them. My friend owns this place and he gave me them on the house."

Sophie warms to Ross more at his honesty. "That's okay, I don't mind being the first to buy the drinks on a date."

Ross shakes his head. "No, but it would be a kick in the ego to me. My mother brought me up to be a gentleman." Sophie narrows her eyes at him, unsure if he was being a dinosaur or not. He smiles, "Chivalry isn't always a bad thing, and if I get these ones, then I will expect a round bought back," there is a twinkle in his eye as he speaks, "so that means you won't leave too early." All the annoyance seeps from Sophie at his words.

She hates men treating her as a mere female, but Ross seems to be nothing like that. She hopes not, for reasons she didn't want to admit to herself at that moment. She hands over their empty glasses and smiles, taking a deep breath.

"Okay. Thank you."

"So, same again?"

"Yes, please." Another smile crosses her face as she sits.

Bringing back the drinks, Ross hands Sophie hers. "So, what do you do for pleasure?" Ross winks at her as he asks the question and she giggles, like a schoolgirl.

"My job doesn't leave me much time for hobbies, but I do like Formula One, and cars, and cars going fast, and the sound of cars going fast." Her silvery blue eyes glint with pleasure. She notices Ross reposition himself in his seat.

"Me too, though not as much as you, I think." Her face flushes as he smiles.

"Aye, cars are my thing." She shrugs, shyly, "So, what do you do for work?"

"I work at a jewellery shop in the Argyle Arcade."

"You enjoy it?"

Ross nods mid sip of his beer. "Aye. It might not be everyone's idea of a perfect job, you know dealing with customers, and some people have even told me it's a 'girly' job, but I love it. What about you?"

Sophie takes a gulp from her pint, trying to give herself time before she answers. She doesn't know why she started this conversation; she tries to avoid answering that question at the best of times. She doesn't want to lie to Ross but can't tell him the whole truth either. Deciding to go for the middle ground of a police officer she opens her mouth to talk.

A booming voice talks before she can get her words out.

"Our Sophie Peterson here's a specialist car dealer, aren't you, and still as gorgeous as ever, I see."

Dynamic Entry

Sophie's heart stops in her chest and her blood runs icy in her veins as the sound of the voice shudders through her. She lifts her head, praying that she's mistaken at recognising the strange accent, but she's not. It's Jason Hamilton. The one guy she desperately didn't want to see again. The person she thought she had taken down when she worked in Northumbria. The man she'd warned her DI and Belle about. The man she had now to be Sophie Peterson for, and now the guy who was making her lie to Ross on their first date.

"Jason, what, eh, what are you doing here? In Scotland?"

Jason grins down at Sophie. His chocolate brown eyes sparkle with want mixed with danger. My business needed a fresh start, somewhere new after…" Sophie swallows hard, hoping Jason hadn't worked out that she was the one who got his business busted, or that she is actually an undercover cop. She also hopes that he doesn't speak too deeply on what his type of business is, or how she was involved. Drug and gun running tended to dampen the mood of a date.

"Understandable." She mutters, Jason gives her a knowing nod of his head. She hoped it was knowing why his business needed to move and not for anything else.

"Aren't you going to introduce us?" He looks at Ross who has been staring at Jason with wary interest and Sophie clears her throat.

"Eh, Jason this is Ross. Ross, Jason." She doesn't venture any more information. How do you explain to the man you're having a first date with, that the man interrupting them is an ex-mark who should've been put into prison three years ago? She knows she needs to stick to her original pseudonym of Sophie Peterson, specialist car dealer, come gun runner, with drug running being thrown in for good measure. Her stomach free falls when the realisation that she is going to need to be her with Ross now hits her.

Jason extends his hand to Ross and the men shake. She can see Jason tensing his muscles and giving what he calls 'a real man's handshake'. She sees understanding in Ross that the handshake is a pissing contest and gives a squeeze back. Another plus for Ross.

"Nice to meet you, Ross, I'm an ex-business partner of Sophie's from once upon a time. But now I know we are back in the same city I will be using her services again."

Sophie plasters a grin on her face, hopes it's believable and nods. "Are you looking for a new car?" Her heart is hammering in her chest, trying to break free as she slips back into her old role.

"Maybe, amongst other things." Jason gives her a pointed look that speaks louder to her than his words. She needs to contact Belle or her DI to let them know the news. News that will be good for the investigation, news that probably explains why there's been a surge in guns and drugs in the West End area of the city but is decidedly bad news for her.

Jason hands her his business card with a smirk on his face. "I'm sorry. Did I interrupt your date?" Ross nods and smiles at Sophie.

Her heart restricts, she really likes Ross. They were getting on like a house on fire, plus he is as sexy as hell. She wants to see him again but doesn't want to pull him into her world of lies and being someone else.

She tries to convince herself she doesn't need to worry about any of that yet as it's only been one date, she takes the business card from Jason.

"Sophie, if you give me a call and we can get something organised," Jason says. He rakes his eyes all over her again then grins, taking his leave. Sophie watches as the perfectly sculpted figure walks away from their table and over to the bar. Looking back at Ross she looks deep into his gorgeous navy-blue eyes and knows she's in trouble.

CHAPTER FOUR

As soon as Ross heard the accent of the man mountain standing at their table, he knew it was the same arrogant arsehole who tried to walk through him in the lane. He watches the interaction between Sophie and the stranger with a mixture of interest and worry.

Sophie had been relaxed, or at least on the way to being relaxed until he arrived. Now her body language was stiff and closed. She was smiling at the man mountain named Jason, but it wasn't the same smile she had given him when he called her beautiful. That had been a real smile and one that had taken his breath away. He didn't like the atmosphere that Jason brought with him, nor did he like the dangerous want shining in the man's eyes when he looked at Sophie. In fact, everything about the interruption felt off, but Ross felt he couldn't say much about it. It was after all only a first date; they hadn't even gotten to the subject of second names let alone second dates.

Jason gives his apologies for interrupting and leaves. Ross can see Sophie physically relax. Letting her shoulders fall, as well as her expression. As quickly as the pained look in her features disappears a smile appears as she looks at Ross. Then her smile increases exponentially as does his heartbeat.

"A friend of yours?" The question is out of his mouth before he can stop it. Sophie's eyes dull slightly at the mention of Jason, then she physically shudders, although she tries to cover it up.

"Someone I used to do business with, before... and going to do again, apparently." There is resignation in her voice as she talks but pushes it all aside and concentrates on Ross. "Anyway, enough of him. What sport you into? Football by any chance?"

Ross bursts out laughing. "Is this your way of asking what team I support, or what school I went to?"

She shakes her head vigorously another blush rising on her cheeks. "Oh god no, sorry. I don't get into all that crap, I don't care what school you went to or what religion you are, I just hate football is all."

He sniggers with a glint in his eye. "That's good to know. So you'll be glad to know that I don't go in for football all that much, rugby is the sport I like to watch, but I'm more of a swimmer myself."

"Not a gym fanatic, then?"

A cold sensation runs through the pit of Ross' stomach at her words. His mind crashes back to his ex-girlfriend's slights of being weedy and not man enough looking. Then it bounces to Jason, the man mountain standing at their table all muscles and pecs. The smile slides from Ross's face. "No, not for me... sorry." Why he was apologising was beyond him. He knew he hadn't resolved all his body insecurities his ex-girlfriend instilled in him, but he didn't normally allow it to affect him during a date. He wonders if Sophie was into the broad, muscular type like Jason. Her voice brings him from concerns.

"Why are you sorry?" Sophie asked.

He shrugs, hoping his insecurities weren't shining through as bright as he felt them. Sophie places her hand on top of his on the table making him look up and into her bright blue eyes.

"Personally I think people can take it too far with the gym and the building up muscles and everything, that they end up looking ridiculous. I mean take Jason for example; he just looks uncomfortable in his own skin." The coldness in Ross' stomach starts to dissipate at her words, relief flooding his system knowing she wasn't attracted to the mountain. Heat floods his veins at her next words.

"Whereas you, you are as sexy as hell." Her hand flies to her mouth, she had obviously not meant to say those words out loud. "I'm sorry that was a bit forward."

"That's okay, I like you telling me I'm sexy." They smile at each other,

"Good, I like telling you you're sexy." Ross grins as Sophie beams her real smile at him as she says his words from earlier back to him. They stare deep into each other's eyes both seeing interest and desire shining back at each other.

Their date continues with more drinks and relaxed conversation, each of them learning more about the other and cementing their mutual attraction. All through their date Sophie and Ross are engrossed in each other's company and nothing else. Certainly not Jason's curious stare. Never once did his eyes leave the couple, his mood swinging between lust to hatred, but always with the undercurrent of danger that continuously sparks in him. He watches as Sophie and Ross stand from their seats and walk towards the door, Ross' hand resting on the small of Sophie's back.

Anger and jealousy bite at the back of his throat. He should be the one holding Sophie. He's the one that spent the best part of six months wooing her and he would've gotten her into his bed if she hadn't had to go away on business or if he hadn't been busted and nearly sent down.

Dynamic Entry

Bumping into her tonight was a great twist of fate Jason decides. He also decides that now their paths have crossed again, he would be making her his, even if it was only for one night. Anger thrums through him.

Jason drains his pint and follows the couple out of The Pub and down onto Argyle Street. He stands at the end of the buildings and watches as they both climb into the same taxi. His anger ramps up to dangerous levels as he rips his phone from his blazer pocket and punches a speed dial number.

Before the worker on the other side of the line can say anything, Jason starts barking orders at him. "You! Has that fucker paid yet? In fact, never mind if he's paid, he's late. Get the fucker and bring him to the warehouse, yes, the fucking new one, I only have one, you fuckwit! I'm going to have a word, teach the bastard a lesson." There's a pause in his rant as his worker talks.

Jason takes his phone away from his ear and stares at it, exasperation and incredulity evident in his expression at his worker's question. "Yes, I want it to happen now. I'm not going to wait until fucking Christmas, now am I? Why do I even pay you, you dumbshit piece of crap? Go do what I tell you to do, I don't care what or who you're doing, you work for me, end of!" He smashes his thumb into the screen, ending the call and growls at some passers-by who were giving him dirty looks.

Throwing his arm out he flags down one of the many taxi's driving on Argyle Street and climbs in, spitting the warehouses address to the driver as he fastens his seatbelt.

CHAPTER FIVE

Sophie wakes up the next day and smiles at the memory of the night before. Ross was everything she looked for in a man. Funny, warm, kind, tall, not a gym monkey and sexy as hell. He also knew how to be a gentleman without it being too old fashioned, he understood that women, or Sophie to be exact, needed their independence, their place in the world.

She quite liked his chivalrous moments like walking with his hand on her lower back and opening the taxi door, normally this would have grated on her but not with Ross. She even enjoyed when the taxi pulled up outside her house and Ross walked her to her door. She enjoyed it so much she replayed the memory back over in her mind.

"Could you wait two minutes whilst I walk my date to the door please?" Ross asked the taxi driver, whose response was a gruff 'whatever, meter's still running'. Sophie started to object as Ross exited the car, but he wasn't listening to her. Once she got out, he placed his hand back on the small of her back and walked the short distance from the kerb, up her drive, past her Racing Green X plate XJS convertible Jaguar. Ross made a noise of appreciation as they pass, making Sophie like him little that bit more.

Once at her door Sophie looks into his dark blue eyes and sees the desire there. She wanted to look into those eyes forever, and that thought scared her.

Dynamic Entry

"I had a really good night tonight." His statement brought Sophie from her almost hypnotic state of staring into his eyes.

"Me too, actually."

"You didn't think you would?"

She looks down and shrugs. "I don't normally enjoy dates, but this one was different." She thinks about mentioning the interruption by Jason, but she doesn't want him spoiling the warm feeling she was feeling holding Ross' hands, so she pushes the thoughts aside.

"I'm glad this one was different and enjoyable." He pulls on her arms, bringing her closer into his chest, wrapping his left arm around her waist he brings his right hand up to her face, brushing his thumb over her cheek bone. She feels him pause for a second, letting her pull away or stop him, but all she does is stare into his eyes. The light silver blue of her eyes sparkles in the summer moonlight. He brings his lips slowly to hers until he softly brushes them together. Sophie was uneasy with men who pushed too much, but as he kisses her gently, she is left wanting more. She blinks as he stands back and asks if they could see each other again. To Sophie's surprise, she agrees.

They exchange numbers as the taxi driver sounds his horn, obviously getting annoyed.

"I better go before he leaves me here. I'll phone you and we can get something arranged, okay?" Sophie can only nod her head, not sure where her voice has disappeared to after the brief, but very romantic first kiss.

Ross turns and leaves, waving from the taxi as it pulls away.

The memory has Sophie touching her lips, feeling the tingle left there from the kiss. Giving herself a shake and laughing, she gets up and goes for a shower before heading into work.

Once there she finds Belle in the incident room and pulls her aside.

"Hey, I need to talk to you."

Belle stumbles to the side and stares at her friend. "Oh, okay, well good morning to you too. Is it about your date last night? How did it go? Did youse get freaky? Is that the problem is Ross not freaky? Or is he too freaky? Wow, if he's too freaky for you he must be wild!" Belle was on a roll and Sophie was losing patience.

"Will you shut up!" Belle's eyebrows shoot upwards at her friend's tone and Sophie instantly feels guilty for talking to her best friend so sharply. "I'm sorry, it's just, I need to talk to you before the boss gets in. I'll tell you everything about the date at lunch, but for now sshh." Belle gives her friend a nod of understanding, then listens intently as Sophie talks. "Right, well, my worst nightmare came true last night. It is Jason that we're investigating."

Belle's eyes go wide and she has a look around the room before answering, making sure none of the other officers were listening to them. "How'd you know that?" Her voice is a gruff whisper.

"He interrupted my date last night."

"Oh shit!"

Sophie gives her friend a grunt of a laugh. "I know. He arrived at the table without a sound. I'm always on watch but I was looking at Ross and we were talking, I didn't see him until he was telling Ross I was a specialist car dealer."

"Oh shit!"

"I know. Then I had to go back into my pseudonym because the bastard came in and called me by my full name. Sophie Peterson, so now any relationship that starts between us starts on a lie, and —"

"Oh shit. You want a relationship with Ross?" Belle interrupts with a grin.

"Will you stop saying 'oh shit'! And that is not the point at the moment, Belle."

The smile slides from Belle's face but stays in her eyes. "I know but —"

"But nothing. The point is, Jason's back and that means I need to go back undercover." She didn't want to think about what she wanted from Ross. For the first time since forever, she'd relaxed with a guy and not worried about being dismissed as 'only a female'.

"Ah, shit, again!"

"Urgh, I know, again! I need to tell the boss. I thought we'd enough on him to put him away, but for some reason, after I left it all went to hell in a handbasket. It was a tough assignment; I mean that man is a proper psycho and definitely a sociopath. He always got what he wanted, regardless of the consequences, the man is dangerous."

"Well, this time we need to make sure we get him proper. Now come and update the boss on the breakthrough." Sophie nods feeling like she'd just been handed a life sentence. "Then you can tell me all about this relationship you want with the sexy Ross." Sophie's stomach makes a flutter at the thought of Ross then drops at the thought of having to give it all up before it starts.

****

Ross walks into The Pub for his daily lunch. He is still on a high from the date and kiss he shared with Sophie the night before. The image of the hulking Jason and Sophie's reaction to him plays on his mind, but he pushes the thoughts aside. Instead, he concentrates on the easy way they spoke with each other and the lighthearted banter. Sean coughs to get his friends attention then laughs.

"They thoughts X-rated about last night?"

Ross brings his attention back to the here and now, then gives his friend the middle finger with a smile. "Fuck off! No, they weren't X-rated. I, unlike you, are a complete gentleman."

Sean snorts out a laugh. "Aye right, and watch your language when the lunches are on."

Ross holds his hands up in an apology. "Sorry, I will watch my mouth. Now there may have been an odd time that I was something of a cad, but Sophie is different."

"Oh god, not again. They're all different and special and 'the one'." Sean's use of air quotes makes Ross squirm and blush. Trying to save face he retaliates in the only manner he knows how to with his friend.

"Fuck off, again!"

Sean laughs out loud. "Okay, okay, keep your trousers on. So you want your usual?" Ross nods and grabs the newspaper trying to stop his mind going back to the night before.

CHAPTER SIX

Jason wakes up with a smile on his lips. He had gone to the old mechanic's garage he called the warehouse to deal with the customer who owed him money.

It wasn't a lot of money, a thousand pounds, but it was the principle of the matter. The cokehead promised he would pay him back and he hasn't so Jason couldn't be seen to let that slide; he had a reputation to uphold. The beating he gave the man had been quite cathartic. It got out some of the anger and jealousy he had felt at seeing Sophie with that other guy, but he knew it wasn't enough, not for the message he wanted to send to his other customers and certainly not enough to take away all of the anger he felt due to the fact that he hadn't had Sophie in his bed, yet.

Not having the correct equipment or clothes with him that night, Jason had chained his prisoner up in the warehouse with the promise he would return the next day to finish the job, and Jason always kept his promises.

Rising from his bed he gets into the shower, as one must be clean to torture and bring living hell down on another human being. Although in Jason's opinion drug addicts weren't human. They were pieces of shit that snorted shit up their noses and let that shit control them, unlike him, other than alcohol he didn't let anything but the best of everything in or near his body.

His body is a temple, and he looks after it with a finely tuned routine of organic food, exercise, and weightlifting, the steroids he took were only to enhance his routine. He was in control of everything in his life, nothing controlled him.

Standing in the shower Jason thinks back to the start of the night before when he walked into the bar and realised the gorgeous blonde sitting at one of the tables was Sophie. The same gorgeous blonde he'd let get away before having the chance to taste every inch of her body. He'd been about to make his move when she announced she had to go away on business. It wasn't long after that that his world crashed around him.

He'd been arrested but managed to get away with it all due to the idiots bumbling something or other; and now he's back and so is she, he will get his taste this time around.

The thought of Sophie's blonde hair falling over her lean body and pert breasts makes Jason hard. Taking himself in his hand he fantasises about everything he would do to Sophie once he gets his chance, and he will get his chance, he always gets what he wants.

Getting into the rhythm he likes, Jason brings himself to his climax with a grunt. Images of Sophie playing on a loop in his head. He finishes getting washed and climbs out.

Within the hour Jason is walking into his warehouse, dressed appropriately for torturing someone in overalls.

His nostrils are assaulted by the stench of ammonia and faeces. He opens his mouth to breathe as he slams closed the door behind him.

"You dirty bastard!" He screams at his prisoner. Picking up the hose Jason blasts the prisoner with water, running the spray from his face to his feet and back again, trying to wash away some of the mess. All the time yelling. "You fucking, dirty, coke headed bastard! How dare you piss and shit all over my warehouse. It isn't bad enough you're a dirty bastard liar and thief, but you go and defecate yourself on my property!"

He drops his voice to a low dangerous growl. "I've been lenient with you over the money you owe me and the product you've effectively stolen from me and this is how you repay me, by shitting all over the place? You dirty fucking bastard!" He slams his boot into his prisoner's already swollen face, making his head snap violently backwards so it bounces off the concrete floor. His nose explodes again. His body shakes with the withdrawal of drugs mixed with his quickly dropping temperature, anxiety, fear, and adrenaline.

Jason stops soaking the prisoner and stands over him watching as he convulses on the cold floor, disgust written on his face. The prisoner starts moaning and begging for another chance to pay, but Jason is having none of it. He draws his foot back and kicks the shaking man in the gut lifting his body from the cold concrete floor with the force of the contact. The prisoner spews bile onto the wet concrete angering Jason further.

Pulling on the Nitrile gloves that he takes from his overall pockets, he grabs his prisoner up, yanking his arms that are still shackled in chains. Jason holds him up with one hand like he weighed no more than a newborn baby and throws punches at his face until tears run down the prisoner's mangled face, mixing with blood and mucus, as he tries to beg for his life.

But all his mumbles and gurgling fall on deaf ears. All Jason can see is red, and all he can think about is his prisoner taking him for a fool and Sophie being fucked by her date last night.

Only once his arm is tired and the prisoner's face is an unrecognisable bloody pulp, does Jason drop his prisoner in a heap on the floor. The prisoner had at some point in the attack passed out. Jason retrieves a chair and rope, unlocks his prisoner, then ties him roughly to the chair before bringing him back to the here and now.

Once his prisoner is conscious again Jason walks around the chair in circles, naming all the things he would like to do to him; then he starts to laugh maniacally, singing in his strange mixed up accent about cutting out the tongues of everyone who'd crossed him.

He rhymes off names and dates of where and when the incidents happened. He stops dead in front of his prisoner and grins an unhinged manic smile. His perfectly straight, white teeth almost glowing in his mouth, he bends down on his hunkers so he's face to face with the bloody mess of the prisoner.

"Oops, I think I've said too much. You know what that means don't you?" His voice is light and airy, teasing and playful. The prisoner shakes his head, he tries to blink but his eyes are swollen shut from all the beatings he has received. Jason gives another light laugh. "Well it means two things, no no, wait, maybe three. One, if I want to continue my song and not have you hear it, I could cut off your ears." A gargled choking sound comes from the bloody face. "Or two, I could let you hear everything, but take your tongue so you can't tell anyone my secrets." Another laugh comes from Jason, "Or three, even better, in my opinion, I do both. What d'you think?" The bloody mess tries to shake his head and mumbles his protests through his broken teeth and jaw, but Jason grabs the mangled face and roughly pumps it up and down in a nodding gesture. "You want both? Good man!" He says proudly as he slaps his prisoner on the back. The man can only drop his head and moan having no energy or hope left.

Jason stands and walks over to the workbench that had been set up the night before with all his preferred tools of his trade. He walks from one end of the bench to the other, touching and caressing all the tools, picking up some to feel them in his hand.

He feels the weight and the fit of them in his palm, all the time whispering to himself, or maybe the tools, about how nice they are, what he could do with them, why he likes them so much. This part of the process, he feels it is the most enjoyable part, his favourite part.

The process of killing someone is his least favourite part. It means all the fun stuff has been finished and the messy bit started, but it is a necessary evil of his choice of career. He can't be seen as weak, not in attitude, not in personality, not in body, and certainly not in business. If people played by his rules, the rules that he explains with great care and detail to them before they sign the contract, then he wouldn't need to show them the extent of their consequences.

Settled in his own mind that what he is doing is not only necessary but not his fault, he picks up the meat cleaver and strides purposely back over to his prisoner. Grabbing a fistful of hair in his gloved hand he straightens him up.

"You can't go to sleep, you silly boy, this a good part." A groan comes from the gaping hole of a mouth. Jason rearranges his hands so he's holding the prisoner's throat. "Now what first do you think? Your tongue or an ear?" He muses for a second. "I need you to hear what's going on, but I don't want you to bleed out too quickly, or choke on your blood so…" Another second of pondering, "ah ha! I know, I'll take your fingers instead." The fearful protests are drowned out by gurgling screams as Jason lays the prisoner's hand on his knee, fingers flat, and brings down the cleaver with his full might on top of them.

He laughs maniacally as he rips the cleaver from where it had embedded itself in the prisoner's knee, the stumps of his fingers fall to the ground at his feet.

"Weren't expecting that, were you?" Jason snorts in his prisoner's face. There is no sound from the prisoner, only deep breathing as Jason takes one ear in his hand and starts to saw away until it has been completely dissected from the body.

Settling into his job Jason grabs a pair of secateurs from the workbench, then grabs the prisoner's tongue. Snipping in one fluid motion he cuts the tongue free from the mouth and hands it back to its owner.

Blood and saliva pour from the wound as Jason starts with the killing of the tortured man. He changes weapon and stabs the prisoner repeatedly in the chest, a serrated combat knife in each hand. His boxing exercise for the day Jason thinks to himself as he stabs.

Once finished, Jason drags off his saturated gloves and overalls, dumping them on the mutilated body. He lifts his phone from the workbench where he left it to keep it from getting blood splattered. He taps at the screen until the number for the worker from the night before is on the screen for him to dial. He shouts down the line as soon as he hears the call connect, not giving his worker a chance to answer.

"You! Get down here and clean up. There's a barrel down here you can use." He cancels the call before the worker can reply, then leaves heading back to The Pub hoping Sophie's a regular there.

****

Dynamic Entry

Come lunch time and after her meeting with her DI, Sophie desperately needs to get out the ever-bustling incident room. Her boss had been more than happy to put her back into her old pseudonym, but not ecstatic when Belle explained about the high-end cars they would need.

Sophie thought her boss was going to have an aneurysm right there and then. His answer was to talk to the powers above and cross his fingers, but he would not be holding his breath. Sophie had nodded before turning to leave, but her boss's next question had had her stopping her dead in her tracks.

"We could use your car Sophie, is that not a classic?"

Cold rage had thrummed in her veins, no-one was allowed near the driver's seat of her XJS. "Not a fuckin' chance, Boss!" Belle stifled her giggle as Sophie charged from the room, leaving the DI speechless in her wake.

As the friends settled into the same table at The Pub as the day before Sophie looks around, hoping she would catch Ross on his lunch as he mentioned he went there every day he was working. Belle makes gushing noises.

"Awe, that's so cute, looking for your man."

Sophie throws her a look. "He's not my man… and I'm not looking for him… I'm just looking, as I always do." She knew it was stretching the truth, and she knew Belle would call her out on it.

"Aye, right! Anyway, you promised me you'd give me the low down on last night at lunch, so here we are at lunch… spill!"

Sophie sighs. She doesn't know where to start explaining her date, it was all mixed up. One minute she was ready to leave when she thought he was a dinosaur, and then she was melting because of his gentlemanly behaviour. Then just as she started to relax and enjoy herself, a first for her, Jason interrupts them giving her a night of worry and now a job she didn't want to take on, again.

She takes a deep breath and starts to talk, telling her friend most of what happened on her date. She did, however, leave out how romantic her feelings were and prayed that Belle couldn't read them in her eyes. Her prayer went unanswered.

"Oh my god! You really like him, don't you?" Sophie starts to answer but is cut off by a now over excited Belle. "Aye you do, don't even try to deny it, I can see it in your eyes. You even liked it when he walked you to the door, I could tell by the way your eyes went all gooey and soft and you smiled!" The word 'smiled' came out more like an accusation than anything else.

Sophie blushes. Never had she been so see-through with her emotions, but then again never had she had emotions for a guy after their first date. She stomps on her thoughts of emotions, not wanting to go there.

"Okay, so I thought he was nice. At least nicer than any other date I've been on." Belle rolls her eyes and starts with her sarcastic answer.

Sophie's face falls and before anyone can say anything there is a hulking presence beside them, talking in a strange accent.

"Sophie, we meet again. I hope my interruption last night didn't put too much of a dampener on your date... or maybe I do."

Sophie makes her smile brighter by sheer will power. "Hi Jason, everything went well, thanks." Sophie's heart starts pounding like a bass drum in her chest as she puts all her concentration on speaking to Jason and controlling her tone.

"Ella this is Jason, an old customer of mine from down South, Jason this is my friend Ella." Jason holds out his hand and Belle takes Jason eyes Belle and Sophie takes the hint.

it in a shake. Sophie notices how small Belle's hand is encased in his and can see her eyes widen.

"Wow, you're huge." Belle grins up at him.

He turns his full attention to Belle. "That I am!" He winks, making Belle shudder. He turns back to Sophie. "So, Sophie, when can we meet up and talk about these cars I'm going to buy from you?" Sophie grins at him. She may not want to do business with him, and she may not have the go ahead to buy the cars needed, yet, but she sure as hell wants to go car shopping with someone else's money!

"We can meet up next week, say Monday and get a list organised, how does that sound?" Jason had brought his phone out as Sophie spoke and was typing furiously into it. Belle smiled throughout.

"Excellent, it's a date then!" Both women resist the urge to shudder.

"Hmm." Sophie is non-committal.

"How about here at seven?" To Sophie that sounded too much like an actual date.

"Well…"

"I'm afraid she's got a mates date with me that night, but that's not until seven, so during the day would be fine."

Jason cuts his eyes to Belle and the atmosphere around them intensifies, Sophie clears her throat. "How does coffee in the shop across from the arcade in Buchanan Street sound? About ten?" That still sounded like a date, but less like a date than a night in the pub to Sophie.

Anger flits across Jason's face but he quickly masks it. "Fine, Monday at ten." He takes Sophie's hand in his and brings it to his lips, brushing her knuckles in a kiss. "Till then." He smiles at Sophie then nods to Belle before taking his leave. The friends look at each other and then exhale loudly.

"Wow, that was intense." Belle is first to say the obvious. Sophie swallows the sip of water she'd taken. "It was that. Right back to the office to let the boss know I'll be needing those cars sooner rather than later."

The friends pay for their lunch then head out towards the car park on Mitchell Street just as Ross steps into the lane. He catches a glimpse of Sophie's honey blonde hair as they turn the corner.

CHAPTER SEVEN

By Friday, Sophie was ready to scream. She had been cooped up in the Incident Room, kept out of the way, off the streets they were covering and away from the people they were following until she met with Jason on Monday morning to 're-immerse herself in the world of guns and drugs.

She had spent much of her time in the office thinking about all that had happened to her when she was working in Northumbria. She made lists of how she acted and who she was the last time she lived the life of Sophie Peterson.

She was never taken seriously when she worked there, not by the powers that be higher up or the gang she'd worked with. She'd had to prove herself time and again. She knew she did a good job, better than good as she was the only person who had a shared interest with Jason. The only person who could get close enough to find out the information they needed, but as usual there was talk that she got the information because she was female, that Jason only accepted her into his circle so he could fuck her.

She was never given the credit that it was her knowledge of cars that got her accepted and her instinct and investigating ability that got the information needed to break the gun running and drug dealing business. It was all her hard work that gave them enough evidence to convict Jason and his workers, and it was nothing to do with her that they messed it all up and he got away with it all.

She'd told her bosses of the sexual advances Jason was putting towards her and she was told to use them to her advantage. They never came right out and said sleep with him, they wouldn't dare, it's not the seventies or eighties anymore, but they loosely hinted it wouldn't be frowned upon. She felt sick every time she thought about Jason and his advances.

It had started with him brushing his hand up her arm, smiling at her, putting his hand on her hips as he walked past her. He would make sure they were together in cars or sitting at tables. She would remove his hand from her knee, and he would smirk at her, lust and desire mixed with the constant danger in his eyes. She had taken self-defence classes as a precaution, but the sheer size of Jason was intimidating, and that was exactly what he played on and used to try to get everything he wanted.

She wasn't well liked by some of the workers in Jason's business. Any females she came in contact with didn't like her because of the attention Jason stowed upon her and the males didn't like her because she could drink them under the table and out talk them about cars and other 'man' stuff. She didn't care though; she didn't like any of them.

She hadn't thought the way she'd been treated down there had affected her much until she came home. Once home she'd pushed all romantic gestures away as sleazy and picked fights with her male counterparts. It took Belle calling her out on her behaviour in work for her to relax around her male colleagues, but she hadn't managed it in her love life.

The thought of her love life brings her thoughts to Ross. He had been flitting in and out of her mind since their date. Sometimes she relished the idea of being romantically involved with someone, other times it butted against her belief that she didn't need a man. She'd been burned before by relying on a man. The one man she should've been able to rely on her whole life, her father.

He'd never miss a chance to undermine her mother and remind Sophie she was nothing but a female before walking out of their lives and into the happy family he had made alongside their unhappy one. Surprisingly enough, her father's 'other' wife gave birth to two boys.

As much as she tried to resist the feeling, she knew instinctively that Ross was different from her father, different from all the men she had dated. He had made her relax and not argue with the romantic gesture of being a gentleman.

But admitting to herself that she liked Ross was one thing. Doing something about it was something entirely different, especially now he thought she was Sophie Peterson, the car dealer and doing business with Jason. She didn't want to start any relationship with a lie and she certainly didn't want to get Ross involved with Jason, but she couldn't help wanting to see him again, maybe even get into the relationship that Belle was always pushing her towards.

Her personal phone pings on her desk bringing her from her musings of relationships and makes her heart rate leap with anticipation that maybe, just maybe it would be Ross contacting her. Then her heart kicks up another notch when she sees that very name flash on the screen, announcing his text message.

*Had a great time on our date. Would love to meet again tomorrow? We can meet someplace, or I can pick you up and go for a meal? *

Her stomach flutters. She desperately wants to meet up with Ross and enjoy his company, maybe even see if they could deepen that kiss, but she still has a niggle in her gut about lying to him about her real name. She doesn't want to hurt him or get him hurt. Telling herself she can keep the two areas of her life separate and promising herself she will tell him the truth if things get serious between them, Sophie texts him back.

Sounds great. Meet you at the pizza place next to The Pub at 6?

Only seconds pass before Ross' reply beeps into Sophie's phone.

Great, can't wait to see you. Xx

Sophie stares at her phone, her heart pounding in her chest at the x kisses at the end of Ross' message. She's turning into a lovesick teenager she thinks to herself.

Belle walks into the Incident Room and reiterates Sophie's thoughts back to her.

"Wow, you've got it bad for your lover boy."

Sophie's head shoots up and she eyes her friend. "What? No I don't" Her voice is too high, so she coughs and tries again, "How do you know it's even him I'm thinking about?"

Belle coughs over her laugh. "A wild guess, going on the dreamy way you were looking at your phone, but you just confirmed it."

Sophie's face flushes as she drops her head in defeat. "Aye, it was Ross I was texting. We're meeting up again tomorrow night for pizza, but he is not my lover boy." Guilt crashes through her at the thought of getting involved with someone whilst she's working under a pseudonym, especially since he believes she is that pseudonym.

Sophie tries to explain her feelings to Belle without coming across pathetic and lovesick.

"I don't want to lie to him, but I can't tell him the entire truth either, or at least not yet. I don't know him enough to trust him with my job." Belle nods her understanding. They have both agreed that it's hard enough when people start new relationships without adding in the complication of their undercover job. "Part of me thinks I should just walk away from it all before it gets started, but," She blows out a huge sigh then shakes her head. "I really like him. I feel all the stupid sparks people talk about, and I was relaxed when I was with him." Belle's eyebrows are in her hairline at hearing Sophie talk about feelings, sparks or even being relaxed on a date and in a man's company.

They had only known each other in passing before Sophie had been seconded to Northumbria, becoming closer after Belle called her out on her behaviour when she returned. It was the best thing that could've happened to Sophie.

She had opened up to Belle over drinks that same day about her treatment by the brass down there, and then to her astonishment, she continued her confession by telling her now best friend all the sordid details of her father and his two families.

By the time the story was finished Bell had explained that she could understand why Sophie didn't trust men, hated romantic gestures and was fiercely protective of her independence as a female. Her father was a suave charmer and her mother fell for it at every turn.

"Wow, he must be something," Belle says. "Listen, I think you should still see him, keep him separate from work though. The only thing you need to keep from him is your second name and job. Everything else you tell him is the truth, then if things go well and you feel better about trusting him, then you can have that conversation, and if the relationship is worth its salt then it will survive."

Sophie nods her agreement with her friend. Her heart dances at the thought of things between her and Ross getting to a point where they have a relationship where she can trust him with the truth regarding her job.

"Right enough about lover boy and your romance, what's the boss said about the cars and Jason?" Belle asks.

The thought of getting to buy cars sends a thrill through Sophie, but it's soured by the thought of who she would be buying for. "Still not sure on the cars. I might need to be more creative on Monday about how long it may take to buy what he's going to ask for, if I don't get a decision, or make him pay upfront." The friends talk further about the case and Sophie's new involvement in it.

****

Getting the text back from Sophie agreeing to another date had made Ross the most blissfully happy person in Glasgow. He had thoroughly enjoyed their first date earlier that week, even if Jason had interrupted them making things awkward for five or so minutes, but Sophie had relaxed again and, he guessed, had had a good enough time to give him another try.

Ross knew he felt differently about Sophie than any other girl he'd dated and it both scared him and thrilled him at the same time.

Dynamic Entry

Since their date on Tuesday night Ross hadn't stopped grinning and that had become infectious with his customers, much to his boss' delight.

He sold a record number of diamond rings that week, everything from engagement rings to full eternity rings. He was full of compliments of how suited together the couple were or giving romantic hints and tips to the nervous customers on how best to pop the question.

"I'm loving the fact that you're in love. Your sales are through the roof."

Ross' head snaps up at his boss' words. "I am not in love, it's my fantastic salesman technique that's selling them."

His boss gives him a wink as she agrees with him sardonically. "Aye okay then. Whatever it is, keep it up, it's good for business. Now off you go for lunch." He gives her a salute before heading out the shop for his daily pub lunch.

Arriving at The Pub, he finds Sean in a state of anger. He's shouting at one of his bar staff to be more vigilant of the customers who came in, especially when he wasn't about. Ross sits at his usual spot at the bar and motions for Sean to come over to him. He orders his lunch from the young waitress as Sean slams into the bar stool next to him with a growl.

Ross eyes him. "What's your problem?"

Sean lets out another growl before answering. "There was a fight in here last night between two customers. It started from nowhere and escalated, quickly. I was upstairs taking a break when I got the call to come down. There was blood and teeth everywhere. I managed to get them separated and chucked them out on their arses, never to come back here again."

Ross listens intently to his friend but is confused at Sean's anger. "Aye, but that's not the first fight you've ever had to break up in here, so why are you angry at the staff? It's not their fault if arseholes come in and start crap."

Sean blows out a breath. "I know, but there was more that night too after closing. Someone spray painted the back door with a gang sign, or at least I think it's a gang sign, an' there's scuff marks on the back door too, like someone has tried to crowbar the door open. Then some guy came in as soon as I'd opened this morning asking if there'd been any trouble and if so, his boss could help."

Ross' eyebrows furrow in confusion. "What like protection? So do you think it's all connected? The vandalism and fight and then the offer of protection?"

Sean shrugs. "I don't know, but my gut says aye. My immediate thought was a protection sting racket thing, but this isn't the movies or gangster country, it's Glasgow."

Ross dips his head to the side. "Could still happen, there's gangsters in Glasgow." Ross ventures his opinion as his lunch arrives.

Sean shrugs again. "I guess, but there's no fuckin' way I'm letting anyone get their muscle in here. This place is mine!" The thought of muscles brings Jason to Ross' mind and a shiver runs through him. The guy was all muscle, bad attitude, and danger.

"Just be careful, and if anything else happens contact the police. DO NOT deal with it yourself."

Sean stands and slaps his friend on the back. "No worries. I'm not going to put my licence in jeopardy, but if I see them outside of here, you just never know how people can trip." Sean leaves Ross to his lunch and his thoughts.

His mind starts thinking about the fight and graffiti damage to the bar and how his friend would deal with it all, but that train of thought brings his good mood down, so he changes his thoughts to Sophie and their up and coming date.

How sexy she is and the things they could do to each other. The thoughts swimming in his head make it uncomfortable to sit and in need of a cold shower before going back to work.

He finishes his lunch, pays the bill, adjusting himself enough to stand and walks from the bar, hopefully without anyone noticing, and waves to his friend as he leaves internally hoping that nothing comes of the bad feeling they both have about the incidents in and around the bar.

CHAPTER EIGHT

Jason hasn't bumped into Sophie over the few days, even after he'd waited for her in the first place he'd seen her, The Pub. This had annoyed him to no end, but on a positive note, the time he'd spent sitting at the bar had made him think. The bar was always a hive of activity and was rarely empty, so always making money. Enough to afford protection and even some of his security officials, there didn't seem to be any muscle keeping an eye on anything other than the one guy, who in Jason's opinion is nowhere near 'muscle', and as a good citizen Jason is only too happy to provide some security and protection, at a price.

To prove his point of the lack of security and the need for some, Jason had set his workers some tasks. First, they had to start a fight during a quiet time to see what happens, how the staff respond to it. To his delight as the fight started and got going there was only a young female working, so no-one who could physically step in to stop the fight until the guy came from the kitchen area and calmed everything down with a few punches of his own before throwing the fighters out.

Jason had seen the same guy every time he'd been in, so he concluded that he was the manager or owner. After that, Jason's next step was to test the nighttime security. Not too much that the police could be notified, but enough to get an idea if there is security around The Pub's perimeter, lights or CCTV and such.

Dynamic Entry

Again, another worker had been put to work spray painting graffiti the walls and back door along with scratching up the door, then reporting back.

To Jason's surprise and gratitude, the job was easily done. There seemed to be no security measures at night, even though The Pub is situated in a poorly lit, dingy lane. Happy with his findings, Jason sets about making plans to introduce himself to the manager/owner to present his case of lack of security and how he can provide it, along with protection from future attacks.

With that plan in his head for later, he sets off to meet another new customer, or bait as he calls them, with a spring in his step.

He loves taking on new bait; someone he can make money from either through interest from their loan, or payment for goods and/or services, that is until said bait pisses him off and either doesn't pay or thinks they can get a better deal elsewhere. That is when he needs to show his nasty side, his 'don't fuck with me' side and cut out peoples tongues, or cut their fingers, toes off and then, maybe, take their lives all together, all depending on their crime against him plus his mood at the time of dishing out their punishment.

The customer he is about to meet had mentioned he was only interested in buying a gun, but Jason was an amazing salesman and with his own private dealer back in his business he was sure he could persuade the customer to spend a wee bit extra.

Getting out of his clapped out, rusted 60 plate Audi A1 in the hotel car park, Jason feels the strange sensation of embarrassment. No businessman of his standing should be subjected to such a heap of a car. He feels it brings down his credibility when he arrives at meetings in anything less than an up to date Jaguar.

He decides he doesn't want to wait the full weekend, until Monday to meet up with Sophie so sends her a message telling her so.

Need to meet earlier than Monday.

Smiling to himself at the thought of meeting Sophie and getting a new car, Jason enters the lobby of the new affluent hotel on Hope Street.

Visions of Sophie in all stages of undress, sitting in his new car dance in his mind, making it very hard for him to walk comfortably.

Arriving at the restaurant area Jason forces all thoughts of Sophie from his head and concentrates on the meeting about to take place. As much as he's desperate to have Sophie, he can't let himself lose focus.

He is quickly seated at a table and orders himself a pint of lager to wait on his customer.

Thankfully he doesn't need to wait too long as the customer arrives promptly, which he likes. They greet each other with firm handshakes and backslapping. Menus are brought and more drinks ordered, then they get down to business.

"So, Mr. Baxter, you're in the market for something shiny?" The customer looks around the restaurant furtively as Jason gives an arrogant laugh. "Please, no-one's listening, plus this is not my first rodeo, I am not going to be saying anything incriminating within earshot of people." He rolls his eyes with a smirk, then pins his customer with a dangerous look. His tone is low and threatening. "I am not stupid or new to this type of business, unlike you seem to be, Mr. Baxter." The customer shifts in his chair then straightens up, trying to appear more confident than his voice suggests.

Dynamic Entry

"Well, eh, this isn't my usual line of work." Jason grins, he loves it when his new bait is a newbie to his world of guns and drugs, it makes them more pliant.

"That's okay, we all start somewhere. Now, why don't you give me an idea of what you're looking for, discreetly, and I'll see what I can do for you?"

The customer gives a short nod and takes a deep breath, rubbing his hands together, then down his suit trouser legs before speaking again. "Well, you see, this will be a one-off purchase."

Jason makes a humorous sound at the back of his throat, but the customer continues. "I need it for one job, then I'm getting rid of it."

"And the job is,?" Jason prods, looking for more sales, but also for incriminating information to have in case he needs to control the man.

"Well, I don't really want to say." Another furtive glance around.

"I need to know Mr. Baxter so I can get you the right equipment. There is no point turning up to do a plumbing job with a cement mixer now is there?"

The customer looks confused and shrugs. "I need to get back what's owed to me. They're not admitting they owe me anything, so I'm going to tan, eh rob, their shop and take whatever I want,"

Jason nods. "So, the shiny thing is for what? Protection whilst you do this, a guarantee to get what you want, a warning to say that you're serious or all of the above? Oh and do you plan on using it?"

The customer looks a bit wide eyed with shock but tries, but fails, to cover it and come across confident. "Em, aye, all of that."

Jason smiles, he understands that his customer wasn't planning on using the gun at all by his reaction to the questions. "Well, in that case you'll need a getaway car and a driver that's not linked to you."

A half nod from his customer is all Jason needs.

"Excellent," he continues. "Well, you might be best with a semi-automatic. Something you can wave about, threatening like and use as a warning, but not do as much damage as say a fully automatic would. You could be in, get what you want and out in a matter of minutes." The more Jason talks and paints the scene, the more vigorous the customer nods at him. "Plus if you take the car and driver, and IF anyone clocks the car it can't get traced back to you, and if need be, we can get the plates changed. A fool proof plan." The customer is smiling but wringing his hands together as he looks at the table, then around the room.

Jason smirks imperceptibly then quickly looks like the epitome of empathy, even though he doesn't have an ounce of it in his body. "I understand this choice has been pushed onto you. I'm guessing that this is not how you envisioned this situation would come to a conclusion, but needs must..." His tone hardens as he leans forward. "And you don't want to look like someone who gets the piss taken from him, do you Mr. Baxter?" The customer swallows hard, then shakes his head, not wanting to disagree with the looming, menacing figure sitting across from him. A satisfied smile spreads over Jason's face, knowing he has his customer exactly where he wants him. Terrified to say no and desperate to please.

"Now, I understand you probably haven't thought about a getaway car, let alone budgeted for it, so I will do you a deal. I'll let you pay everything in installments after a deposit of five hundred pounds and I'll even drop my finder's fee as the car was my idea. Now you can't say fairer than that now, can you?" The question was followed by a glare of pure warning and a dare to challenge it.

Dynamic Entry

Mr. Baxter swallows again before agreeing, the pit of his stomach falls away from him, like he had just done a deal with the devil. "Fantastic!"

Jason takes his customer's hand in a crushing handshake. "It's a done deal. I'll arrange another meeting to go over the contract and the full amount due." Without dropping the customer's hand Jason pulls him closer so he is leaning over the table. "Remember though this handshake is a gentleman's agreement and so I class it as binding as the signed contract, understand?" A wild-eyed nod is all the customer can manage as a grin bursts onto Jason's face. "Excellent. Now I've got other business to attend to, so if you excuse me, I need to leave." Jason leaves the customer sitting slightly stunned at what had transpired during the meeting and with the pleasure of paying the bill.

****

Looking at her phone again, Sophie's stomach drops as she reads the text form Jason.

"FUCK!" She shouts into the room. She doesn't want to meet up with Jason at all let alone any earlier than Monday. Meeting him on Saturday was definitely out as she'd planned on spending the day getting ready for her date with Ross, a first for her, and didn't want anything or anyone bringing her mood down that day.

Looking up from her phone on her desk, she sees her DI and Belle looking at her. Looking between them she knows how her next conversation is going to go.

"What?" She keeps her tone to a small growl.

"What's all the screaming about?" Her boss eyes her as Belle questions her. "Is it Ro-"

Sophie throws her friend a look. "No! It's Jason, he wants to meet earlier than Monday."

Her DI grins. "Excellent. See if you can meet him tomorrow."

Sophie's head snaps to look at her boss as Belle's eyebrows disappear into her hairline. "It's Sophie's day off tomorrow and she's, busy. Why doesn't she see if she can meet him today at some point?"

Sophie whips her head round to her friend. She had thought Belle was backing her up when she first started talking, until she threw her under the bus.

"Today?" She asks, and her DI smiles.

"That sounds like a fantastic idea, Belle. Sophie, text Mr. Hamilton and meet up today."

Sophie narrows her eyes at Belle then smiles grimly at her boss. "Fine, but if he can't make it today it's staying Monday, and what about the cars? Am I telling him I can get them, regardless of what he wants?"

The DI mutters something about payment and Sophie working something out, then walks away. Sophie turns her attention back to Belle and motions to the empty, plastic chair on the visitor side of her desk.

"I'll deal with you in a minute!" She states and Belle shrugs then smiles sweetly. Sophie stamps out the text to Jason, jabbing her screen with her thumbs.

Only other time I can do is today, failing that it stays Monday as planned.

Throwing her work phone onto her desk in disgust she glares at Belle. "What was that?"

Belle tries for a look of innocence. "What was what?"

"That!" Sophie points to the space where their DI had stood. "With the boss, I thought you had my back, but instead you threw me under a bus. With your 'maybe today' shit!"

Dynamic Entry

"Don't you mean threw you under a muscle car?" Sophie catches the glint in her friend's eyes, but she hasn't calmed down enough to enjoy Belle's poor attempt at humour.

"I'm in the right mind to run you over with a muscle car! Some friend you are. You knew I wanted this weekend free from work stress."

Belle waves away Sophie's fears. "Ach, it'll be just like pulling off a plaster, it'll only sting for a second then you'll get used to it. Although the sting will probably not be as good as getting spanked, that sting changes into a heat like —"

"SHUT UP! I do not need to know where the rest of that simile is going, in fact I didn't even want to know that much."

"Got your mind off being angry at me though didn't it?"

Belle smiles and Sophie slumps her shoulders in defeat and smiles back. "In a sick and perverted way, aye. Now help me work out what I'm going to wear tomorrow night." Belle claps her hands as Sophie's work phone beeps with a text message coming in. They both stare at the offending object.

Sophie picks it up and looks at the name on the screen, then looks up at Belle, all the excitement about her date gone from her face. "Guess it's show time." She opens the message.

Excellent news, we'll meet this afternoon for lunch. The carvery place at The Fort near the cinema at 1. See you outside first, can't wait to see your gorgeous face again. x

A shiver runs up Sophie's spine as she reads the message, then she gags as she reads it again, only out loud for Belle's benefit.

"Oh that guy's got it bad for you. A kiss an' everything."

Sophie's stomach turns at the thought of any kind of kiss from Jason. "He was like this three years ago. I dodged his advances daily and told him no numerous times and in numerous ways. My main reason was I didn't mix business with pleasure, he got angry if he thought I was just outright saying no." Belle's eyes widen.

"Please be careful. D'you want me to come with you?"

Sophie shakes her head. "No, thank you, but no. He won't talk business with someone else there. I learned that the last time too. Keep your phone and your work phone on you and if I need back-up or a way out, I'll text or phone you. You could stay in the vicinity though."

Sophie rises from her chair as Belle nods her agreement. "Right, I better go inform the boss, then make myself presentable for my meeting."

Belle squeezes her friend's hand in support as she walks off. "I'll meet you at the pool car," she shouts at Sophie's back and gets a wave as an answer.

CHAPTER NINE

Jason grins at his phone as Sophie's reply of 'fine' comes through. He loves it when a woman plays hard to get and Sophie definitely plays hard to get. But that didn't matter, as Jason always gets what he wants one way or another, so he isn't worried, he will get Sophie in his bed.

Getting into his seaside themed bathroom, Jason winces. He hates the décor in the house but as he is renting the premises and he can't redecorate. At least his lease states he can't decorate, but he has decided that the bathroom is beyond his patience and so it will be getting ripped out and his lease ripped up. He pushes his thoughts of decorating to the side to concentrate on freshening up for his meeting with Sophie.

After a quick wash and a splash of aftershave followed by a change of clothes into dark navy jeans and a tight, white, low cut V-neck t-shirt coupled with his untied boots and he's ready to go.

Climbing into his Audi A1, he gives himself a smile in the rear-view mirror. Soon he will have a better car and a gorgeous woman to help him expand his ever-growing empire. He is going to be the most notorious, untouchable and best-looking gangster in Glasgow, or even better, Scotland.

Reversing into the parking space nearest the carvery, Jason spots Sophie standing by herself. He takes a moment to check the area around the restaurant for anything suspicious and is satisfied that all is well. He doesn't suspect Sophie is anything other than what she says she is, someone who can get high end cars amongst other things, but he is always careful.

After checking out the area, he takes another second to check out Sophie. It's a warm Friday afternoon in July and she is dressed to suit in a baby blue tailored linen dress that comes to just above her knee and white wedge sandals. Her honey blonde hair, which has been straightened to within an inch of its life, falls down her back to her shoulder blades. The only problem with the picture of perfection, Jason thinks, is the frown of stress marring her features. He smiles to himself, he's just the man to rid her of that frown and get her screaming his name in ecstasy.

****

Sophie sees Jason climb from his beat-up Audi and is shocked. He does need a new car, she thinks, and a bigger one too.

Watching him prize himself from such a small car would be amusing if it weren't an Audi and it wasn't Jason she was looking at.

He walks up to her with a sneer of a smile on his lips and a partial bulge in his trousers. He encompasses her in a hug before she can move back, so she stands there still and unmoving. Not wanting to make a scene this early in the investigation.

"Sophie, you are looking as gorgeous as ever this afternoon. Let's get inside out of this scorching sun, with your skin tone it wouldn't take much to burn." He places his hand on the small of her back and walks her into the restaurant.

The feeling of Jason's hand on her makes her skin crawl. She can feel the sweaty heat coming from him through the thin linen material of her dress and it's disgusting. Nothing like the sensual heat she felt when Ross placed his hand low on her back as they walked from the bar.

She reminds herself to breathe as he pulls her seat out for her, the only saving grace she can settle herself with is he pulled out the chair she can see most of the restaurant from, a must for her.

A waiter arrives at their table and smiles at Sophie after giving Jason a cursory glance. Sophie notes the way Jason's facial expressions change from barely guarded desire to all out anger in the second it took the waiter to smile at her and open his mouth to ask Sophie her order.

"We'll both have the carvery and bring a bottle of the house red!" Jason spits at the waiter gruffly. His strange mixed accent becoming thicker with anger. The waiter turns to look at him with a strange, mixed look of surprise and disgust.

"Okay, we have a Barefoot Merlot or —" Jason holds up his hand stopping the young man from talking.

"I don't care, I'm guessing it'll be cheap shite in a place like this, just bring a bottle." He waves the waiter away and turns his attention back to Sophie, who has given the waiter a tight smile of apology.

"That was a little rude, was it not?" She asks Jason with defiance in her voice. Jason settles into his chair more, looks Sophie in the eye and smiles, before batting away her question.

"Not really. When I ask for something, I expect to get it, I don't expect twenty questions. I know what I want and I always get it, it's as simple as that!" He looks down at her, his hands steepled. "I don't mean to come across as arrogant and I know I do sometimes." He opens his hands to her, making his body language appear open and readable, but Sophie can still see the danger in his eyes and the solid set of his overconfidence in his shoulders. "Forgive me, please?" He drops his hands and encases hers in his.

She notes how small hers seem in his and a cold shiver runs down her spine, giving her gut feeling more oomph. She pushes her fears away, knowing at that moment, or any moment with Jason was not the time to give out fear pheromones.

Giving him a smile and a nod, she retracts her hands from his. She uses the excuse of pulling her handbag from the seat beside her to get a new reporter's notebook and pen from it so it didn't look like she was pulling away from him. Jason grins.

"Desperate to get to business, or just talk cars? We've plenty of time for that, I would like to enjoy a semi-decent meal with you before we get bogged down with work. I mean so much has happened since I last saw you." He stares at her intently as she ties to gauge his thoughts. She knows she'd gotten away clean from their last investigation, so she didn't think he suspected her, at least she hoped not.

"Okay, let's get some food." She stands from their table, but Jason blocks her way and her view.

"No, you sit, I'll bring you over a plate."

She bristles at his words. "That's okay, Jason, I can... I mean, I prefer to pick my own food. I'm a big girl now." She barely holds her sarcastic tone in check as she steps around his hulking frame.

He walks behind her, his hand once more on the small of her back, and a touch too low for her liking. "Ah, I forgot how feisty you can get when a man tries to do nice things for you." His breath is on her neck, causing goose bumps to erupt on her skin. She holds in her shudder. "I bet you give up all power in bed though and become completely submissive." Ice runs through her at his words.

She stops walking and turns to look into the dangerous brown eyes staring at her. "I never give up my power." Her voice is stern to put her point across. "And I told you the last time, I don't mix business with anything else." She turns on her heel and marches to the counter, thankful there is no-one in front of her to be served. Jason smirks behind her.

They sit down with their meals and Jason pours them both a wine from the bottle, Sophie tries to stop him.

"The drink drive limit in Scotland has changed, you're not allowed any alcohol now." Jason gives her a small laugh.

"We're eating and we'll be here long enough for it to be out of our system. If not, I'll get one of my workers to pick us up. You going straight on me?" He eyes her with humour and she gives him a smile.

"I prefer to keep my licence clean. I enjoy driving my cars too much to get a ban."

"Understandable. It is part of your livelihood after all isn't it?" She gives him a nod as he continues. "I'm guessing you're wondering what happened three years ago?" Sophie's motions stutter, her fork piled with roast beef inches from her mouth.

"Well..." She places the food in her mouth, an excuse to not say anything else, hoping Jason would fill the silence. She's not disappointed.

"Well after you left, I got a feeling we were being watched. Then a month after that my warehouse got raided by the police early one morning, but I'd moved most of the stuff because of my gut feeling, so they didn't get much. They did have some information on me, so I realised I had a mole. I found it and dealt with it. He won't be talking again, that's for sure." Images of severed tongues flash through her mind as she swallows down her food along with the anger she is feeling at hearing what had happened after she left.

"Will he be doing anything again?" She asks as guilt creeps through her.

"Oh yeah, just not talking, or eating solids. No tongue left." Her stomach flips and her food turns sour. "Sorry, not a pleasant subject to discuss whilst we are eating, but at least everyone understands the warning it was." She nods and pushes her food around her plate, then takes a gulp of her wine, telling herself internally that Belle could drive home. "So, anyway, I should have gone down for three years, but they didn't have enough on me so here I am, free as a bird." Sophie plasters a grin on her face.

"That's good, and no problems since?"

"Nope, no-one would dare. I brought my business up here to Scotland as I saw a gap in the market and my face isn't as well-known up here, yet, and low and behold, I meet back up with you, it must be fate. My favourite car dealer and personal it girl." Another sneer comes her way making her push her plate away completely, all thoughts of food and hunger gone. She picks up her glass and takes another large gulp of her wine.

"I'll get my friend to pick me up." She answers the unasked question. "So, talking of cars, what do you fancy this time?"

Jason smiles then snaps his fingers at the waiter. "You, clean this away, we have business to discuss."

The waiter clenches his teeth as he walks towards their table. "Certainly, sir, could I get you anything else, tea, coffee, manners?"

Jason growls at the young man. "No, I don't think so, just some privacy, if you don't mind!" He waves the waiter away, as he turns his full attention to Sophie.

"And would the lady wish anything?" The waiter's voice is light and flirty, Sophie smiles and Jason growls again.

"NO, she doesn't! What part of privacy do you not understand?"

Before the waiter can respond Sophie speaks. "Thank you, but no, I'm fine." She gives the waiter another smile then waits until he is out of earshot before turning her anger onto Jason. "You will watch how you speak to people in my company Jason, or I will refuse to work with you." Her tone is stern.

He holds his hands up again. "I'm sorry. I will hold my tongue around idiots. Please forgive me, again." Another smirk crosses his face and it's all Sophie can do to hold her temper.

"That's okay, as long as we're clear. Now down to the good stuff, cars." For the first time since she met Jason that afternoon Sophie feels a genuine smile form on her lips.

Jason smiles back at her, a glint of desire in his eyes. "Well I need to get rid of that god forsaken Audi I have just now. It's an embarrassment with the amount of rust on it, plus it's too small for my muscular physique. Stupid fucking car."

Sophie stifles a laugh as she replays Jason getting out of the smallish car. "They're not that small, but I'm no Audi fan either. You looking for a Jaguar again?"

"Yes, big boot needed again, obviously. I'm also in the market for something fast and nippy that I can rent out for other business. I'm going to have a driver and a change of plates for that one."

Sophie gives a low whistle, that's a big order she thinks to herself. "Okay, so, first of all I'll need cash to pay for it all." Jason's eyebrows go into his close-cropped brown hair. "I was burned a few months ago with someone not paying the first time I asked and the deals I do are non-refundable, so I'm not gambling my own money again."

Jason nods his agreement. "I understand, totally. Did you get your money back or do you need me to have a word?"

Sophie places her hand on his making herself look relaxed. "No, it's sorted, but thank you for the offer. I know I can count on you." The words burn at the back of her throat, but she is warming back into her pseudonym.

She pulls out her phone and taps on the screen to bring up pictures of the cars she wanted to show Jason "So, you have the XF with the 540 litre boot like you had down south, or you could go for the F Pace which has a 650 litre capacity. It's also much better looking and more sophisticated than the Range Rover so many people are jumping about in."

Jason muses the cars over. "I think the F Pace this time, we'll be able to get more merchandise in it, don't you think?"

Sophie's eyes sparkle at the thought of car shopping. "Oh aye!" They continue talking cars and drinking wine until after five when Belle texts Sophie to give her excuse to leave. They ask for the bill and Sophie pulls her purse from her bag, Jason waves her away.

"This one's on me, please."

Sophie is taken aback by his manners so much she nods her agreement at not splitting the bill. "I'll be in touch with the details of my business account for you to transfer the money once I've found the perfect cars for you."

Jason tries to take her into his embrace when they stand, but she places her hands on his chest stopping him from getting any closer. She feels how solid his chest is as he pushes forward and presses a kiss on the side of her mouth. Power emanates from him

"I look forward to hearing from you." She fights the urge to wipe her mouth as she says her goodbyes and walks away, feeling his gaze on her backside as she goes.

CHAPTER TEN

Ross walks into The Pub after work on the balmy Friday night. It is Sean's only night off that month, and he'd requested his best friend's company, urgently. They tried to meet up for a drink on Sean's day off, but Ross knew there was more to it this time.

He sits in his usual barstool but finds himself looking over to the table where he and Sophie had sat together earlier that week. The two burly workmen sitting at the table frown at Ross making him turn back round sharply. He orders his pint, then thinks about his date and everything he wants to do to Sophie the next night on their date.

He couldn't explain why he was so nervous but excited about it. Sean sidles beside him.

"Dare I ask what's going through your mind or is it X-rated, again?" Ross blushes at Sean being able to read his mind so easily, then blushes even more at blushing. Sean laughs. "Oh fuck, you got it bad, an' whatever you were thinking must've been filthy! Come on," Sean nods to the seat in the very back corner they normally occupy on their nights out. It's private enough for them to talk, but Sean can still see what is happening in his bar. Never really off duty. Ross follows him and sits before giving his friend his answer.

"Fuck off!" He states as they sit.

Sean laughs, then chokes on his beer, then laughs again.

"Aye, you wish! Anyway, not my fault I can read you like a book. Looked good whatever you were doing." Ross' mood drops. He's never felt annoyed at his best friend for ribbing him over any of his girlfriend's, but for some reason he does this time. He puts it down to his nerves. Not wanting to look too deeply at why he is so annoyed at his friend or nervous he changes the subject.

"What's the urgency about the night out?" Sean sobers.

"Mind I was telling you about the fight an' the graffiti an' everything?" Ross nods his answer as he takes a drink of his pint. "I had the same guy in asking about it. Wee weedy guy. I told him to fuck off and he laughed, he fuckin' laughed. He then walked to the door, turned around and asked if I was sure, that it was my last chance."

Ross' eyebrows shoot up. "Last chance for what?"

Sean shrugs and takes a gulp of his pint. "I don't know, but I don't like it. I've said it before and I'll say it again, this pub is mine and no-one messes with it, or me." Ross can see the anger in his friend's eyes. Sean had worked his fingers to the bone and himself nearly to death to get The Pub up and running and where it is today.

"Has there been anything else happened since, any more damage or fights?"

"No, nothing, yet." A silence falls over the friends as they contemplate in their own thoughts what hasn't been said.

The front door bangs open and Sean's head shoots up to see a giant of a man walk in. Ross curses under his breath, bringing Sean's attention back to him.

"He's been in here a few times, someone you know?"

Ross looks over at Jason. "Someone Sophie knows, but I don't think she likes him all that much, and I don't like the way he looks at her."

Fiona Morgan

Jason looks over at the friends and smiles. It's a dangerous smile full of self-belief and contempt.

"Is that jealousy talking?" Sean asks with a wink.

"No, she totally clammed up and her body language became taut when he arrived at our table the other night. She'd only just started to relax and then he arrived and interrupted us and bang, she tensed right back up."

"You think he's bad news?"

Ross gives another shrug. "I honestly don't know, but I don't fuckin' like him." Sean nods his agreement. The friends try to continue their night with their usual banter and humour, although Sean keeps one eye on Jason.

An hour later, two more customers enter sitting at the bar, a few seats away from Jason. Sean notices them and clocks that it's the same guys he'd thrown out earlier that week. He decides to wait and watch before sending them packing.

After fifteen minutes Sean becomes aware of voices being raised. The friends look over to the bar area at the same time as the first punch is thrown between the two customers who had arrived together. Sean is on his feet and moving fast, but it's Jason who is there first.

He stands in between the fighting men, holding them at bay from each other with a hand on each man's chest. The men make a show of still going for each other, but Ross can see that it is more for show than an actual fight. Jason stands and grins at Sean.

"Would you like me to dispose of these gentlemen outside for you?" He directs the question towards Sean. His strange mixed up accent has a mocking undertone to it.

Sean grabs one of the men by his shirt and hauls him towards the front door, shouting behind him for

Ross to bring the second man. Both men go without argument and with a sly glance at Jason.

Once outside, Sean explains to them in no uncertain terms that they are no longer welcome in his pub and the police would be contacted if he saw them even breathe on his front door. The fighting men, no longer fighting, walk away after some apologies. Ross and Sean share a look, neither sure what had happened exactly, but both knew it was connected to the incidents earlier that week and the mountain of a man sitting in the bar.

Once back inside Sean walks over to thank Jason, Ross stands beside him. Jason turns to face their friends.

"Well that's a turn up for the books isn't it? I only came in for a quiet pint and here I am doing my civic duty of breaking up fights." Jason's brown eyes glint with humour and challenge.

"Aye, well thank you for stepping in Mr. ...?" Sean eyes him suspiciously.

"Hamilton, Jason Hamilton. You are very welcome, but can I ask, does that kind of thing happen often?"

Sean straightens, his shoulders going back and pushes his chest out. "No, this is a respectable establishment. Now can I get —"

Jason talks over Sean. "I understand, but I've heard through the grapevine that there have been some fights earlier on in the week, was there not?" Sean starts to answer but is again interrupted by Jason. "So I was wondering if you could use some security in and around your premises. Some door men or security officials. If so, I could help out there." Jason smiles a megawatt smile. His teeth perfectly straight teeth and dazzlingly white. Ross physically flinches at the brightness.

"That's very kind of you Mr. Hamilton." Ross can see his friend is barely holding back his anger at Jason's offer. His jaw is as tense as his clenched fists. "But I have my own bouncers at the weekend and I'm here every day. So thanks, but no thanks."

Sean turns to the barmaid and gestures to Jason. "Get Mr. Hamilton a drink on the house as way of thanks for his help." Sean gives Jason a tight smile and walks off. Before Ross can follow Jason places a hand on his arm and starts talking to him.

"It was so lovely to meet with Sophie today." Ross looks down at Jason's hand then back up at him, trying to dampen down the feeling of jealousy and nausea at hearing Sophie's name on Jason's lips. "How did the rest of your date go the other night?"

Ross grins. "Amazing, thank you. We're seeing each other this weekend, actually." Ross sees the flash of anger on Jason's face at his words, even though he covers it quickly with a mask of calm control.

"Really? She didn't mention it at lunch today."

"Well, Sophie is a very private person who likes to keep business and pleasure separate." Ross is talking on instinct from the feeling he got from Sophie on the subject of Jason and then he prayed it was true.

Another flash of anger mixed with impatience makes Ross think he's hit the mark and a nerve with his instinct.

"Yes, and don't I know it!" Jason growls deeply. "I'm sure you will have a nice time, but if I know Sophie, which I do, she's not one for staying with people. She's not really a people person." Ross smiles, knowing Jason is grasping. "Oh and while I have your attention. If I were you, I would try to convince your pal there to play nice and take my help if he likes his bar." Jason slaps Ross on his arm a few times as he grins and turns his back to the bar lifting his free pint to his lips.

Ross stands for a second, slightly shocked at the thinly veiled threat. Coming out of his shock enough to walk back to his table, making a mental note to question Sophie on Jason's business.

"You okay?" Ross asks Sean as he sits down, still feeling some jealousy from his own conversation with Jason.

"Don't know, to be honest. I'm pretty sure he's behind all this." Sean motions with his chin towards Jason. Ross follows Sean's gesture to see Jason smile smugly at them.

"Aye, I think you might be right about that one. I'm going to ask Sophie about him tomorrow night, although the thought of him, even in conversation, being involved in our date perturbs me. Sean agrees with Ross' sentiment as their night continues with both men keeping one eye on the mountain of a man at the bar.

****

After Sophie and Belle get back to the police station, Sophie gives her DI a quick rundown of what had transpired between her Jason and that she needed to go car shopping. The only fact that made her happy about the entire situation. The DI was pleased at her progress with getting close to Jason again and that she had managed to get around the issue of payment, ensuring Police Scotland wouldn't be footing the bill.

Coming out of her debrief Sophie finds Belle.

"You got anything planned tonight?" She asks her best friend.

Belle looks up to the left, making a show of thinking about her plans before answering. "Nah, ready meal for one and shite T.V. why?"

Sophie wrings her hands, feeling so far out of her comfort zone she could be on Mars talking to Martians. "I was thinking you could come over to mine, we could get a takeout and some beers and, maybe, help me pick out something to wear for tomorrow night?" Finding out her whole family life was a lie had left Sophie with trust issues, which in turn made making friends a tricky past time, but since meeting Belle she was getting better.

"Awe look at you are getting all girly." Sophie stops wringing her hands and folds her arms across her chest as Belle continues to talk, "wanting a girl's night and picking out an outfit for a date."

"Do you want to help me or have your lonely dinner for one?" Her tone is defensive, though Sophie knows Belle will see past it.

"I would love to help you."

Sophie blows out a breath. "Good, but I don't want any of your mushy shit, just because this is a first for me, understand?"

Belle manages to look shocked. "Me? Would I?"

Sophie hears the friendly sarcasm in her friend's tone and smiles. "Never!" She counters with her own.

The friends go to Sophie's end terrace house, situated on Roman Road in Motherwell. She knew it wasn't anything special, but it was hers and hers alone. No-one, especially a man, could get their greasy hands on it.

Getting in the front door, Sophie drops her handbag and jacket on the stair bannister where she always leaves them, then heads through her cosy golds and browns living room into the pastel pink kitchen to grab the takeaway menus and two bottles of Stella Artois.

Dynamic Entry

Belle follows her into the kitchen. "This kitchen never ceases to amaze me. I still can't get my head around the fact that you, of all people, have a baby pink kitchen."

Sophie holds out one of the beers. "It's pastel pink, not baby pink so shut it, or there will be no beer, no food and no girly shit of picking out clothes."

Belle makings a zipping motion over her smiling lips. "Okay, no more talk about your pink kitchen. So what we eating and what kinda date is it going to be tomorrow?" she asks as she opens her bottle with her teeth.

"Belle! Stop that! How many times have I told you about doing that, you are going to break your teeth! Honestly it's like being your mother sometimes." Belle sticks her tongue out at her friend as she laughs.

An hour and a half later the friends are fed and have the buzz of alcohol thrumming through their veins. They head upstairs to Sophie's bedroom. Belle sits on the white pine bed in the light grey room as Sophie pulls out clothes from her wardrobe.

"I'm not wanting anything too skimpy or sexy. I want it to say I'm interested, but not easy."

Belle nods. "Okay, well that shouldn't be too hard. You said dinner, then The Pub?"

"Aye, we're going to the pizza place next to The Pub, so I want to be able to eat, so nothing too tight, but I do want him to think I'm sexy, without it being too obvious,"

"So, let me get this right, you want to look sexy, but not too sexy and be comfortable?" Sophie gives her a nod as Belle starts looking through the clothes. "Don't want much do you?" Sophie rolls her eyes and hopes Belle can't see the worry behind them. "Don't worry, we'll get you something fabulous to wear." The friends spend the rest of the night fitting out Sophie for her date until they are both more than a little tipsy and badly needing sleep.

CHAPTER ELEVEN

Saturday night rolls round far too slowly for Ross' liking, but eventually, after many hours of waiting, planning and re-planning the date and how he'd bring up what he was expecting to be the touchy subject of Jason, it was here.

He had spent far too long getting ready again, and again he refused to acknowledge, even to himself, why that was or why he was so nervous. Sophie, he knew, was unlike any other woman he had dated. She was strong willed and stubborn, fiercely independent and would take no prisoners. Which he feared left her vulnerable as coming across as harsh and cold, but he could see a softer side to her when she relaxed, which he didn't think she did often.

Making his way from Queen Street train station he takes some deep breaths to try to calm his racing heart. He walks down Buchanan Street and turns into Mitchell Lane towards the pizza restaurant and stops dead in his tracks when his eyes land on Sophie walking down the lane from the other direction.

His heart beats itself into his throat at the sight of her in her full length flowing turquoise summers dress with white linen box jacket draped over her arm. Her straightened hair is pulled up at the sides then left to flow around her shoulders. Her make-up is light save for the red lipstick making her lips pop with colour and oh so kissable. They reach each other and Ross swallows his heart to speak.

"Wow, I mean you look, wow!"

Sophie smiles shyly as an unreasonable blush climbs up her cheeks. "Thanks, you look good too."

Ross looks down at his navy jeans and crisp white shirt. "Although if I was wearing bright white, I would be panicking about dropping something down it. I'm bad enough with just a jacket." Ross snorts out a laugh.

"I know what you mean, I'll probably need a bib." They smile at each other before Ross opens the restaurant door, letting Sophie walk in first with his hand at the small of her back.

Ross notices as she quickly checks out which table would give her the best view of the restaurant and makes a beeline for it. He also notices the way she looks around checking in a three sixty circle before choosing a chair. He had wanted to pull it out for her, but she was half seated before his hand touched the back of the chair. He makes his way around the table to sit across from her.

"Is this seat okay?" He points to where he is sitting.

"What? Oh aye, eh I mean yes, sorry." A waitress comes over with their menus, asking if they would like to order drinks. Ross can see a flash of something in Sophie's eyes. He takes a hold of Sophie's hand on top of the table, sending shivers running up his arm.

"Ladies first, what would you like to drink?"

The flash of Sophie's real smile has his heart stopping. "Thank you."

He smiles back and they order their beers. Then Ross brings the conversation back.

"You don't need to be sorry."

She gives him a shrug of her shoulders. "I like to be able to see what's happening, it's a work thing." The words are out her mouth before she can think about them.

"See any potential customers?"

Dynamic Entry

She blows out her breath, glad Ross didn't pick up on her slip and takes a sip of her pint. "Hmm, something like that." They order their dinners and the date continues smoothly, both of them finding out different things about each other.

With their meals finished, Ross offers to pay the bill, but is shot down by a fierce look from Sophie. He backs down, knowing he has still to bring up the subject of Jason and his interest in The Pub.

"Okay, dutch it is then, but can I tell you it's okay to let yourself be wined and dined, and your eyes are seriously sexy, especially when you get heated up." He feels more than sees the softening of Sophie's stance at his words as they hold hands again and gives an internal jump for joy.

Sophie smiles. "Maybe I'll try that the next time we go out then." Her words of a next date bring bigger smiles to each of their faces.

****

Jason walks into The Pub and looks about. Knowing that Sophie had a date with Ross that night had almost driven him to distraction during the day, so much so that he'd given one of his customers a good beating due to the way they had looked at him.

Wanting to kill two birds with one stone, Jason decides to wait on Sophie at the bar, assuming they would end up there and that way he could lean on the owner to take on his security at the same time.

Sitting at the bar, Jason keeps one eye on the front door and the other on the doorway behind the bar. He's not waiting long when Sean walks through from the kitchen area and Ross and Sophie walk in the front door.

Fiona Morgan

****

Sophie and Ross make their way into The Pub and head towards the bar. Sophie asks about drinks and Ross answers without argument, then they both see Jason at the same time and both tense, but Sophie is first to speak.

"Hi Sean, two lagers please." She turns to Jason, "Jason, I'm surprised to see you in here tonight, I'd thought you'd be working. Isn't Saturday night a busy night for you?" Her tone is stern even though her insides are on alert. Ross stands slightly behind her but to her side, she feels his presence and finds strength in it, that should alarm her, but instead she finds comfort in it.

Jason gives a wry smile. "I have my workers out there doing all the grunt work for me, so I thought I would pop in here for a few, this bar is beginning to grow on me." She sees the glint in his eyes and her stomach drops, she's seen that glint many times before and knows it means he's planning something. Something illegal and more than likely only profitable to him.

Sean has the drinks poured and places them on the bar, Sophie turns with her purse in hand, Jason and Sean speak at the same time.

"On the house."

"I'll get them."

She glares at Jason, then smiles at Sean. "Thank you, both, but I can pay my way." She pulls a ten-pound note from her purse and hands it over, feeling the anger emanating from Jason at the look she threw him.

Ross lifts his pint and motions for Sophie to lead the way from the bar. She heads to the same table as before, now thinking of it as her table and sits.

Ross gives a small laugh and sits beside her. "I thought it best to let you pick the table as it seems to be a thing for you."

Her heart swells slightly at his kindness and words. "Thank you and I am sorry, but it is kinda a thing. Will that be all right?" She inwardly berates herself for asking the question.

"Why wouldn't it be all right? Everyone has their own things. Just as long as you don't spend the rest of our date watching that man mountain down there."

Sophie's head is drawn to Jason as a shudder of revulsion courses through her. "No fuckin' danger of that happening." She turns back and looks deep into Ross' amazing navy eyes, her voice softening. "Not when I have you to look at."

She leans into him and places a gentle kiss on the side of his mouth, making his pulse hammer in his neck. "Wow!" It comes out as a squeak, so he clears his throat before attempting to talk again. "Not a fan of Jason's then?"

She snorts out a laugh. "No, not really, but it's work, so I need to be nice to him." She takes a gulp of her pint before she can say much more.

"He's not a nice man, is he?"

Ross' question leaves her floundering slightly for words, so she opts for shrugging instead. "I think he's trying to pressure Sean into paying for protection for this place." Ice runs through her veins, followed swiftly by molten anger.

She knew he was planning something, and now she knows it's a protection racket. Another charge to add to the sheet when they got one.

"I'll talk to him, tell him this place is off limits to him, now let's not talk about him anymore, it's a bit of a mood killer." Ross grins and agrees eagerly, changing the subject to cars instead, a subject that Sophie could talk for hours on.

After a few more beers, the couple call it a night. Both of them were aware of Jason's stare during their date and were thankful when he'd came up and said his goodbyes. Sophie physically relaxes once he'd exited the building.

Standing outside in the dimly lit lane Sophie is aware that she didn't want to say goodbye to Ross just yet, but also how much it must have cost Ross in a taxi the last time. She takes a deep breath and says how she feels before she can back out of it.

"As much as I want to go home, I don't want to say goodbye." She takes another breath so as not to lose her courage. "Normally by the second date I'm ready to scream, tell them to fuck off and just walk away, but with you, with you I want you to walk with me." An embarrassed laugh bubbles out of her.

Ross pulls her into his embrace. "I think that might be the nicest compliment anyone has ever given me." He kisses her forehead. "It's cheesy!"

"It's also how I feel too." Sophie takes a sharp intake of breath as Ross' lips descend on hers. She wants to start the kiss slow and soft, but as soon as she feels her mouth open to his she is lost, finding his tongue with hers. After long minutes she breaks the kiss, panting with desire and needing air.

"I know Motherwell is a long way away from Shettleston, and things aren't going to end up going all the way tonight, but, come home with me?"

"Aye." It is the only word he could summon at that moment as she raises up on her tiptoes and kisses him again.

CHAPTER TWELVE

Jason hadn't slept very well on the Saturday night after seeing Sophie out on a date with that idiot of a man. He wondered how someone so small and weedy could ever satisfy a woman, Jason strongly doubted that he could. He had eventually fallen into a fitful sleep, dreaming of all the things he could do to Sophie, all the ways he could get her to submit to him, so he could have complete control over her every sexual need and desire.

He had awoken with a pounding in his head and a throbbing between his legs. Getting up he walks to his badly decorated bathroom and takes himself in hand, stroking himself hard and fast as he revisits his dreams of Sophie. He comes hard, but he doesn't feel satisfied, knowing the only way he will get full satisfaction is when he empties himself into the warm wetness of Sophie.

Once he's showered and dressed, Jason decides he doesn't want to wait about any longer for his cars.

The car on order for his customer will be needed as soon as he can get it, and the sooner he gets his other car the sooner he can shift more of his product, which in turn makes him more money. He pulls out his phone and starts his message to Sophie.

Need to get a move on with these cars, especially the one ordered for a job. Need to meet up today for lunch to get the ball rolling. Text me back.

It was a demanding text, but he was a demanding person. As it is Sunday, he heads out to start some of the collections from the businesses he provides protection too. No rest for the wicked, he thinks ironically to himself as he closes his front door.

Climbing into his A1 Jason makes a phone call, ordering two of his workers to meet him, barking the addresses and time down the phone. He may be a body builder and can lift 300kg, but he isn't stupid. There is always safety in numbers and if there is more that one of them there more of an unspoken threat.

Starting his car he pulls out of his driveway heading to one of the pubs he provides security officials to first. It's a dark, dingy and dirty pub, but one that not only uses his bouncers, but always pays up on time and more for the extra protection of being associated with him. This should make the bar untouchable.

He had heard rumblings that one of his drug runners was boasting to all who was listening about how he was making easy money. He had also heard that the inebriated big mouth had nearly said his name. That was something Jason wouldn't stand for. The confidentiality contracts he made all his workers sign weren't for nothing.

He enters the darkness of the pub and tries not to touch anything. The barman who is standing behind the bar polishing glasses with a grubby kitchen towel stops what he's doing and smiles, showing off what little of his yellowing teeth he has left in his mouth. The two security officials bounce from their seats at the bar like their arses had been set fire to. Jason eyes them.

"I see I'm paying both of you to work hard!" It was more of a statement than a question and the burly men grumble their apologies and excuses. Jason points back at their seats and orders them to sit, then turns his attention back to the barman. He keeps his tone friendly, but his face is stern, his smile increases as the barman produces a grimy white envelope from under the bar and pushes it across the bar top with his dirt ingrained fingers. Jason lifts it, managing to not touch the barman's skin.

He knows he doesn't need to check the amount but takes a quick peek before depositing the envelope into his inside pocket with another grin.

"Always a pleasure coming to my favourite customer." He butters up the barman, then sobers again. "Now, about this ned the other week, the one running his mouth about my business and his involvement in it. Anyone know where I can get my hands on him?" The barman winces, he doesn't want his bar to be involved in anything, messy. He pays his money and his pub stays safe.

Jason gives the security officials a pointed look. The burliest of the two speaks first.

"He normally comes in here about one-ish on a Sunday, so..." He leaves the rest of his sentence unsaid, not really wanting to think about the outcome, let alone say it out loud, they all knew what their boss was capable of. Jason rockets between his toes and heels, a Cheshire cat grin spread over his face.

"Excellent! Well, once he arrives get him a pint on the house and keep him here. I'll be down to see him for a wee chat." Panic flashes over the barman's face.

"Eh, em, Mr., eh, Mr. Hamilton. I, eh, I don't mean to be disrespectful, but, eh, would, it okay not to, ye know, here?" Jason gives the man an understanding look.

"Don't worry. I'm only picking him up. I don't shit on my own doorstep, that would be unprofessional of me, now wouldn't it?" The barman nods, relief covering his face at the news. Jason thanks the barman again for his payment and continual loyalty to his business then takes his leave.

He spends the next few hours going around various pubs and houses collecting drug money, loan payments and one other protection payment. Most of the payments are made with no quibbles or excuses except one, but Jason is being the considerate loan provider so has given the customer in question a reprieve for this month, as long as he gets double payment, plus ten percent interest the next month. The customer was all too happy to agree to the terms, knowing the alternative would be bloody, unpleasant and unbelievably painful.

Come one o'clock, Jason has finished with his rounds, so he orders his workers with him to meet him back at the dingy bar. Before they enter, Jason goes through what he wants to happen once they are inside.

The workers have to surround the ned and Jason will talk to him. Depending on the ned's answers and Jason's feelings, depends on whether he gives the men the nod to lift the ned and place him in the back of the transit van or if he was getting left to finish his day in peace.

The workers nod their understanding, but all three knew what the outcome of this meeting would be.

They enter the pub, taking a second to let their eyes adjust from the bright July afternoon to the dingy, windowless pub. The security officials, thankfully, this time aren't sitting on barstools and are actively standing at the door, as per their job description.

They grunt their hellos and nod in the direction of the ned without being prompted. Jason turns in the direction of their nods to see the greasy, wild eyed twenty something male sitting with a rather bored looking female goth beside him. A frisson of excitement runs through every nerve in Jason's body at the thought of what was about to happen.

He walks towards the dark corner the ned has chosen to sit in, followed by his workers, and gives the barman a friendly nod before sitting across from the condemned man. His workers follow suit one sitting either side of him on the cushioned bench seat blocking him in like a pair of bookends. The goth is made to move tables for the meeting. The ned has the good sense to be afraid as his deer caught-in-the-headlights expression shows.

"Ah, eh, Mr. Hamilton, it's eh, nice tae, eh, can I git ye a drink?" The ned goes to stand, but the workers have a hand on each shoulder, forcing him back into his seat and holding him there.

"No, we're not staying long. Only popped in for a chat like." The ned gives a lopsided smile as he raises his pint to his lips.

"Aye, whit about?" He says the words into his pint as he pours the rest of the golden liquid into his mouth.

Jason's arm shoots forward, the heel of his hand slamming into the base of the glass, pushing it up into the ned's mouth and nose with a thrust strong enough to make the pint glass explode into cubes and so breaking the ned's front teeth and nose.

The workers hold the ned in place as he screams in pain at the assault on his face. Jason is up out of his seat, the small round table pushed into the ned's stomach pinning him to the back of his cushioned seat. He grasps the front of the ned's t-shirt, pulling him forward, pushing the table further into his stomach, as the goth girlfriend looks on in shock.

"I hear you've a big fucking mouth. You've been boasting about how fucking easy it is working for me?"

The ned's face blanches. "Eh, I never actually used your name, boss." The ned thinks his clever answer will be his saving grace, but his cocky attitude only makes Jason angrier.

Jason pulls the ned closer again, until they are practically nose to nose, the table pushing so far in it feels like it's touching the ned's kidneys.

"You said enough! If it wasn't for the fucking barman interrupting you would have said it and more, dickhead!" Anger pulses through Jason's veins, thinking about how easily the idiot in front of him could've made problems for him and his business.

He takes a deep, cleansing breath before speaking again, this time in a calmer, colder voice. "Now I can't abide people with big mouths, so, we're all going for a ride!" Jason uses the table to shove his chair back with a flourish and gives the two workers a nod, signalling to them to escort the ned into the transit van.

Standing up fully, Jason straightens his top and runs his hand through his short light brown hair, making sure everything was in place before walking over the bar, feeling the eyes of the goth girl on him. He pulls out a wad of cash from his pocket and throws a one-hundred-pound note on the bar.

"Here's something for the use of your bar and the pint. See you in a week." He points at the barman with a grin, throws a warning growl to the goth, then walks out of the dark bar back into the bright sunshine. He pulls out his Gucci sunglasses from his inside pocket and climbs back into his Audi, the beat of dance music blaring through the speakers thrums through his body, helping him prepare for the lesson he was about to teach the ned.

****

Waking up in bed with Ross was a surreal feeling. A feeling she wondered if she could get used to. She rolls over and feels his slender but solid frame lying next to her.

Memories from the night before buzz through her mind. The unusual feeling of not wanting the date to end, of not wanting to go home alone, but not wanting to come across as easy. She was always one for sticking to her decisions once her mind was made up over something, but last night she thought she would waver in her decision not to have sex with Ross, that last night would be the first time she would change her mind, but she didn't, although they did nearly everything else.

Ross had been the consummate gentleman, pleasing her without pushing. They kissed and caressed each other's bodies in every way possible without having full intercourse and never once did Ross make her feel lacking. No, he did the opposite, he made her feel sexy and wanted and wanton, and dare she even think it... loved.

Ross turns on his side and smiles, his eyes still closed. "Why are you smiling?" A quizzical frown forms on her forehead.

"'Cause I'm here with you." The easy answer slips from his lips in a sleepy tone.

"You don't know what I look like first thing in the morning, I mean I could look like a troll."

Ross opens his eyes and smiles again. "Aye, but you'd be a sexy troll!" He pulls her into his side and kisses her soundly on the lips. Normally she would pull away, frightened of morning breath, and getting too comfortable in bed with someone, but this morning she melts into his arms, letting herself enjoy the feeling of being there together.

She hears her work phone buzz and knows it will be Jason. She had planned on ignoring it, it was Sunday after all, but seconds later her own phone beeped with a text message. Both phones having different alert sounds.

Ross pulls away to look at her. "Mr.s popular this morning are ye no? An' why the two different ring tones?"

"Two phones." Her answer leaves her lips as her fuzzy brain kicks in. His quizzical look has making an internal monologue of 'shit' increase rapidly.

"Why two phones?"

She takes a deep breath, deciding that she needs to stick to the truth as much as she possibly can without giving away her actual job, just yet. "One's a work phone and the other is my personal one. I don't mix both." She can tell that Ross is pondering her words by the look in his eyes.

"What number do I have?"

She's taken aback slightly by his question. "Personal, obviously."

He smiles, but it's short lived as a frown replaces it. "What about Jason, what number…"

"Work!" Sophie answers before Ross can finish his question, making his smile beam again at hearing it.

"Has there ever been anything between you two?"

Sophie's stomach rolls as she disentangles herself from their embrace, a coldness settles in from not being near him. "Never! And there never will be, not in a romantic or even in just a sexual sense. I'll tell you what I tell him, I NEVER mix business with pleasure." Her tone is harsh and defiant at the thought of Ross thinking she could find Jason even remotely attractive, then she remembers he doesn't know the background, so softens her voice and cuddles back in trying to lighten the mood. "He's not my type. I don't like dodgy arseholes." Again her mouth is quicker than her brain. She hopes Ross wouldn't latch onto her words, but it's to no avail.

Dynamic Entry

"He's dodgy? Like just a bit dodgy, dodgy dealings, or like, pure dodgy, dodgy dodgy?"

Sophie looks at him bemused. "He's not nice and not really straight or narrow, and I'm not talking about his physical stature, and how many times can you say the word dodgy in the one sentence for god's sake?" She gives Ross a peck on the lips and climbs from the bed, pulling a t-shirt over her head before heading to the toilet.

She stops at the bedroom door and looks back. "I'm straight, my business is straight, my dealings with Jason are business, what he does with the cars I supply is up to him. Now I need to pee, then, when I get back can we not talk about him anymore. Especially since we're in bed." Ross gives her a huge smile and a resounding affirmative answer as she leaves the bedroom.

In the bathroom she reminds herself that it's her day off and there is a sexy guy in her bed, so not to look at either phone. Both can wait, especially the work one.

That text, she knows will be from Jason and that it will be more than likely be about the cars he wants. She reminds herself that she will be getting pushed and pulled into the life of Sophie Peterson twenty-four/seven for the foreseeable future, so, she muses, this is her day off and she is going to take it.

She flushes the toilet, washes her hands then gives her teeth a quick brush before going back into her bedroom, her heart pounding out of its permanent residency of her chest.

Ross is climbing out of bed when Sophie arrives back, she admires his lean body as he stretches wearing nothing but his trunk shorts.

He catches her eye and smiles. "Bathroom." Relief courses through her, she's not ready for him to go home.

"Okay." It's all she can think of to say. He walks past her, stopping to give her a quick kiss.

"I'll be back." She grins, a blush rising up her neck at the thought of him reading her thoughts.

Left alone, she gives into temptation and has a quick peek at her phones. The personal one is from Belle asking about the date, she sends a quick text back saying she would inform her tomorrow, then turns the phone onto silent. The work phone is from Jason, as she had guessed. He was pushing for the cars which meant he was looking to expand sooner rather than later.

She puts the phone on silent and throws it onto the chest of drawers with a thud. Ross comes up behind her, wrapping his around her waist.

"Work stress?"

She turns in his arms to face him. "Nothing I can't ignore for now."

She pulls him back into bed, his weight pushing her onto the mattress; she pulls him down further until their lips meet and all thoughts of Jason are pushed from her mind.

The feeling of Ross' mouth and hands all over her skin and inside of her isn't enough. She places both palms flat on his chest and pushes slightly. Ross breaks their embrace, panic flashing through his eyes, making her decision all the more certain.

"Did I hurt you?"

There is genuine panic in his tone, and she smiles. "No, I…"

"Do you want me to stop?" He goes to move his body from hers, but she grabs him tighter, wrapping her legs around his waist.

"No, I want more. There is protection in the top drawer on your side. Ross, I want you, all of you." Her forwardness shocks her, and she waits for the doubt or the niggle in her gut telling her to back off, to not get too close to start, but it doesn't come, so instead she pushes her hips up, grinding into his.

"Are you sure?"

She takes his handsome face in her hands, bringing him down to kiss him deeply. "I've never been more sure of anything in my life." And it was true, even her gut felt it.

CHAPTER THIRTEEN

The rest of the morning and into the afternoon the lovers send their time together going downstairs to eat then back upstairs to make love again.

Sophie had never felt intimacy like it. In her mind intimacy caused feelings and feelings caused problems and hurt. She'd witnessed first-hand what intimacy could do to a woman, make them so pliable they would be blind to what was staring them in the face. Endless derogatory remarks and affairs until eventually another fully made family, that took precedence over theirs, took away your husband, leaving you with nothing. No husband, no father for your child and no confidence in life to start again and no reason to keep living.

After growing up watching that happen to her mother and having her father walk out on them, Sophie had vowed to herself to never let a man into her life in such a way that he had power over her. She had fought all her life to be the strong independent woman she was today. Taking all males to task if they even considered her to be inferior, never allowing anyone in far enough to see the cracks in her tough veneer. But Ross felt different, he seems like a decent man. He never once made her feel inferior, even when he was being charming and acting like a gentleman.

She hoped they would continue whatever this was, maybe even turn it into a relationship, then she would need to tell him about her job and the omission of who she really is. She hated that he had been caught up in this web of half-truths but promises herself she will explain all as soon as she felt things between them were stable enough and there was trust on both sides.

It was late Sunday afternoon before Ross leaves with a kiss she would feel for hours to come on her lips and a promise to be in touch later. After a long hot shower, easing muscles that hadn't been used in a long time, Sophie orders herself a Chinese takeaway and boots up her laptop. It may still be her day off but looking at cars could hardly be called work for her.

Many hours later and with gritty eyes Sophie messages Jason.

Found some cars, can meet up tomorrow to show you.

Her work phone rings instantly in her hand and the call recording app she downloaded kicks in to record her conversation as she answers. Her voice is full of the fake happiness she'd perfected the last time she was undercover investigating Jason.

"Jason, how's things?" She's good at her job she thinks to herself.

"Ah, my gorgeous Sophie. Things have been, messy here, but tidied up now, thankfully. I thought I would've heard from you sooner though." His words grated on her, she hated the way Jason expected her to be at his beck and call.

"Well, Jason, I have other things to do, other clients to look after, so I can't always drop everything at the snap of your fingers. We had this discussion the last time we worked together. Plus, car hunting can be a tedious matter." She injects some humour into her voice knowing his anger would've been pricked at her admonishment.

"I'm sure it was hard labour for you Soph."

Sophie detected the sarcasm in his tone but chose to ignore it. "So you want to meet up and show me some cars?"

"Well you wanted a push on them, so I found some. I'm going to try and get some wiggle room on the price. I'll show you the ones I think are best and do the deal, all you have to do is pay."

A chuckle comes from down the line. "Okay, so I'll pick you up."

Jason knew he would be shot down with this, but he pushed it anyway. "We can go for lunch and drinks, I know your feelings on drinking when you're driving."

An indiscernible huff comes from Sophie. "No, I'll meet you, I'll need my car to go do the deal later."

"Okay. What about that nice pub you've started frequenting? Seeing you with me in there might loosen the arsehole who owns it up enough to take my offer of protection." Sophie can hear the dangerous lilt in his voice as she squeezes her eyes shut. She needed to put the brakes on him 'protecting' The Pub.

"No! And that bar is out of bounds for your protection. I've got that one!"

Another chuckle comes down the line. "Touchy about that bar, aren't we? Didn't know you were in the protection business too, trying to be in competition with me Soph?"

"No I'm not in the protection business, but I don't want that bar targeted, as a favour to me, if you will." She knows that her statement would come back to haunt her, but she couldn't let Ross, Sean or The Pub become any more involved in this sordid life than was necessary.

"Hmm, okay my gorgeous Soph, only for you. Now why don't you meet me at my office in Blythswood Square, number nineteen, that way I can transfer the money or give you cash, whatever is easier for you."

Sophie is shocked at the quick change of plan and the niceness from Jason, but she doesn't question it and agrees a time for the next day, then cancels the call, glad to be off the phone but also happy that the case has taken, what feels like a giant leap forward.

She types out an email to her DI, spelling out the basics and arranging a meeting with him the next day before she leaves for her meeting with Jason. Then she phones Belle from her own phone, not wanting to wait until the next day to talk to her friend.

"I wondered if you'd get back to me today." Belle gushes in a mock angry tone, one similar to how a father might use on a daughter sneaking back into the house far too many hours later than what was her curfew, or at least she assumes that's what it would've sounded like if her father had stayed around long enough for that to happen. "Good date I take it? On second thought, I can hear your grin, so maybe I don't want to know!"

Sophie grins at the memories, thankful that her best friend couldn't see her blushing. "I never said anything so how can you hear my grin?" She hears Belle sniggering.

"I heard it through the silence, so it was good then? Are you seeing him again? Oh my god you went all the way with him, didn't you?"

Sophie knew Belle was an excellent police officer, but even she couldn't have worked that out from the mostly one-way conversation. "How the hell did you come to that conclusion Belle?"

Her friend starts to screech down the phone. "I knew it, I bloody knew it! You're going to marry him, I can feel it in my waters, as my dear departed mammy would say." Sophie shakes her head at her friend.

"If you must know, aye, we slept together, and we did it lots and it was good, better than good, but it didn't happen until this morning, then Ross left and I ended up looking at the text on my work phone and so doing some work and arranging a meeting with the Jason and one with the boss before that. I've found some cars that would be suitable for Jason, so I suppose we should get this show on the road, so to speak." Belle makes a sound of agreement and the friends spend the next hour talking about the case and what would be the best way for Sophie to continue to be Sophie Pearsons with Ross whilst him knowing her as Sophie Peterson.

****

His Sunday ended on a relatively high, Jason thinks to himself. Not exactly how he had wanted it to turn out, but a step in the right direction none the less.

He will be seeing Sophie tomorrow, will be in receipt of a decent car for his business soon, plus the idiot with the big mouth has been taken care of, sending a message to everyone involved with his business and probably some who weren't, that he wasn't to be fucked with. He is Jason Hamilton, master of his universe and all who live there.

The loudmouth ned wasn't as loud or mouthy when they'd bundled him out of the back of the transit van when they arrived at the warehouse. He had been rendered mute with fear by that point, though he found his voice box for screaming once the torture started.

Jason had gone through his usual routine of talking through all the possibilities of violence that could happen as he caressed his tools. He preferred to think of his weapons as tools.

In his own mind Jason isn't violent and the word weapon conjures up images of violence. No in his own mind he is a businessman, a workman you may, so, as a workman he has tools.

The ned had been boasting about the size of the packages he had to carry, so Jason had taken away the ned's ability to carry anything. Using the ned's own knees as a chopping board again, Jason had hacked off his hands at the wrists with the meat cleaver he had used not too long ago on his other customer. Satisfaction had filled Jason as he continued to tell the ned everything he had done wrong then removed the offending body part.

Didn't listen to the instructions given to him, off came his ears. Walked about with the product, off came his feet. Looked at the product, out came his eyes. This was the most gruesome torture Jason had ever given out, but the more he warmed to his subject the more of a thrill he got from it.

The two workers helping to hold the ned down grimaced every time Jason swung his cleaver or used his knife, but neither of them said anything for fear their boss' wrath be turned on them.

Eventually, after half an hour of chopping and stabbing, Jason decided to end his victims suffering. He was almost dead from blood loss as it was, so taking the secateurs, Jason pulled out the ned's tongue and sniped it clean off. He thrust it into the ned's limp hand, growling that he wouldn't be talking about anything anymore to anyone. As the ned took his last breath, Jason dumped his bloodied tools back onto the workbench, turned back to face his workers who were white with shock.

"Right you two, clean this mess up, I've got other business to attend to." He walked away leaving his overalls in a bloody heap behind him.

CHAPTER FOURTEEN

Monday morning rolls around and Sophie rolls out of bed alone. She'd missed having Ross in her bed the night before but chastises herself for being soppy. She had, however, allowed herself to text him goodnight then grin like a giddy schoolgirl when she received his goodnight text back.

Getting ready in the morning was a task Sophie took on with determination. She needed the mask of the make-up before she could leave the house knowing she was meeting Jason.

She keeps her daytime make-up light, then starts on her hair, one whiff of humidity or rain and her curls spring to life. That meant by living in Scotland with all its rain she was fighting an ever-losing battle to keep her hair straight, but it was a battle she chose to fight every day.

Satisfied that she was ready to face the day, and Jason, Sophie leaves her house, lifting her light rainproof jacket as she goes. There had been a few weeks of bright sunshine and warm weather, so rain in biblical senses was overdue.

Climbing into her XJS Sophie takes a moment to appreciate her car before pulling out of her driveway and heading into Pitt Street. As always, she is aware of the cars around her, making sure she wasn't being followed.

She arrives at the police station and parks her car in the furthest away space, hoping no-one parks next to her and dinks her door. Getting inside she immediately heads for her tea, then finds Belle and her DI, giving them both a briefing of her conversation with Jason the night before and her plan for the day ahead. The DI gives them the nod for Belle to go with Sophie, although she was told to keep her distance when it came to the meeting with Jason.

Sophie has heard back from some of the sellers and arranged a time to see the cars, making sure she has time to have the meeting with Jason to get his money transferred into the new bank account that had been made for her.

So with her plan of action in place and everyone happy, Sophie grabs the keys to the silver 2015 BMW 335i Coupé pool car and heads towards Blythswood Square.

****

Jason preens himself in the mirror in the bathroom in his office. He always spends at least half an hour to forty-five minutes getting ready in the mornings. Showering, shaving just enough so he had the perfectly fashioned day old growth of stubble, then blow drying and styling his light brown hair until it is sitting in the gelled sharp side pattern that makes him look groomed to perfection, but this morning he took longer, knowing he was seeing Sophie.

He had to be at the top of his game if he was going to get through to her that mixing business with pleasure is a good idea and that come hell or high water they will be together he had to look too good to say no to.

He walks back into his office as the intercom buzzes. One look at the CCTV monitor tells him it's Sophie at his door and she's looking sexy in her pencil skirt suit. She always comes across as a woman never to be messed with or underestimated, which many men have to their own demise.

He buzzes her in and blows out a breath to centre himself. Sophie walks through the short corridor to the door stating Jason's name and enters without pausing to knock. Her mobile phone is already recording to catch any conversation between them.

Jason walks from behind his desk to greet Sophie with a kiss on both cheeks, his hands grasping tightly onto her shoulders. She keeps as much of a distance between them as possible and her arms stuck by her side.

"Soph, you are looking the optimum of sexy businesswoman today. Please sit and show me these cars."

Sophie takes the visitors seat at the desk placing her phone on top of it. She pulls out her convertible laptop and using it as a tablet she swipes at the screen bringing the screen to life, showing the screen saver of an Aston Martin Valkyrie, Jason eyes her.

"A dream of yours? What model is that one?"

He nods towards the car on the screen. "It's a Valkyrie. Two of my loves rolled into one. Fast cars and strong warrior women." Jason gives her a disdainful smile. In his book women are not warriors, they should be there to do his bidding. Ancient societies, in his mind, had the right idea. Keep women to do as you please with them.

"Hmm." Is all he can muster as an answer. "Well, what about my cars?" With a flick of her finger and some taps on the screen a 66 plate F Pace black Jaguar materialises on screen. Jason takes hold of the tablet and marvels at the beast.

"Wow, that is something else, and it's boot's bigger than the XF?" Sophie nods.

"Aye, 650 litres. That should be enough for what you need, will it not?" A glint in Jason's eyes lets on more than he is aware.

"Oh yes. So what's this coming in at?"

"Forty grand. It has low mileage and I can deliver it as early as tomorrow, provided the money is available." Jason swallows down his retort about being more than capable of having that kind of money and reminds himself that Sophie was only looking after herself. Something that should be commended.

"Ah, Soph, you know I'm always good for the money, but seeing as you explained about a previous situation, I'll transfer the money right now." Sophie releases her breath.

"Excellent, now do you want to see the other car? The one you need for an order?" Jason nods. "Now this one isn't flashy or fancy like you requested, and an Audi, but the only Audi I like." A white 1983 Audi Quattro flashes into the screen and Jason sits back in his seat with a grin on his face.

"That there is a getaway car." Sophie's eyes widen at the slipped confession but recovers her composure before Jason can notice.

"It is that, it's in fantastic condition considering its age." She swallows with a car salesman's grin then continues. "This is coming in at five grand, which I think is a steal, even if it is an Audi." Jason's pulse is thudding in his neck at the thought of everything coming together.

He will have the cars he needs to conduct his business and also prove his class and status, plus the 'messages' he had sent out by way of his customers/victims will let all of his counterparts in the city understand how serious he is. So all he needs now is the girl, and not just any girl he wants Sophie and as Jason has already proved to himself time and again, he always gets what he wants.

"Excellent, if you give me your bank details, we'll get the money transferred plus your payment too." Sophie nods and smiles.

The transfer took seconds to go through. Sophie packs her tablet away and stands, a grin bursting from her lips.

"Well Jason, I will be in touch when the cars are ready. Hopefully it won't be too long." She holds out her hand for Jason to shake. He clasps her small hand in both of his large ones, encasing them in his grip, then jerks her arm in towards himself bring her into his chest. He removes one of his hands from hers and snakes it around her waist bringing their pelvises together. He splays his hand round onto her lower back, his fingers caressing the curve of her buttock.

"Now Soph, I'm sure we can do a better thank you than a handshake, after all the years we've known each other." Sophie forces her hand from his grip and onto his chest, pushing at the solid mass of muscle but he doesn't budge.

"Jason, we've been through this. I do not mix business and pleasure, and we both need each other in business." She pushes again, and again feels a second of resistance before Jason loosens his grip on her back.

"Ah Soph, you are killing me, yes I do need your business, but one day my beautiful Sophie we need to be together." She keeps her grin glued to her strained face to lessen the blow.

"So you keep saying Jason, now I better go and get spending your money." She extracts herself from his grip altogether and gathers her bag heading towards the door.

"One day Sophie." Jason mutters from his standing position at his desk. Sophie turns back.

****

"Goodbye Jason." Her voice is calm and business like. and she has no idea how she made it come out the way it had. She heads back out onto Blythswood Square and into a summer rain shower. She's not normally thankful for the rain as it makes her curls spring to life, but today she feels the rain cleansing her from Jason's touch.

Belle is waiting in the BMW that's parked outside the office building and she eyes her colleague as Sophie steps back into the driver's seat.

"How'd it go? You look a bit stressed."

Sophie gives a shudder. "Not stressed, just grossed out. He was getting touchy again."

Belle's eyebrows go into her hairline. "Touchy?"

"Hmm, nothing too bad just trying to cuddle me instead of a handshake with a quick rub over the top of my arse, things like that. Plus he insists that we need to be together at some point." Belle visibly shudders at the thought.

"Nah, you're all right." The friends agree with Belle's sentiment. "So, you want to do lunch before or after the car dealers?"

Sophie's checks the time; she'd hoped to catch Ross at lunch time in The Pub. She mentally laughs at herself and how she feels over Ross so quickly. "Let's get food, then shop. Need the sustenance to enjoy the afternoon."

Belle shrugs her agreement with Sophie. "I can do that, and maybe see the sexy barman too." With a smile on both the friend's lips Belle pulls the BMW out into the quiet road, heading towards Mitchell Street.

****

Ross sits on his usual barstool after ordering his lunch. He is eager to talk to Sean, wanting to know if there had been any more trouble or if he'd heard if Sophie had spoken to the mountain man about backing off. He wasn't sure what she could do about Jason, if anything, but he didn't want his friend's business being targeted by thugs or gangsters.

He pulls over the bars newspaper and tries to concentrate, but every time he hears the front door opening his head snaps round in the hope that Sophie would come in for her lunch.

They hadn't arranged anything, but he still hoped. God, he thought, he was turning into a lovesick puppy.

The door opens and he turns his head. A smile breaks out across his face at the sight before him. Sophie walks in with Belle on her heels. She looks over to the bar and flashes Ross a dazzling smile, the one that makes his heart stop then stutter back to life with a thud. It was her real and relaxed smile and it was just for him.

Sophie stops at the bar, standing next to Ross, their matching smiles giving Belle something to snigger about.

"Hi."

"Hey."

Again they both stare and smile at each other and Belle groans. "God, is this what your dates are like? They must be feckin' boring!"

Ross laughs and Sophie growls at her friend. "No they are not like that; we can actually be quite articulate with each other." Ross' sardonic tone makes Sophie laugh.

"Thank god for that!" Belle looks between the lovers. "I was thinking I would need to join youse and show you how it's done." She wiggles her eyebrows comically as Sophie shrieks.

"BELLE!" Belle shrugs then jumps with a squeak as a voice booms from behind her.

"You an' me both!" Belle spins round and slams into Sean's chest.

It's Ross' turn to growl. "Maybe we could make it a double date instead of us being creepy third wheels on their date."

Belle smiles up at Sean. "I quite like the sound of that." Belle and Sean stand smiling at each other until Sophie clears her throat bringing them back into the here and now.

"Sean, have you had any more trouble?"

Sean drags his eyes away from Belle, bringing his attention to Sophie, sobering as he does it. "No, not for a few days, thankfully."

Sophie nods her head in understanding. "Good. I, hopefully, have stopped it, but if you have any more trouble let me know, okay?" All eyes are on Sophie.

"Aye, okay, thanks, so, does that mean I need to pay you protection instead of that giant dickhead?"

Sophie shakes her head with a laugh. "No, that's okay, I'll get Ross to pay me for services rendered." Her cheeks glow red at her own words, not meaning to say them out loud. Belle snorts out a laugh.

"Dear god Ross what have you done to my friend? I've never heard her talk, dirty!" Laughing, Belle turns to Sophie, pushing her towards the table they have claimed as their own. "Right you, lunch before you do or say something really bad." Sophie smiles at the two men standing with them as she allows herself to be pushed to the table.

They finish their lunches and pay the bill. Ross had come over to say his goodbyes, followed by a short, chaste kiss for Sophie and the promise to phone her later that night.

They leave the bar and climb into the BMW pool car, heading towards the first address where Sophie is looking to buy the first car from. Belle fidgets in the seat next to her.

"Right, out with it. I know you're dying to ask." Sophie demands.

"You're really into him, aren't you?" asks Belle.

Sophie pulls the car into the kerb at the address they needed. "Aye, I am." She blows out her breath at the confession.

"You gonna tell him the truth? About the job?"

"I can't, well at least not yet. I mean it's only been a week or so, but I am going to need to have that conversation at some point. I just want to make sure I can trust him and not only with my job." Belle bites her lip and Sophie can feel her annoyance at her friend growing. "What now?"

Belle blows out her cheeks. "Not all men are like your dad." Sophie can see Belle hold her breath again. This is a touchy subject and one she didn't want to be brought up right before they went into to do a deal for work.

Sophie grinds her teeth. "One, do not refer to that man as my dad. He fathered me, then fucked off. Two, I know not all men are like him, and for what it's worth I don't think Ross is like him at all but, then again my mother didn't think he was a lying cheating bigamist, so, I think I'll take a wee bit longer than a week to make my mind up, if you don't mind!" Her tone is snappy as it always was when the subject of her father arose. She takes a deep breath to clear her mind from him and get it back into the game of car buying. "Right forget that arse and let's get in here to buy this car for another arse." Belle gives her a short nod.

They knock on the front door of the semi-detached house and a fifty something man answers. Sophie's eyes widen at the sight before her. The seller could have bought the Quattro in the eighties and kept the clothes he was wearing when he bought it.

The shiny grey suit with the sleeves pushed up to his elbow nearly blinds them as it glints in the sun as it chooses that exact time to peek out of the rain clouds surrounding it, and the pair of loafers with no socks completes his outfit. Belle whispers in Sophie's ear.

"The eighties called, and they want their suit back."

Sophie coughs her laugh away, then greets the man standing staring at her with her most confident smile. "Hi there, I emailed yesterday. I'm here to look at the Quattro you have for sale." The seller grins and makes a sound at the back of his throat. Sophie flashes him another smile, knowing he has just underestimated her as a mere female who knows nothing about cars.

Half an hour later Sophie drives away in the Quattro as Belle drives the pool car. Mr. Eighties hadn't known what had hit him when Sophie had started talking, pointing out 'faults', bringing the price down by fifteen hundred pounds. She had managed to make the seller think he was getting the best deal he could get.

CHAPTER FIFTEEN

Sophie pulls her XJS into her driveway and hears her personal phone ring. Pulling it out she smiles as she sees Ross' name flash on the screen.

"Hey there." She opens her car door and rustles as she collects her bags.

"Hi, I hope you don't mind me calling?"

"No, not at all. Just give me a minute 'till I get in."

"You just getting in from work?"

Sophie drop her bags on the floor then flop into her couch with a humph, checking the time as she sits, nine o'clock. "Aye, sometimes car shopping can be a long and tiring day." She and Belle had taken the Quattro back to the station to get a tracker device fitted to it before Sophie takes it to Jason the next day. She had stayed a bit longer to fill out her notebook for that day and to go over more paperwork.

She'd also spent time staring at the incident board trying to commit the faces of Jason's known workers to memory for future reference. She feels bad for the lie, but technically, she thinks, she did do car shopping.

"I'm sure it is. Did you get what you were looking for?"

She smiles down the phone at his question, glad he is semi-interested in cars and her. "Aye I did. I'm going to drop it off to Jason tomorrow, then I have another one, maybe two, to get for him." She can hear Ross makes a noise at the back of his throat. She hopes he isn't going to go down the road of telling her she can't work with Jason, but he doesn't, and their conversation continues smoothly.

Dynamic Entry

They end it with soppy goodbyes and promises to speak the next day and to organise a double date with Belle and Sean.

****

The next morning Sophie goes through her usual morning ritual of putting on her makeup, straightening out her curls and drinking her first cup of tea of the day.

She adds in a good morning text to Ross to her ritual, making herself smile. She muses at how quickly she had allowed him into her life and without too much of a fight. She pushes away the warm fuzzy feelings that that thought brings to her heart and heads out the door.

Once at the station she parks her XJS in her normal, far away spot and heads into the canteen for another cup of tea before her meeting with her DI to go over their plan of action for the day. Grabbing her tea, she spots Belle sitting at a table so wanders over and sits opposite her friend.

"You look lost in thought, anything I can help you with?"

Belle's head snaps up and a blush rises on her cheeks. "You probably don't want to know, I was thinking about Ross' friend, Sean."

Sophie shakes her head. "You're right, I probably don't want to know."

Belle throws a scrunched-up napkin at Sophie with a laugh. "Don't be cheeky! So, are we getting a double date sorted? I mean, I think you and Ross need help talking to each other, and, well I think I need to get to know Sean better, you know he's kinda part of the case with Jason threatening protection."

Sophie gives her friend an eye roll. "Aye, I'm sure we can get a double date organised, and for your information, Ross and I can talk to each other just fine, in fact we were talking about the double date last night when he phoned me."

Belle's eyebrows go up in interest. "Oh, so it's getting serious is it? Talking on the phone at night and everything."

Sophie can hear the friendly teasing in Belle's tone. "Maybe." She answers coyly. "I think Sean is taking a night off in two weeks, so it'll need to be then." She checks her watch, "Right we better move our arses and get up to the boss before he comes looking for us." Sophie lifts her cup to take with her.

An hour and a half later Sophie and Belle leave the station, Belle driving the same BMW pool car as the day before and Sophie driving the Quattro.

The techs had fitted the GPS tracker and shown Sophie where they had hidden it. Sophie took the time to have another once over the Audi to remind herself of all the redeeming qualities of it. She wanted everything straight in her head before handing it over to Jason.

She had phoned Jason when they were in the meeting with their DI, they arranged to meet him at the same carvery restaurant as before at the Fort shopping centre.

Somewhere public was perfect for Sophie, her discomfort whilst being alone with Jason grew with each meeting they had. She had brought the situation up with her DI and was told to watch her back and remove herself from the situation immediately if she felt at risk in any way. She had bit back the sarcastic retort and eye roll that her body demanded she give her boss, it wasn't worth the hassle she would more than likely bring down on herself, plus she was still trying to be nicer to the male population after Belle's admonishment three years ago. Old habits were hard to break, sometimes.

Sophie parks the Quattro and takes a deep breath. She checks that Belle is parked five rows away from the front of the restaurant as per their plan. She's to stay in the car and only come in if Sophie sends her a SOS message.

Taking another deep breath she exits the car and walks into the dark gaping hole of the front entrance. After a quick scan of the restaurant, Sophie deems that she is first to arrive and so she picks out the best vantage point seat possible. Not perfect, she thinks, but the best the layout had to offer, she sits and waits on Jason, remembering that he liked to be late, keep people waiting on him and if possible, make an entrance.

The man loved himself and truly believed everyone in his presence should bow down to him. She wonders if he makes his customers lurch at his feet when he walks in to do his dodgy deals, she smirks at the thought.

Jason chooses that moment to walk up to her table with a predatory grin.

"Ah, beautiful Sophie, are you that happy to see me?"

Sophie brings her business face into play, inwardly berating herself for getting caught looking happy to be meeting him. "You know me Jason, I love selling cars." She motions to the seat she wants Jason to take, the seat across the table from her, but he ignores her, taking the seat directly next to her and grins as he settles in.

"The conversation may turn more private," He explains his choice of seat, "so the closer we are the less chance there is of others hearing us." He winks at her, making her skin crawl. "Now, what would you like to drink?" Jason clicks his fingers to gain the attention of the young waitress. Both women roll their eyes at the gesture.

Sophie starts to order herself an orange and lemonade when Jason stops her. "Please share a wine with me, to celebrate the first of our new business deals."

Sophie eyes him warily, then reluctantly agrees. "Okay, I have my friend picking me up, so I can have one."

Jason nods with a glint in his eye. They order their drinks then go to collect their food. Once they're all settled back at the table, Jason starts with his bullish gentleman act.

"Sophie, I wish you would let me be a gentleman and bring you your food and then drive you home."

Sophie clenches her teeth to contain her annoyance. "Jason, I am not a child. I am more than capable of collecting my own food and even feeding myself, and as for getting me home, I have another meeting after this, so I wouldn't want to put you out." She gives him a sickly-sweet smile.

A lascivious smile crosses his lips when Sophie mentions feeding herself, but it was closely followed by a look of annoyance at hearing she had more meetings. On her first undercover assignment with Jason he had tried to monopolise her time and her 'business'.

"Well, yes, I'm guessing your business is flourishing being back in your natural country?"

Sophie swallows against another wave of anger that washes over her at Jason's condescending tone. "Aye, very much so, thank you." She retorts, thickening her Glasgow accent. They finish up their meals and wine. Jason orders another wine, and Sophie takes a toilet break to breathe.

Dynamic Entry

After the breather, and a quick text to Belle letting her know all was going as expected, Sophie settles herself back into her seat.

"Remember the drink driving laws have changed in Scotland, so you shouldn't be driving even after one glass of wine, let alone two." Jason waves away her warnings and she makes a mental note to add drink driving to the list of crimes to add to his charge sheet. "So, keys." She puts the keys to the Quattro on the table in a veiled attempt to finish up the meeting.

Thankfully Jason takes the hint and they pay the bill with Sophie demanding she pays half, then they head towards the car. Jason places his hand on Sophie's hip, then pulls her towards him as he wraps his fingers around her slim waist as they walk. She is pulled in tight to his side when they arrive at the car. She tries to extradite herself from his embrace, but he grips on tighter, his fingers digging into her flesh, almost to the point of pain. He leans into her ear and takes a deep breath in before talking.

"I forgot to say in the restaurant, but I am in the market for a semi-automatic gun. Is that something you could get for me?"

Sophie swallows, takes a deep breath, then fixes an apologetic smile on her face. "Ah, sorry Jason, no. I never got around to finding contacts in that area since I moved back up." Again she tries to remove herself from his personal space, but again he tightens his grip even more.

"I would make it worth your while, Sophie."

She forces another smile, hoping it reaches her eyes enough to convince Jason her faked sincerity. "I'll see what I can do, but don't hold your breath, I don't see it happening." Jason gives her another squeeze, this time causing a pinch of pain in her waist and then he lets her go.

"Okay, but I need it soon and I don't want to use my contacts down south, and I don't have a reliable supplier up here, as of yet." Glad to be freed from his grasp and the unspoken threat, Sophie takes a step back, putting distance between them again.

"I can only try." She lies, there is no way she can produce a gun, her bosses are wanting much more evidence of drug running before they put themselves in the position of arresting him. Jason nods his understanding then places a chaste but wet kiss on her cheek.

"Okay. I'll be in touch soon." They part ways and Sophie blows away the disgust she feels rippling through her.

CHAPTER SIXTEEN

Two weeks had passed since Sophie delivered the Quattro to Jason. There had been no evidence as to what he needed the car for other than his slip of the tongue about it being a get-away car. Sophie had de-briefed her DI with all the information she had gathered from Jason and continued to search for the F Pace Jaguar that Jason had requested.

The first one she looked at was not up to her standards for the money the seller was asking so she was continuing her search.

She and Ross had met up a few times over the weeks and text or spoke on the phone every day. Sophie could feel her defences slipping more and more each time they were together, and to her pleasant surprise she wasn't freaking out about it. If anything, she felt almost giddy about where their relationship might go. A fact that Belle loved pointing out to her.

The double date had been organised for the first Saturday in August. The days had gone by with a countdown from Belle and a million questions of what she should wear. Occasionally she would dress up her barrage of questions by asking Sophie what she was going to wear, but quickly turned it around to her, again. Sophie found it endearing that her friend was excited about their double date, and even admitted to Belle that she felt the same.

Eventually the day if the date arrives as does Belle at Sophie's front door. The back seat of her sixty plate Volkswagen Beetle is full.

Sophie holds her front door open as Belle humphs in armfuls of dresses, skirts, tops, trousers and shoes.

"Did you bring your entire wardrobe?" Sophie enquires as she closes the door after Belle's third and thankfully last trip to her car.

"No, just my going out stuff," says Belle. She gives Sophie a sweet smile as they enter the now destroyed living room.

"Holy shit Belle, my living room looks like a jumble sale threw up in it," says Sophie. Belle pushes past her, stepping over the pile of shoes she'd dropped near the coffee table.

"It's not that bad. Now here, go open these as we search for outfits." Belle brandishes two mini bottles of Prosecco. Sophie takes the bottles from her friend but scrunches up her nose.

"Not really wanting to get half cut before we go out, Belle."

"I know, I know, but it's only one each, you'll be fine." Sophie rolls her eyes, not a massive fan of the fizzy wine, but she pours it to appease her friend and maybe to get her own nerves under control.

Two hours later and Sophie has sipped half her way down her drink. Belle has been on a roll the full two hours trying on outfits and getting her and Sophie's hair and makeup just right. Sophie had insisted her hair be straightened as is her normal preference, but she was overruled by Belle who sat and expertly gave her loose curls with her straighteners, all the time complaining about how she was curling hair that is naturally curly.

Sophie eventually throws Belle a look that makes her hold her tongue. Once the friends are ready, Belle in a sleeveless red and black peplum dress with black killer heels and Sophie dressed in tight black skinny jeans, a black strapless, fitted top, and black spiked heels, they phone for a taxi to head to the train station.

"So what's the plan for tonight?" Belle has asked this question numerous times over the past fortnight and Sophie has answered it in numerous different ways.

Sometimes she gave a straight, truthful answer, but other times, especially nearer the end of that week she answered with absurd answers. The most absurd being Ross and Sean are aliens and they were going to take them to their home planet to create a new species. Sophie had earned herself a missile being launched at her for that answer. Thankfully it was only a scrunched-up piece of paper.

"For the umpteenth time, we are meeting the boys at The Pub for a drink, then we're getting something to eat, probably somewhere near the bar as Sean doesn't like being too far away from at the best of times, but especially at the moment after all the incidents and with Jason wanting to 'protect' the place, then it's back to The Pub for more drinks, then home on the last train."

Belle pouts at the last part. "If you want to pay a fortune in taxi fares you can, but I ain't."

Sophie eyes her friend who's continuing to pout, "What?" Belle looks up. "What happens if I don't get lucky from the date? Or if I do get lucky? I mean, it's obvious you're definitely getting lucky!"

Sophie rolls her eyes. "Firstly, stop saying 'getting lucky' we are grown ass woman, secondly if things go well between you and Sean and you wish to stay that's fine and your decision, if things either don't go well, or at least don't go that well and you are going home, then we are going home together, and if that happens then we are going home on the last train. I won't be bringing Ross home with me. You worried about this date by chance?" Sophie has a quick flick through her memories as they climb out of the taxi and onto the platform in time for the train pulling up, she can't recall ever seeing Belle so jittery over a date before.

Settling into their seats Belle shakes her head vigorously, then she shrugs before nodding and letting out a sigh.

"Aye, and I don't know why! I mean I've been on loads of dates, but Sean's, gorgeous. Don't you think he's gorgeous?" Belle has a dreamy look in her eyes as she asks, and Sophie would laugh if she didn't have the same thoughts and probably the same look in her eyes over Ross.

"Not compared to Ross. No, he is it for me." Sophie snaps her mouth shut at the connotations her statement could take. The dreamy look fizzles out of Belle as she eyes her friend.

"Really, there'll be no-one else for you? Who are you and what have you done with my friend who says that no man will ever be it?"

Sophie waves away her friend's question with what she hopes is indifference. "So I'm enjoying his company at the moment, that doesn't mean it's going to anywhere, I mean, it's been a month, if that, I think."

Belle grins at Sophie with a knowing noise coming from her lips. "I'm so happy you have found someone you 'enjoy their company with'" Sophie bats away Belle's hands as she makes air quotes. "And I'm glad I had that conversation with you three years ago, who'd have thought it would lead to us double dating!"

With a smile Sophie nods. "Aye, who'd have thought."

****

Dynamic Entry

Ross and Sean are sitting are sitting at the bar, their first pints in front of them, both their legs bouncing on the bar stools and their nerves palpable around them. Ross looks at his friend, taking in all the nerves he was feeling.

"I know you think it's a pile of crap, and only a sales pitch, the uncanny way I matchmake people, but I do think you and Belle are right for each other, and I'm not trying to sell you a diamond."

Sean blows out a breath and slows his leg bouncing. "Aye, cheers! That makes me feel so much better, not that I'm needing to feel better." He lifts his pint and tilts it towards Ross in a 'cheers' gesture that says much more than his sarcastic reply.

The waitress serving behind the bar that night sniggers at her boss and his friend then brings their attention to the front door as their dates walk in. Ross loses all his breath watching Sophie walk in.

Her slender figure on show in her tight jeans and top. He can't believe he is even friends with such a gorgeous, amazing, albeit private and sexy woman, but here he is going on a double date, hoping to get her back into his bed at the end of the night.

He was trying not to hope too much as it was ungentlemanly, but the teenage boy in him wasn't listening.

As the two women come to a stop in front of them, Ross notices traces of nerves and insecurities in both of them. He stores away that piece of information about Sophie, registering that she's not always the confidant, take no prisoners female she portrays in all the other areas of her life. She has her moments of needing reassurance and love like everyone else.

The men step down from their seats, Sean taking Belle's hand in his and kisses her knuckles making her physically swoon with a girly giggle. Ross clocks the eye roll Sophie does at her friend as he takes her into his arms in a close embrace, enveloping her in his warmth and placing his mouth at her ear so only she can hear his yearning.

"You look amazing, I really hope I get to undress you from that outfit at some point." He brings his lips to her in a firm but sensual kiss. He made sure not to say that he needed to undress her that night as he didn't want to push her.

He can see Sophie's face and feel her body heat at his words

"Thank you, you're looking good yourself, and, we'll see about the undressing," Sophie replies. She gives him a smile then turns to the other couple on their double date. "So, we getting a table?" Sean orders the women's drinks as Ross leads them to the table he knows Sophie will want. She gives him a look of gratitude and desire as they sit.

The date continues with the couples enjoying each other's company. The food, drink, conversation and laughter flow freely. Sophie couldn't remember the last time she'd felt so happy or relaxed, that was until Sean asks his next question.

"So, family; who has what? Brothers, sisters?" Sophie's stomach falls to the floor, as her spine straightens with steel.

Belle throws a look at her friend before answering first in a too cheery tone. "Well I have a bigger brother and sister, twins."

Sean nods then turns to Sophie. "Sophie, what about you?" He looks expectantly at her as she takes a deep breath and plasters a smile on her lips.

"I have Belle."

There is silence around the table until Ross speaks. "I'm an only child too, so I steal Sean when an older brother is needed." Sophie gives him a shy smile as a thanks for his input into the conversation, and the answering reassuring squeeze to her knee settles her.

CHAPTER SEVENTEEN

The night finishes long after the closing time of The Pub and long after the last train has left Glasgow Central Station for Motherwell.

The conversation topic had been changed from families and the relaxed atmosphere of earlier had resumed, thanks to Ross and to Sophie's great relief.

Sean offers for them all to stay above the bar at his residence in one of his two spare rooms.

Ross is gentlemanly enough not to assume Sophie will share a room with him so he is more than pleasantly surprised when Sophie asks Belle if she would be fine on her own. He holds his breath for the reply, although he's not sure why.

They go up to their bedrooms and close their doors. Sophie is silent as she strips from her clothes and climbs into the double bed in only her lace boy shorts, the cool sheets making her shiver. Ross climbs in beside her and pulls her close into him so they are chest to chest, he tries to dampen down his arousal, but knows it's a losing battle and can only hope that Sophie understands he's a man, but would never do anything she wasn't comfortable with.

"You okay?" His voice is soft and full of concern.

"Aye, but thank you for changing the subject when it came to families, I don't discuss mine." A pain shoots through his heart at her words and the pain in her tone.

"That's okay, I could see you were uncomfortable." He feels her take a deep breath.

"My father had two families. Me and my mother and his other, better family." She hadn't meant to say the words, to explain her family problems, or her father's choice. She had never admitted that awful truth to anybody except Belle, and certainly not to someone she was dating.

Ross squeezes her tighter, letting her know he is with her, not letting her go and she continues to talk. "He was a charmer, had the gift of the gab, the perfect car salesman." A cynical laugh comes from her throat without her permission. "Ironically that's where I get my love of cars from... him."

She spits the last word out, then takes a breath, blowing away her hatred. "My mother couldn't do anything right, not even have the correct sex of child. It didn't matter that I shared his one true love, it mattered that I wasn't a boy. When I found out about the other family, I realised that no matter what I did or didn't do, I would never be as good as them, that family consisted of three boys." Tears had formed in her eyes and fell silently down her cheeks. "He continuously told my mother how stupid she was, how she could do no right. I never seen it, but I'm sure he beat on her too, but she took him back every time. She ignored the fact he had another family and took him back into her bed." Ross had been rubbing his thumb over her back throughout her confession. He has questions and anger is burning through him.

"Did he ever hit you?"

She pulls back from his embrace to look up at him. "No, I don't think he cared enough to have any emotions for me. I was a hindrance, he had to provide for me, albeit a pittance, and that was it, nothing more."

She sniffs into the darkness and Ross brings his hands to her face, rubbing away her tears. "That's why

I don't trust men. Especially charming gentlemen. Plus in the fo ... car trade, women are looked down on. Cars are boy's toys, not anything a mere female would be interested in."

Ross picks up on her near slipup but puts it down to a slight slur from the alcohol they have consumed. He brings Sophie back into his embrace, kissing her soundly on the lips.

"Does that mean I'm not charming or a gentleman?" There is humour in his voice and Sophie lets out a small shaky laugh.

"No, you are both charming and a gentleman and I'm beginning to think I might be able to trust you." The air thins around them as her words settle into both of them.

"Thank you." He knows those simple words do not convey how much her words mean to him, but they are the only words he has at that moment in time. She reaches up and kisses him and he pours all his feelings of rightness into it.

****

Sophie smiles into the darkness, unsure why she confessed her biggest shame to Ross, but is glad she did.

Never had she felt so relaxed in a man's arms and now she felt the extra weight she always carried about with her had been lifted from her. She turns around in his arms and snuggles further into his embrace and falls into deep peaceful sleep.

Early on the Sunday morning the four friends are sitting around Sean's small kitchen table, all of them feeling better than they probably should be considering the amount of alcohol they had consumed the night before. Sean is bustling about asking who wants tea or coffee, Sophie's ears prick up at the mention of tea.

"Oh a tea would be heavenly." Her tone is longing. Belle laughs and shakes her head as Sean stops mid pour with the kettle in his hand to look at Sophie.

"I'm guessing you a tea jenny then, Sophie?"

A slight blush creeps up her face. "Em, maybe." She grins easily, still breathing easier from her confession the night before.

"There's no maybe about it, I never see you at work without a cup of tea." The words leave Belle's mouth and Sophie curses inwardly. "Aye well, buying cars and drinking tea go hand in hand."

Sophie shoots her friend a look that would kill and she gets an apologetic look in return. Ross looks between the women.

"Good to know, if I ever need a new car or if I'm ever in the bad books." Sophie brings her attention back to Ross at his words.

"Always good information to remember." She grins, her heart growing at the thought of Ross wanting to get out of her bad books before doing anything to get into them.

Sophie accepts her tea from Sean and takes a sip, testing the hot liquid then groans with satisfaction.

"Oh Sean, now that is a cup of tea!"

Ross turns to his friend, a flare of jealousy in his chest.

"Heard anything fae that Jason guy?" All eyes land on Sean.

"No, thankfully. He's been in on his own and with other people, but he hasn't said anything, he just gives me a strange nod."

Sophie takes in his words. "Good, he might have got the message, but still, any problems give me a shout." Sean answers her with his thanks, then offers to drive everyone home, explaining that he realises they may not want to take the walk of shame of getting on a train home in the same clothes they left in last night. They all agree to the plan and finish their drinks.

****

Jason finishes up some of the collections from his protection rackets. The client with the missed payment had paid his double payment, much to Jason's surprise and disappointment. As much as he was draining himself at the gym every day, pushing himself to his limits, his levels of patience over not having Sophie in his bed plus his gun problem were thinning, and the only way to improve his mood and get his patience under control was to get his problems solved or at least to cause physical violence to sooth him until they were all solved. He had thought he would get his violent itch scratched by another missed payment, but it was not to be. He would never bring his wrath down on a customer without good reason, he wasn't a monster.

He places his takings into his house safe and checks the time, not wanting to be late for his meeting with his new customer, Mr. Baxter.

He pulls his Audi A1 into the hotel car park and peels himself out. He curses the car and Sophie for making him wait on his Jaguar F Pace.

Getting seated in the same restaurant as before, he makes a mental note to send a text to Sophie asking when his next car would be available. He replaces his phone into his dark jeans pocket as his client walks through the cluster of tables, looking decidedly worried and a wee bit sweaty as he sits across from Jason.

"Ah Mr. Baxter, how have you been?" Jason sees the man take a deep breath and a deeper swallow. He feels the tension rolling of off his client and can feel a tingle of excitement at the base of his spine. He might just get his violence after all.

"Mr., eh, Mr. Hamilton... I, eh, I... well you see..." Jason holds his hands up to stop the stuttering man from torturing his ears anymore.

"Mr. Baxter, what seems to be the problem? You haven't changed your mind, have you?" The client blows out another breath as he relaxes imperceptibly until Jason sits slightly forward, imposing his large presence further onto him. "We have a deal Mr. Baxter." Jason's voice is low and threatening. "A gentleman's handshake and, at least to me, that's as binding as a written contract, and I did explain that. So, sir, tell me, do you have a problem?" The air around them hangs heavy as the client opens and shuts his mouth like a goldfish gasping to find the right words.

"No, no. Mr. Hamilton there's no problem, no. It's just, I might not need the, items I ordered." A murderous look crosses over Jason's face, making the client backtrack furiously. "I mean, maybe just postpone the order as everything got worked out and I've calmed down since I last saw you, so..." Jason smiles, amusement dancing in his eyes.

"So you and this shop owner have kissed and made up, so everything's okay? Whatever he did to disrespect you is forgotten and forgiven, so I'm down a deal? Is that what's happening? Am I understanding the gist of the situation correctly?" Another deep swallow comes back at Jason. "Are you that soft and easy Mr. Baxter? You can forgive and forget so easily? I mean did this person not disrespect you and your family so much that you were angry enough to want to scare them? Bring destruction to them? Did they not take money from your pocket, so food from your families' mouths? And now what? All's fine?" Jason's aggressive tone had shifted to one of mocking as he asks his last question. "Are you even a man Mr. Baxter?"

The client bristles. "Yes I am a man!" Mr. Baxter tries to infuse his voice with confidence, but it falls flat.

"So can I ask Mr. Baxter, did you receive your money back?" A sad shake of the client's head gives Jason his answer. "Well, you can't get out of this deal without paying what you owe me, and you are still owed money, so may I suggest you carry on with your plans and sign on the dotted line that way you can get money for the repayments." Jason pushes forward a piece of paper and a silver Parker Pen, followed by a growl and a look of pure challenge and danger.

The client gives another deep swallow knowing he is caught between a rock and a hard place. Be out of more money with nothing to show for it and be in the cross hairs of Jason Hamilton's anger or continue with his original, knee jerk reaction of a plan, maybe recoup some, all, or even more money that he's owed with the risk of getting caught by his so called friend and, or the police.

Another furtive glance into the dangerous chocolate brown eyes of Jason and the decision is made. The scribble of his scrawl of a signature is rushed onto the document. Jason notices that nothing was read or checked over; not even the amount or payment breakdown. Today may be a good day Jason thinks, then flips the document round and with a flourish signs his own name before folding it away into his inside pocket along with his pen.

"Best decision you'll ever make Mr. Baxter. Now, a timeline. I have the car; a beautiful Audi Quattro and I'm waiting on the shiny thing you ordered. That should be available in about a fortnight, at the latest, so your first payment of two hundred pounds per month, that's payment and interest together will be due the week after that. Now," He holds his hands up to ensure he has his client's full attention before continuing. "I am being incredibly generous here Mr. Baxter, and only charging you ten percent interest on this deal as it involves money being taken from your family, but, if you miss even one payment I will be charging you the full amount of thirty percent, and I will add on my finder's fee, you remember I waived that due to it being my idea to get the car?"

The client nods his head, his eyes wide at the monthly payment, but far too frightened to say anything. "Excellent, well I'll be back in touch once I have everything required for the job." He drains his now cold coffee and throws down a five-pound note, noticing that his client never got the chance to order anything.

Smirking he leaves the hotel and climbs back into his too small Audi. He never got his violence, but nevertheless he feels significantly less stressed than he did going into the hotel due to the extra money he will be bringing in, so he heads towards Mitchell Lane, hoping he might Sophie in The Pub.

CHAPTER EIGHTEEN

Sophie made it to the Wednesday of the new week before hearing from Jason. She was glad of the respite as it gave her time to catch up on her paperwork, study his known associates and workers more and search for another F Pace Jaguar.

She had only just decided on one when Jason's call came through. A shiver runs through her at the coincidence. Taking a deep breath, she puts a mental picture in her mind of Sophie Peterson and answers the phone.

"Jason, what do I owe the —" Jason cuts her off, thankfully, as the word pleasure was starting to stick in her throat.

"Yes, yes. I've been waiting on you getting back to me, Sophie." Sophie notes the strange mixed up accent is somewhat frosty and with more of a South African twang to it.

"I've even been in that bar you're so fucking desperate to protect, but you've not been in!" Sean had contacted her on the Sunday and the Tuesday, letting her know that Jason had been in but he hadn't mentioned protection again. She was grateful for the information, even if Sean didn't understand for what reasons she needed it.

"I don't live in The Pub Jason, nor do I appreciate your behaviour, which is verging on stalking me. If you want to meet with me, phone and we can arrange a business meeting like people who do business together normally do," Her tone is stern and her anger is simmering at the words and behaviour presented to her.

Her anger tries to get the better of her when she hears his chuckle coming down the phone at her.

"Now Sophie, you know we could be so much more than just business associates if only you'd say the word." His last words come out as a growl and Sophie wonders if that is Jason's idea of sounding sensual.

Another shiver ravages her and she's glad he can't see her. "No! Jason, we've been through this, and anyway I'm with Ross now and I'm a one guy woman." She hadn't wanted to part with the knowledge that her and Ross were an item and she certainly didn't want to put Ross in the middle of her undercover work, but the words were out now.

Another growl comes from the other end of the line. "Anyway, enough about him, what about my car and gun?"

Sophie takes a deep breath she was so glad she was recording the conversation. "I'm going to look at the car tomorrow so all going well I'll have it to you by end of play. As for the gun, I've told you I don't handle them anymore." Although she had never sold him a gun, she had spoken about buying and selling them when she worked in England. Thankfully she had always gotten away with her excuses three years ago, but she could tell he was getting suspicious about it this time round.

"I thought you could get anything?" His tone was trying to mock her.

"No Jason, maybe down south I could get more, but up here I deal with cars and cars only. I've explained this to you." Her own mocking tone meets his and she knows this will make him angry, something she doesn't want, but she can't help herself.

"You've did it before, so do it again!" The anger in his demand is evident, she clenches her teeth as she answers.

"I'll see what I can do, and I'll contact you tomorrow if I get the car deal done. Goodnight!" She doesn't wait for an answer as she ends the call. She leaves a note on her DI's desk requesting to speak to him the next day. She needed to see where they stood on giving the bad guys a gun.

She groans, as much as she loves her job and enjoys being undercover, she hates being undercover and working with Jason. She hates being around him or even just being in contact with him.

When she was in Northumbria, she'd learned to despise him quickly, at least this time she felt more supported with her colleagues and superiors than she had down there.

She tidies up her paperwork and heads to the door of the incident room. She takes one last look around before turning out the lights, she's last to leave again.

Once home Sophie pours herself a white wine, picks up her own phone and phones Ross, she needs to hear his voice and kind words he always speaks to her to take away the feelings of disgust lingering in her after her conversation with Jason.

Ross answers after only a few rings, his soft warm voice soaking through their invisible connection in the airwaves and into her body, making her relax for the first time that day.

"Hello you, how's things?"

A wave of emotion washes over her and lodges in her throat. It may have been only just over a month they had been seeing each other, but he had gotten through her tough girl defences. "Hi, I'm fine, kinda."

Ross makes a noise down the phone encouraging her to tell him more.

"I was on the phone to Jason," she says. He is wanting the other car asap, so is being a bit grumpy. I just wanted to hear your voice to get his out my head."

She didn't know how she felt about relying on Ross to make her feel better after a bad day, but she was pushing that worry away.

"I hope I can live up to your expectations," he gives a soft laugh down the phone, "been a tough day?"

She smiles to the empty room at his concern, wishing he was there with her, or even lived within walking distance so she could be closer to him if needed. "Not really, just spent half an hour on the phone to him. I should be picking up a car for him tomorrow so that will mean a meeting, but I've survived all the meetings up to now so I'm sure I'll survive this one too."

Ross makes a growl at the back of his throat. "Please be careful, I don't like the way he looks at you, like he wants to devour you, possess you."

His tone is serious but tender at the same time, it brings another smile and wash of emotion over Sophie. "Why Ross, are you jealous?" She enquires in a playful manner, although part of her is desperate to know the answer.

"No. Not of him, but neither do I trust him. I know your feelings towards him are as romantic as toothache."

Sophie gives a chuckle at his analogy. "You're right there, I wouldn't want either. I'm more than happy with the hunk I'm with." The lovers talk for another hour, laughing with each other and enjoying the easy flow of their conversation. They say their goodbyes and hang up the phone, feeling completely relaxed, Sophie falls into bed with a smile playing on her lips.

****

Picking up Belle from the train station, the friends head out to see the F Pace Jaguar. An excited butterfly

Fiona Morgan

bounces around Sophie's stomach. The thought of buying a car, even if it isn't for her, is thrilling.

Belle looks at her friend then rolls her eyes. "You're all excited over this aren't you?"

Sophie shrugs her shoulders, going for nonchalant, then nods her head like a child at Christmas. "Aye, but it's a gorgeous car, so how can I not be excited?"

Belle gives her a quizzical look. "But it's not even for you, and you're buying it for someone you don't like and who's going to be using it for criminal activities."

Sophie's shoulders slump, her excitement dwindling slightly at the thought of Jason and what he planned on doing with the car. "You're a buzzkill!" Then a thought hits her, "But, after we do an amazing job of bringing him down, we will be able to confiscate it under the Proceeds of Crime Act and it will be used for good again!" She gives her friend a short nod, her excitement back in a rush full of stomach flips. Belle agrees with her as they pull up in front of a gleaming Royal Blue Jaguar F Pace.

An hour later the friends are headed towards Blythswood Square and to Jason's office. Sophie parks the F Pace and tries to slip out of the SUV in a ladylike manner but struggles with its height. Belle walks to her from where she had parked their pool car with a barely covered laugh forming on her lips. Sophie throws her a stare, then shakes her head.

"Don't even start, I'm not that short, I at least hit five foot."

Belle holds her hands up in defence. "I never said a word. Now, you ready to go in?"

Sophie pats the front pocket of her light-weight navy blazer where her phone would be recording her meeting. "Aye, got all the paperwork, got the keys, and got my big girl pants pulled up to deal with his highness!" Giving her friend a smile she turns and enters the sandstone building into the lion's den.

Once in she sits in the guest chair she sat in on her last visit. Jason sits on the other side with a leering grin on his face. Sophie knows she doesn't have a single inch of skin on show, other than her hands and face, but she still feels like Jason can see her naked.

She pushes aside all her worries, knowing she has back-up outside in Belle and that she could raise the alarm for more back-up if needed. She smiles brightly at Jason before speaking.

"So, you are now the proud owner of a gorgeous Jaguar F Pace. There are the keys and the V5. The logbook and manufactures manual are in the glove box, and he's sitting outside all shiny and waiting on you." Sophie slides over the two sets of keys and all the paperwork across the table and removes her hand quickly so as not to touch Jason as he reaches forward at the same time. He gives a smirk at her actions, and Sophie knows he is loving the feeling of power he thinks he has over her.

"Excellent, and you had enough money in the account?"

"Yes, you know I always get a better deal than anyone else, that's why you do business with me." She smiles again, this one more genuine, though not the one she saves for Ross. She's proud of getting the car at a discount, even if it was for a criminal.

"Very true my gorgeous car dealer. Now I'm going to ask again about this gun as I need to get it. You did say you would see what you could do, and I wouldn't like to think you're lying to me, or, god forbid went fucking straight on me?" She hears the underlying threat laced through his tone and Sophie understands that she's being tested.

Thankfully she'd had that conversation with her DI about the gun and they agreed to do the deal, but with a twist.

"I may be able to help you. I had a dig around and came up with a Beretta." A grin covers Jason's face thinking he has won, thinking he now has something over Sophie, something to keep her in his pocket.

"That's my girl. Right I'll contact you and you can get it to me in the next few days, Saturday maybe."

She shakes her head. "Nope, Saturday is out, I'm busy."

A growl comes from Jason. "Busy fucking Ross I guess?"

She swallows her anger. "That is none of your business and keep your mouth clean!" She pins him with an angry glare and squares her shoulders. "As it stands, I won't have the gun until Monday, so I'll get it to you then."

"Fine!" He spits the words out. Sophie knows he doesn't take kindly to females dictating to him what will or won't happen, or even giving him a telling off, and she smiles inwardly. At this point there is nothing he can do other than agree, he needs the gun for his deal, and he needs to keep Sophie coming back to him.

Sophie stands and they say their terse goodbyes. Walking back out into the summer's day Sophie takes a deep breath and blows it away, glad to be away from the intense, dangerous atmosphere that always surrounds Jason.

CHAPTER NINETEEN

Closing time on Friday and all the staff working at Saltire's Jewellery has decided to go for a celebratory drink at The Pub after another exceptional day selling diamonds.

Settling down at the table, Ross puts the last of the drinks in front of their owners. His boss picks up her glass with its decanted Irn-Bru in it and holds it aloft.

"Well team, you have pulled it out the bag this month with sales, which makes me feel better about going on maternity leave soon. But I have to say that the person who kick started this selling spree and has kept it going, all thanks to him being in love, is Ross."

A cheer goes up and Ross feels the heat in his face. "I am not in love," His brain is screaming 'yet', but he keeps that piece of information to himself as another round of noise goes up from the table.

"Oh my god! It is love!" His boss exclaims none too quietly, amusement dancing in her eyes. "You are always in love when you are seeing someone, but this time you're not, oh I can feel a wedding in my waters. Just make sure it's after this one comes out so I don't look like a beached whale in the photos."

Ross rolls his eyes at his boss. "You never mind feeling anything in your waters, that bun's not ready to come out yet, and if anything comes from my relationship with Sophie it's not going to happen in the next three months, so I think you're safe." His boss gives a happy clap of her hands and the conversation moves on to safer territory.

Fiona Morgan

It moves on everywhere except inside Ross' head, his boss' words of love and the bizarre explanation of why its love goes around in a loop. He wonders if after only a month it could be love. He knows for definite that he's never felt this strongly for anyone after such a short space of time, if ever no matter how much he thought he was in love any other time.

After a few more hours, their numbers have dwindled, and the boss stands to leave. She gives Ross a cuddle and whispers in his ear.

"I love seeing how happy you've been over the past month, especially after getting me and my wife together, plus I've made my decision on who'll be running the shop when I'm squeezing this bambino out. Congratulations."

****

The look of shock on Ross' face makes Sophie panic ever so slightly. Walking in to see her boyfriend with a pregnant woman's arms around him whispering in his ear made her feel emotions she wasn't used to, then he goes and smiles a full megawatt smile. She swallows down the ridiculous jealousy clawing at her, chastising herself for letting her mind go there automatically and reminding herself that Ross is not her father. She tells Belle to order her a pint as she makes her feet move towards her boyfriend. That word; boyfriend, she thinks to herself, does things to her emotions.

Ross spots Sophie walking towards him and his entire body lightens.

"Sophie!" He steps forward and takes her in his arms, giving her a quick kiss on the lips before turning to everyone left sitting at the table. "Everyone, this is my girlfriend Sophie." He pulls her closer into him by her waist. "Sophie this is my boss, Louise and some of the work." Sophie's stomach flips as he introduces her as his girlfriend. She swallows down her slight panic, letting her happiness at the word replace it and smiles her shy hello to everyone.

Belle takes that moment to walk up, handing Sophie her pint. The friends finish their introductions and Sophie gives Ross another kiss before they leave to sit at their usual table.

CHAPTER TWENTY

2 Weeks Later

Sophie smooths down her hair, hoping the lingering moisture in the night air wouldn't spring her curls to life, but she knew it was a losing battle.

Standing waiting outside the warehouse with a handgun in the holdall on her shoulder was a daunting feeling. The back-up team she had sitting in cars out of sight was doing little to calm the nerves skittering up her spine. She walks towards the door to the side of the large roller shutter, glad she had worn her exercise clothes, a hoodie and trainers as the ground is uneven under her feet, so would be difficult to run on, if the need arose.

She approaches the door and holds her arm out to rap her knuckles on the door, but it opens with a whoosh before she can make contact with the steel.

The man standing before her is not Jason. He doesn't come anywhere near Jason's size. In fact he's lucky if he reaches 5 foot two inches. Sophie takes a step back trying not to show recognition of the thug in front of her and she plasters on a smile.

"I'm here to see Jason." Her voice is solid, not giving the thug any hint of fear. She had read his rap sheet and profile so knows he is not a nice man. What he lacks in height he makes up for in aggression and violence. One would say he showed signs of small man syndrome.

"Aye, I know, the boss told me to stay here an' fuckin' wait fir you, an' by the way, I think ye'll find yir late!"

Anger creeps over her, one thing she is never is late! "I think you'll find I'm not! Six o'clock was the agreed time and that was the time I arrived." Her tone is indignant. "So…"

The thug interrupts her. "I wis telt hauf five, so I've been fuckin' aboot for hauf an hour waitin' on your skinny arse, now, hiv ye got the piece the boss asked fir or no?"

"Well, you getting the wrong information is of no consequence to me, I arrived on time, and yes, of course I have it!" She gestures to the bag slung on her shoulder.

The thug bristles at her words. He'd dearly love to teach her a lesson but is on strict orders from Jason to leave her alone.

"Right, moan then." The thug turns to walk back into the warehouse.

Sophie's laugh rings out in the quiet wasteland. "Aye, see no, I'm not going in there, alone, with you." She straightens, fully asserting her height, taller than the thug, and tries to project strength.

The chuckle that leaves the thug's snarling lips is enough to freeze the puddles at their feet.

"You feart hen?"

The glint in his eyes warn her that she should indeed be frightened, but she couldn't show it, she would never show it.

"Not of you, but I am also not stupid, so here." She takes the holdall from her shoulder with a gloved hand and thrusts it towards the thug.

"Hmm, gloves. I think you might be a bit feart." Another chuckle comes from his sneer.

"Again, just not stupid, now are you going to take this or am I taking it back to where it came from and you can explain to Jason why he doesn't have all the equipment he needs for this job?"

The thug's eyes darken as he takes the bag from her. "You're lucky the boss has a 'hing fir you, making you out of bounds for us mere workers, or I'd hiv you screaming in seconds." Sophie daren't think what the threat could mean.

"Lucky me." She throws back in disgust.

The thug shakes his head. "Right, you need tae fuck off now so I kin take this tae the boss the night. He's got the meetin' the morra."

A small smile plays on Sophie's lips at the information the thug had inadvertently let them know. "Gladly!" she says. She turns back to her car, throwing a saccharine sweet 'goodbye' over her shoulder.

She walks the few streets away until she meets Belle in the pool car where she radio's in her instructions for the two uniform officers to get to business, then the friends head towards the station to start their paperwork for the night.

The thug locks up the warehouse, anger rolling through him. He doesn't trust her, but he has been told to hold his tongue about her and like her. He isn't stupid; he wouldn't go against his boss.

He's a mile away from the warehouse when the blue lights flash in his rearview mirror. He curses loudly in his Corsa and pulls over, doing a mental check list of what he could be getting pulled for. Speeding? No. Insurance? No. MOT? No. Lights? He thinks they are all fine. He rolls down his window and glowers at the male police officer standing at the side of his car.

"Can I help you?" He sneers through the opened car window. The officer bends down to peer inside the car and eyes the holdall sitting on the passenger seat.

Dynamic Entry

"Yes Sir, did you know you had a tail-light out?" The thug growls, then contains himself. There was no way he was going down for a taillight.

"No officer I didn't. I'll get it fixed tomorrow."

The officer gives his head a nod before asking the thug for his name and drivers licence. The thug knows he would be in trouble if they searched the car, so continues to try and play nice with the officer and hands over his licence then holds his breath.

Taking his time, the officer makes a show of looking over the thug's licence, then hands it off to his partner for him to radio in the details for the check. They are well aware of who they are talking as per Sophie's call out for them to pull him over, but they need to make the search seem like any other ordinary stop. The officer bends his knees into a near seated position with his arms on the open window. "So have you been anywhere special tonight?"

The thug keeps his face straight as prickles of panic start running up his spine, he needs to keep his anger in check and try and get away from this situation. "No, eh, just finishing up at work."

The officer makes a show of looking at his watch. "Hmm, working a bit late. That your bag, the holdall?" A nod is all the thug can give, not wanting to trust his voice not to give anything away. "Any chance I could get a wee look?"

Anger burns in the thug's stomach. "You got a warrant?"

The second officer nods that they have the go ahead to make the arrest. "No, I don't have a search warrant, yet, but you do have an outstanding warrant for your arrest, so it looks like you'll be coming with us and I'll get to see in that bag anyway." Lead settles in the thug's stomach, Jason is going to kill him for this.

Fiona Morgan

****

The next morning Jason paces his office floor, his anger levels are at fever pitch. Another of his workers is standing next to the overturned visitors chair. He had made the mistake of trying to sit down but his boss wasn't for having it, demanding he stand.

"What the fuck happened? Why was he fucking pulled over in the first place?" Anger is rolling off Jason and filling the air in the small office. He is standing toe to toe with his worker, his spittle flying in all directions, but mostly over the worker's face.

The worker opens his mouth to talk but can only sputter, so gives his boss a shoulder shrug instead.

Bad idea. Jason explodes. "DID YOU JUST FUCKING SHRUG AT ME YOU LITTLE WANKER? DO NOT, AND I MEAN DO FUCKING NOT SHRUG YOUR FUCKING SHOULDERS AT ME! FUCKING ANSWER THE DAMN QUESTION!" He takes a few deep breaths trying to calm his anger and bring his volume under control. "You took his call, tell me, why was he pulled?" The worker drags a deep breath in, desperate to wipe his face, but knowing he daren't for fear of losing his fingers.

"I... eh... he... said —"

"Spit it out! He said what?"

"A broken taillight. He had a broken taillight, that's why he got pulled." There, the words were out, now all the worker had to do was brace for the next eruption of anger.

The eruption never came. Instead Jason became still, uncharacteristically still, the only emotion showing was the murderous look in his hazelnut brown eyes, the worker would swear to all his friends later that he could see lightning shots of gold flash through

157

them as his boss' anger bubbled and fought its way out of him.

"He got pulled because of a traffic violation? Because of a blown light? Mr. 'I don't get caught because of stupidity like all the other morons'! The guy that insists on having all his paperwork, MOT, and insurance up to date, plus drives at the speed limit on jobs to not arouse suspicion, gets pulled on a busted light?" He pauses for a second getting his thoughts in order. "So why did the pigs search the car?"

The worker swallows hard, that exact question had been asked. "He had an outstanding arrest warrant. I think it was for —"

Jason's roar stops the worker mid-sentence. "ARGH!! I don't give a flying fuck what the warrant was for, he shouldn't have it!" Jason had gone back to pacing his office like a caged animal trying to contain his anger until he heard about the outstanding arrest warrant, but now went still again. He had to, if he didn't stop moving, he would move over to the worker and start swinging his fists, and he wouldn't stop swinging them until the worker had no face left.

It was not this worker's fault and they do say 'don't shoot the messenger', but god he wanted to punch fuck out of someone for this major and unneeded set back.

The first thing he warned all his workers about was outstanding warrants. He'd seen too many jobs get ruined and men get busted because of something stupid, and if memory served him right the cocky bastard that had gotten himself arrested was the first to shout about his clean record and the pains he took to keep it that way, lying bastard!

"Did he say anything else?" He growls his words, trying somewhat unsuccessfully to regain control of his anger.

The worker swallows again. "Aye, well he said... eh, he thought... eh —"

"SPIT IT THE FUCK OUT!" The roar leaves Jason's lips without his permission. He hated losing control of anything and at that moment he felt like he was losing control not only of his anger, but of the job he was getting paid for and his staff! Unacceptable. The roar also made the worker stutter and stumble more over his words.

"Aye... well, eh... he thought... that, eh, that fancy burd ae yours is involved.".

Jason locks the worker with a stare. "Sophie? Why did he think she is involved? Was she there when he was arrested? Was she the one to pull him over?"

"Naw, but it happened minutes after he left her."

Jason pondered the information for a second, before dismissing the worker, with a warning to keep his ear to the ground.

He thought some more about Sophie being involved in the arrest and dismisses it again, albeit not entirely.

He types out a text to her 'checking' that all went well with the hand over, then sits back to plan his next steps.

****

Sophie is lying in Ross' bed, in his arms, when she hears the text beep through on her work phone.

They had landed the same midweek day off so had a midweek sleep over. She had known Jason would contact her that morning after the arrest of his thug the night before, although she was surprised the contact was in the form of a text message, as she fully expected a curse filled rant of a phone call. Ross pulls her closer into his chest.

Dynamic Entry

"I thought you were taking today off?" She revels in the warmth of his arms.

"I am, but I'm guessing Mr. Hamilton doesn't care for time off, or at least he doesn't care for my time off."

Sophie feels Ross move to face her. "How do you know it's him texting you?" Sophie tenses at her slight slip up, but tries to relax, hoping that Ross hadn't noticed too much.

"We had a business deal last night, so I kinda expected contact from him today." Not a lie she thinks to herself as she turns in his arms so they are face to face and nuzzles into his neck, nipping it playfully with her teeth. "But anyway, never mind about him. We are on a full day off together, so, what do you fancy doing?" Ross pulls her even closer, running his hand down her bare thigh and lifting her leg over his hip, bringing their bodies even closer together, making them both forget all about Jason.

"Hmm, well, it's been a long time since I had a day off to share with someone so beautiful so I would normally go for a swim." His hands didn't stop caressing her back and down over her raised hip to her backside and up again as he talks. His length growing against her stomach. "So I'll need to give it some thought. I'm sure there will be food involved and maybe a drink or two, there will definitely be kissing involved." He claims her lips in a powerful kiss, she feels love in his kiss and pours it into her own kiss...

They both break the kiss for a much-needed breath. Sophie grinds her hips into his, feeling bolder than normal under his caresses.

"I think this is the best way to start the day, then after we can think of what else to do." Ross kisses her again and they can both feel each other's smiles as they deepen the kiss and explore each other's bodies until they both climax once more.

Exhausted after their love making, Sophie drifts in and out of sleep in Ross' arms, feeling wonderfully at peace with herself, her surroundings and with Ross, which is a particularly significant shift in her personal life.

She feels the mattress move as Ross de-tangles himself from her, but she is too spent to protest his movements even though a part of her does mourn his absence.

What feels like seconds later due to sleep, Sophie feels the mattress dip under Ross' weight as he climbs back in and strokes her bare arm to rouse her. She comes too with a smile.

"You hungry?" Ross' blue eyes are kind and smiling as he gazes deep into her and she is reminded of the hypnotising feeling she felt looking into them the first time they met.

"Hmm, aye. You want to go out?"

Ross shakes his head. "I've made you breakfast in bed. It's not much, tea and a roll 'n bacon." He gives an apologetic shrug of his shoulders at the merge offerings. Sophie pushes herself up the bed until she is sitting, firmly holding the covers to hide her nakedness, her every nerve flashing and twitching in alarm at the kind gesture.

"What? Why, why did you do that? I didn't ask you to do that. You didn't need to…" Her voice trails off as Ross' expression changes from happiness to confusion.

"I know you didn't ask me to do it. I wanted to do it."

"Why?" The question explodes from her like an accusation.

"Why? What do you mean why? Because I wanted to, because you're my girlfriend and I like doing nice things for you." The moment should have been nice, romantic even, except Sophie was treating him like he had asked her to commit a bank heist.

"So you can butter me up, make me pliable so you can use me? Romance is... is-"

She is comparing him to her father, again. She doesn't want to, but the words come out anyway. He takes her hands in his, but the firm grip she had on the covers under her arms never falters.

"Sophie, I am not doing this for any reason other than I wanted to. I was hungry after making love and I guessed you would be too, so as you slept, I cooked. That's it. There is no ulterior motive here." He takes a deep breath. "I am not your father."

His final words seem to penetrate Sophie as she relaxes, making the covers fall from her stranglehold on them, baring the tops of her breasts.

"I'm sorry. I just don't know how to deal with it when people — men — do nice or romantic things for me as it normally means they want something from me."

"I do want something from you," Ross says as Sophie tenses. "I want you to be my girlfriend, to be with only me, and to trust me, so do you think you can do that?"

Fear and guilt slide away leaving a fuzzy feeling in her chest at being called his girlfriend. She could do that; she could be his girlfriend. She wants to be his girlfriend more than she's ever wanted to be anything to anyone, but trust was a big thing. Could she trust him? With her life? Her heart? Her job? That was the million-dollar question.

"Girlfriend, I can do one hundred percent and I am working on the trust thing." She takes the roll from him and gives him a quick kiss trying to assuage the guilt that had started to crash through her again.

Ross climbs back into bed with his own roll then turns to answer Sophie.

"I know —" He sees her still staring at him, uncertainty in her eyes. "What's wrong Sophie?"

Sophie's heart is screaming at her to tell him her secret, but her head has blocked all the words from passing her lips, leaving her staring at her boyfriend like she is an oil painting.

"I... I" Her ringing phone brings her from her confusion and a frown to Ross' forehead. The ringing phone is her work one.

"You'd better get that; he seems to be eager to contact you."

She feels a coldness form between them so places her roll on the bedside table then moves towards him taking his roll away from him and then his face in her hands.

"I don't care, I'm enjoying breakfast with my boyfriend right now. I will need to contact him later, but I'm not letting him interrupt the moment where we've agreed we're serious about this relationship." She brings his lips down onto hers and lies back down into the bed, making his body follow hers.

"Now seeing this is the first time I've been in a proper, serious relationship, can I suggest you make love to me, so I know what it's like not to just have sex." Ross kisses her soundly. Pulling back he looks deep into her mesmerizing blue eyes.

"It's never been just sex with you." He gives her a hungry smile as her heart soars, hoping beyond hope that his words are true.

CHAPTER TWENTY-ONE

Jason slams down his phone onto his desk. If he was in one of the cartoons from his childhood there would be steam whistling from his ears, he was that angry. Why wasn't she answering? Was she behind the arrest of his worker or was the worker full of shit and bad luck?

Before he can get too much further into his thoughts his office video doorbell chimes. He has a quick look at the CCTV monitor on his desk to make sure it's who he's expecting then buzzes in his visitor. This is a meeting he is not looking forward to.

Telling a customer he can't deliver has never been his favourite pastime, but losing money is even further down his list of favourite things to do.

"Mr. Baxter come in, sit." Jason greets his customer with as much friendliness as he can muster, due to circumstances. The customer sits at the allocated seat and wrings his hands, nerves are rolling off him. Jason watches the customer with his shrewd business eye and decides to hold back his information on the gun. "So Mr. Baxter, what's the matter?"

The customer squirms in his seat making the faux leather squeak. "Well, you see Mr... eh, Mr. Hamilton. I would like... I mean, everything is sorted with the... eh, problem I was having and you see... I don't need the eh... eh... items anymore." Jason's heart rushes in relief at not losing business over the fuck up of his worker, but he refuses to show his relief on his face, so keeps his expressions deadpan.

He can see Mr. Baxter takes his facial expression as a threat and smiles inwardly as he stammers on. "I'm, I'm sorry Mr. Hamilton, I mean, I... I didn't mean to mess you about. You know how it is when tempers flare and families are involved. I will pay for your time... obviously, it's just, I shouldn't have been as rash is all." Jason's face darkens, his customer thinks he can throw him a bone of compensation, that is not how these things work.

"Oh well now, Baxter, that is very kind of you." Jason's tone is low, guttural and dangerous, just like the glint in his brown eyes. "But that's not how this works. Not only have you wasted my time, you've wasted my employees time and my contact's time. That's a lot of man hours to waste. Plus I have already paid out for the getaway car and the gun."

The customer looks like he is physically shriveling in the chair as Jason talks. "So, you will be paying the agreed amount on the contract, plus a cancellation fee of two grand which takes your total to five grand and if I remember correctly, which I always do, your first payment of two hundred, but is now four hundred, is due this Sunday. Would you happen to have that on you today? You know, to save me time coming to get it?" The customer's face pales even more and moves his mouth to talk but it is bone dry.

Jason knew he didn't know how he was going to pay the money owed to begin with, but now there is even more added.

He shakes his head, the only movement he can muster. Jason's face is like thunder and the customer would swear he could see gold lightening flicker through his eyes. "Well in that case I will be seeing you on Sunday for your first payment, of four hundred pounds.

Dynamic Entry

Jason stands and growls, signalling for his customer to do the same. The customer rises to his feet, desperate to get out of the office and away from the overwhelming, dominating, dangerous power that is Jason Hamilton.

Mumbling his apologies and agreements, the customer scurries out into the pouring rain and takes a deep breath. He walks away from the office building on Blythswood Square.

Jason sits back down in his executive chair and blows out a breath of relief. The meeting could have gone so differently if he had had to admit he didn't have the gun and probably more violently if he actually did have everything in place, but overall, he came out on top. Something he always does.

He pours himself a protein drink and makes a note to go to the gym later that day. He needed to get rid of some energy and pent up aggression. As of late the main way he was exercising, getting out his aggression and getting his itch scratched was through torture and murder.

His email ping's, drawing his attention to his computer and away from murder. The ping is an invite to a charity black tie event with a plus one.

The event is being held by a person who Jason is interested in meeting and doing some business with. A person with clout in the Glasgow underworld. He quickly emails back his acceptance, wonders where his tuxedo is, then realises he is being noticed in the right circles. Life is going his way, and with Sophie at his side as his plus one, there will be more things going his way.

****

Fiona Morgan

Their day together had been perfect, Sophie thinks as she closes her front door that night. After admitting to being in a serious relationship and making love again, Sophie had felt everything had turned magical. Soppy she knew, and definitely unlike her, but true.

They had headed to The Pub for some lunch and liquids, then to the cinema. They had chosen an action film that was showing although neither of them seen much of it as they had been the archetypical 'young love' couple, sucking at each other's faces in the back row of the cinema.

Sophie gives a small laugh into the silent, empty house at the memory and touches her lips, trying to feel Ross' lips there one last time before giving into reality and the phone call she knows she needs to make.

Pulling off her leather jacket she hangs it over the back of her couch and makes her way through to the kitchen for a beer. She sits on her couch and lifts her work phone. There is a missed call and a text message from Jason demanding that she phones him at her earliest convenience, or before. She snorts out her derision at him and with a growl she stabs at the screen to place the call.

She'd be putting in an hour's overtime for the call, working on her bloody day off! She knows she won't get it, but that is beside the point.

The ringing tone echoes down her ear until the gruff, strange accented voice she'd learned to despise comes bellowing through the phone's speakers.

"Sophie, I was wondering when I'd hear from you." She bites back the curses she wants to rain down him, and vows that one day she will tell him exactly what she thinks of him.

"I'm not at your beck and call Jason," she says. "We've had this discussion. Now what do you want,

167

I'm a busy woman." She hears a disgusted noise coming down the line at her.

"Yes, I know you've been busy with that idiot you're fucking and so neglecting your customers. In fact, you've neglected your work so much one of my men got arrested last night after your drop off."

She clenches her teeth in anger. "First of all, my relationship is none of your concern and will not be brought up as a conversation, ever. Secondly, I have not been neglecting anything, especially my business. If your imbecile got himself arrested last night that's his fault not mine. He's the one that got caught, and may I point out that he must have been pulled for something unrelated to the firearm as it happened after the deal."

A humph comes through the phone. "Yes. The idiot had a busted tail-light so got pulled- how do you know he was pulled over?" Ice flows through her veins. Did she just blow her cover? She didn't think so.

"A logical deduction. He said he was taking the piece to you that night, so I guessed he wouldn't be stupid enough to be wandering about Glasgow with an illegal weapon in his possession, or is he that stupid?" She blows out a silent breath, hoping that Jason would buy her lies.

"No, he isn't quite that stupid," there's a pause, "but anyway, I don't need the piece anymore; the client has pulled out." Sophie closes her eyes, glad that the gun wasn't on the streets anymore and that whatever crime Jason's client had planned was now off, although she worried how that would affect her investigation.

"But something else has come up." Jason continues, interrupting her thoughts.

"And?"

"And I need you to go to a black-tie ball with me. My presence has been requested and it will introduce me to the people who are further involved in the underworld in this city than me. It should also get my foot into their business and so make a better name for myself." Her every instinct is screaming 'no' at her.

She knows Ross would not be happy at her spending time with Jason at such a public event, even if it is for work and she sure as hell didn't want her face known to all the gangsters in Glasgow. That would make for tricky work in the future, but she knows her bosses will jump at the chance to collect more evidence on Jason's deals and maybe get more names and faces of the underworld. She was screwed. She would need to do it.

"I'm not sure, Jason, I'll need to check my diary." A lame excuse, she knew, but it was all she had at that moment.

"I'm sure you will find your diary is free that day." The dangerous tone he uses with her sends a chill through her veins. "And I'm more than happy to provide you with a wardrobe for the night; everything from shoes, dress, to the sexy underwear I might even get to see at the end of the night."

A shudder wracks through Sophie, making her find her voice. "I have my own clothes and it will be a cold day in hell before you get to see me anything but fully clothed."

A chuckle comes down the phone at her. "Whatever you say my gorgeous girl. Now I need to go, but I will get back to you with times."

She cancels the call and shivers, draining the rest of her beer. The thought of spending any time with Jason makes her skin crawl, but an entire night as his 'date'? The thought repulsed her. She heads to the kitchen for another beer, she was going to need a few more of these to banish the thought of her big night out.

Dynamic Entry

CHAPTER TWENTY-TWO

The two couples are on their second double date. It is the week before Sophie needs to attend the ball with Jason and she needed to break the news to Ross. She has been putting it off all week, ever since Jason had told her about in the hope that one of the powers that be in the ranks above her decided that the assignment would be too expensive, take up too many man hours, or even put her in too much danger, but it was not to be, they all signed off on it, thinking it would be a great way to get as much information as possible on the underworld of Glasgow.

The couples had been out for dinner and were settling into 'Sophie's' table at The Pub for the rest of the night, having agreed that they would all stay in Sean's flat above the bar. The men were at the bar collecting drinks, leaving Sophie and Belle to talk.

"You've not told him yet, have you?"

"No, I can't find the right words. I mean what do I say? Sorry honey, but I need to go to a black-tie ball with the man you despise, but it's for work, so that's okay?"

Belle nods. "That sounds okay. I mean it is the truth isn't it."

Sophie nods, then shrugs. "As close to the truth as I can go, at the moment." Belle nods absently for a second.

"When are you telling him, about everything?" Sophie opens her mouth to talk, then snaps it shut as Ross and Sean arrive with their drinks, putting them down on the table. Sophie closes her eyes and prays that Ross didn't hear any of her conversation, but her hope is short lived.

"Tell him what? And who's 'him'?" Ross sits next to Sophie placing his arm around her shoulders, rubbing the bare skin lovingly, making her guilt eat at her more. "Jason that you're not working with him again?" Sophie can hear in his tone that he is trying to make it into a joke, but she can also hear the serious undertone.

Her independent side is pricked to anger at the thought of Ross, or any man telling her what to do and she decides to hold onto that emotion by a slither to get her through her guilt and white lies.

"No, I will not be telling Jason that, as I need his business," Her anger dissipates at the thought of her next words. "but I do need to tell you that I need to go to a ball with Jason next weekend."

Ross blinks a few times trying to understand her words. "A ball?"

"Yes, a black tie do, party thing."

"Why? I mean why does he want you there? Although I can guess why!" Sean and Belle watch the conversation like they were at Wimbledon watching a match on Centre Court.

Sophie tries to ignore the confidence shaking thought that Ross may think she isn't good enough for such a posh night out and has only been asked so Jason can get her into his bed, but then reminds herself that she doesn't get knocked down by anyone, especially the man she is falling in love with. That thought hits her hard, she is starting to fall in love with Ross, but pushes it aside to continue their conversation.

"He wants to do business, he trusts my opinion on business deals, so has asked me to go with him. It is purely business!"

Ross humphs. "Maybe for you, but not him!" He spits out his last word with venom.

"Well as you said, it is for me, and it is something I need to do for my business, so that is all that matters!" The lovers stare at each other, neither wanting to back down, but neither really wanting the argument either. Sean is first to speak to break the silence.

"Well, if it's a work thing and not personal choice thing, it might give the dickhead something other than trying to screw money out of me to concentrate on."

Sophie turns to Sean, her anger still bubbling. "Is he still trying to get protection money from you?" Her anger is evident in her voice.

"Not really, but he does still come in and stare a lot, but listen, it's fine, he's buying his drinks and staying to himself, so I can deal with that." Sophie nods.

"Okay but let me know if he tries anything again and I'll talk to him, get him to back of, again!" Sean nods.

The friends get back to their night out and after a few laughter filled hours they finally retire into their respective bedrooms at too late an hour.

Sophie notices Belle following Sean into his bedroom and smiles, happy that her friend is finding happiness outside of work, as was she. The thought stabs her heart with guilt. Her feelings for Ross are growing every day and even though she doesn't want to admit it, she is falling in love with him, hard.

Something she never thought would happen, or even wanted to happen, but it is happening all the same. She closes the bedroom door and stays facing it, gathering her thoughts and feelings, promising herself that she will tell Ross the truth about everything, her name, her job and her connection to Jason as soon as she knows how he feels. If he ever says they three important words, she will open up her life and her heart to him.

Dynamic Entry

****

Ross watches as his girlfriend closes the door and stays there, her back to him. He wonders if she's still pissed at him for going slightly Neanderthal on her over the ball business with Jason. He could tell she hadn't been happy at his choice of words or probably his tone of voice either.

He would never stop her or even suggest she couldn't do anything, but the fact that it's a night out with Jason, and not just any night out, a high class night out, something he could never give her, with someone who is built like a mountain, who can fill out a tux much better than he could, is sending his jealousy over the edge.

He pushes his self-deprecating thoughts out of his mind and slides his arms around Sophie's waist, pulling her against his chest until she is nestled in his arms, where she belongs.

"I'm sorry I sounded totally against your work tonight. I would never do or say anything to stop you working, I just don't trust him! He always seems to have an ulterior motive when it comes to you, and I get a bit worried." She leans further back into him, leaning her head to the side, inviting Ross to take her neck in a kiss. He obliges her invite.

"Why would you be worried?" She asks. She closes her eyes, enjoying the feeling of his lips on her neck.

"He looks like the model of a man that every female wants."

She turns in his arms to look deep into his navy-blue eyes as she speaks her next words. "Not this female! Never this female! This female wants you and only you." She threads her fingers into his hair and gently pulls him down until his lips are brushing hers.

"He has nothing on you." She crushes her lips to his, pouring her life and soul into her kiss, just for him.

Ross responds, all thoughts of not being enough leaving him, his kiss is full of passion and love.

The three words that keep running through his head are something he didn't think would happen for real, but the feelings are there, nonetheless.

Embracing his newly admitted feelings, he slows the kiss down, pulling Sophie closer into his embrace. He turns them and walks them to the bed, never breaking the kiss until he lowers them both down to the mattress. He looks down on her, love rushing through his system and in that moment he knows there is no one else in this world for him except Sophie and the thought lights him up, makes him feel all sorts of gushy things he has never felt before all the other times he was 'in love'.

Sophie stares back at Ross self-consciousness evident in her eyes the longer he stares at her, regardless of the love shining in his eyes.

"What's wrong?" Her voice is thick with passion as Ross grins at her.

"Nothing, I'm just thinking how much I lo — beautiful you are." He nearly confessed his feelings for her, but hadn't wanted to freak her out, there would be time for that, he would need to take they words slowly.

Her answering smile melts him. "Thank you." They smiled at each other another second before Ross takes her lips again, leaning on her body so she can feel what she does to him.

Sophie grasps into his shoulder as he pushes into her fully, he loves the feeling of him being inside her, both of them connected. They enjoy each other's bodies fully until they fall asleep wrapped in each other's arms thinking of their love for each other.

Dynamic Entry

The next morning, after breakfast, Sean drives them all home. Ross walks Sophie to her front door. She brushes her fingers down his face and he shivers.

"I need to do some work this morning; but why don't you come over later and maybe bring a change of clothes for work tomorrow?" Excitement bursts through him.

"Definitely." He kisses her goodbye before bounding into to Sean's Silver 2014 Nissan Juke.

"You are in deep my friend!" Sean states as he pulls away from the kerb. Ross grins like the cat who'd got the cream.

"Oh aye, and I love it!"

CHAPTER TWENTY-THREE

Every night since the last weekend Sophie and Ross have spent together either at her house or his. They were loving being in each other's company and loving each other, even though neither of them had said the words, but they both felt it deep inside them.

The Saturday morning of the ball arrives with Ross in her bed and her curled up around him. She loves the nights they had spent together. She never thought she would enjoy sharing her space with another person full time, but if the topic of moving in together came up, she wouldn't be totally against the idea. She smiles to herself and turns in Ross' arms, hooking her leg over his hip.

"Morning." She kisses him with a grin on her lips and the early morning summer sun starting to peek through her blinds.

"Good morning. You going into the office this morning?"

She had had to cover herself for work by saying she worked out of an office space in Pitt Street, which technically, she mused to herself, wasn't really another lie. "No, I'm taking this morning off since I am working tonight." She feels Ross stiffen in her arms at the reminder of her night out. "You working this morning?"

She kisses his jaw feeling the morning stubble scratchy against her lips. "Aye, although I would rather stay in here with you. Will I see you tonight, before you go out, or when you get home?"

Dynamic Entry

Sophie stops her kissing descent.

"I don't know. It's going to be a late night; I wouldn't want you to stay up just for me."

He pulls her back up until she is straddling his thighs and kisses her softly. "I would love to stay up just for you and I want to be the last person to kiss you goodnight."

She looks deep into his eyes. "No-one will be kissing me goodnight but you, ever."

Ross' heart scuds a tattoo in his chest at her words. "Ever? That's good to know, maybe now I can believe that you'll come back to me."

Emotion chokes Sophie at the thought of Ross worrying about losing her. "Hey, tonight is business and only business. I am not going anywhere. I'm yours and if you know me at all, you'll know I have never said that to anyone, ever." Ross embraces her face in his hands and brings her down for a kiss.

The kiss starts gentle, a caressing of each other's lips, but quickly turns hungry, both of them taking and giving in turn until they break apart, both of them breathing hard. Sophie adjusts them so Ross is full inside her. Panic flashes on his face at not having protection on.

"Soph —"

"I'm on the Pill, I trust you, and I want to feel you, all of you. Do you trust me?" He thrusts his hips up again as he speaks over the lump if emotion in his heart and throat.

"Aye."

At eight o'clock, both Sophie and Ross are dressed and sitting on her couch with their respective cups of tea and coffee.

"You didn't need to get dressed; you could've stayed in bed." Ross grins at her.

"I know, but I thought I could run you in and maybe you can sell me something pretty to wear tonight, so I'll have you close to me all night." He grins again.

"That I can do."   .

****

Jason stands under the iconic clock in Glasgow Central train station at seven o'clock, a nervous, angry energy running through him.

He had offered and pushed to pick up Sophie from her house and drive her to the ball, but she was dead against it, to the point she was refusing to go, so he pulled back on his insistence.

He needed her to go to this ball with him, he had plans for them after the business of the evening was concluded. Oh yes, tonight was the night Jason would have Sophie under him, on top of him and on her knees for him.

He adjusts himself to a more comfortable position after his thoughts and smiles at the approaching Sophie, feeling the need to readjust himself again at the sight of the gorgeous honey blonde walking towards him.

****

Sophie is feeling highly over dressed in her red one shouldered, fitted, open backed, full length evening dress that splits at the front showing off her lean leg. Her new silver glittery platform stilettos clicked loudly on the tiled floor underfoot as she grips tightly on to the matching box clutch bag. She hopes she isn't over dressed once she gets to the ball and looking at Jason in his tux she shouldn't be.

Dynamic Entry

She comes to a stop in front of Jason and takes in his attire. In a tuxedo he should look sharp and sexy, instead he looks uncomfortable; like his suit is choking his body instead of accentuating his well-defined muscles.

An image of how Ross would look in a tux flits across Sophie's mind, bringing a smile to her lips. She sees Jason's lips curve up into leering grin in return, wiping the smile from Sophie's face instantly as she internally kicks herself at her inability to keep her emotions for Ross off of her normally unreadable face.

"Sophie, you are looking spectacular tonight." Jason takes her hand and brushes her knuckles with his lips. She tries to repress the revulsion shuddering through her. This is going to be a long night.

"Jason, let's get this over with." She extracts her hand and starts to walk towards the entrance to the Grand Central Hotel that is situated inside the train station. Jason grasps her elbow, stopping her in her heels.

"Now, now Sophie, there's no need for an attitude; and in case you've forgotten, you are my date for the night, so you will act accordingly." His dangerous growl is a warning as he pulls her into his side and places his arm around her waist, his fingers gripping her hip bone possessively.

Sophie doesn't want to poke a hungry bear, but she also doesn't want to give Jason any hint that this night is anything other than business, so she plasters an apologetic smile on her face as she looks up at him.

"I'm sorry for my attitude, working on a Saturday night isn't my usual MO." Jason's fingers tighten on her hip and Sophie winces at the pain.

The couple arrive at the ball and Sophie is in awe at the grandeur and elegance of the ballroom, the chandeliers are exquisite. The many tables are decked out in whites and purples, and the attendees screamed money, ill-gotten money, but money all the same.

Looking around at the females attending the ball, Sophie realises she no longer feels over dressed, but she does however now, feel watched. She pushes her paranoia away and plasters on her undercover smile, hoping that every criminal in the ballroom believes it.

The night continues on with Sophie smiling, trying to drink as little wine as possible; even though Jason seems to be on a 'get Sophie drunk' course and her taking in every face she possibly can.

After standing with Jason as he concluded some business deals with Glasgow's finest in the underworld, Sophie concludes that the night had been organised as a pissing contest; each man trying to outdo the others by bragging about how many cars they had or crimes they had committed.

Many times she's caught herself rolling her eyews and has had to squeeze close her fists tight to feel the bite of her fingernails in the palm of her hand, her reminder to play nice and keep her cover. During a particular boring conversation Sophie excuses herself to escape to the ladies.

Taking a deep breath, she smooths out her hair then types out a quick text to Ross, wanting to be herself for a second before going back into her cover as Sophie Peterson. She takes another deep breath as she touches the diamond and ruby collarette she'd bought at Saltire Jewellers that morning. The memory of picking it out and Ross' fingers caressing the nape of her neck as he fixed the clasp for her as she tried it on, and the smile that broke from her lips at the delicate way it twinkled in the bright shop lights came bidding to the front of her mind along with the nervous way Ross packaged it up and handed it over with the cryptic words, 'I've put something extra in the box, if you want to use it later on when the ball has finished.' Then he'd kissed her soundly where they stood on the shop floor, his boss standing in the corner grinning with a knowing glint in her eye.

Once Sophie got home, she'd pulled apart the box until she'd found what Ross had been talking about. A silver door key. A key to Ross' house so she could go there after the ball.

A thought that the gesture had been brought about through jealousy flitted through her head, but she pushed it away, telling herself that Shettleston is much closer than Motherwell to the centre of Glasgow, and so it makes much more sense to stay with Ross, plus she couldn't deny herself the truth, she wanted to go home to Ross at the end of the night, in fact she wanted to go home to him at the end of every night.

A crash of the bathroom door being opened brings Sophie from her thoughts. She looks up to see an incredibly sparkly, incredibly fake tanned female almost growling at her.

The female's eyes danced and sparked barely held in anger. "How the fuck did you weasel your way into his bed?" A picture of Ross flashes across Sophie's mind before her brain kicks back into gear and she realises the woman is talking about Jason. She plasters on her undercover smile.

"I'm sorry, but who are you?"

The female sticks her fake chest out further than should be physically possible. "I'm the one who should be with Jason tonight, not you!" A scorned woman, Sophie thinks quickly to herself.

"Well feel free to be there again, as I am not, nor will I ever be in his bed," Sophie says. "I am here as a, business sounding board, for want of a better term."

The female becomes indignant. "Well, he's out there telling everyone he'll be fucking you tonight no matter what, an' you're in here saying no fuckin' way, how's that going to work out then, an what's wrong with being in his bed?"

Sophie stares at the woman wide eyed and wondering what part of this scorned woman's rant to deal with first, that Jason was telling people they would be sleeping together by the end of the night, and by the sounds of it he wasn't above taking her by force, which is sending alarm bells off in her head, or the fact that the female has done a one-eighty and is now demanding to know what problem Sophie has and why she is so against sleeping with Jason. Her head was starting to hurt.

"As I have said, I am not, nor will I ever sleep with Jason, regardless of what he is saying," she says.

Sophie side-steps around the female, but the woman grabs Sophie's arm, stopping her escape.

"He has his sights set on you and if you know Jason, then you know he always gets what he wants." The dark warning was loud and clear to Sophie and one she would take heed of, but at that moment in time she couldn't look weak.

"Thanks for the warning, but he won't be getting his own way with me." With her head held high, Sophie strides from the bathroom into the cacophony of noise that is the ball in full swing.

Jason spots Sophie walking from the ladies' room and walks towards her.

"Where have you been?" He growls into her ear, his nose touching her jawline. He takes a deep breath of her and Sophie swears she hears him moan in pleasure. She jerks her head back but can't get away from him due to the grip he has on her waist, his fingers stroking higher up her ribcage.

"Well the ladies, obviously, since that's where you just saw me come from." She thinks about trying to tame her sarcastic tone and facial expression and tries to convince herself that she had at least attempted to do that, but she couldn't hide her disgust for this excuse of a man, it was too overwhelming. His fingers curl further into her ribs, digging painfully into her flesh.

"Watch your mouth! I'm trying to show you a nice time so we can get to know each other better before I make you mine, but all you're doing is trying my patience and being bitchy." Her movement is restricted with the vice like grip he has on her and sweat breaks out down her back as a chill runs through her at Jason's sheer size and strength.

Her back-up wasn't as strong as she would have liked but had hoped that being in such a public place would placate Jason enough, then all she had to do was not leave with him.

"I am here on business and I have told you too many fucking times now Jason, this," she motions with her free hand between them both, "is strictly business and business only. Now you do not get to talk to me like that and get your hands off of me!" She gets angrier with each word and is happy about it. She will use the anger along with her training to get away from him, if need be.

The thought of how she might be able to get away has just finished crossing her mind when she feels her feet move without her permission.

Jason is moving them both quickly through the large ballroom, his grip even tighter than before and her shoes clicking loudly on the wooden floor.

He takes them out of the highly populated area into a deserted, dull room, he slams Sophie against a wall then turns her to face him. He plasters his body against hers, spreading her legs as far as they can go in her tight ball gown.

Sophie can feel his growing erection pressing against the apex of her thigh. She knows she's in trouble but tries not to panic, swallowing her fear down and holding on to her anger.

"Who do you think you're talking to, bitch? I've been plenty patient with you, and you know I'm not a patient man!" The growl of his tone matches the dangerous, golden thunder glinting in his brown eyes, which only increases her heart rate as she frantically tries to go through escape plans in her head along with fighting her own panic. "So now you are going to give me what I've been waiting for since Northumbria and what I was planning on having at the end of the night, you're pussy." Sophie smothers the whimper trying to escape her lips, but she still feels Jason's smirk against her cheek as he lands a kiss there.

Her fear is feeding his excitement. She tries to dampen it down, swallowing away the panic again and forcing herself to concentrate on the here and now and not on his hand which is painfully squeezing her breast.

"So you're going to add attempted rape onto your rap sheet, are you?" she says. "Along gun and drug running, and probably murder." She tries to wriggle from his grip to cover her movements of taking one of her shoes off but remains on her tiptoes to further conceal the plan which at the moment goes as far as taking a shoe off.

"There's not going to be anything attempted about this," he moves his hand down her body and between her legs and back up again to her shoulders, "so to answer your question, yes I am going to be adding rape to my C.V. and yes it will sit there beside everything else you just said and more, so just remember that when we are fucking, there's no point fight me, I always win!" He licks up the side of her face and round the shell of her ear. A shiver of fear runs through her without her permission, but she straightens her back, putting back the steel that she is known for.

"Not this time!" Sophie growls back as she sinks her teeth in Jason's neck hard enough to make him slacken his grip.

She grasps the opportunity to swing her box clutch bag, making contact with his shoulder as she drives her knee into his groin with enough force to physically move him, making him drop to the floor. Having got her shoes off she is free to run like a bat out of hell, praying to any and all gods that she could get out of the room before Jason could summon the strength to move again.

Bursting through the door to party she rushes through the throng of people, pushing and jostling them from her path out of the building, leaving a streak of disgruntled party goers until she is standing on the pavement in front of the train station in her bare feet, looking for the nearest taxi. She pulls her phone from her clutch and hits the speed dial for her DI.

"I got a confession, now I need an out!" She doesn't wait for a reply as she jumps into a waiting taxi, never seeing the female from earlier standing behind her listening to her every word.

CHAPTER TWENTY-FOUR

Ross checks his phone for what feels like the millionth time that night. It is almost midnight. Sophie's last text had come across as stressed. He knew she hadn't wanted to do business with Jason, but he was getting the feeling there was more to it than just business, although his gut told him it was nothing romantic, at least not on Sophie's side.

He knew she was all his where that was concerned and he loved it, loved her. The realisation that he knew she was his and only his should've brought forth shock from him, but it didn't, instead it brought forth peace and rightness in his world. That peace was short lived as Sophie bursts through his front door, using the key he had given her.

"Sophie, am I glad..." He takes in her appearance. Her dress is crumpled and ripped at the split almost to her waist from her long strides from running, her feet are bare, and her hair is falling out of the bobby pins that had so perfectly held it up in a sophisticated knot.

Her cheeks are red from exertion and streaked black from her tear run mascara, and her normally sparkling, mesmerizing silver blue eyes are shimmering with more unshed tears and fear.

Ross rushes forward, pulling Sophie into his embrace. He feels her flinch before allowing herself to be enveloped in his arms and breaking down.

****

Dynamic Entry

Feeling Ross stroke her bare back soothingly as she sobs massive cathartic sobs in his arms is something Sophie never thought she would do, but being there in his arms is helping all the stress and fear she has been feeling since Jason pulled her into the empty room leave her body.

She had always thought that showing a man emotion in the form of tears was weak, had thought if she let a man into her heart, she'd lose her independence, but at this moment in time, in Ross' arms, she didn't feel weak. She is beginning to feel her strength come back, taking that strength from her boyfriend, she felt safe and, dare she think it, loved.

Her sobs start to calm, and she looks up to see deep into Ross' eyes. Worry and love shine back at her and she gasps at the feelings running through her. As she was sitting in the taxi waiting impatiently until she arrived at Ross' house, everything she'd been through this night made her admit her feelings towards him. She loves him. She loves him with everything she is, which means she trusts him.

"Sophie! What happened?" He walks them over to the couch and sits. Sophie takes a deep breath and blows it away.

"Jason got a bit handsy, I bit him and hit him with my bag before kneeing him in the balls and running. I grabbed a taxi and came here."

Sophie can see rage surge through Ross at the knowledge of Jason touching her in anyway, and going by her appearance, her ripped dress and black tears, she guesses he can work out it was more than 'just getting a bit 'handsy', it must look and sound like exactly what had happened, she had had to run from him and his advances. The rage in his eyes is quickly followed by relief and love that her first instinct after getting away from danger was to get to him.

"You need to report him. Do you want me to phone the police?" The worry and kindness in his tone nearly breaks the hold Sophie has on her emotions as tears fall freely from her eyes and she hiccups a sob.

"No, I'll put it, do my, a report tomorrow. Just now all I want is a shower and to be held by someone I lo, by you." She stopped herself from saying the words burning in her throat. When she said they words for the first time, she needed Ross to know to know they came from her heart and not her fear.

Ross nods. He's confused at the words she used about the report and he wonders if there is something she isn't trusting him with, and it also stung that she'd changed her sentence when he'd held his breath for those three little words he was desperate to say himself, but he couldn't, wouldn't voice they words tonight though, not after everything she had been through. No tonight he would give her exactly what she has asked for and needed, a shower and to be held by someone who loved her, and he loved her more than he needed his next breath.

"Do you want any help in the shower?" He sees Sophie smile. It had felt like days since he had seen her smile when in fact it was only hours ago in his shop.

"Yes, I think I will need some help." She smiles another genuine smile, making her eyes dance with lust. Much better than the fear that had danced in them when she first entered his house Ross thinks to himself.

The lovers shower, Ross taking care of Sophie in such a heartbreakingly tender way. Washing her hair and rubbing away the night

All clean, the lovers get dried and Sophie brushes out her towel dried hair, her soft curls bounce around her face and down her back and she grumbles.

"I love your curls; I don't understand why you dislike them and straighten the life out of them so much." Ross takes a breath before speaking again, "Do you think on our wedding day you could leave your hair curly?"

Sophie stops brushing her hair and stairs at Ross. Her heart is hammering a tattoo in her chest, beating out the word 'yes' as her brain tries to take in the conversation and how she feels about it all. "Our wedding day?"

Ross kicks himself internally, he was pushing too far too fast he hadn't even told her he loved her and he was talking about their wedding day, but the words were out now and he meant them, so he'd have to own them.

"Well, yes, I hope so anyway." He moves to stand in front of her and takes a deep breath in before continuing again, "Sophie, I know you have trust issues and you don't really believe in happily ever after or fairy tales, but I want forever with you. You are my happily ever after. Sophie, I love you with all my heart and more. Now this isn't a proposal, I know you're – we're not there yet, but I am hoping that one day we will be." He is breathless by the time he has finished talking, wanting to get everything out before Sophie could stop him or he backed out of his confession.

Sophie continues to watch Ross, searching his face and eyes for any hint of a lie or deceit, the way she'd been trained to do at work, and she found none. Now there was nothing holding her back from saying the same words back to him except herself and her job, and after tonight she'd be taken off the assignment with Jason, then even her job wouldn't be holding her back. Ross starts to speak, telling her she doesn't need to say anything, but she stops him with a kiss. An ice melting, life changing kiss. One that leaves them both breathless.

"I never wanted, or thought it possible, for me to fall in love, or trust a man enough with any part of my life, but I do Ross, I love you more than life itself. I want forever with you and only you, nobody else." Tears are flowing from both of their eyes as Ross nods his head, struggling to get words passed the Dumbarton Rock sized lump that has lodged itself in his throat.

"It will always, only ever be you. I am an open book with no secrets." Sophie winces at his words.

She has an enormous secret, but she will explain it all tomorrow, tonight she has said the words she wasn't expecting to say or hear, so all she wants now is to be happy and loved. She kisses him soundly again as they fall onto the bed, making love to each other until they are both spent and sleeping in each other's arms.

CHAPTER TWENTY-FIVE

The next morning Jason wakes with violence throbbing to get out of him. His plans the night before to have Sophie in his bed or at least him having her without her consent didn't materialise.

After she'd bitten him then kneed him, he could hardly breathe never mind run after her for at least five minutes after she'd ran. By the time he'd got himself back to a standing position and out of the hotel door she was gone. The only person standing in the cool night air was an ex-girlfriend, telling him she needed to tell him something. At that moment in time he didn't care what her mouth had to say, he was only interested in seeing it stretched around his length.

He'd taken what he'd needed from the warm, pliable body in his bed the night before, but now it was morning he wanted nothing else from her, but the ex seemed to have other ideas.

"Jason please listen to me. She's trouble." Jason finishes pulling on his trousers and looks at the woman in bed. In his topless state he knows she is admiring his body and he can't help but show it off more, that is why he looks after himself so well.

"Fine, what is it then?"

The ex squirms in the bed. She wants to touch his chest, she wants to have sex with him again, this time she wants to have sex where she gets as much out of it as he does, and after what she is about to tell him she hopes it might be on the cards, but her gut is telling her otherwise. "Last night I overheard that bitch talking on the phone when she was running to get her taxi."

"Aye, phoning that wimp of a boyfriend I expect, and what?"

"No, it wasn't the boyfriend, I think she's police."

Jason stills. This wasn't the first time someone has said that statement to him, and at times he hadn't listened. He'll listen this time.

"What do you mean?" He growls.

"When she ran out last night, she was on the phone an' I heard her say 'I got the confession, now I need an out.'" The ex sits on the edge of the bed. The loud smash of Jason's fists against the makes her shrink back into the bed.

Anger mixes with and magnifies the feeling of needing violence that throbs through his veins. He so wanted to take the pathetic female in front of him and pulverise her for her words, he wanted to disbelieve Sophie would be a rat or a pig, but his gut was screaming at him that his ex was telling the truth.

Bile rises in his throat, but before he could do anything with the violence raging within him, he receives a text.

Mr. Baxter doesn't have his first payment.

Jason sees red. No fucking way was anybody taking him for a fool, not today, not any fucking day! With a growl he stabs a message into his phone in answer.

Get him to the warehouse. I'll meet you there, bring tools.

He looks at the female still on his bed and growls again. A female is the reason he took his eye off the ball and now he might be on the police's hit list. A dangerous glint of thunder flashes through his eyes and his muscles seem to bulge on their own.

Dynamic Entry

The ex scrambles from the bed and Jason takes a step forward, blocking her escape. A whimper comes from the ex, followed by a scream as Jason's fist makes contact with her cheek.

A red mist descends on Jason as he draws his fist back, snapping it forward into the female's face with a sickening crunch for a second time. Then he grabs her blonde hair, dragging her from the bed and ramming her into the wall before pulling her back and repeating the action again and again and again until she crumbles to the floor, ripping a lump of hair from her scalp as she slips from his grasp, but Jason is far from finished with her.

He lifts his sock covered foot, thrusting it down onto her face and chest, but it's not his ex's face he sees as he lifts and thrusts his foot down for a second and a third time, but Sophie's.

The vision in front of him feeds his need for violence that morning. Lifting the limp and broken body he slams his ex into the wall one last time and holds her there by her throat, pushing against her windpipe until he feels it fold and crumple beneath his fingers and her life is over.

She didn't even fight back, which disappoints him. He drops the lifeless body to his bedroom floor with an anticlimactic thud and a disgusted grunt. He is going to need to clean himself up, putting him behind schedule.

After showering the blood from himself, Jason pulls on his 'work clothes' thinking dryly to himself that he should've had them on an hour ago when he took his anger out on his ex. With a shrug he leaves his house and the dead body in his bedroom, shouting into his phone to a worker to come and clean up the mess in there.

Jason pulls up at the warehouse and walks in expecting to see his customer tied to a chair and for the

Fiona Morgan

first time that day, he isn't disappointed. The customer
is bound and gagged and terrified. Just the way Jason
liked.

"Ah Mr. Baxter, you beat me here, good, as I don't
like waiting, but you already know that, don't you?"
The customer nods his head frantically, his eyes
darting about with fear. "Now I hear you haven't made
your first payment, so do you care to tell me why that
is?" The customer mumbles incoherently behind his
gag. Jason rips the tape off with practised precision
letting out a roar of pain from the customer. "So are
you going to tell me why you are holding out on me,
Mr. Baxter?" He shakes his head.

"I'm not Mr. Hamilton, it's just, I don't have the
money. I'm really sorry Mr. Hamilton, I told you the
last time and I'm not using your services, so I thought
if I could explain everything to you, you might
reconsider my bill?" The hope filling the customers'
voice was palpable.

Jason laughs. "Oh, I am going to reconsider your
bill Mr. Baxter, and how do you think that's going to
work out for you, eh?" Jason pulls on overalls and goes
over to his tools, all laid out just the way he likes them
so he can go through his routine of touching and
caressing them. Checking them and touching them,
talking all the time he needs before deciding on a pair
of pliers.

Walking back to his tied up customer Jason smiles.
A full bodied, dangerous smile. The workers with him
would swear they'd seen the thunder and lightning in
his crazed eyes again before an eerie calm comes over
him.

Picking up one of his customer's fingers, Jason slips
it into the pliers and snaps it backwards, breaking it in
an ungodly angle. The scream that comes from his
victim's throat is also ungodly. Jason continues with

the fingers until all ten are sitting broken with bones pushing out of their boundaries within the skin.

For the next hour Jason tortures and beats his customer with precision and glee. He delights at the broken feet and ripped out toenails, almost takes sexual gratification when he feels his victim's ribs bend and snap as his punch connects with such force he moves the chair with Mr. Baxter in it, until finally he lifts his claw hammer and bends down to his victim's ear.

His voice is low and growling. "I don't know or care if you can hear me, but now you understand what happens if you can't pay, I take your life as payment." He stands to his full foreboding height, slightly to the side and with a gleeful goodbye, Jason swings his hammer, striking Mr. Baxter on the temple with the full force of every tensed muscle.

He lifts his arm and swings again, and again, striking every part of his victim's head and face until there is nothing left of Mr. Baxter's head but pulped brain matter, bone shards and every bodily fluid possible.

Throwing down the hammer Jason steps from his blood-soaked overalls and removes his gloves. Even though the need for violence that was thrumming through him has been satiated for a time, after two murders, he can still feel his anger demanding to be settled, so he pulls his phone out and stabs out a text to Sophie.

Meet me at my warehouse, no arguments

He turns back to his works, who are frozen with fear at the viciousness of their boss' attack, their eyes snapping from Jason to the mutilated body and back again. A strange haunting laugh comes from Jason at their reaction.

"Taught him a lesson, didn't I?" Again the workers look between the body and their boss. "Right, make sure that bitch Sophie gets here. Do not clean anything up until she arrives and then make her help. It'll teach her a lesson about double crossing me, plus it will incriminate her in the murder; then keep her here until I phone you. If she tries to weasel out of it, remind her she owes me a favour since I left that fuckin' bar alone, and if that doesn't work, remind her how dangerous I really am. I'm going after that arsehole she loves since she came after me." He turns on his heel and leaves, kicking up dirt as he fishtails his F Pace towards Glasgow city centre and Saltire Jewellers.

****

Sophie is sitting with her DI in their incident room, going through her debrief from the night before. Her head is banging and her eyes are stinging under the harsh fluorescent strip lights, but her sorry state wasn't because of any alcohol she'd consumed the night before, but from the stress of thinking she had messed up her assignment, and the lack of sleep from celebrating her and Ross' new step in their relationship that was to blame.

Her work phone buzzes with the incoming text as it lights itself up on the table. She grabs it to read Jason's message then sags in her seat, suddenly feeling even more weary and a lot older than her twenty-seven years. Her boss' eyes light up.

"Great we can bust him."

Sophie shakes her head. "Fuck no! Not when I'm there. I need to keep my cover as much as possible. I was introduced to a load of gangsters last night and I'd rather they didn't find out my what my actual job is, thank you very much." Sarcasm dripped off her final words, and Sophie inwardly smiles, being in love hasn't made her soft in all aspects of her life, thankfully.

"Oh calm down." Her DI starts, "You need to go, you need to see what the fall out is from you biting him, then kneeing him."

Sophie's indignation rises in her throat, but she manages to keep her voice low and calm. "That bastard was sexually assaulting me and had threatened me with rape. I don't care what the fuckin' fall out is." Her boss stares at her, "Fine. But I want back-up with me and at a safe distance."

The DI nods, "Sophie, I'm sorry, I shouldn't have made it sound like you did wrong, you did what you needed to do to get out of a bad situation, a really bad situation and I thank the lord that you are safe and unharmed. I didn't mean to sound chauvinistic. Now it's Sunday, so not hunners of us kicking about. Take whoever you want, but as you said, keep them at a safe distance, so as not to blow your cover." She can only nod, too stunned at her boss' apology. As she rises from her chair the DI speaks again. "And Soph, stay safe."

"I will, thanks." She gives her DI a smile and walks through the door to leave his office. Finding someone to be her back-up, she leaves the station heading to what she hopes is her last shift on this god-awful assignment.

Sophie climbs from the pool car, ducking her head back in the door.

"Right Ben, stay here. This is close enough I can run to you, but far enough away to be inconspicuous. Keep your phone on you and the radio on in case you need to give me any information, though text me it if you have to. Stay out of sight as much as you can, and congratulations on your move to CID." Ben flashes her a smile as she closes the car door and walks in the direction of the warehouse.

She walks through the gates and spots two young, worried looking men standing smoking at the door to the warehouse. Straightening her shoulders and setting her 'don't fuck with me' face on she strides up to them.

"Morning boys, your boss requested the pleasure of my company." The two workers eye each other warily until one of them finds the courage to clear his throat, straighten to his full height and speaks.

"Aye, well, he's no' here, but he telt us you've tae help us, so moan." He shrugs his head in the direction he wanted Sophie to follow through the door to the warehouse.

With her heart beating rapidly in her ears and her stomach screaming at her not to go, she follows behind worker number one and senses number two bringing up the rear. They enter and the door closes behind them, blocking out the strong summer sun. The smell of blood and death is the first thing Sophie recognises in the dull building as her eyes adjust. She'd been around enough crime scenes to recognise the smell straight away.

Looking around her eyes settle onto the bloody, brain splattered corpse sitting slumped in the chair further into the room. Worker number two behind her gives her a push to get her to move forward, towards the gruesome scene as she hears worker number one confirm her whereabouts down the phone, she guesses to Jason. Her stomach bottoms out. This is not good.

"Right, you're going to help clean this up, as apparently it is partly your fault for making the boss angry last night, plus you owe him a favour an' he's calling it in."

She turns to the worker who is talking, her blue eyes blazing in anger. "No fuckin' way is any of this my fault, and there is no way I am touching anything in here. This man's death is not my responsibility. Favour or no favour."

The worker smirks. "I think you'll find you will help! It's either that or you'll end up the same way, well that is after the boss has his way with you, like he's planned. You'll be begging to die, begging him to kill you before he's finished!" A sickening shiver runs through Sophie knowing that was Jason's plan the night before at the ball.

Her personal phone buzzes in her pocket alerting her to an incoming text and she drags it out. Coldness runs through her as she reads.

*Hostage situation at Saltire Jewellers. Ross inside. Think it's Jason. B *

She fights to control her breathing, keeping her panic at bay, to keep her facial expression and voice neutral.

"Sorry boys, but business calls. I need to love you and leave you." She takes a few steps towards the door, but the workers close in on her.

"Sorry, no can do. Boss' orders."

She eyes the young men before her, she could fight them if it came to it. "Not my boss. Now unless youse want to end up with a bullet in your brains, I suggest youse move out of my way." She moves her hand, faking a move to get a gun. "Youse have no idea who I work for, or what fresh hell I can bring, now move!" She growls her last word and walks away, trying not to break into a sprint.

The workers aren't sure if Sophie was bluffing or not, but they had seen enough that morning to know that there was a chance she wasn't. They both winced when she moved for her gun, then watched as she left.

They would tidy up the body, then probably leave the country to get away from their dangerous, strange-accented boss.

Back out into the bright sun, Sophie does sprint to the pool car and dives in. Ben is gunning the engine and squeals away before Sophie's door is closed.

Sophie radios in the gruesome scene she is leaving behind, demanding a team be sent over there, but without full sirens, so as not to alert the workers cleaning up. Replacing the radio, she turns to her partner for the day.

"Have you heard about the hostage situation?" Ben glances quickly over at her and nods.

"Is that where we are going?" Another nod. "Well get your foot down, where's the stick-on light?"

"Don't have one."

Sophie rolls her eyes. "What do you mean we don't have one?" Ben opens his mouth to explain but doesn't get a chance. "Never mind, just drive, fast!" Ben presses down on the accelerator and weaves his way on to the M8 motorway.

As he moves the car through the Sunday traffic, Sophie spots a fully marked police car, all flashing lights and blaring klaxon's and she gestures to Ben.

"Catch them and use them as a toe to get through the traffic, with any luck they will be going to the same place as us. Ben does as he's told and pulls in behind the marked police car, keeping closer than any braking distance as they manoeuvred their speeding cars towards the cutoff they needed.

CHAPTER TWENTY-SIX

Jason and another worker walk into the Argyll Arcade, nodding their polite hellos to the door men as they walk past them, making a bee line for Saltire Jewellers at the bottom corner of the arcade. Jason makes his way inside as his worker skulks about at the doorway.

As he enters, Jason spots a heavily pregnant woman standing talking to the very person he was looking for, Ross.

Arriving at the counter Jason places his hands on the glass countertop and grins. Ross looks round, noticing his pet peeve, customers leaving their sweaty handprints on his clean glass, before he realises that the customer is Jason. Now he knows that his day is about to go to hell in a handbasket, but he has no idea just how far down to hell he is about to go.

He excuses himself from his boss and walks over to the dangerous looking mountain of a man smiling at him.

"Jason, how can I help you?" Ross sees a flash of thunder and satisfaction crosses Jason's eyes as he removes his hands from the counter, bringing them to the waistband at the back of his perfectly fitting jeans.

Ross watches Jason's muscles roll with a cold feeling settling in his stomach. The coldness didn't come from the feeling of lacking that amount of bulk on his lean body as it had before, but from the thoughts of what those muscles could have done to Sophie the night before, if he had gotten his own way.

"Ah, my nemesis." Jason spits out the words in his strange mixed up accent. "You have something that I want, and she ran away from me last night, the bitch." Ross starts to chastise Jason for name calling Sophie, but Jason throws him a look that could've cast him to stone. He closes his mouth, the cold feeling in his stomach turning to ice and moving through his veins.

"So," Jason continues, "I'm going to get my revenge by taking something of hers, namely you!" Jason pulls out the Beretta handgun he had managed to purchase that morning. Ironic, he thinks to himself, it's the exact same make of gun that Sophie had bought for the deal that never was.

Ross' eyes widen as they take in the gun in Jason's hand and he instinctively goes to press the panic button, but Jason is quicker and sticks the gun into Ross' chest. "I wouldn't if I was you." In the corner of the room, behind the counter, the door to the office opens and the very pregnant Louise peeks out. Quickly but quietly she closes the door and lifts the phone receiver, praying that the rest of her staff stay downstairs in the staff area where they are safe.

Jason barks out an order over his shoulder to his worker, still skulking about the door, to keep anyone from entering the shop, then brings his attention back to his victim.

"Now, tell me something, Ross, what work does our Sophie do, exactly?" Ross looks at Jason confusion written all over his face.

"What do you mean, she buys and sells cars for you, and I'm guessing for other people too." Ross had never really pinned Sophie down on what she did for a living, exactly, she had always been vague when the subject was brought up. He'd always thought it was part of her trust issues due to her father, so never pushed, thinking she would tell him everything eventually, all that was really important was that she was legal, which she had assured him she was.

"She has you believing that, too, does she? Fuck she is good." Ross goes to moves his arm towards the panic button again, but Jason aims the gun slightly to the side, just past Ross' shoulder and squeezes the trigger.

An explosion of noise echoes throughout the shop and has Louise opening the door again, tears running down her cheeks.

Ross grimaces at the ringing in his ears and the pain beating a pulse in his shoulder. Jason's aim was off and the round he wanted to use as a warning had passed through the side of Ross' shoulder before embedding itself in the wall behind him.

Jason roars for everyone in the shop to gather on the shop floor. Ross holds his injured arm, fear and confusion battering him inside. All of Ross' colleagues gather around him and their boss, their fear palpable in the air around them.

Taking a deep, painful breath Ross locks eyes with Jason. "Listen Jason, it's me you want, let everyone else go, especially my boss, I mean she's pregnant. Please." A cruel laugh falls from Jason's lips.

"I don't fucking think so, I mean really, does it look like I care who's pregnant and who's not? Now as I was saying, our Sophie, what does she do? "The other staff stand close to Ross, all of them holding onto their boss, all of them praying that nobody else gets shot, or that the pregnant lady doesn't go into labour.

"I've already told you Jason, she sells cars." Ross' words come out through gritted teeth as he breathes through his fear and pain. Jason gives another laugh.

"Well I've got news for you, dickhead, your precious girlfriend isn't in car sales, she's a fucking cop, a dirty, two faced, lying bastard of an undercover cop." More confusion covers Ross' face until the hurt hits him. His ex-girlfriend didn't think he is good enough because of his lack of muscle and his slender build, but his current girlfriend didn't think he was good to tell the truth to.

The pain ripping through his heart out stripped the pain in his shoulder. In the background they hear the police sirens. "Sounds like we're getting company."

Minutes later a female voice echoes through the opening of the shop. "Mr. Hamilton my name's Sian Young, I work with Police Scotland and I would like to talk to you for a bit if I may?"

****

Sophie loudly, and with many expletives, urges Ben to drive faster, keeping as close to their lead car as possible so they could share in the opening up of traffic. She half wishes she was driving her XJS as it would be sharper and nippier at accelerating than the Vauxhall Astra pool car.

After what feels like hours, but was really only minutes, they pull into the pedestrianised area outside the Argyll Arcade on Buchanan Street and Sophie rushes from the car before Ben can bring it to a full stop. She hears Ben comment something about running from a moving vehicle and something about Formula One driving, but she is too focused on getting to the shop and to Ross to listen.

She skids to a stop next to Sian, demanding an update. Sian obliges and Sophie starts to shout into the shop, ignoring her DI's words to let the other officer handle the negotiations.

"Ross are you and everyone all right?" Sian rolls her eyes at Sophie's complete disregard of the steps in the negotiator's handbook. Sophie shrugs her shoulders, too intent on hearing her boyfriend's response to care.

Jason eyes Ross with the always present dangerous glint. "Ah, sounds like your liar has arrived."

Ross moves forward, desperately wanting to shove Jason's words back down his throat.

"Oh no you don't, I'm in charge, always!" Jason growls as he waves his gun at Ross.

He stops his waving and thinks for a second before motioning for Ross to step from behind the counter. Grabbing him by the back of his neck, Jason pushes him forward, pressing the gun into the small of his back, as he growls at the other staff to follow them. They walk to the edge of the shop premises.

Sophie gasps as she sees Jason pushing Ross in front of him with the rest of the staff bringing up the rear, every face a mask of fear.

Guilt floods her system at all the innocent lives being embroiled in the mess that her assignment is turning into. She could have sworn she'd gotten out clean. Taking a deep breath Sophie rushes to get to Ross seeing the blood drip from his arm, but Belle puts her hand on Sophie's shoulder stopping her, just as Jason aims his gun at her. She stops short.

"So here you are Sophie, or is it even Sophie?" he says. "I mean it might be Susan maybe, or, bitch even?"

Sophie winces. She can see blood drip from Ross' fingertips and how hard Jason's fingers are gripping into his neck. She didn't get out clean.

"Jason, let Ross and the others go! This has nothing to do with them. This is between you and me."

Jason snorts out a laugh. "Ha, you would like that wouldn't you; WPC Sophie, charging in to be the hero, saving the weakling of a man you are dating, or are you just using him too?"

"Ross is no weakling believe me, he is more man than you'll ever be, I am no hero, or a WPC for that matter."

"Oh so not a plod then? So what, a Sargent? Chief Super? Or higher even? Sleep your way to the top, did you?" Belle presses further into Sophie's shoulder in a non-verbal warning.

Sophie swallows back the retort that would normally spew from her mouth about working her way out of her uniform on her own merit and grit, but she will not allow Jason the satisfaction of seeing how much he is affecting her.

"What do you want, Jason?" she asks.

A smirk flashes across his face. "I want you to tell your loving boyfriend how much you've lied to him, and me, then I'm going to take his life, just like you're trying to take mine."

Black shadows on the glass roof distract the worker, who had been standing quietly as a passerby and he pulls his gun out. Jason sees his worker draw his gun and looks up, also.

Ross takes the distraction as an opportunity to try and rip free from Jason's grip as a shot rings out followed by another and another. Glass shatters as more shots ring out mixing with people screaming and orders being barked.

Sophie dives towards Ross, trying to block him from all the shots that are flying past them all. She lands on him with a thud as a burning white pain emanates from her shoulder blade.

Ross lands with a thud with more burning pain in his shoulder. He looks at Sophie lying on top of him with her eyes closed and a paleness that scares him. He shouts her name over and over to get her to open her eyes, his heart soars with hope as her lids flutter and

Dynamic Entry

she murmurs his name, then she flops like a rag doll in his arms as his hope disintegrates.

CHAPTER TWENTY-SEVEN

Ross pushes himself up the hospital bed as Belle walks into his room, careful not to pull on his drips or move his bandaged shoulder too much. Belle sits on the blue hard plastic visitor's chair and gives Ross a warm smile, hoping he won't throw her out.

"I've phoned Sean and he's on his way and I've spoken to the staff nurse, a nice woman called Eveline and explained who he is, so he will be allowed in for a bit, but not to stay too late," she says.

Ross nods his head then opens his mouth. Nothing comes out so he closes it and tries again. "Where's Sophie?" His voice quivers when he utters her name, but he coughs to clear it. "If that is even her real name." His tone changes to clinical but still with a hint of hurt and sadness.

Belle closes her eyes. "Yes, her name is Sophie. It's only her surname she changed for the assignment." She blows out a breath, "Ross, I can't explain everything as that is Sophie's job, but I will say that I backed her decisions and still do."

"So she's not in car sales then?" Belle shakes her head, ignoring the sarcasm in Ross' voice.

"No, she's a police officer, like me, but that's all I can say, as I said, the rest is up to her to tell you, but please know, everything else she said and done with you was real, was her."

Ross gives her an unbelievable snort and a shrug of his good shoulder. "So, where is she? She was on top of me and I couldn't wake her," his stomach drops. "Is she okay?"

Dynamic Entry

Belle eyes him with sympathy and a touch of fear. "She's in surgery."

Confusion worries his eyebrows. "Surgery? Why?" Panic laces itself through his veins.

Belle takes a deep breath before answering. "Jason noticed the armed response unit on the roof getting into position for their dynamic entry." Ross looks at her with a blank expression as she continued. "The guys on the roof, they were getting into position to bust through the ceiling and take Jason out, but he opened fire. Sophie jumped in front of you, to stop you getting shot again, but she got caught in the crossfire instead. She was shot in the shoulder; near her shoulder blade I think." Ross' face blanches of all colour, he points towards the cardboard sick bowl on his bedside table. Belle rushes it to him just in time.

Ross empties his almost empty stomach into the piece of cardboard at hearing what Sophie did for him. She'd jumped in front of a bullet to save him. His heart swells with love for her, but it quickly deflates when he remembers the point that she'd kept her real identity and so her real life from him. Just like her father did with her.

He cleans himself up and apologises to Belle, but she waves the apology away. Tears form in his eyes, breaking their barriers they glide silently down his cheeks.

"I fell in love with her you know, and her me, apparently," he says "We had told each other just last night how much we loved each other and were even talking about our wedding and how I wanted her hair to be curly and how this relationship was forever, but now — " he was babbling with emotion.

Belle leans in and grasps his hand. "Listen Ross, I have never seen her so happy with anyone, never known her to be with anyone. Certainly not in the serious way she is with you, and I have never seen her so split over her job as she had been these past few months. Normally she has no problem going undercover and playing her part, but this time it damn near ripped her in two. Now I know a semblance of that was due to the dickhead she was covering, but it was mostly due to the fact she had to keep her full life from you. It killed her. As I said, I can't say too much as it's up to Sophie to explain everything to you and how she feels about you, and all going well that should be tomorrow."

"What do you mean, 'all going well'?" The door opens and Sean walks in as Belle talks and wraps his arms around her. "Well," she blows out a breath as tears pool in her eyes, "the person I spoke to, I don't know if it was the surgeon or someone else, I can't remember, said that where the bullet had gone in could cause severe blood vessel and nerve damage and may, I mean it sometimes can lead to an amputation of the limb. She had me down as her next of kin on all our work stuff, so I had,"

Belle's voice breaks and Sean pulls her closer making calming noises into her hair. She pulls herself up again, takes another deep breath and fixes Ross with a stare. "I've given them permission to take her arm if they can't save it, or if it's a case of it or her." The enormity of the situation and her decision crushes Belle and she grabs onto Sean, needing his arms and his strength enveloping her.

Ross' stomach rolls again, the thought of having to make a decision of that magnitude doesn't bare thinking about and his heart is breaking for the strong, best friend of Sophie who is currently using his best friend as human tissue for having had to make such a decision.

He is also, however, trying to protect his own heart from being any more broken than it already is. Yes, he loves, (or loved as he is trying to convince himself) Sophie and yes, he is beyond worried about her, but he has to remember she lied to him. She led a double life, excluding him from the truth, from her truth, exactly like her father had with her.

Knowing all of that he questions if he can believe and trust anything that has come from her mouth. How she didn't fancy muscular men like Jason, how sexy she found him and his body, and that she wasn't sleeping with Jason all along. He mentally chastises himself for his last thought. He knows in his gut that she hated Jason, but the rest?

A muffled buzz pulls them all out of their own thoughts. Belle pulls out her phone and her face drops. Ross watches on as she stares at the text.

Need you down here, NOW!

Ross' stomach plummets as Belle mutters something about an emergency with Sophie and runs from the hospital room.

Sean walks over to his best friend and asks the only thing that comes to mind, even though he knows it's the most useless question in the history of useless questions.

"You all right?" The laugh that comes Ross' lips is anything but reassuring.

****

Jason lies in his hospital bed desperately wondering why he can't feel anything in his legs.

He runs through the events of the last few days when he had planned on taking Sophie to his bed after he had wined and dined her at the ball, but then it all went wrong, so he'd went to plan B to take her by force, but again it all went wrong and the bitch somehow got the better of him.

He'd been expecting his dick to be sunken into her, not sunken nearly back into his body. He had had her exactly where he had wanted her, frightened of him; in his arms and frightened. Then he realised she had gotten the better of him in more ways than one.

She is an undercover cop.

He had planned to take everything away from her, her boyfriend, her career, everything and everything was going to plan, she was there watching him point a gun at the person she cared about the most. He'd seen the terror in her eyes when she realised she'd been caught out in her lies, but then the dark shadows on the roof above distracted him and spooked his stupid worker, and that's when it all went to hell in a hand basket.

He can't remember who shot at Ross first, him or his idiot worker, and he can't even be sure if the armed response team actually got any rounds off. But what he was sure of was, it was his own worker that shot him.

He felt the bullet go in through his back and up his spine before he fell to the ground and felt nothing from his waist downward since. He had thought he'd seen Sophie dash in front of Ross then go down as he'd fired his gun, but he wasn't too sure.

Several emotions play through him at the thought of Sophie risking her life for Ross. First was anger that he never got to take away something from her, the way she was trying to take everything away from him, secondly there was bemusement that she would pick the weedy, wimp of a man over him and his perfectly toned temple that is his body, but lastly was regret,

regret that he never got to take her body as his, and now she may be dead.

A smile spreads on his lips at that thought. He may not have taken her body but taking her life would make up for that. That probably would have been the plan after he had raped her anyway, he wouldn't have been able to let her live and talk.

Pushing all thoughts of the event aside, Jason tries to concentrate on moving his legs.

He watches the lumps that are his feet under the covers and thinks about them moving. Nothing. He silently repeats the word 'move' over and over again in his head, but to no avail.

Getting frustrated, Jason turns his attention to his arms and fingers lying on the outside of the covers, after a second they move without a problem, so he turns his attention back to his legs and toes, again he puts all his might into moving the hulking muscles in his legs or even just wiggling his toes.

Again and again he tries and tries, screaming out loud for his limbs to work, but nothing happens.

He presses his head back into the lumpy hospital pillow and closes his eyes, tired from the exertion of not being able to move his legs. A nurse comes into his room at hearing the raucous he was making.

The nurse is looking at him with sympathy in her eyes that she is trying and failing to mask.

"Now Mr. Hamilton what's all this noise about?" Her voice is kind, but with a 'don't mess with me' steel to its undertone.

"Why can't I move my legs?" He spits out the words accusingly at her.

"Well, now, Mr. Hamilton, that is something the doctor will talk to you about when she gets back. It won't be too long." Jason opens his mouth to complain about having a female doctor when a tall female walks in, her long strawberry blonde hair flowing behind her.

If Jason had met her out with the hospital, he would be chatting her up and wooing her into his bed, as they weren't outside, and she was apparently his doctor, he hates her on sight.

Females aren't good enough to be anything other than playthings in his opinion. He glowers at her and she gives him a tight smile.

"Mr. Hamilton, I'm Erin McGuire, your brain and spine specialist. I'm sorry for your wait. I was working in a different hospital today but the staff here wanted me involved in your case as soon as possible."

Jason huffs at her. "So I've had to lay about waiting on you? I don't wait on anybody!" He stares at the doctor with pure disdain,

Erin takes in a deep breath. "Again Mr. Hamilton, I'm sorry. Now I've been through your notes and would like to do some quick tests of my own on you. I see from your notes and your scans and x-rays that you received a gunshot wound to your back and that the bullet travelled up your spine some." Another huff comes from Jason, but it is to cover the ice-cold fear that is filling his veins.

Erin's voice brings him back to the room. "Can you feel this, Mr. Hamilton?" Jason stares at the beautiful woman standing at the bottom of his bed, with what looked like a knitting needle in her hand dragging it up the sole of his foot.

He didn't feel a thing, not even the covers being moved up baring his legs making the cooler temperature of the hospital ward hit them. Fear slides through him again. How can he run his empire if he can't walk? Anger follows the fear, overpowering it.

"Of course I can't feel it, you are hardly touching me, I am a man if you haven't noticed and so I have a higher than normal pain threshold!" Venom drips from his every word.

Erin takes her time to carefully remove the knitting needle implement and move it further up the patient's leg. "Okay, what about now?" Erin presses her implement firmly into his leg, although being careful not to puncture the skin.

The answering growl of 'no' was enough to tell everyone in the room he felt nothing.

Erin pulls the bed clothes back over his legs and moves up to Jason's hands and arms, blocking his view with her body she presses into his skin, trying to get a reaction or any sort of feeling from him.

A jerk from his arm as he pulls it away is enough of an answer that he has feeling in his top half.

"Yes! I felt that! Maybe if I had a real doctor, a male doctor who could do their job it would be a different story on my bottom half!"

Erin swallows. "No Mr. Hamilton, the reason you can't feel anything from your waist down is due to the bullet that is embedded itself into your spine and nothing to do with me being female."

"Well operate and take the fucking thing out!"

Erin tries to keep her composure and professionalism but inserts steel into her tone.

"I would ask that you keep a civil tongue in your mouth whilst you are in this hospital, Mr. Hamilton, or you will not be treated. Now, I cannot operate due to where the bullet is, it is far too risky, and you could end up with paralysis of your entire body." Erin softens her voice at her diagnosis. The patient maybe a horrible man, but he doesn't deserve a bad bedside manner when getting such a devastating diagnosis. "As it is, we are looking at total paralysis from the waist down,"

The words rattle around Jason's head. Paralysis. Nothing from the waist down. The doctor is still talking but he doesn't hear a word of what she is saying, and anyway, what would she know, a female specialist? She is obviously wrong.

"I want a second opinion; a male opinion!"

Erin takes a step back, as if she had been slapped. "You are entitled to a second opinion, Mr. Hamilton, but you cannot dictate if it is a male or a female specialist, both will have the same outcome. Plus it may help you to know that I am the highest and most sought after in my speciality." Jason makes a noise of disdain at the back of his throat as his future of being reliant on idiots and bed bound spans out in front of him.

An angry blackness descends on him, darker than anything he has ever felt before. His growl turns into a roar and if he was able to move, he would be up out of his bed with his fingers around the lying bitch of a doctor's throat, but as it is all he can do is grasp at her and make noises.

Erin and the nurse take a step away from him. He may not be able to get to them, but his behaviour is still startling. They walk away leaving him to his anger with Erin prescribing a sedative if he didn't calm down.

CHAPTER TWENTY-EIGHT

Sean helps Ross sit up in the hospital bed and grimaces when he sees his friend bite his lip to get through the pain.

"You know you can cry like a big Jessie in front of me. I won't tell anyone."

His attempt at humour is met by a glare. "Fuck off!" The words come through gritted teeth.

Once settled, Ross fixes his friend with a stare. "Do you think she's all right? The emergency. I need to know if she is okay." Worry laces the pain in his voice.

She may have lied to him and ripped his heart out and danced all over it, but he still loves her, he can't switch off that emotion that quickly. Not the way he did with his ex, but then he thought that was love, when it was nowhere near it. Sean checks his phone for any news from Belle. Nothing.

Sean looks at him. "No news is good news. Belle will let us know, or she'll get someone, a nurse or another officer, to give us an update. Now while we wait, are you going to tell me what happened?"

Ross goes over the events of the hostage situation, how he was glad his boss, Louise, hid in her office so she and her baby wouldn't get hurt and that it was probably her that phoned the police.

He described how terrifying it was to have a gun pointed at his head and chest, how he thought he would never get to see Sophie or indeed Sean again. He continues to describe the pain as the bullet tore his skin open, moving through him until it burst out the back of his arm and embedding itself in the wall, and then the feelings of regret at not being confident enough to just push the point of love and life and marriage like he had so desperately wanted to with Sophie.

From there, he tells his best friend of the feelings of absolute anguish as his heart was ripped apart, shattering into so many millions of pieces that it would never go back together the same way when he found out the woman he loves, truly, desperately loves lied to him and lived a second life, her real life, that he wasn't part of.

"For what it's worth," Sean leans forward, determined that his friend hears everything he has to say, "I was shocked when Belle told me what was happening. I know it's different, to some extent, between Belle and me as we're not at the serious stage you and Sophie are at, although I do hope it gets there, so it still smarted. Then, after Belle explained it all, and how it all came about I understood why she and Sophie made the decision that they did, and I know for a fact that the only things she lied about were her second name and her job. Everything else, all her feelings for you are true. She can't hide the way she looks at you, believe me, I've seen it."

Ross shakes his head. "The trust is gone. I can't believe anything she's said or will say, she may as well have cheated on me."

Sean closes his eyes. Ross can see his best friend is fighting the anger rising inside him at his words. "Don't throw it away, at least hear her out, then you can make your decision." Sean's phone buzzes in his pocket with an incoming text, pulling it out to look his heart drops.

Not looking good, she's had an allergic reaction to something, think it's the anaesthetic, giving her *epinephrine and trying to start her heart again. I'm scared. xxx**

Sean looks up at his best friend, his own fear staring straight back at him. "That is if you get the chance to talk to her again."

Ross tries to speak but nothing comes out, fear has a grip of his vocal cords and it isn't letting go. Never in his life has he seen his friend so worried looking, not even when his business was on the verge of collapse. He tries again.

"What do you mean 'if I get the chance to talk to her again'? Sean what's happened? Is Sophie alright? Sean?"

"No." It's the only word he can get out. How do you tell your best friend the woman he loves but is angry at may be dying?

"Sean, Sean what is it? Sean fuckin' talk to me!" Ross' shout brings Sean back to the here and now and the nurse into the room; warning them about noise levels.

Sean apologies and calms Ross down before explaining what he knows.

"Sophie's in surgery, but she's taken an allergic reaction to something, they think it is the anaesthetic, they've given her epi- something but," he squeezes his eyes shut, not wanting to say his next words, "they are trying to, to restart her heart." Silence ensues his words.

It grows around them, enveloping them and barricading them in their own worlds and their own thoughts. Ross is the first to break the silence, shattering it to pieces with his roar of grief and pain.

****

Fiona Morgan

Belle paces back and forth over the small family room. It's dull in the room, there are no windows and there is only a side table with a lamp sitting on it, which is throwing out the most pathetic excuse for light, as it tries to cut through the dullness.

She can see that it's the hospital's way of trying to make the room look homely and warm, but all she can see is darkness and depression. She thinks that the overhead light, the 'big light' as her mum would call it, would be better, but decides against turning it on, knowing it would be too harsh and garish for a room that needs to be calm.

She isn't sure what lighting would be best, in fact she isn't sure what would be best for anything if she is being honest with herself. She doesn't even know why she is thinking about the lighting situation in the room when her best friend, her non-blood sister is having her heart jump started like a car battery, all the while there is a bullet in her shoulder and she might lose her arm.

Tears pool in her eyes before spilling over, breaking what little self-control she had on her emotions. She breaks down, wishing she was being held by Sean to make her feel better and wishing she could hold Sophie.

After what feels like hours, and well after her emotional melt down, a nurse that she had seen before walks into the room, his face is pale, but not pinched with worry, Belle hopes that that is a good sign.

"Belle?" Belle stands and rushes to the nurse. She looks into his eyes, searching them for information like she would in the interrogation room.

"Is she...?"

The nurse closes the door and smiles. "Sophie made it, she's alive," he says. "They have her heavily sedated with something she isn't allergic to. They did manage to get the bullet removed after they stabilised her, so she doesn't need to go through another surgery."

Belle nods her way through everything the nurse is saying with tears streaming down her face. She's alive!

"Can I see her?" she asks excitedly.

"She's sleeping heavily," He blows out a breath at the beseeching look she gives him, "You can peek in through the window, but that's it. Then it's best you go home and get some sleep; she is going to be out for the rest of the night." Belle nods her head, then grabs the nurse into a fierce hug of thanks, he gently hugs her back then peels her from him, a wet patch on his tunic from her tears.

"Sorry, I need to let her boyfriend know she's okay. He was brought in at the same time."

The nurse shakes his head. "That's okay, I've sent word up to the ward. Nurse Eveline is telling him, and your boyfriend is coming down here to get you."

Belle stands staring at the nurse grateful for every word he has uttered. She grabs the nurse into another hug, emotions overwhelming her. "Thank you." She mumbles into his shoulder. She realises she isn't just thanking him but every doctor, surgeon and nurse that was involved in getting her best friend through the worst day of her life.

The nurse takes Belle to Sophie's room and she peers through the small window into the private room where Sophie is sleeping. More tears trace down her face at the sight of how small her strong and beautiful friend looks.

She feels arms wrap around her waist and she looks up. Sean pulls her closer, embracing his girlfriend in his strength.

"She'll make it through, she's a tough cookie." He feels Belle's nod as they turn to leave, heading back to his flat above The Pub.

Fiona Morgan

CHAPTER TWENTY-NINE

Ross wakes with a start, sweat pouring from him as his nightmare disperses into the dawn of the new day's light.

He reminds himself that he's safe. Jason can't get him. They are in two entirely different hospitals on the opposite sides of the city, one in the North and one in the South. He then remembers that Sophie is alive and his heart soars, but not out of the woods entirely and a short stab of pain lances his heart.

He presses his buzzer, needing to get to the bathroom, but not able to move due to his drips and pain. The kind nurse from the day before is back and smiling at him. She takes one look at him and frowns, seeing the sweat covering his brow.

"You feeling okay, Ross?" Her voice is soft and concerned, but there is always the no nonsense undertone to it.

As much as Ross finds Eveline to have a caring and kind bedside manner, he certainly wouldn't like to get on her bad side or say no to any medication. He smiles at her trying to convince her that he is fine and not falling apart at the seams.

"Yes, I just need the toilet." She gives him a look all over then nods. She unhooks his drips and together they shuffle to the toilet door. He assures her he'll be fine getting himself back to his bed, so she leaves him be.

By the time he is finished and back at his bed, Eveline is there with the blood pressure pump and thermometer. She hooks him back up and sets the blood pressure machine on, taking his temperature and pulse all at the same time.

"Hmm, no temperature, and everything else looks fine." She smiles, "I was worried when I came in and saw the state of you." Ross dips his eyes. "Bad dream?" He feels a flush climb his cheeks. Real men aren't meant to blush with embarrassment, just like real men aren't meant to have bad dreams or be built all straight up and down, not a hulking muscle in sight.

Yes, he was lean, and he did have muscles from swimming, but nothing like Jason's muscles or the broad chested muscle guy his ex-girlfriend always wanted him to be, or who she eventually left him for. He had thought Sophie liked him for the way he was built, liked the way he was built, but now he can't be sure. He can't be sure of anything she said during their relationship.

"Is there any news on Sophie? Have they woken her up yet?" He berates himself for caring, he shouldn't care, doesn't want to care, she lied to him, broke his heart and got him shot, but he also can't help himself, he loves her, he can't turn his feeling for her off that quickly.

Plus she did jump in front of a bullet for him and nearly die. That's got to count for something hasn't it?

"As far as I know she was still under sedation during the night to let her body rest. I will try and find out more for you." Eveline pauses before speaking again, "Talking is the best way to solve most problems."

A look of despair and defeat pass over Ross' face as he shakes his head. "I can't believe anything that comes from her mouth, I think."

"I think, deep down you want to believe everything she says and the only way to know for sure is to talk to her," says Eveline."

Ross looks up. "Will I get the chance? Will she-" He breaks off, not wanting to give voice to his greatest fear.

"All going well Sophie will come around from the sedatives just fine, then it's up to both of youse." He nods, emotion clogging his throat, making it impossible for him to speak. Eveline gives him a reassuring smile before heading from the ward, leaving Ross alone with his thoughts.

****

The next morning Belle is by the bedside when Sophie starts to come around. She knows her friend is going to be groggy, disoriented and in pain. What she didn't expect was her friend to wake up with no fight in her.

Sophie opens her eyes, confused as to what she was seeing, the walls didn't belong to her bedroom or Ross' bedroom, they didn't even belong to the room above The Pub that her and Ross had slept in the times they had double dated with Belle and Sean.

She moves her head, making pain shoot over her upper body and her eyes land on Belle, who has a smile on her lips and tears of relief in her eyes.

"Hey, you, how you feeling?" The sound of her best friend's voice, full of concern and love is more than Sophie can take as everything from the past few months avalanches over her, bringing forth every emotion she has ever held back to the forefront of her mind and beyond.

Noises come from Sophie, sobbing and wailing and noises she has no control over. In fact, the more she tries to control and suppress her ugly crying the more the noises come out of her, making her sound like a whale in distress. Belle rushes up onto Sophie's bed so she is close enough she can hold her carefully, holding as a mother would hold her baby, making soothing noises as her heart breaks for her friend. Only once in the three years of knowing Sophie has she ever seen her express any emotion other than anger or annoyance, but never to this extent, and then she started dating Ross, Belle witnessed her friend start to feel so much more than annoyance and anger, so this was something of a first and somewhat unnerving. She had never seen her friend so broken, never thought it could happen.

Belle fishes a piece of kitchen roll she has in her pocket and hands it to Sophie, letting her pull back as her sobbing noises lower to a pitch that humans can hear and then lower again until the sobs are an occasional hiccup sound.

Sophie takes the proffered hankie and fresh tears fill her eyes. "It's clean…well, kinda."

Belle assures her with a sad smile.

"A communal hankie?"

Belle nods and shrugs. "A family hankie!"

More tears flow from Sophie. "Thank you for being my only family, although for a minute there I did think Ross would be my family too, and Sean, but I guess I fucked all of that up." A fear hits her square in the chest, making her flinch. "Is he okay? Was he injured badly? Did Jason get him again? Have I killed him?" Her voice breaks with her last words. Pain physical and emotional wash over her making her incredibly tired and wrung out.

Belle squeezes her hand again, trying to sooth her. "He's fine. His injury was a flesh wound, the bullet skimmed his upper arm, a through-and-through, although it barely went in. He's in ward three on an antibiotic drip for precaution, but other than that he is fine. Confused and worried, but fine, and anyway, if Jason had shot and killed him, which he didn't, it wouldn't have been your fault. You didn't get Ross shot; you saved his life. You jumped in front of him, to save him and you got yourself shot doing so."

Tears flow from Sophie's eyes as Bell speaks. She never knew she had so many tears in her, thought she had used them all up when her father left them and vowed to never make them again, but here they are, flowing down her face.

"What have you told him?"

Belle blows out a breath. "Your full name and that you're a police officer, the rest I said was yours to tell. I have told Sean my side of everything. He's not going to say anything to Ross until you have had a chance to talk to him and explain, and for the record Sean understands and I think that once you explain everything Ross will too."

Sophie gives a short nod. "He doesn't hate me?"

"No, he loves you too much for that."

Feeling slightly more at ease, Sophie's eyes flutter closed again, but she forces them back open. "I'll ask the nurse when I can go see him, or if he can come to see me." Her eyes close again and Belle smiles, blowing out a breath of relief at seeing her friend relax.

"I'll organise for Ross and Sean to visit you. I don't think you're up to getting out of this bed just yet. And I don't want you to ever die on me again, do you hear me?" Sophie gives a tired smile with her eyes still closed. She's half asleep but can still hear her friend the fear lacing her friend's voice. "I love you Sophie Pearsons." Sophie hears herself say 'I love you too' to her friend but can't determine if she managed to say it out loud or if it was only in her head before she fell into another deep sleep.

CHAPTER THIRTY

Sean walks into the room that Ross is in and is shocked to see an empty, made bed. He looks around in a panic until his eyes land on his friend coming from the toilet, fully dressed, but still in pain.

"What are you doing up?" Ross grimaces a smile then sits on the powder blue padded patient chair leaving Sean to pull over an orange, hard plastic chair to sit on.

"I'm out of here!" Ross says. "Just waiting on my prescription, then I'm free to go." Sean gives him a nod.

"What?" Ross' tone comes across defensive.

"Are you sure you're ready to leave? What about your wound?"

Ross tries to shrug but ends up wincing. "It's a flesh wound. Antibiotics were for precaution only and I can go to my own doctors to get the stitches out, so just some painkillers to get, then that's me homeward bound. You wouldn't mind hanging about to take me home, would you?"

Sean nods, then looks about uncomfortably. "Aye, well, I mean I have the bar covered until tonight, but-" Belle walks in interrupting Sean. He's glad for the interruption.

"Belle!" Sean grins at his girlfriend before landing a kiss on her lips.

"Hi sexy," she smirks, her face glowing after his kiss. Ross groans.

"Hi Belle, how's Sophie?" Belle smiles at Ross and moves to place a light kiss on his cheek.

"Sore, still sleepy, but not as sleepy as yesterday and giving the nurses a run for their money at pill time, she wants to come down and see you, but, she's not allowed out of her bed yet, due to her almost dying, so I said I would get you to go see her. Youse have a lot to talk about."

Ross winces at the reminder that Sophie nearly died. "Is she ready for visitors? I mean, other than you?" His voice is rough with mixed emotions.

"If you mean, does she want to see you, then the answer is yes. She wants to explain everything and hopefully move on, with you."

Ross nods then blows out a breath. "Okay, as soon as I have my —" Nurse Eveline picks that moment to walk into the room carrying a paper pharmacy bag.

"Paracetamol, busy place in here." Eveline nods her hellos to the visitors. Belle is first to speak,

"We're just taking Ross up to see Sophie."

Eveline smiles. "That's a great idea. Youse can talk everything through, get everything sorted, then get back to being in love." Eveline's eyes twinkle with happiness.

Ross grunts. "Maybe."

She hands him his prescription with a pointed look. "Give the lass a chance to explain, if you don't, and throw it all away, you will regret it."

Ross takes the paper bag from the kind nurse and gives her a half smile. "I'll try and thank you for everything."

"That's okay, it's my job, now on you go and don't get shot again please." Ross gives a snort of a laugh followed quickly by a grimace.

The three friends arrive at the window of the private room where Sophie lies sleeping. She is paler than normal, and her hair has a curl to it from not being straightened.

Dynamic Entry

Ross' heart lurches in his chest at the sight of the vivacious woman he loves with all his heart and soul. He has never seen her so still or so deathly pale.

Even when she had been working all day, dealing with the horror that is Jason and came back to him weary and low in mood, she still had a fight in her, a smile and happiness for him, but now there is nothing.

He wanted to ask if she was still with them, definitely still alive, but he refused to even think of the D word that she had already been once the day before, but she moves ever so slightly and he lets out a breath he didn't know he was holding.

Belle takes his hand and squeezes. "Hey, she may have left us for a minute or two, but she came back."

Ross sees the tears threaten to fall again from Belle's eyes, he nods his head, his voice not working again.

****

They enter the room as Sophie opens her eyes. She sees Belle first and smiles as she tries to push herself up her bed to a sitting position.

The pain is too much, so she slumps halfway. Sean steps forward, and between himself and Belle they get her sitting up and as comfortable as possible. She smiles her thanks at Sean and then her eyes find Ross and her heart stutters. Guilt and shame flush over her with relief closely on their tail.

"Hi." She squeaks, her voice scratchy from sleep. Ross bobs his head in response.

"Ross has been discharged, so I thought it would be easier if we all came to see you." Belle aims for a light and airy atmosphere, but it falls flat.

"So how's the food been? I've seen some of his, and it looked hellish." Sean tries to make small talk, but

Sophie can't ignore the elephant in the room anymore. She fixes her eyes onto Ross' gorgeous navy-blue ones and takes a deep breath.

"I'm sorry." The atmosphere is thick in the small room.

"Was any of it real?" This is the first Ross has uttered to her since walking through the door and the words shoot through her and penetrate deeper into her than the bullet had. Tears flood her eyes again, but she defies them to fall.

"Yes, as Belle has already told you, the only things I lied about were my second name and my job. I was put in a position that I had to lie to you. I was about to tell you my real name when Jason arrived and answered for me, so I had to go with it. I wanted to tell you, but I couldn't risk the operation."

Ross takes a step forward, anger rolling from him. "You didn't trust me or was I just not worth the truth? Not man enough for it?"

"What? No, it's not like that Ross, I —"

"Oh, so what is it like then? Am I your bit of fun on the side, nothing serious so you could just string me along... oh no I've got it, I know what I was, I was part of the ruse wasn't I? I was part of your secret life, your hidden life." He lets out a derisive snort, "Like father, like daughter." Sean and Belle both raise their voices, but it's Sophie's low, deadly calm voice that breaks through to Ross.

"Get out... now!" Not needing to be told twice, Ross turns on his heel and walks through the door, leaving Sean sputtering apologies for his friend.

"It's fine," Sophie reassures him, "it's not your fault, but if you don't mind, I would like to be on my own." Sean nods and gives her a kiss on her forehead.

She has never felt like part of a family since the day she found out about her father's preferred family, but that one gesture from her new friend, after everything, made her feel like a loved sibling, making her hurt even more for what she may be losing.

"I will talk to him and kick his arse," Sean says. "You concentrate on getting better and not dying, I like having you as a sister." He gives her hand a squeeze before turning to Belle, "I'll wait on you outside." She nods at her boyfriend with a tight smile before he walks through the door, closing it behind him quietly.

Sophie speaks first, before Belle has even turned back to look at her. "I'll be fine. I always am. I got over being rejected by my own father, so I'll get over this." Belle could see the unshed tears threatening their barriers of Sophie's eyelids. She can also see the pain, mental, emotional and physical all playing out on her face, but she knows her friend won't give into her feelings whilst she was there, if at all. There was only that one time Belle had seen Sophie break down, and that was the time she told Belle the full story of her dad, but even then, there had been copious amounts of wine and vodka involved that night.

"This is different." She takes a deep breath and blows it out before continuing, "Sophie, you know what he said isn't true, don't you? He's hurt and angry, you're nothing like your father." Sophie casts her eyes down, shame, guilt and fear crash through her. So much so she can't bring herself to speak.

She didn't know what to believe, but it is leaning towards Ross being correct, she is her father's daughter. A tear tracks its way down Sophie's cheek. With her voice breaking at the sight of her broken friend Belle talks, "Let me know if you need anything brought in. I love you." All Sophie can do is nod at her friend, the emotion lodged thick and burning in her throat making it impossible for her to talk.

Once her room door closes behind Belle a noise leaves Sophie. The noise is somewhere between a strangled sob and a scream, a noise that Sophie has never heard leave her body before. On the other side of the door Sean pulls Belle into his arms, as her legs buckle from under her as her own emotion takes over.

CHAPTER THIRTY-ONE

Sean and Belle catch up with Ross at the front door to the hospital. His face is an impassive mask of nothingness, except for his eyes which are shot through with red.

Nobody talks as Sean drives them from the hospital, and after a rather awkward goodbye to Belle, Sean drives them back to The Pub.

The friends still haven't broken breath to each other as Sean pours them both pints and they trudge upstairs to his apartment.

Sean is first to break the heavy silence.

"You, my friend, are a dick! A selfish, pigheaded, untrusting dickhead of a man!"

"Untrusting, unfucking trusting? Is it any wonder? She lied to me; our whole relationship was a lie!"

Sean growls at his friend. "No it wasn't! Right so she had to lie to you about her last name and her job, but that was due to circumstances out with her control, Belle was the same, but everything else she said and done has been her, one hundred percent, and you know it. You just want to play the martyr because that bitch ex of yours done a number on you. Well guess what, Sophie's not her. Sophie is an amazing woman, an amazing woman who fuckin' loves you. In fact, she loves you so much she took a bullet for you. She threw herself in front of a mad man with a gun and got shot, all so he wouldn't kill you. She might lose her job because she broke protocol, in fact as far as I'm aware she basically threw the whole damn protocol book out the window to save you, and she nearly lost her life doing it all, and you throw her dad at her, that was the biggest dick move ever! I wouldn't be surprised if she walked away from your ass and you end up losing the woman you should marry." Breathless from his diatribe Sean drains his glass and lifts Ross' empty one.

Ross had sat motionless as Sean spoke, staring at one of the knots in the hardwood flooring, but as his friend stands to get more beers, he lifts his eyes to meet Sean's.

"She did die."

Sean stops in his tracks.

"What?" Confusion covers his face.

"Sophie, she did die. Remember, they had to restart her heart after the allergic reaction."

Sean drops his head and shakes it. "That just makes you an even bigger dick. You never even asked her how she was feeling this morning." He blows out a breath, like he's trying to blow away all the bad atmosphere in the room. "I'm going for more drinks." He walks from his living room leaving Ross with his thoughts.

He was the injured party here, wasn't he? If it weren't for Sophie lying about who she was and what she did for a living, then Jason wouldn't have held a gun to his head or shot him, or even have been in his shop. But, he thinks, if he was going down that train of thought, if she had given Jason what he wanted, sex and her body, then he wouldn't have been in the shop either and neither of them would've been shot.

His stomach sours at the thought of Sophie willingly giving herself to Jason. Another thought hits him in the chest. The night of the ball Sophie rushed into his house in a mess, claiming that Jason only got 'too handsy.'

He had known there was more to it, but he hadn't pushed it. His stomach rolls and sours once again. Maybe Jason got what he wanted from her. He shakes his head, no, they made love that night and she wasn't in pain, just shaken up.

Then he remembers their other words, their words of weddings and love and trust and, honesty. 'I am an open book with no secrets.' Those were his words, but she had hinted at the same, hadn't she?

His stomach now turns to stone and falls from its living space in his body, it didn't matter, she'd lied, pure and simple. His ex may not have thought his body worthy enough to love, but Sophie, she didn't think him worthy enough for the truth, and that knowledge stung.

Sean walks back in with their fresh pints and sits down, watching his friend intently.

"What?" Ross' tone is sharp and he knows it, but he needs to hold onto his anger to get him through what must be the breakdown of his relationship.

"Have you come to your senses yet?"

Ross looks at his friend, his pain both physical and emotional warring in his eyes. "She lied." His voice is an icy monotone of emotionless nothing.

Sean shakes his head. "Only because she had no choice. You, however, are choosing to be a dick!" Sean stands, "I'll be downstairs if you need me." He leaves Ross sitting with his own thoughts again.

****

Jason has been moved to the spinal unit of the Queen Elizabeth University Hospital. He has given every person who helped move him or give him care, hell every time they came near him.

Having no family to speak of and certainly none in Scotland and no friends, only workers, meant he had had no visitors. He was okay with this, as he didn't want anyone to see him in this sorry state, plus it wasn't as if he could physically see anyone unless they bent over him as he is flat on his back for what may be the rest of his life.

Anger floods him again at his situation, so much so that a plan starts to formulate in his head. He still needs to get his revenge on Sophie for all of the lies and for attempting to snare him in her undercover sting.

He obviously can't do it himself, but his workers can. He presses his buzzer to alert a nurse that he needs assistance. He is sure that they draw straws to see who's turn it is to come and get abuse thrown at them and that thought gives him immense pleasure. In fact, it's the only pleasure he has had since he has ended up in this godforsaken hospital.

State-of-the-art hospital, but they can't fix him or his spine. Another thought enters his head: Does he want to be fixed? Obviously, he doesn't want to be paralysed for the rest of his life, but, would they charge or jail a person in his condition? He thinks not, and this gives him more pleasure. To be able to get away with everything he has ever done. Amazing.

A very toned male nurse enters the room, his tunic style uniform, a tight fight which shows off his well-maintained physique to perfection. A shot of jealousy spikes in Jason's blood. If he is left in this sorry state, he may never again know the joys of pushing himself until he feels the burning in his thighs, or even dead weightlifting. His body will wilt to mush. Anger follows the jealousy as he looks at the nurse.

Dynamic Entry

"So, Jason, what can I do for you?" The nurse's tone is pleasant and friendly, but Jason's isn't.

"If it was up to me, you'd be doing fuck all for me," Jason snaps, "but as you idiots can't fucking fix me, and I'm not allowed to move just yet, you can make a phone call or at least send a text for me."

The nurse rolls his eyes and bites the inside of his cheek. "Now remember, Mr. Hamilton, there is no need to talk to people in that abusive manner and you've already been told that if you continue to do so, you will be denied treatment. Now, are you allowed a phone? I thought you were under police custody."

"I'm allowed phone calls in prison, so if you don't mind, please!" He tacks on the 'please' in a saccharine sweet tone he didn't even know he could manage.

"Well since you said please." The nurse is hesitant, but lifts the phone, "What do you want?" Jason explains who he wants to text and the content, keeping it basic and legal, then dismisses the nurse, wanting to be alone to go through his new plan in his head.

CHAPTER THIRTY-TWO

Two weeks after the shooting and Sophie is still in hospital and feeling like a caged tiger. Belle has been in every day at some point to see her as had Sean, even some of her colleagues from the station had been in to see her, some to take her statement, but hey they came, unlike Ross.

She had heard nothing from him since he explained, so plainly, that she was a liar and no better than her father. She had been devastated when he left and for days later, then, the realisation that he was right to hit her. She is no better than her father, but unlike her father she isn't going to put anybody through her lies, especially not someone she loves and would call family. So the decision was made for her, even if she had always known deep down, she would never have a proper relationship, or a family of her own.

Belle comes in with a smile on her face until she sees the scowl on Sophie's. "Still no word from Ross?" she asks.

"No, and I don't think I will," Sophie says, "and to be honest, I think it's for the best. He was right, I am no better than my father. I lie for a living and I don't want to pull anyone else into it like my father did. Although technically I did pull him in and got him shot for the pleasure of it. So no it's all for the best."

Belle stares at her friend, astonishment covering her face. "What?"

Sophie can hear the exasperation and confusion in her best friend's tone but chooses to ignore it. "You heard," Sophie continues. "I don't know why I even let myself get that close to someone; I mean other than you. I should've known better. He was right, I am a liar, that's what I do as part of my job. Plus I'd always promised myself that I wouldn't put anybody through what my father put me and my mum through, which I ended up doing anyway, so it's the spinster life for me. I don't mind being known as the bitch that hates men."

She continues to talk, trying to convince herself as well as Belle that this was the best way. "But on a positive note, you and Sean got together so I guess it wasn't all for nothing." She'd tacked on the end bit as emotion had been catching in her throat and she hated it.

She had had made peace with her breakup with Ross, or so she had thought. So why now was she feeling this god-awful, heart-shattering pain? The little voice of hope at the back of her head spoke up, again, as it did every time she thought about her broken relationship. Have they actually broken up? No one actually said the words 'we're over' or 'done' or anything resembling a break-up, she had only told him to get out. Her heart squeezed in her chest again.

Belle watches as Sophie's final expression masks her face. It is hard and emotionless, just like it was nearly four years ago when she arrived back from Northumbria.

"You can't live like that Sophie," Belle says. "You love him and he loves you, you know he does. He's just hurting and confused at the moment."

She gets a mirthless laugh in return. "He will be hurting, I got him shot!"

Anger spikes in Belle's veins. "No you didn't! Jason shot him, that's on him, not you! And he's healing fine, the bullet just grazed him a bit, kinda." Sophie sends a silent thank you to any deity listening that it was only a flesh wound that Ross had received and nothing more serious.

"Is his boss, Louise, alright, and the baby?" Sophie asks.

Belle nods her head. "Yes she's fine and so is the baby. She was in the office during most of the incident and it was her that called it in. They kept her in and on a baby heart monitor to observe the baby for any signs of it being in distress, but all was well and she's back at work, at least for another week or so until her maternity starts. Ross hasn't gone back yet. He's been advised to start with a visit, then built it up with a phased return."

"Am I going to be dragged over the coals for my part in the shoot out?" asks Sophie.

Belle gives her a look. "It was hardly a shootout, the armed response unit was still trying to get into position for their dynamic entry when Jason saw them through the glass on the roof, he went to shoot Ross and you jumped in the way." She gave Sophie a disapproving, pointed look. "His idiot friend tried to shoot and god only knows what happened with the dodgy gun he had as he managed to shoot Jason in the back and as far as I've heard he's still in the spinal unit, paralysed from the waist down and the friend is getting held on remand at Barlinnie."

Sophie gives her friend a look of disbelief. "And that's not a shootout?"

Belle shakes her head, "Nope. Our guys never got a chance to return fire. The idiots did it all the shooting and managed to mess themselves up, and as for your part, I honestly don't know what's going to happen. The boss just shakes his head and shrugs. I think he's trying to put off doing anything about your part, as he knows we would all do the same if we were in that position, even him."

Sophie nods. "At least the operation wasn't a complete waste. We'll still get him, won't we?" The hope in her voice is palpable. She couldn't stand it if everything she has been through is for nothing.

"Of course it wasn't a waste, and yes, all your hard work has paid off, we'll get him on everything and more now."

A wistful look passes over Sophie's face. "I'm glad some good is going to come out of it and not just two gunshot wounds and broken hearts."

Belle leans over and cuddles her friend, trying not to squeeze too hard on her wound. Pulling back she fixes Sophie with a look any mother would be proud of.

"You and he are not finished, do you hear me?" she says. "Youse will get through this, even if me and Sean need to lock you in a room until it happens. You deserve your happy ever after Sophie, more than anyone I know."

The friends move their conversation onto the safer topic of Sophie being freed from the hospital. She is adamant she is going home to her own house in Motherwell, but little does she know that Belle will be staying with her for a few days and Ross will be making an appearance. Both Belle and Sean are determined over this.

****

Sean walks downstairs and into the bar area, double checking that everything is running smoothly as he is going to be away for the afternoon.

He's going for lunch with Ross then taking him into Saltire Jewellery for his first visit prior to his return, then, after that the plan is to get both Ross and Sophie together to make them talk until they both see the error of their ways, and to do that, Belle and himself were not above locking them in a room.

They need Ross to see the situation for what it was and for Sophie to stop believing the worst in herself. He blows out a breath, there are also some selfish reasons for him and Belle pushing for their two best friends to be able to be in the same room, their own relationship.

It would make for some awkward double dates if the other couple hated each other.

He spots Ross at his usual spot at the bar talking and laughing with the girl working behind the bar, his hand on her arm. A feeling of protection towards Sophie runs through him, like she is his sister and his best friend is cheating on her. He makes his way over and sits beside Ross, ordering his lunch and an Irn Bru to drink. Normally he would've taken the order to the kitchen and retrieved his own drink, but he wanted to give his barmaid something to do, get her out of Ross' eyesight.

"How you feeling about today?" he asks.

His question is terse and Ross gives him a strange look. "Fine, well fine until you asked me with that tone of voice. Should I be worried?"

"No. It'll be fine." Still he couldn't get a friendly lilt to his tone.

"So what's with the growl?"

"I didn't growl, I only asked a question." Sean pauses, then does give a growl, "Were you flirting with my staff?"

Ross pins his best friend with a stare. "No, well not really. But what is it to you? I am single, am I not?" This had been a question that had been running around his head since he was ordered from Sophie's hospital room, did they actually split up? He had started many times to contact her, had full text messages typed out ready to be sent until the burning knowledge that he wasn't good enough to be trusted came back to him with a sickening thud to his chest and he would delete the whole thing.

"Well to be honest I don't know, but neither do you!" Sean says. "You need to talk to her, let her explain fully and listen to what she has to say. Plus over the months I've known Soph, especially the past few weeks she's become like a sister to me. I don't want to see her get hurt."

Ross stares at Sean. Pride tries to burst from him at how his friend has accepted the woman he loves, but he quickly stamps all over that feeling. He can't be feeling things for Sophie if he is to get over her, hence the reason he was trying, without success, to flirt with the barmaid.

Their lunches arrive and Ross pulls his anger over him like a cloak of protection.

"So, you're taking her side then?" he asks. Sean drops his head.

"I'm on no-one's side, so shut up and eat your lunch," says Sean. The friends eat in silence.

They walk into the Argyle Arcade and Ross notices his breathing increasing as does his heartbeat. He also notices the sweat starting to bead on his forehead, it starts to trickle down his spine and it covers his palms making them clammy.

He feels his eyes wandering upwards towards the glass ceiling. He snaps his head back down, telling himself internally that there is no-one there. Sean notes Ross' reaction to walking into the arcade.

"You okay?"

Ross blows out a breath. "Aye, I'll be fine. Let's get this over with."

"Moan then." Sean slaps his friend on the back. Ross grunts in pain, his wound not quite fully healed.

Sean grimaces. "Sorry."

Ross waves off the apology, gritting his teeth and breathing through the pain. "It's fine, it's not as sore as it used to be, only when some arsehole hits it!" Ross injects some humour into his tone. Sean reiterates his sorry, only with his laugh somewhat stifled. The pain and good-humoured banter manage to take his mind from the panic attack that had been starting.

The friends arrive at the entrance of Saltire Jewellers and enter without hesitating until Ross finds himself standing in front of his heavily pregnant boss.

"Hello boys, what brings you here today? A big diamond for Sophie, I wonder?" She looks expectantly at Ross.

The smile falls from Ross' face. "No, I'm here for a visit, and I think we've split. I've to build myself up to coming back, and need to be back in time for your maternity leave starting, that is if you still want me to cover for you? Or if I still have a job." He feels anxious at the answers he may receive and the angry look on his boss' face wasn't helping.

"Why wouldn't you have a job?" she says. "You're the best sales person I have, plus you saved everyone 's life, you put your own life before all of us by asking for us all to be released from the crazy shit that was happening in here, and what do you mean you and Sophie may have split? You better not have broken that girl's heart!"

Ross drops his head; he can't bear to look his boss in the eyes. He knows what he said to Sophie was horrendous, maybe even unforgivable, but he had his reasons.

Sean's voice brings him back from trying to assuage his guilt. "Oh he did that and more! Called her a liar!" Ross' eyes snap to his so-called best friend. He'd just been thrown under a bus.

Dynamic Entry

"You did what?" His boss is furious and he doesn't like it.

"Calm down, you need to think —"

"Calm down?" Her voice raises several decibels, so much so Ross looks around for customers. Her voice then drops to an eerie quiet. "Never in the history of anyone, especially a pregnant woman, being told to calm down has anyone calmed down! Now the pair of youse two dunderheads get down those frickin' stairs to the staff area and send all them down there back up! I will meet you there!" The men walk behind the counter and open the door to the staff area as a shout echoes from behind them. "And get the kettle on!"

Once they are alone in the spotless black and white staff room Ross glares at Sean who is sitting on a recliner chair, as he starts to arrange the teas.

"Did you have to say that about me messing up with Sophie? I didn't mess up, she did, remember!" He stirs the teas with too much force and the smell assaults his senses bringing forth a tsunami of memories of all the times he made Sophie tea, which was a lot, that woman loved her tea.

Emotion catches in his throat, if only she loved him as much, he thinks. Shaking his head to rid himself of the memories, he throws a teabag at the open bin with as much force as possible only for it to hit the white tiled wall and slide down, positioning itself between then rim of the bin and the wall.

"You had better clean that up, you're not the boss in here yet you know!" His boss makes her way down the rest of the steps one at a time, picking up her tea she sits on a dining room chair. "Right, so, tell me, Sean, what's this idiot done?" Ross lets out a growl as he cleans up the tea splashes on the tiles, then sits on the black leather couch as far away from Sean as possible as he explains, in explicit detail, the horror of everything Ross had said to Sophie as she lay in her hospital bed recovering from being shot and nearly dying.

All through the story Louise shakes her head and lovingly rubs her baby bump. She turns and looks straight at Ross. "You are an arsehole!"

Sean sniggers. "That's what I said! Oh, and a dickhead!" Ross throws him another murderous look.

"What were you thinking? And to class her in the same category as her dad?" Louise asks. "Unthinkable!"

Ross growls again. "Neither of youse should know about what her dad did." It was his only come back. He knew he'd messed up. He knew he was an arsehole, but he had been hurt, physically and emotionally. He was still hurting.

"We're not saying anything to anyone about it —"

Ross cuts Louise off. "She lied! She lied about her second life."

Sean gets up and walks to the other side of the room to get even further away from his friend. "Shut up you idiot! I swear to god, it's just as well you're over that side of the room or so help me, I'd swing for you!" He says from his standing position across the room.

"Well she did!" exclaims Ross. "She didn't think I was good enough to tell me her secret, let alone the truth. At least my ex only thought my body wasn't good enough."

"Oh my god!" Louise starts, "Is that what this is all about, that craziness of your ex? Sophie is nothing like her and the situations are entirely and completely different, and you know it!" She takes a deep breath and holds her hand up to stop Ross from starting to talk. "Yes Sophie should have told you about her job and everything that it entails, but I'm sure she had her reasons for going along with her undercover name with you considering her job and everything that it entails and what was happening with it all. Plus, I'm sure she was going to tell you everything, maybe she just never got the time as everything came to a shooting match," Ross shivers at the thought of the shooting.

"And did you not say she told you she loved you the night before?" Louise continues. "That you knew there was something else she wanted to tell you, but you hadn't given her the time she needed for her to tell you?" Did you not say that?" Ross lowers his head into his hands while Louise goes on. "In fact, it was seconds after you said that, that the crazy guy came in here and everything went to hell in a handbasket!"

This time Ross pushes himself from his seated position, not able to sit any more, but not able to get away either. "That's when I thought she had wanted us to move in together, or... or... go on holiday or something, not that she had a full other life that I had no idea about."

Louise shakes her head again. "I think you're wrong. Her dad had a full other life; kids, a partner, a house, the lot. You are, were, Sophie's life. The rest was just a job. A job she went above and beyond in and put her life on the line for us, you, me, the staff here and my son! I think you need to get your head screwed on a different way and see this for what it is. Plus I think you'll find she told you the most important secret in her life, all about her family!" From the corner of his eye Ross sees his best friend nodding his agreement.

CHAPTER THIRTY-THREE

Sophie sits in Belle's living room, agitated. She hated sitting doing nothing but felt weak and stupid after trying to walk to the shops from her house.

It would normally be a five-minute walk and she thought she was healed enough to tackle it, but her body had other ideas and was certainly not healed enough. Seeing her blood seeping through her white t-shirt made her realise she wasn't ready to do such a walk and that she needed to phone Belle to come and collect her to take her home. So here she sat, bandaged back up and feeling like a fool. Her only silver lining was Ross couldn't see how broken she really was, inside and out.

She hated feeling so weak physically and emotionally; she had promised herself she'd never let a man make her so vulnerable and emotional, but she had let it happen. Ross had her heart and he'd thrown it back at her, along with her sordid secret.

Tears flood her eyes again, she had thought she was all cried out, but again her body had different ideas and she wasn't.

The living room door opens, and she hears voices floating through. Voices she didn't want to hear. Frantically she wipes at her face, rubbing away the tears flowing freely down her cheeks.

"Soph," His voice sends her head shooting up to see the only man she will ever love standing looking at her and her heart breaks again.

She can see Ross looking into her red rimmed eyes and knows he will see her pain. So much pain and she so desperately wants him to take it all away for her. She chastises herself internally, she doesn't need him to take away her pain.

He takes a step forward, but Belle brushes past him talking as she goes.

"Sophie, are you okay? Are you still bleeding?" His heart sinks, but it's Sean that speaks first.

"Bleeding? What happened? Sophie why are you bleeding again?"

Belle answers. "One of her wounds opened up a bit because she walked to the shops. She phoned me to go and get her. She knows she's not fit to be kicking about like that, but nooo, out she goes." Tears of embarrassment sting the back of her eyes. She swallows her embarrassment down and grabs hold of her anger.

"And she is sitting right here." Sophie spits out. Ross smiles. Yes, she thinks, I'm still here and still as feisty!

Sean sits beside Sophie and pulls her carefully under his arm, placing a gentle kiss on the top of her head.

"And we are all glad you are sitting right there, all of us." He turns to look straight at Ross, "Aren't we pal?" He clenches his teeth to speak.

"Yes, aye, very much so." He remains rooted to his spot on the carpet, uncertainty rolling off of him.

Belle clears her throat and subtly as possible she nods to Sean. "Sean, can you come and help me do... something?"

Sean gives Sophie another kiss on her head and whispers in her ear. "I think I need to teach my girlfriend how to be subtle. We'll just be in the kitchen, talk to him, he loves you and he is miserable. I canny cope with him like this." His eyes glint, trying to lighten the mood.

Left on their own Sophie tries to push herself up to a more confident level, but it brings a wave of pain. She grimaces then feels Ross sit next to her, his hand going automatically to her knee.

"Are you okay?" he asks. She notes the caring tone to his voice, but anger and embarrassment tinge hers.

"I'm fine!" She breathes out her pain.

Ross breathes in and swallows. "I never said a proper thank you for saving my life. I don't think I said 'thank you' in anyway or shape or form, and I'm sorry about that, but, thank you. If it wasn't for you, I would probably be dead."

She shrugs her shoulders. "I was only doing my job." She could see the sting her barb left, and she thought she would take delight in it, but she didn't, if anything it made her feel even more miserable, just like Sean had said Ross was.

****

Finding a time when a worker could come and see Jason was hard. They had to get their timing right and dodge any doctors or nurses and of course the police.

Eventually they ended up with twenty minutes, just enough time for Jason to get an update on the business and find out what was happening with the useless piece of shit that shot him.

"So is the money still getting collected?" The worker rolls his eyes and Jason turns his head witnessing it and the smirk on his face. "I can still move my head and see you remember, and there is still plenty of people to do my bidding, so watch yourself." The worker straightens and Jason grins. Paralysis or no paralysis he's still not someone people want to mess with!

Dynamic Entry

"Sorry boss, eh, aye Grotty's got everything under control and he's got someone on the police to find out what's happening with your case and he asked if what's his face got out, an' then he's gonna have words wa him like."

Jason nods his head, enjoying the little movement his broken body can still achieve. "That's good, Grotty knows all the ins and outs and won't fuck anything up."

The worker hides his knowing smile. "Right keep the protection side of things up, there's stuff in the boot of the F pace, get that shifted asap and tie up any loose ends then I want Grotty to look into that bitch policewoman and get her and her man sorted. The worker opens his mouth then shuts it again.

"What is it?" Jason demands.

"Well..." The worker shrugs, "I mean, won't the polis be waitin' for that move? You know like a revenge attack an' that?"

Jason rolls his eyes and, in his head, he is out of his bed and squeezing the life from his worker's neck, but he knows in real life that can't happen. "I don't fuckin' care what the pigs will be waiting on, she needs to be brought down from that pedestal she is on, and taking him out will hurt her even more, a win-win situation, so get it fucking done!" Anger and frustration roll over him. His every fear of not being in control and losing everything is materialising in front of his eyes.

Needing to be alone, Jason growls at the worker to come back in a few days with some good news. The worker stands and stretches making Jason's anger bite again at the back of his throat.

Seeing the worker leave the well-toned nurse picks up the phone and dials the number for the police station, passing on the information of the worker visiting Jason to the contact he was told to stay in touch with.

Fiona Morgan

CHAPTER THIRTY-FOUR

Ross and Sophie sit in silence for a heartbeat, Ross is unsure if he should remove his hand from Sophie's knee or leave it there. He decides that since they may not be together anymore it is probably inappropriate of him to be touching her in what feels like an intimate way, so removes it, then misses their closeness immediately.

"I told you my real first name and was about to tell you my job," Sophie starts to talk, wanting to explain her side of things, "when we met in The Pub for our date, then Jason arrived at the table and spurted out my undercover name and job. I hadn't seen him for three years and was shocked that he was standing in front of me at that table, in that pub, in Scotland. The last time I spoke to him was in England and to be honest I thought he would've been put away for something, even though the idiots down South wrecked all my hard work, I thought they would've got him on something, but no. Anyway, my training kicked in and I had to run with what he was saying."

Ross nods, some things starting to fall into place. "You were going to tell me everything when we were on the date, so why didn't you tell me when we were alone?"

Sophie closes her eyes and shakes her head. "It doesn't work like that. Before Jason butted in, I was going to tell you my real, full, name and that I was a police officer, but I wouldn't have told you about the undercover part. Not until we were further into the relationship and I knew we were serious. It isn't just me, or my job and life that is on the line when I tell people what I do. It's Belle's and everyone else on my team."

Realisation settles into Ross' mind. Yes, she may have lied, but not out of deceit or badness, but out of circumstances and protectiveness. So nothing like her father. Guilt assaults him, not taking its time to wash over and through him but barging into him like a tsunami.

"You were eventually going to tell me everything?"

She nods her head; Ross can see she's fighting her emotions.

"I was planning on telling you when I got home the night of the ball," Sophie says, "but then everything went wrong when Jason attacked me, then everything we spoke about, I didn't want to sully that with my lies and then everything went wrong again with the shoot out."

Ross slowly nods his head. "I'm sorry. I was angry and hurt and confused and, and I threw your dad at you."

He sits his face red with his shame crashing through his guilt with just as much force. "You are nothing like him. I-" He looks her full in the eye, facing his guilt and shame. "I'm sorry. I love you so much and I messed up. You died for me and all I could see was my ex and me not being good enough."

Tears roll down his face as he fronts out the error of his ways and prays to all gods and deities mythical or not that Sophie will see the truth in his words. "Please forgive me?" The silence stretches out between them, Ross's eyes pleading for forgiveness, pleading for an answer, pleading for anything until he can't take it anymore, "Sophie, please, say something."

She takes a deep breath and blows it out. "I never thought I could love anyone, thought I would never let anyone in, I wasn't worth loving. If the one man who should love me unconditionally can't love me, then why should someone choose to love me? But I did. I fell in love with the most amazing man, someone for the first time, ever, I felt I could trust and I felt loved. I was letting my guard down, in all areas of my life, I was willing to put my life and the life of my best friend and colleagues in your hands."

Ross felt things were going in the right direction, she was going to forgive him, but that happiness was short lived, "I gave you my deepest darkest secret and you threw it back in my face. Used it against me, told me I was exactly the same as the person who destroyed my childhood, my trust and at one point, I thought, me," She takes another deep breath, "and through doing that reminded me why I shut down love, shut down my emotions." She wipes away the tears that have been flowing freely down her face.

Straightening her back, putting the steel back where she believed it belonged, she speaks again, "So you, Ross, I do forgive you. I did lie to you and at that point in time all you knew was I lied and you got shot because of it, so I understand why you said what you did and I am sorry for what happened to you, my job was never meant to involve you, but I also want to thank you for the reminder of how I should be—on my own, no one near my heart. So, I'm sorry, I should never have started a relationship with you. I shouldn't have started a relationship with anyone. I know they aren't conducive to my job and life."

She takes his hands in hers, feeling his skin on hers for the last time. "Ross, I love you, with all my heart and everything I have, I love you. Everything I said, everything I felt between us and for you is, was the truth, I was never anything but me with you, but I'm not made for this. I can't be who you need me to be, but please don't take that as a slight on you, and please let go of what your ex said to you, you are perfect exactly the way you are."

Taking his face in her hands she kisses him one last time, trying to scorch the memory of it into her brain to keep her warm on the nights she knows she'll be cold without him. She breaks the kiss and places her forehead on his, "I'm sorry." She stands with a grimace and walks from the living room, her heart breaking without her permission with every step away from Ross she takes.

Belle and Sean hear the living room door close and Sophie's sobbing disappearing up the stairs. They look at one another then move from the kitchen. Standing at the living room door they take in the quiet devastation on Ross' face.

"Pal?" Sean tries, but Ross shakes his head.

"It's over." Pain erupts inside of him. Belle closes her eyes. She gives Sean a kiss then she turns heading up stairs to find her friend.

****

Instead of moving thousands of pounds worth of cocaine from Jason's F-Pace to his cramped Fiesta, Grotty decides to take the whole vehicle. It's not like his now incapacitated ex-boss is going to use it again is it?

His plan to take over Jason's empire is going amazingly well. Jason becoming paralysed through the incompetence of one of the idiots he employs was a stroke of pure luck and the push Grotty needed to start making his dream come true.

Driving past the warehouse Jason had used for his beating's Grotty notes the mass of police activity still on going. Jason got sloppy, he thinks to himself, he let his lust for that female rule his head.

He was living and breathing getting that cop into his bed until everything he did surrounded her, giving her all the intelligence she needed to take them all down. Well not all, Grotty had always made sure he wasn't around her, he also made sure he was never a part of the 'activities' dished out in the warehouse, and if for some reason he had to be in that building, he made sure he was in full overalls, gloves and hat. No DNA of his will be lying about, nothing to connect him to Jason or any of the murders that he committed.

The worker that Grotty had sent in to visit Jason phones him with the update. He explains everything that their boss wants Grotty to do in his absence and Grotty would do it, but not to line Jason's pockets; no, he will be lining his own. The business was now his.

****

Belle sits in the situation room listening to her DI explain what was happening with the investigation into Jason. The occupants of the room collectively held their breaths, thinking that all of the work, all the sacrifices they, and more so, Sophie, had taken would be thrown away since their main suspect was paralysed.

"The case still stands." The DI's words ring out and the room breathes again. "Jason remains in custody in hospital, unguarded, as he won't be going anywhere, plus we have intelligence, thanks to Sophie, on many of the others working for him that we can take down on any number of charges." There are mutterings of pleasure all around the room.

"How's she doing?" A random voice from the back speaks up.

The DI looks at Belle, who reluctantly takes her cue and stands. Clearing her throat she starts. "Well, she's still quite sore, but she's improving every day. Her wound is clear and healing and she's hoping to come in for a visit soon."

A murmur of encouragement floats around the room. The DI finishes up the meeting by asking everyone in the room to make sure the case against Jason and his workers was watertight. Every t crossed and i dotted, and just to add to the pressure he reminds the team that they are doing it all for one of their own who was shot in the line of duty.

There is more muttering and chatter as the team stand and leave, most of them stopping at Belle's side to give their best wishes and messages to pass on to Sophie. Her heart swells but tightens at the same time. If only Sophie could see how well respected and loved she is, she might not be shutting herself away from emotions and love again.

As the last of the stragglers leave the situation room, Belle gathers her papers and heads towards the door, only to be stopped by her DI.

"So, what are you not telling everyone about Sophie?" He eyes her with a hint of suspicion as only a detective can.

She takes a second to think if she should share her worries about her best friend. "It's true, her wound is healing and her health is improving, although I think she is sorer than she lets on and I doubt she is taking the full dose of her painkillers, but," She lets out a sigh then continues, "she is devastated about the split between her and Ross and so has reverted to her closed off self. Not letting anyone in, hating most people, especially men and trying to be a machine again. I'm worried about her. " The DI drops his head. "I remember Sophie that came back from England, angry and entirely too self-sufficient. Thankfully she found you that time to help bring her out of her anger and get her to accept help, but is that going to work this time?"

Belle shakes her head. "I don't think so, to be honest. I don't know anything will at this moment in time."

"Is Ross not understanding her position?"

Belle shakes her head again. "It's not that, he apologised and says he's come to understand everything, but it was too late for Sophie. She'd already convinced herself his first reaction was the right one and she is a liar and not worthy of being loved. She even says she exactly like her father."

"Did I make the wrong decision to place her back into the the assignment with Jason?" The DI's guilt is palpable.

"There was no decision to be made. Circumstances and Jason decided it all for us." They both nod at each then move the conversation on to arrests.

CHAPTER THIRTY-FIVE

3 Months later

Ross turns the shop keys to the left starting the mechanism to lift the shutter guarding Saltire Jewellers. The familiar feeling of underlying panic settles in his chest which replaces the constant feeling of how badly he messed up with the woman he loves.

Getting in he turns off the alarm and stands breathing. Every day he talks himself into work. Being the manager now means he can't let everyone down. He goes through the motions of reminding himself there isn't a lunatic mountain of a man with a handgun storming the shop to shoot him and destroy his life as he knows it. A rattle on the partially opened shutter shakes his anxiety and pulls him from his daily musings.

"You okay boss?" The part time sales assistant asks as she brushes her fingers over his shoulders as she walks by.

He takes a sidestep, trying to remove her fingers that want to linger on his shoulder. "I'm only the temporary boss, and I'm fine, thanks." He walks towards the office.

"I'm putting the kettle on; you want a coffee?" she asks.

"A tea please." His breath comes out in a puff. He needs to stop drinking tea, he never drank tea until him and Sophie parted ways and now he drinks gallons of the stuff. "No, sorry, a coffee... yes a coffee." Karen smiles at him before walking down to the staff area. Ross slumps in the office chair. God, he misses Sophie.

Pulling out paperwork he forces himself to concentrate until he hears the voices of more staff arriving and Karen arrives at the office door with his coffee. Giving him a faux shy smile, she hands him his mug, he takes it from her and returns her smile with a lopsided real one of his own.

"Thank you, Karen. Is that everyone in?" She nods making her light brown ponytail bob and swish with the movement. "Okay, I'll be out in two minutes to go through today, and Karen," she turns back to look at him, her eyes full of hope, "thank you for the coffee, it's just what I needed." She smiles at him again, a smile that she has given him many times, but one he is only now realising is flirty.

Maybe it's time to move on from the heartache that Sophie left behind when she walked away from him, from them, even if it was him that gave the push to begin with, "Karen, would you like to go out for a drink after work and maybe a meal, just round to Sean's?" In for a penny, in for a pound he thinks to himself as he pushes away the nagging feeling of doubt and something akin to guilt eating at his stomach. Maybe going to The Pub isn't a good idea on the off chance that Sophie walks in, but he pushes that thought away too.

"That would be lovely Ross. To be honest I never thought you would ask." She sends him another smile, this one coupled with a wink. His stomach drops again.

****

Sophie walks into the room and feels every set of eyes on her as she passes all the desks heading towards the kettle for her morning ritual first cup of tea in the office before heading to her desk.

She had spent an hour that morning looking in the mirror trying to fix her hair and make sure she was dressed properly for someone who had been shot, had had a near death experience and presumably been the talk of the station for three months in the intern.

As she waits for the kettle she tries to flatten her hair again, not being able to lift her arm for as long as it takes to straighten her hair was really starting to grate on her and she couldn't keep asking Belle to do it, she had her own life with Sean. The thought of Sean brings Ross into her thoughts and pain slices through her mostly healed wound and her body winces against her will.

"How you doin'?" She looks around to see her DI hovering over her with something akin to worry in his eyes.

"I'm fine," she grates out, "ready to come back, and I've been cleared to come back from the Doc too, so don't start on me!" Defensive much? She muses to herself, but pushes it away, she needs to channel the old Sophie again, the 'before Ross Sophie', the hard bitch Sophie.

"I know, I've read the report, but at least for today I need you at your desk writing reports and setting out what other information we have about the other members of this gang." A small growl creeps up her throat, but she swallows it down. She hates doing paperwork, but it's a necessary evil in the job. She takes her tea, grunts her okay's and walks to her desk.

Belle comes in and another colleague grabs her.

"Do you feel the atmosphere in the room? Sophie is back, so guesses that's where it is coming from." Belle gives a quick look around the room to see what the colleague is talking about.

Dynamic Entry

A few colleagues are whispering at each other and one brave soul is offering words to Sophie who is glaring holes into them. "

Thank goodness she can't turn people to stone or has laser beams that can be shot from her eyes or the poor sod talking to her would be dead." The colleague continues.

Belle throws them a look of disgust. "Well, she's still in pain, so give her a break." Belle walks towards Sophie and the brave soul.

"Good morning!" She announces cheerfully as she reaches Sophie's desk, "And how are we all on this fine winter's day?" Belle gives another bright smile to Sophie and their colleague.

"I'm fine!" Sophie grits out through her teeth. The colleague mutters how nice it is to see Sophie back at work and skitters away to whatever clique they are part off. Sophie rolls her eyes then faces Belle. "Why are you so damn cheerful?"

"Because it's a beautiful day and my best friend is back at work, what isn't there to cheerful about?" Belle sits at her desk next to Sophie's then rolls her seat over. Sophie gives her a saccharine sweet smile.

"You don't have to spend the day at your desk writing up reports, you can be out and about doing 'real police work', as all the punters say." She drops her hands onto her desk after doing her air quotations, and tries to squash the wince of pain, but Belle still catches it.

"You o —"

"Don't! Don't ask it, don't say it, don't even think it! I'm fine, I'm here and I am not an invalid!"

Belle puts her puts her hands up and backs off. "Okay. But if you must know I'm sitting at my desk all day too. I've got reports to do and I'm here to help you type if you need." Sophie softens towards her best friend.

"Sorry."

Belle smiles and winks. "Nae bother." The friends fall into their natural work mode as Belle fills Sophie in on all the office gossip, plus how and where their investigation into Jason is going.

****

Grotty walks into the hospital and slips unnoticed into Jason's room. His unsuspecting ex-boss lies perfectly still, too still. A thrill shoots up Grotty's spine at the thought of his plan to take everything from Jason. It wasn't that he disliked him, it was just survival of the fittest in this game. Clearing his throat Grotty starts to talk.

"You awake?"

Jason opens his eyes and moves his head. "You'll need to move closer; I'm only allowed to sit up for so many hours a day, they're resting my spine, apparently."

Grotty stands over the bed peering down. "You're no looking too bad for getting shot."

Jason gives out a mirthless laugh. "Thanks, not feeling too bad, even though that may be because I can't feel anything from the waist down. So I hear you're stepping up to the mark for me. Taking over the reins, for just now?"

A flash of fear that Jason knows about his plans to take over the business shoots through him, but he calms himself before talking. "Aye, need to keep everything moving, keep the money coming in. You been charged with anything?"

"They've charged me with attempted murder and false imprisonment, but I can't see any of it sticking."

Grotty makes a face of disbelief. "How?"

"Well, they're not going to charge, take to trial or imprison a paraplegic, are they? He grins a wicked grin. "I'll be free to carry on as normal soon enough."

Grotty gives him a sceptical look then shrugs as the men carry on their conversation about the business with Grotty picking out what information he wants Jason to know and leaving the rest out.

"Right, that all sounds like everything is going to plan. Now I want you to get another plan into action about getting revenge on that bitch and her man!" Grotty mutters all the correct words of agreement that he knows Jason wants to hear but has no intention of doing anything for him.

CHAPTER THIRTY-SIX

Two weeks back into the job and Sophie has finished all her debriefing and paperwork, had her interview with internal affairs and is back to working the case to bring Jason down once and for all. Life altering injuries or not she is determined to get him put away this time.

Through her time working close to Jason the names of some of the workers stuck in her head and she wonders out loud, as Belle drives the pool car, whether someone had taken over the protection business and the sale of the drugs. Belle turns to her.

"I was thinking the same. I mean he wouldn't just let the business go, it's his income and being injured and in police custody didn't stop others, so I don't see it stopping him. You got someone in mind?"

"Hmm, a few, but one guy stands out for me, Grotty. He was always there in the background or whispering in Jason's ear, but never seemed to want to get his hands dirty, never done any work, but told others to do loads, you know the type, perfect managers."

Belle nods her agreement. "You have anything on him?"

Sophie does a mental check of her memory banks trying to find something on Grotty. "I think I do; I'll check my notes; it will definitely be in there. It's a hunch at the moment, but I think he's the best bet." Belle pulls the car into a space behind The Pub.

"Right lunch time." Sophie groans. As much as she loves Sean and the food he serves a nervous panic fills her when they enter. Meeting Ross is not high on her list of things to do.

"He might not be in, but I think it would do you good to see him. Youse belong together."

Belle's words are all Sophie needs to remind her of her strength. "I do not belong to anyone, and I don't need to see him and I am certainly not worried about seeing him again!" The steel in her voice holds, which she is grateful for.

"Nobody said you were worried about seeing him, 'till you, just there." Sophie throws open the car door and climbs out, closing it behind her without saying another word.

The friends walk into the bar and Sophie heads straight towards her table. She stops dead as she notices people sitting there. Her stomach falls to the floor when her eyes land on the table's occupants.

Ross sits with Karen sipping on his water, Sophie can see him trying to quell his nerves.

She glances at Sean and sees the look he is throwing at his best friend. He is pissed at him, and she guesses Sean had told him so.

The waitress arrives with their lunch, which brings Ross' attention away from his water and back to the room. He looks up and smiles at the waitress, but it falls from his face when standing behind her is Sophie. She remains standing stock still, but her face paints a picture of a thousand feelings; hurt, anger, betrayal, being only a few.

Karen lifts her eyes and follows Ross' gaze, smirking when she sees Sophie. Sophie bristles.

"Ah Sophie, it's nice to see you out and about. Are you back at work already?"

The sickly-sweet tone of Karen's voice brings Sophie back to here senses, and she pins Karen with a look that she tries to make friendly, but knows she is failing miserably and it is full of disdain. "Yes, I've been back for a while now. Nothing keeps me down!"

Ross stares between the women.

"It was just awful what happened in the shop, we were all affected by it. It's astounding how one decision can affect so many people, but luckily Louise was there to alert the police, or it could have been so much worse." The implication that Sophie was to blame for the incident was not lost on her.

"Yes, I'm sure everyone who was there on the day is indebted to her, as am I," says Sophie. "So much so, in fact, she has become a close friend of mine since the incident." Ross' eyebrows shoot up at this information, but Sophie refuses to acknowledge his surprise. "Although I don't recall you being there, sorry I didn't catch our name." Bitchy she knew, but that was who she was again, and she had to keep herself together.

"Sophie, this is Karen, one of my, co-workers, and no she wasn't in that day, it was her day off." Sophie sees the look of incredulity on Karen's face and took a small triumph in it.

"I'm glad to hear that not everyone employed by Louise was involved and in danger that day, and yes, it was great that Lou could contact the police, or it may indeed have been worse for some."

She turns her attention back to Ross and clicks her tongue. "Well, I will leave you to your, date?"

The waitress arrives back with a pot of tea and sits it in front of Ross. Emotion catches in Sophie's throat. "You're drinking tea?" Ross nods, and Sophie can only nod back, her emotions fighting to get out. Out of everything that she thought could break her bitch demeanour she never thought it would be a pot of tea that succeeded. She makes her excuses and leaves before her emotions gave her away.

Dynamic Entry

Getting to the bar she wrestles herself onto a bar stool next to where Belle is standing talking to Sean.

"We're sitting here to eat, there's no seats left." Belle looks around at the empty tables and the one that is occupied then nods.

"Okay, here it is then." Belle turns back to Sean, "What's going on there?"

Sean shakes his head and shrugs. "They've been in a few times together. Mostly after work. I've tried to talk to him about it, but he tells me to butt out, so I have. Sorry Sophie."

She waves away his apology. "It's fine, he's free to do what he wants. Even if she's using him. But any way, have you had anybody back in about getting protection since Jason?"

"Nobody that has come right out and asked about it, but I do think people have been in." Belle opens her mouth to speak, but Sean carries on, "I didn't say anything to you as nothing has been said to me and I can't be sure, I just think I recognise the guy from coming in with Jason, but if there is anything said I will let you both know." The girls both nod, then place their lunch order.

****

Walking back to the arcade Ross can still feel the cold shoulder he has been receiving from Karen since their conversation with Sophie at lunch. He hadn't really been in a talkative mood after seeing Sophie so wasn't too bothered with the silence.

Guilt has sat heavy in his stomach at hearing and seeing the walls and barbed wire she had built around herself again, exactly as they were when they had first met, and he knows he is the one to blame for her resurrecting them again.

They arrive at the entrance of the arcade and Karen turns around sharply, making Ross pull up quickly behind her so as not to walk into her.

"A co-worker? Are you serious? You introduced me as your co-worker." The more she speaks the louder she gets, until it is a shrill and Ross is sure only dogs can hear her. "I thought we were dating. I thought this was a thing! Us!" Ross stares as do the people that are milling about looking in the bright shop windows. "Nothing was ever spoken about us being a thing or a couple. We've had a few drinks, so I went with the least complicated explanation."

"You wanted space between us in case she takes you back."

Ross snorts out a laugh as pain lances through his heart. "She's not taking me back; she broke up with me and I'm trying to get over her."

"Well, not with me you're not. I'm not a rebound girl"

He rocks back on his heels, relief flooding through him. "I'm finishing this before it gets started, since I'm just a co-worker!"

"Okay, so does that mean you won't be using me to get my bigger employee discount or the extra hours you've been hinting at?" Karen dramatically steps back as if he had slapped her, then turns on her stiletto heel and strides away.

Ross feels a twinge of disappointment at himself for his accusations and words. His mother didn't bring him up to be so crass with other people's feelings, even though he knows they were true. He walks back into the shop with a cloud hanging over him and gets on with the rest of his day.

CHAPTER THIRTY-SEVEN

Belle and Sophie come back from Barlinnie prison and from interviewing the worker whose aim was so off he shot Jason and to their amusement he sang like the proverbial canary, spilling all of Jason's secrets.

The drugs, the protection racket, the tortures and murders all four of them that he knows about. With his testimony, all the physical evidence they have found in the warehouse as well as the evidence gathered by Sophie they should have an open and shut case for the Procurator Fiscal to go to court with and no defence lawyer in their right mind would choose to defend it.

All they needed now was more evidence on Grotty, who Sophie is adamant is taking over Jason's business, and they would have it all shut down for good.

They are sitting in the cafeteria sipping lukewarm tea basking in the glow of what they are claiming as a massive win for the case.

"Well that went better than expected didn't it?" Belle asks with a smirk.

"Oh aye it did! Thank god something is going right in this case."

Belle frowns. "Other than the shootout, everything has gone well in this case."

Sophie rolls her eyes. "You said it wasn't a shootout."

"Yes, well, I may have changed my mind about that. I mean bullets were flying so it kinda was. Sorry" Sophie waves away the words not wanting to think about that day.

She sees her therapist and talks about it with them, that is enough at the moment. "Anyway, since we're talking about subjects you don't want to discuss, Sean told me Ross and Karen have split up." Sophie notices her heart rate quicken at this news and she stamps on it immediately.

"And why should that interest me and why are you grinning like a cat with two tails?"

"Well, it was after he spoke to you, she apparently went in a huff and told him it was over, even though they weren't actually together, as such. So he's single again!"

"How can they split up if they weren't together and why do I want to know he's single? We are over, he called me a liar, he was right, I broke it off, that is how my life is best being."

Belle softens her tone. "You still love him." It wasn't a question but thinking of the answer hurt like hell.

"I will always love him; doesn't mean I can have him or that I want him." She pulls her emotions around her, burying them back behind her defences where they had slipped from. Belle squeezes her hand.

"Okay, whatever you say. Now let's go tell the boss what new information we have." The friends walk back to the incident room with their good news.

****

Parking outside Jason's office in Blythswood Square, Grotty climbs from the F Pace and opens the tailgate, pulling three black bin bags full of cocaine out, happy that the deal he'd just made to buy them was the best he, or anyone, could get, now all he had to do was get the drugs split up and sent out to his ladies to sell them.

Dynamic Entry

He knew keeping some of the working girls in his pocket would come in handy, and now that he was the ruler of all in this small corner of the Glasgow underworld everything he touches will turn to gold.

Giving his girls the drugs to sell is like killing two birds with one stone and then having his cake and eating it with the protection racket on the side. Not able to add any more idioms to his thoughts, he smiles.

Getting into the office Grotty drops the bags. He had been looking forward to getting into the office without anybody with him but didn't want to appear too eager to those watching so waited a reasonable amount of time before broaching the subject with Jason. The visits with Jason were getting less and less, just enough to take in anything he needed, Grotty wouldn't leave him completely, well not completely at the moment anyway, there will be time for that.

Using the fact that the police were more than likely watching to explain away the visits becoming more infrequent.

Now he was inside the office he could see there wasn't a great deal of space to store his product so he stacks them behind the desk whilst leaving enough room for him to sit, which he does and takes great pleasure in rearranging the office chair to his liking, and removing the framed photo of Jason standing bare chested in the gym with a barbell above his head. The man really did think he was a Greek god. Grotty sniggers, well not any more he isn't.

The front door buzzer rings out and Grotty gives the CCTV a cursory glance before releasing the door allowing the visitor in.

In walks a female clad in black leather trousers that are so tight Grotty wonders if they are painted on and a black boob tube top which is basically a strap of leather and covers very little, he wonders how it stays up.

"Ah Grotty, look at this place, it's tiny!"

Grotty straightens his back at the woman's slate of his new premises. "Did I ask you for your opinion? There's nothing wrong with it, and once I get my own décor in it'll be better. Now sit down and I'll get ye some ae the gear." He bursts open one of the bricks of drugs taking some out for his guest to test.

CHAPTER THIRTY-EIGHT

"Right just come for one or stay over like we used to." Belle is almost begging Sophie to go out for drinks that night.

Sophie can feel Belle's desperation to get her out of the house for longer that a workday but she doesn't want to bump into Ross, even though Belle and Sean are determined to get the lovers back together again as they continue to tell her that know they are meant for each other and love is meant to conquer all, eventually.

"Why?" Sophie rolls her eyes at her best friend.

"Well, firstly it'll be fun. Secondly Sean's not seen you for ages and lastly, we have the day off tomorrow, so there!"

Sophie drops her shoulders in defeat. "Sean seen me a fortnight ago, I don't particularly need fun and I can't just have one as I have the car and as a police officer you should know I would be over the drink drive limit, but-"

"That's why you should stay overnight and park the Jag behind The Pub, or better yet leave it in the police yard where it will be even safer." Sophie tries to glare at her friend, but her annoyance has left her.

"Well before you interrupted me, I was going to say, BUT okay, let's have a night out." A squeal of delight comes from her friend as Sophie is bundled into her arms for a crushing hug.

Entering the familiarity of The Pub is bittersweet for Sophie, but the cuddle she receives from Sean along with a kiss on top of her head makes it all better.

Fiona Morgan

She never thought she would call anybody family ever again, but both Belle and Sean were most definitely that. They order pints and sit at the bar to talk to Sean who is working.

****

Ross walks into The Pub after a hard day at work trying to get Karen to do some work whilst ignoring the scathing looks she was throwing his way.

Getting involved with another member of staff wasn't the best idea and he knew it, but to be fair he hadn't been thinking clearly that day, he had been concentrating on moving on from his heartbreak, but it didn't work, if anything it felt worse with the extra guilt it had brought him. Every second he was with Karen felt like he was cheating on Sophie.

Getting to the bar he spots Belle and Sophie sitting there, Sophie sitting exactly in his chair. He snorts ironically to himself then shrugs. They need to speak to each other at some point, their best friends are dating, and things are looking serious for them. He'd never seen Sean so loved up and it was good to see.

Sophie sees Sean lifting a pint glass and start to pour a Tennants. A quick check at her own and Belle's pint find them half full. She looks over her shoulder, past Belle to see the buyer of the pint.

"Rough day?" Sean asks as he places the pint on the bar for Ross to sit next to Belle.

Ross stops to give Belle a kiss on the cheek then picks up his pint and takes a large gulp. "Aye, not the best." He looks over at Sophie and nods, "Sophie." She nods back.

"Ross." Sean and Belle smile at each other and the friends fall into a slightly strained conversation.

Dynamic Entry

Half an hour into their night another couple walk in, Sophie is first to look at them and frowns.

The male has on blue, ill-fitting jeans and a black shirt which also doesn't sit right on him. It looks like he found the outfit at the bottom of a giant's ironing pile and pulled it on. The female is dressed in a short red skirt that barely covered what she'd been born with, paired with a white crop top and white stilettos, not appropriate dress for a cold and damp winter's night in Glasgow, no matter how warm Sean keeps his bar.

Ross follows Sophie's gaze then returns it to see Sophie's hackles rise as she straightens her back.

The male of the couple orders drinks as the female sits at a table behind the friends. Belle turns to Sophie.

"What's up?" Sophie shrugs.

"I don't like them, getting bad feeling from them."

Belle nods her understanding. "Okay, I've worked with you long enough to take heed of that feeling, but we're on a night out, so why don't we just keep an eye on things."

Sophie nods. An hour later the female struts to the bar. Standing next to Ross she runs her hand down his arm and back up in a continuous movement.

"Hi, fancy buying me, a drink?" Ross makes a sideways step to remove her fingers from touching his arm.

"No, sorry. I'm here with my friends." He keeps his tone polite and clamps down on the revulsion flowing through him.

"Awe, I could make it worth your while, and it could even count as part payment, or maybe you want something stronger than this piss water."

Sophie is out of her seat moving towards the female and whispering to Belle 'prostitute' as she passes. "I think it's time you and your friend over there left, this isn't the kind of establishment that requires any of your services."

Sean and Ross look on confused.

"Eh, who the fuck do you think yir talkin' to ya boot?" The female looks at Sophie dragging her eyes from her head to her boots and back again, her tone harsh.

"I am your worst nightmare, hen, if you don't take your wee pal over there and any merchandise you're trying to punt and leave before I call the police and have you done with possession of a Class A drug and him done for being a pimp." Sean steps out from behind the bar and Ross stands beside her. Sophie feels heat radiate from him as she side steps, putting herself in between him and the prostitute.

The male rushes the scene with the kitchen knife he'd brought with him. At the same time the prostitute dives for Sophie, grabbing at her hair like an alley cat.

Belle intercepts the running man with her foot, making him sprawl on the floor and lose grip of the knife. She kicks it free of the struggle as her foot is grabbed and she is pulled to the floor.

Dropping his phone on the floor, Sean runs to grab Belle up from the floor and away from the now unarmed man. Between them both Sean gets the assailant under his knee and press it into his chest, pinning his arms to the floor.

"My phone, the police on the line." Sean manages to grunt out as he presses his knee down again with all his might to try and keep his prisoner where he wants him, all whilst fighting the bucking movements of said prisoner.

Ross tries to get himself between the fighting women and gets nails dragged down his cheek for his actions. He hears and feels Sophie more than sees her ram the female against the wall behind them, pinning her there with her forearm to her windpipe her hand pushing against her sternum.

"You don't get to fuckin' touch him." Sophie growls. "He's mine!"

"Grotty will hear about this." The prostitute grins at Sophie.

The thug under Sean's knee continues to struggle to get away from the crushing weight on top of him as he grunts for the prostitute to keep her mouth shut. Sophie leans closer to her prisoner pressing her full body weight into her and with a grin of her own.

"Oh, I'm counting on it."

Belle is giving the bar address to the police operator, then heads to Sophie who still has the prostitute pinned to the wall. She leans in and whispers into her ear.

"Sophie don't go too far, or you'll put the investigation in jeopardy with a police brutality accusation. Sophie hears her and eases off a touch.

Within minutes police officers arrive at The Pub and start to apprehend the prostitute and her companion then take everyone's details and initial statements, asking them all to go into the station the next day to give a full statement. The girls assure the young officers that they will all be in to give statements, keeping their cover stories from the investigation in case the prisoners haven't been privy to all their boss' information.

Sean locks the door behind the police officers. Ross mentions that that is the first time since his grand opening of The Pub. Which Sean explains that he doesn't want any more customers coming in that night, they all had had enough excitement for one night.

The four friends need the peace and solitude of the empty bar and their own company. He walks back into the bar area to see Ross pouring them all fresh pints.

"You after a new job?" He jokes, as they all start to relax for the first time since they realised there was a prostitute trying to sell drugs in the bar.

Ross smiles and shrugs as Sean takes a seat next to Belle giving her leg a squeeze who then turns to Sophie.

"Sophie, I need to ask you, how did you know she was a hooker?"

Both Belle and Sophie throw him a look of disbelief. "Are you kidding me? Did you see the way she was dressed?"

He shrugs, "It's a Wednesday night!"

Belle shakes her head at her boyfriend as Sophie continues, "Then there was everything she was saying to Ross about buying her a drink and that it could be as part payment. Plus the guy she came in with was wearing clothes that were far too big for him and the dark blue of the shirt showed up all the white powder he'd dropped down himself as he probably tested the merchandise they have been sent to peddle, along with her services. I'm guessing it's connected to Jason and so I would assume it is Coke." Ross sits watching Sophie as she talks, his mouth hanging open with amazement at everything she noticed in the short space of time.

He was the one sitting nearest the door when they came into the bar and he was the one that had the conversation with the prostitute and he never noticed any of it.

Lifting her pint Sophie turns to Ross to see him staring open mouthed. She places her finger under his chin and pushes his jaw closed.

"You'll catch flies."

CHAPTER THIRTY-NINE

Sitting in his new wheelchair, Jason is split in how he is feeling about his situation. He is glad, almost happy that he was up out of bed for most of the day, sitting and able to see the world from his more vertical position instead of staring straight up to the ceiling.

The police had been in to question him, but he had 'no commented' his way through it since he hadn't been in touch with his lawyer and he certainly wasn't talking to one of theirs.

He contacted Grotty to arrange the lawyer they had used many times before to come and see him in the hospital to confirm his hunch that the police wouldn't prosecute someone who is so badly injured.

The lawyer arrives an hour after being contacted, a fact that Jason is pleased with. Injured or not, he still doesn't like waiting and that recently that is all he has done.

He listens to his defence lawyer explain the ways he could try to get the charges dropped and if not, then what his defence should be when his case gets to court. Jason was dumbfounded.

"They'll still charge me and take me to trial? Try me and send me to prison, here in Scotland?" He gets a noncommittal shrug as his only answer. "But I'm in a wheelchair, paralysed from the waist down, doesn't that count for anything?"

The lawyer shakes his head as he answers. "Doubt that will even be looked at. You have previous, a rap sheet that reads like War and Peace, plus you shot a police officer. They do not take that lightly and are going to throw everything at you."

Jason throws his arms up. "And what about me? I got shot too!" His voice rises with his anger.

Grotty smiles. The Jason of old would never lose his temper like that. Take his anger out on an unsuspecting customer in the privacy of his office or the warehouse, yes, but never shout and lose his cool in public. All signs that he was losing control and so another reason for Grotty to take over the running of his business.

There is a strained silence as Jason fumes at the information that he may still be sentenced to a jail term for his crimes regardless of his current health condition.

"So," Grotty breaks the silence, "I've been thinking about the business." Jason scowls.

"What about it?" His tone is demanding.

"Well, I was thinkin', if things are going south for you, why don't you sign over some of your things to me, just for a bit, that way the polis can't get their hands on things, you know under that Proceeds of Crime law." Jason eyes Grotty warily, then nods. "I mean it'll only be the things you want to hide, or I mean keep out of harm's way, the office premises for example, or the F Pace." More nodding from Jason as the lawyer looks everywhere in the room rather than at the men talking.

"Okay, but I get them back once this all dies down and I'm free again." Grotty nods with more vigour than he wanted to show. His plan was starting to come to fruition.

The men discuss the running of the business with Grotty playing his part as second fiddle as well as any Oscar winning actor.

Dynamic Entry

"So you both know what you need to do?" Jason directs his question to both men.

"I'll see what I can do about getting the charges dropped due to your health condition, but I've never heard of it before, so don't hold your breath, and we've discussed the other options for you to think about."

Jason scoffs at the lawyer then turns his attention to Grotty.

"You?" "Oh aye boss, I know exactly what I'm doing." With a sly grin he stands and leaves the room quickly followed by the lawyer, leaving Jason to his own personal hell.

****

Sophie wakes up with a warm body wrapped around her. She lies for a minute enjoying the embrace, not wanting to lose the feeling of having Ross so close to her, but she knows it can't last, then the flashbacks start, she remembers her reaction to the prostitute flirting and then attacking Ross, them getting taken away after being arrested, and then her drinking more, much more; she cringes at the memories.

She had been jealous and protective of him and never in her life had she felt rage of that magnitude than when that woman had dragged her nails down Ross' face. Nobody brought pain to the man she loved, except her, she thought guiltily. Even after everything had calmed down the guilt stayed with her, but even that didn't stop her telling him what she thought of his choice in replacement and exactly why that woman was dating him.

"Aye, so I worked out." She remembers the resignation in his voice and how it broke her heart.

"You deserve better than being used as a way to get a job promotion. You deserve someone who loves you for you, who sees your full worth and appreciates it. Someone who thinks you're amazing and can give you everything you want in a woman and in life." She downs the last of her pint and slides, unladylike, from her bar stool, staggering slightly as she lands on her lager laden feet.

"Whoa!" Ross holds her arms to steady her, "I think it's time for bed for you." Sophie nods sluggishly, tiredness washing over her. Ross steps from his own stool and places an arm around her waist, keeping her steady enough to walk. "I'll help you upstairs, then I'll phone a taxi." They stumble into the spare room and Sophie strips down to her underwear before climbing into the double bed and gestures for Ross to sit next to her on the bed. He sits

"I don't like the woman you're dating, or banging, or whatever youse are doing." She repeats.

Ross brushes the small hairs that have started to disobey her straighteners and curl around her forehead, behind her ear. "I'm not dating anyone or banging anyone for that matter. I stopped seeing Karen as I felt like I was cheating- it didn't feel right, plus I realised she was just after a promotion at work."

Sophie lifts her heavy hand and cups Ross' cheek lovingly. "I'm sorry, for everything."

"Me too." He bends down placing a light kiss on Sophie's lips and they both react hungrily, holding onto each other, drinking from each other's kiss like they had been parched in the desert for weeks.

Ross pulls back first. "Sophie, I can't do this, I mean I want to, but we've both had a lot to drink and I don't want to take advantage of you."

She nods. "Very gentlemanly of you, thank you, but stay at least?"

He caresses her cheek again before standing and stripping down to his underwear also, then climbs into the bed beside Sophie. He holds her close as she drifts off to sleep, both of them feeling like they had won the lottery.

With a sigh and a heavy heart, Sophie moves to extradite herself from Ross' embrace only to have Ross pull her closer to him.

"Don't." His voice is rough with sleep and it reminds her of all the mornings she woke up encased in his arms.

"I can't, we shouldn't." Her voice catches.

"I know, but I can't let go just yet, and going by that sigh, I don't think you want to let go either." Any fight Sophie was trying to hold onto leaves her and she moulds herself back against him. She has missed him so damn much, even though she tries to make herself not miss him.

"But nothing has changed." Ross pushes himself onto his elbow, rolling Sophie onto her back, and leans down kissing her. He pulls back."

"Tell me to stop and I will." He leans down again threading his fingers into her honey blonde hair, hovering his lips a breath away from hers.

Giving into temptation she speaks. "I don't want you to stop." She pulls him down to her, running her hands over his back moaning into his kiss and letting herself go, enjoying every touch and caress the man she loves passes over her body, until she is moaning his name and falling apart in his arms.

Walking towards Sean's kitchen after their lovemaking, Sophie feels like she is walking on air. Reaching the kitchen door she schools her face from beaming to her 'I'm just up, not had my tea don't talk to me!' face and walks through the door.

Ross is at her back smiling like the proverbial cat. Belle and Sean both look up at their friends and then throw each other a knowing grin.

"Thought you were going home last night?" Sean aims his question at his best friend but keeps his eyes on his new honorary sister as a blush rises up her cheeks. Ross grins and shrugs his shoulders.

"Was too far away."

"Ah." Sean gives Sophie a kiss on the forehead good morning as she tries not to blush more.

Once everyone is sitting with their morning teas and coffees the friend's start to discuss when they will go to the police station to give their statements about the incident the night before. They are all relaxed in their wee group, a feeling of contentment settling around most of them except Sophie. She knows she is going to be the one to split the group up again.

CHAPTER FORTY

Finishing their statements, the friend's meet back at the reception are of Pitt Street police station. Pulling Belle to his side, Sean is first to speak, breaking the tense atmosphere,

"Right, back to The Pub for food?" He looks at each of his friends and sees two nodding heads and Sophie looking everywhere but at the group. "Soph?"

She brings her attention to the group. "Youse go ahead, I'll, eh, catch you up."

Belle squeezes her eyes shut. "Sophie Pearsons, it is your day off and you have that, 'I'm going to work myself silly' look in your eyes."

Sophie looks among all her friends. "I will only be an hour, two at the most. I don't want this lead going cold on us, I'm sure last night is connected to everything else, so I want to get a head start on it."

"I didn't think you'd be allowed to investigate last night?" The query comes from Ross who looks like he is trying his best not to be disappointed at her picking work over a day off with him.

"We won't be!" Belle looks sternly at her friend.

"I won't be investigating last night!" Sophie growls back. "I will be looking at any connection, there's a difference, and this is what I do when a case gets a hold of me and you know it! This is my job!" Her words come out harsher than she had intended, but they were mostly aimed at herself. She couldn't let last night with Ross change her mind over the relationship.

As she said, this was her job, and this is what she does. It takes over her life, and that is unfair to Ross, and that is why she has to end things before they got started, again.

"Okay, well I'll come and pick you up in two hours," Ross offers.

"You don't —"

"I know I don't have to, but you're my friend, so I want to and I am." Not wanting to argue any more Sophie nods.

"Okay, thank you." She gives her apologies and her goodbyes then heads back into the maze of corridors that make up Pitt Street police station. Belle turns to Ross.

"I'll stay with her but make it an hour and I'll make sure she leaves." Giving Sean a chaste kiss Belle turns and follows in best friend and partner's wake.

****

Grotty is livid when he finds out about the arrests from the night before. He'd warned both of them not to make it so damn obvious why they were in the bar, and if they thought the police officers were there then they had their orders to have one drink then leave, but no, they go and have a full blown cat fight, get arrested and then remanded in custody the next day, charged with intent to supply a Class A drug and prostitution.

Thankfully someone who owed him a favour was working at the Sheriff Court that day and relayed back the information, or he wouldn't even have known they had been arrested.

Growling under his breath about Jason's stupid employees leading his girls astray, he continues going through all of Jason's paperwork and contracts, signing everything over to himself using Jason's forged signature, which he had perfected. Then it was on to make friends with all the contacts in Jason's diary, explaining that he will be taking over from Jason, in the interim, until he is cleared of this small bit of trouble.

To his surprise, everyone he spoke to seemed happy that Jason had support and even commended Grotty for taking the reins as they knew Jason wouldn't easily let go and would definitely not be the easiest to work for, especially now he wouldn't be able to do his full workouts or keep up his alleged intake of steroids. Grotty keeps his thanks modest, so as not to raise any suspicions of his plan to take over the business entirely.

The front door buzzer sounds and Grotty presses the release with only a glance at the CCTV. He doesn't recognise the male standing there, but he isn't worried, he has his fists as protection and Jason's reputation to play with. The visitor arrives at Grotty's desk, all bravado and swagger.

"Any chance I can get some Charlie?"

Grotty is taken aback by the man's forwardness. "And what makes you think I sell anything?"

"Senga told me, said you'd sort me out, for ma customers like." Grotty's suspicions melt away at the mention of one of his girls, even if it was the one that had been arrested the night before, and pound signs flash in his eyes.

"Aye, I can help you out with that." The men sit across from each other in the small room and discuss amounts, prices, and the frequency of delivery and payments.

Today is a good day, Grotty thinks to himself as he slides three thousand pounds worth of cocaine across the desk and takes the same amount in cash that's offered to him.

"Nice doing business with you Ben, and I'll see you in a month?" Ben nods.

Fiona Morgan

"Oh aye, or sooner, you know if I get it all shifted."
Grotty smirks, "Hopefully sooner then."

Ben makes his way from the claustrophobic office and back out into the crisp autumn wind, and quickly into the Signal Red XJS Jaguar sitting waiting on him at the end of the road.

"You get it all?" Sophie asks. Ben opens the holdall full of drugs, "Fantastic!" Sophie pulls away from the kerb smiling.

"Why didn't we use a pool car?" Ben runs his hand over the perfect magnolia with red piping leather interior of the well-loved car. "Not that I'm moaning, 'because you know this car is amazing."

Sophie throws him a smile; she loves getting compliments about her car. "If Grotty came out and saw a pool car he would've recognised it off the bat, however, I never use my own car at work, so no-one would ever recognise it, but don't and I mean do not mention to anyone that I used this car as part of the job. I've been asked so many times to use it and refused point blank, and using it this time does not mean I'm going to use it again, got it?" Her tone leaves Ben nodding furiously.

Sophie's reputation over her love for her Jaguar and her temper over it precedes her.

Sophie nods back, happy that she can still strike fear into a man. She gives herself a mental self-appreciative smile.

"Right I need to get back to the station, I am meant to be getting picked up in ten minutes and Belle thinks I'm photocopying crap." Ben shakes his head as Sophie puts her foot down on the accelerator, pushing him into his seat as the engine roars and her speed increases. He doesn't miss the smile on her face.

****

293

Dynamic Entry

Ross sits at the bar waiting for the extra hour the girls asked for to count down. He sips his drink then pushes it away, there is only so many cans of Irn Bru one person can drink in two hours.

"You're taking this 'this is my job' thing in your stride. You change your mind about wanting Sophie back?"

Ross shakes his head. "Absolutely not. I'm using this to prove that I can hack being with her whilst she is knee deep in a case. I'm proving that I am patient enough to want her and support her, but within a reasonable limit, so picking her up in two hours." He taps his nose to prove he knows what he's talking about. "What about you?" He throws the question back to Sean who shrugs.

"We both work crazy hours," he says, "so we understand that we both need to work at making time for each other. We'll make it work. This is it for both of us and we know it."

Ross' eyebrows go up. "Never thought I'd see the day you were actively taking yourself out of the dating market."

Sean laughs. "Me neither to be honest, but Belle is a special girl. What about you? I never thought I'd see the day that you'd say you were in love, and actually be in love." Ross sticks his tongue out in a childish gesture. He had spent every relationship 'in love' when he didn't even know the meaning of the words, and now he does, he's fighting for it.

"Sophie's a special lady too," he says.

"That she is. So when you get her back don't fuck it up again!" Ross lifts his can in a salute.

"Not planning on it my friend, not planning on it." Draining his can he steps down from the bar stool. "Right, I'm going to get them, be back soon."

Fiona Morgan

CHAPTER FORTY-ONE

Two weeks pass in the investigation. Ben has collected more evidence on Grotty and they are ready to raid the Blythswood Square office, plus the case against Jason has been handed over to the Procurator Fiscal, which meant it was out of Sophie's hands and hair.

She has done all she can do to bring him down for life this time, now it was up to the PF to do their jobs and convince twelve of their peers of his guilt.

As the two weeks had stretched out Sophie had found herself and Ross texting more and more. She hadn't realised how much she had missed their late-night conversations and playful sexting, but the guilt kept eating at her that she was setting them both up for a fall again. She is still who she is and still does the job she loves; no amount of banter was going to change that.

Belle finds her sitting in the canteen with a lukewarm cup of tea in front of her smiling into her phone. "You ready for the raid?"

Sophie jumps at Belle's words, accidentally hitting the screen and sending the 'aye' message she had been dithering over sending Ross. An answer to his request to see her that night.

A slight panic washes over her until she realises she is actually happy that the decision had been taken from her by the fates, it was meant to be.

"What? Eh, aye, yes. Is everything and everyone ready to go?"

Belle nods. "Hmm, was that Ross?"

296

Sophie dips her head like she'd been caught out stealing sweets, then she smiles, there's no point trying to cover her tracks with Belle, she can read her better than anyone.

"Yes, we've been texting each other again, as friends, so don't bother getting any ideas or your hopes up, I'm still me and I still do this for a job, which can consume me, so nothing has changed. Now talking about our job, if everything is ready, let's get it done." She clears her cup away and leaves the station, ready to get started on her favourite part of her job, taking down the bad guys.

Ben has been in Grotty's office for ten minutes and everyone is in place to storm the office. Sophie's heart rate is beating in a double time tattoo in her chest and she feels like she can hear colours her adrenaline is pumping so fast around her system making her hyper aware of everything going on.

Poised and ready with the big red door key, the officers at the door pull the battering ram back, firing it forward as soon as the DI gives his go ahead.

The banging seems to go on for an age, but it really only took twenty to thirty seconds for the door to buckle and give way, leaving a gaping hole for all the officers to barge through, shouting their arrival.

Sophie enters the office she has been in many times before, hot on the heels of the barging officers. There she is confronted with Ben playing his part of the scared customer in the corner and Grotty standing, surrounded by packets of cocaine stacked into the space behind his desk, with a smug grin plastered onto his face.

"Might have known you'd be behind this, ya cow." He grins at Sophie as she grins back, not letting his self-assured, bizarre smile derail her.

Dynamic Entry

"Of course I'm involved. You think Jason could scare me off? Not a chance. Now what do we have here then?" She gestures to all the wrapped packages behind him as officers start their search. Grotty shrugs.

"Nothing to do with me. As you well know this is Jason's office, I'm just looking after the place for him, you know since he's unavailable at the moment." Another grin stretches over his lips.

"So I'd heard." She retorts.

Belle heads toward the desk, opening drawers and pulling out paperwork. Sophie watches Grotty's every twitch as Belle moves through the desk. She sees him visibly relax when Belle closes the last drawer and his smug grin makes a reappearance. They must have missed something.

"Check for false bottoms in the drawers." Sophie uses her 'I have a hunch' tone to convey her suspicions to Belle who goes back to check the drawers again.

Sophie is rewarded with a panicking flash in Grotty's eyes. Belle taps on the bottom of each drawer until they hear a hollow thump come back at them. She pulls away the false panel and finds more paperwork. After a quick read through she grins at Sophie.

"Paperwork signing everything over to Mr. Crossan here. I'd say we have him on everything in here and probably more. Would you like to do the honours Sophie?" Sophie's heart rate spins out of control with the knowledge that she was indeed bringing down this entire business.

"That I would!" She grins as she steps forward. Grotty lunges for her, but she sees it coming and side steps the lunge, grabbing his outstretched arm and twists it up his back as she slams him face first into the nearest wall.

"I don't fuckin' think so Grotty!" She reads him his Miranda rights as he continues to struggle. She enlists the help of another officer to restrain him as she gets her handcuffs snapped into place on his wrists. "Looks like you're going to be unavailable for the foreseeable too." She nods to two officers, "Get those two back to the station, but keep them apart, don't want them getting their stories straight before they get there." She gestures to Ben who has also been 'arrested'. Then she and the rest of their team go back to searching the office, gathering evidence as they go. All in all, she thinks to herself, a good day's work.

****

Having got home and showered, Sophie sits in her living room phone in hand. She is desperate to phone Ross and tell him all about her day and the raid.

Once upon a time, it was Belle she would recount it all to, but now she only wants to share it with Ross and that thought scares her. They have been back in contact for a few weeks now and it has been great, talking like they used to, but without the worry of the case and her secret hanging over her.

She loves Ross with all her heart, but can she trust herself to not be her father? With that thought she deletes the message she has typed out, a flirty text that all but said she wanted Ross to come over.

A coldness settles in her stomach at the thought of her father and she types out a text to her aunt then sits and lets the coldness wash over her as she waits for a response. It comes within seconds with her phone ringing in her hand. With shaking fingers she answers.

"Hi."

"Sophie, honey," says a voice on the other end of the line.

"Auntie Ann."

"Why? Why do you want his details? Why do you want to meet your dad? After all this time of hating him and you want to, do what?"

Sophie squeezes her eyes shut, what was she doing? Why did she want contact with her father after all this time? "I need to ask him why," Her voice is rough with unshed tears, "I've met someone and I've messed it all up by being like him, with two lives, although not really, but kinda…"

She blows out a breath, "I don't know, it's all just a mess. I just need to know why them and not me!" Holding back her tears she listens to her aunt as she explains that Sophie is nothing like her dad, her brother, and how sorry she is for his actions, but the need to confront him and hear it from the man who left her only grows."

She says her goodbyes and promises to keep in touch then cancels the call with her aunt. She holds the phone to her chest, her emotions in turmoil.

Before she can attempt to get them under control her phone rings again in her hand, she turns it over and a picture of Ross flashes at her. She presses answer as her tears break their boundaries and clog her throat.

"Ross, I think I need you, can you come over?" Her voice is broken. There is silence on the other end. She hadn't even greeted Ross with a 'hello'.

Panic settles in her stomach. Her stubborn side kicks in, telling her that she shouldn't be relying on him until she hears his voice and she blows out a breath she hadn't realised she had been holding.

"I'll be there in twenty minutes." Relief sweeps through her as her tears fall.

****

Ross phones a taxi as soon as he cancels the call and then paces the floor like a caged animal waiting on it. Jumping into the back of it, he fires off Sophie's address and then presses himself into the back seat of the silver Skoda, trying to will the driver to go faster as a million scenarios crash through his mind at the heart wrenching plea Sophie answered her phone with.

Before the taxi comes to a full stop Ross throws thirty pounds at the driver and is running up her driveway, dodging her XJS as he goes. Bursting through her front door he shouts her name.

He stops dead in his tracks at the sight of her sitting on her living room floor, her beautiful silver blue eyes red rimmed and shining with tears as she stares at her phone. Her whole body sagging in what looks like defeat. He crosses to her, bending to sit beside her.

"Sophie, what can I do?" His voice is soft, so as not to startle her. She looks up at him, relief glinting through the sadness in her eyes. She shakes her head like she doesn't have the words to describe her feelings.

She grabs Ross and holds onto him like he is a lifeline. Someone who is there, for her and she lets go of all the sadness that has been building in her for her full life.

Ross holds her letting her sob into his chest, cooing soothing noises at her for as long as she needs. Her sobbing reduces as she starts to talk.

"I, I contacted my, my father." She stutters her words out through fresh tears, mumbling them into Ross' chest. He pulls them both up onto the couch, taking her hands in his so they are facing each other.

"I'm guessing it didn't go well?"

Sophie snorts out a laugh then sniffs in a very unladylike manner. "I didn't get to speak to him. His wife said he wasn't in. I told her my name and asked her to get him to phone me back, she asked if he would know who I was, so I told her who I was. She denied he had children; I mean other than the ones he has with her." She lets out a breath, "She didn't know who I was, he never told her about me or my mum. We really did mean that little to him. It's stupid, but I feel like he's abandoned me all over again."

Ross' heart breaks with her every sob. The need to bring physical harm to her father burns in his throat, but he knows that that's not what will fix this situation, and also the last thing Sophie would want. Knight in shining armour sweeping in to fix her problems is not high on Sophie's wish list. No, what she needs is love and security, and to trust in the knowledge that he loves her, for her, the amazing person she is and that no amount of pushing him away is going to change that. He may have fucked everything up once, but never again, well at least not on as grand a scale again.

"I don't know what to say, other than he's a dickhead. Losing out on knowing the bravest, most amazing and special person I have ever known or loved. But why did you contact him? What made you want to do that? You have always hated him so much."

Sophie pulls back. "I wanted to find out why them. What did I do wrong, and to see if I really am, just like him?" Ross knew Sophie wasn't throwing the 'just like him' statement at him, but he still winces. He squeezes her tighter. "Thank you for being here."

He takes her face in his hands. "I'll always be here for you. I love you." Before she can answer he kisses her, pouring all of his love and hope for her into it. Sophie responds to the kiss.

CHAPTER FORTY-TWO

The next morning Sophie wakes with the familiar extra warmth enveloping her and she remembers the night before, but before she can analyse her feelings her mobile rings. She grabs it and answers without looking at the screen. The ringing wakes Ross.

"Hello?" She starts to get out of bed, but the caller's voice stops her movements.

"Hello Sophie." Her father replies.

"Dad, you?"

"Yes, me, your dad. I'm returning your call, the call that made my wife very confused, which made her ask many questions. So can I ask why? Why did you phone?"

Anger fills her. "Why did I phone?" Her voice raises without her permission. "I phoned to ask, to ask you why you picked that family over me. I phoned to find out what it was I had done to make you walk out. I phoned —"

"Well there was no need for you to be so selfish and phone and upset people now was there! Now like I told that doormat of a mother of yours at the time, I chose them because they were, no, they are the better family. They are stronger, they are boys, not weak doormats like you and your mother." Even after all these years her father's archaic views hadn't changed.

She scrubs at the tears that had formed in her eyes and straightens her spine with steel, reminding herself of who she is.

Sophie feels Ross laying their listening to her conversation. She pulls herself up, showing her resolve. He places his hand on her stomach, and she takes the reassure of his presence and uses it to give her some added strength for what she needs to say.

"Yes I am a female, but I am no fuckin' doormat. I have carved myself a life. I have a job, a damn good job. A job where I work as an equal and I take bad guys down. I have friends and someone I love and," She looks over at Ross who has held her throughout.

Did she deserve his love after everything she put him through? Can she be a strong female even though she finds herself wanting to rely on him being in her life. Now wasn't that the big question she thinks.

Pushing that aside she carries on telling her father how she has made it without him. "And I've done it all without you. I phoned to find out why you didn't pick me and mum, and now I'm glad you didn't. So don't worry about me phoning back and ruining your perfect life as I'm doing perfectly well on my own!" She cancels the call before her father has a chance to reply.

She sits for a second trying to make sense of her feelings and the way that having Ross hold her gave her more strength.

"You're not on your own, or at least you don't have to be." Sophie turns her head to Ross who had pushed himself to a sitting position.

"I don't rely on anyone. I told you that way back at the start. I can't." She swallows away the pain her words are causing her.

"I'm not leaving, push all you want, I'm here, I want to be with you. I'm choosing to be with you." Sophie pushes herself up from the bed.

"I don't think you should." And she walks away from Ross for the second time.

****

Ross steps into his house and closes the door with an angry slam. She walked away from him again. Walked away from them, again.

It had taken him all his strength not to take Sophie and shake her until there was some sense in her, but he knew that would only make matters worse, so he did as she asked and walked away.

With his heart breaking all over again he heads to his kitchen and to the cupboard where he keeps his whisky. A finger or two of Laphroaig should keep the pain at bay he thinks to himself as he pours.

Some hours and many whisky's later, Ross answers his phone to a worried Sean.

"I thought you were coming over tonight for our monthly night out?"

"Ah, shit. Sssorry pal." He slurs then hiccups. "I to'tally for, hic, forgot about it. See she's left me again, but you know what, I ain't giving up! Nope, not me. Fuck that running away. I'm no doing that, an' I'm no letting her do it either!"

He can hear Sean blow out a breath. "Are you drunk?"

Ross shrugs to his empty house. "Maybe, just a smid... smidgen. But I know I love her, an' she loves me!"

"That is very true." Another breath comes down the line, "Right. stop drinking and go to bed, you've got work tomorrow and you don't want to be hungover when you're trying to win back your girl, again."

Ross sobers for a second. "No I don't, and I will win her back then I won't be letting her go ever again." The friends say their good nights and Ross climbs his stairs to bed, hatching a drunken plan to get Sophie back beside him.

CHAPTER FORTY-THREE

Jason's trial starts in Glasgow High Court on a snowy February morning and his lawyer has told him to prepare for the worst. He has pled not guilty to all the charges against his lawyer's advice, as he was still convinced they won't convict a paralysed man, but as he wheels himself into court for the start of his trial doubts start to build in him.

The charges are read out; four counts of murder, shooting a police officer on active duty, possession of class A drugs with intent to supply, and possession of a firearm.

He feels like his foot is tapping and his lower half is squirming, but he knows it is phantom movements, but it still messes with his head.

His lawyer eyes him as he sits in the dock, giving him a wary look at the sight of the sweat beading on his forehead. The lawyer mouths over.

"Jason, are you okay? Do you want a recess?" But Jason doesn't notice it as he pulls at his tie. It is starting to feel like a noose around his neck. He can feel the sweat run down his back and his hands are clammy in his lap.

He resists the urge to wipe them on his trouser leg, he didn't want anyone to know the feeling of panic that was starting to consume him as his heartbeat quickens to what he thinks must be an impossible rate.

He can hear his lawyer talk to the judge, but it's like he is underwater, the sound is muffled and far away. His breathing comes to his attention, why can't he get enough air into his lungs? Why can't he catch his breath?

He starts to wonder, is this a heart attack? He pushes the thought away, his body is a temple, he is as healthy as an ox, except for his lower half, but his heart is strong.

The lack of steroids filters into his mind, but again he pushes it away quickly, he may have injected steroids, but he wasn't addicted, he had gone without before and not had any symptoms, plus, he reminds himself, they are only supplements, not drugs. Not like the crap he sells.

As his thoughts spiral out of control over his predicament his sweating increases, as does his rapid breathing making his heartbeat pick up to an even quicker tempo; then the pain starts.

He clutches his chest, his mind telling him over and over again that he is dying. He is having a heart attack and he is dying. He pulls at his suit jacket, trying to take it off, but his hands are slick with sweat and the sides are tucked between his hips and his chair. The bulk of his well-toned body making everything a tight fit and so more difficult to manoeuvre through his panic.

He struggles more with his jacket, making noises through his gritted teeth as he forces out breaths, although he is taking little air back in. Dark spots flash through his sight and he squeezes his eyes shut tight, trying to clear his vision, but as he reopens them his vision is worse, everything is moving, nothing is staying where they should be as blackness continues to encroach at the sides of his sight.

This all adds to the voice of death whirling around his head, which in turn accelerates his breathing and heart rate in an ever-worsening vicious circle.

Dynamic Entry

He manages to move his right arm, flailing it at his lawyer as his left clutches at his chest, trying to soothe the pain stabbing at his over beating heart. He can hear himself tell his lawyer he is dying but can hear nothing in return over the ringing in his ears. A constant high-pitched noise that is only getting louder as his vision gets darker.

His lawyer is in front of the dock talking, but Jason can't hear anything. His only thought was about his impending death and where did the front of the dock go, and then there is nothing but blackness and silence as unconsciousness takes him under.

****

"HE DID WHAT?" Sophie shouts as a silence encapsulates the small office and all its inhabitants. Belle glares at her DI who is hiding behind Sophie like a coward as Belle explains the events of Jason's day at court.

"I know, it's annoying, but —"

"Is he dead?" She demands to know.

"What? No you can't die from a panic attack."

"You said he was having a heart attack!" Belle rolls her eyes at Sophie's growl but keeps her calm as she throws a look of disgust at their DI.

"No, I said they thought he was having a heart attack so phoned an ambulance, and then he passed out. You went off on one before I could say anything else after heart attack. So, he didn't have a heart attack, he had a panic attack in the courtroom before they could get anything started, so they have had to postpone the case until there is another free spot in the High Court calendar. I think there's still a bit of a backlog due to the holidays."

Sophie nods. "Bloody typical, okay, but was he still going to plead not guilty? Do we know that at least? I mean, how could he plead not guilty, we have him bang to rights, don't we? And what does the scaredy cat behind me think?" She swings round on her heel to face her DI who is standing with eyes as wide as a deer who's seen headlights.

"Eh.. aye, bang to rights," The DI straightens himself and pulls at the sleeves of his suit jacket, "and I am not a scaredy cat!" Belle tries to stifle her snigger to her DI's words and Sophie's sarcastic reply of 'aye right'.

"Anyway," Their DI clears his throat, trying to bring back his authority as he moves from behind Sophie, "he was kept in for observations, but as Belle said, it turns out it was a panic attack. Plus, as far as I know he blew up at the nurse taking blood from him, just swung out and punched her. So, he got arrested, again, for assault. The man is an idiot! A dangerous idiot who will be up in court for everything we have on him and then again for assault on an NHS worker, which the courts throw the book at, so I would put my bet on him going down for a good long time, I don't see him getting out."

Sophie calms at the DI's words. "Good, and with any luck the idiot will plead guilty and I won't need to give evidence. Now what about Grotty? Any word on his court case or plea?"

The DI swallows again. "Aye, he's pleading not guilty to. His defence is to blame everything on Jason. He didn't know about any of the 'goings on' of the business until he took over and was going to turn everything over and make the business legit."

Sophie stands open mouthed at her DI. "Are you shitting me?" She tries to control her raising anger. The DI shakes his head and shrugs, then shuffles his feet.

Sophie eyes him. "You're keeping something from me, spill it, now!"

The DI takes a step towards her. "Let's talk in private." He motions for Belle to exit the office.

Ice slithers down Sophie's spine. Whatever she was about to be told was not going to be good and something she didn't want to hear. Dread pools in her stomach as she watches Belle take the few short steps to leave the office.

She stops and takes hold of Sophie's hand giving it a squeeze of reassurance before walking out and closing the door behind her. Why did that door closing feel like a death sentence was about to be handed down?

"Have a seat Sophie, and before I say anything remember we have a protocol, so certain things need to happen. But saying that, we all have your back." The dread that has pooled turns to lead and settles itself in her stomach with a thud.

"What is it? Just tell me."

Her DI blows out his breath as he sits beside her. "Grotty has put in an official complaint about you. He is accusing you of giving him the drugs to keep and that he was pimping the girls for you, on your say."

Sophie stares at her boss, trying to take in his words. "He's, he's what? Claiming entrapment?"

"No, not entrapment, he's saying you're a —" Realisation dawns on Sophie as she jumps from her chair, cutting off her boss' words before he can utter them.

"DON'T! Don't you dare, don't you fuckin' dare say it!" She raises her hand in apology for swearing at her boss, then continues in an eerily calm voice. "He's accusing me of being, bent? A bent cop? Is that what's happening? Is that what that piece of shit is saying about me?" A nod is her only answer as her head swims.

Her whole career she has strived to be the best police officer she can be, better than every male dinosaur that told her she'd never make it, or said she was too fragile to do any of the undercover assignments she pushed for, and for what? For a lowlife piece of scum to bring it all crashing down with false accusations of being a bent cop who sells drugs and runs prostitutes?

"We all know it's a pile of shit, Soph, but it's an official complaint, it needs to be taken through the proper channels, it will need to be investigated fully, and I have to follow the proper procedures. But on another note."

She drags her eyes to meet her boss', trying to dampen down the anger and utter dismay she is feeling. "You mean there's more? What else can he possibly say after that?"

The DI smiles. "No nothing else from him, but rumour has it you might be up for a Bravery Award." She snorts out a derisive laugh.

"Are you taking the piss? What on earth for?"

Her DI smiles. "Sophie, you never give yourself the credit you're due for the amount of work you put into each and every case you work on. But this award is for getting shot in the line of duty, whilst saving a member of the public, namely your boyfriend."

"He's not my, I mean I'm not sure if we are back together or not, but that doesn't matter, is he up for one too? Ross, I mean."

"I don't know, I'll look into it and-"

"And get his name put forward. He got shot the same as me, and he saved a whole shop full of staff and an unborn baby, not just one person."

Dynamic Entry

The DI nods his understanding. "You really do love him, don't you?"

An icy glare from Sophie has the DI moving on from the subject of love. "Well, as you know, due to there being an investigation, I need to put you on restricted duties. So no contact with the public and your access to the system will be restricted too." Her indignation is clear on her face. She is desperate to fight, but knows it's of no use, so with resignation she stands.

"Fine! I'll be in the cafeteria drinking tea. Sort this shit out quickly!" She leaves the office with a torrent of emotions fighting to be the one she feels the most. She holds onto anger, that one never lets her down.

CHAPTER FORTY-FOUR

A week after her restricted duties commence Sophie finds herself sitting in a Glasgow Sheriff Court witness room.

"How you feeling about giving evidence today?" Belle eyes her friend over her polystyrene cup of vending machine coffee.

"It's quick to be called."

Belle bobs her head. "I thought that too, but Jason's case has been garnering media interest since his melt down in court, so the powers that be must have thought it best to get this one up and running, seeing as they are connected, in a way. But you avoided the question. How are you feeling?" Sophie sighs wistfully, then internally growls, she is not the type of girl to sigh! And she certainly doesn't sigh wistfully!

"I wish the complaint was all dealt with and finished, then the arsehole wouldn't have the defence 'the big bad bent cop did it and ran away!' That way he can change it back into 'the big bad man done it and is now in a wheelchair'. I mean what kind of defence is that anyway? He's a grown man, not a five-year-old in the playground."

"So what you're saying is you're feeling bitchy and a tad sarcastic over giving evidence today?"

Sophie cocks her head to one side to mimic thinking. "Aye that about covers it, but then, is that not me all the time?"

Belle mimics Sophie's thinking stance. "Well on most things, but with Ross, who by the way sends his good luck for today —"

Sophie cuts her friend off from saying more. "I know he does, he told me last night when we were talking." The bitchy, back off tone is not lost on Belle, but it is ignored.

"Oh so youse are talking then?" she asks.

Sophie drags her eyes away from Belle's to fight the eye roll that is demanding to happen. "Yes we've been talking, you know we have, though I'm not sure what else we are after I walked out on him again, but we are talking." The last part came out softer, her bitchy side lessening.

"And youse love each other."

Sophie wasn't sure if that was a question or a statement, but thankfully the Court Officer comes into the unofficial police witness room and shouts her name, saving her from acknowledging it. "See you on the other side."

Belle looks up from her phone and winks at Sophie.

"Check your phone."

Through all of the questioning Sophie can feel Grotty's eyes boring into her, showing his contempt and hatred for her, but she refuses to let it bother her. She didn't get to where she is in her career by being affected by a man and their behaviours, and she be damned if she was going to start now just because she has softened in her love life.

"So Miss Pearsons," Grotty's lawyer speaks again. "I put it to you that during your investigation you struck a deal with my client to run your and Mr. Hamilton's business, but in return you framed him when Mr. Hamilton turned against you and you had to save your own skin." Sophie swallows the laugh that bubbles in her throat. She'd been warned before about laughing at defence lawyers from the witness stand.

"I put it to you, Sir, that that is a made-up story from someone who is trying to save their own skin." The lawyer gives her a look she can't quite interpret.

"Well, isn't it true, Miss Pearsons, that there is currently an investigation into you and your investigation after a complaint was put in against you?" A murmur goes around the courtroom as the Procurator Fiscal jumps to her feet.

"Objection, Miss Pearsons is not the one on trial here and neither is her career." Sophie's blood boils, she hates that she is being put under suspicion in an attempt to keep someone so horrid from being exactly where they should be, behind bars for the rest of his natural life. "This is inadmissible." The PF continues but is cut off by the defence lawyer.

"It is completely admissible, my client's defence-" The sheriff's gruff roar of 'order' brings the bickering lawyers' lips snapping shut.

"Do we have a result from the investigation?" The sheriff directs his question to the PF, but it is Sophie that answers.

"If I may answer Sheriff, the investigation has been completed," she says, "but I do not know the outcome of it. I have been summoned to a meeting once I am finished with court for the day, M'lord." The sheriff furrows his bushy eyebrows then nods his head definitively at Sophie.

"Okay then, we will recess for today and council will meet in my chambers tomorrow morning at nine-thirty sharp with the outcome of Miss Pearsons meeting." He nods his head once more to seal the decision.

The sheriff is taken to chambers and the jury led from court. Sophie dashes out the double doors, blows out her breath and then waits, impatiently, on Belle being told she can leave for the day and her making her way to meet Sophie at the front door.

"What took you so long? Never mind, I know, so do you know the result, is that what the wink was for?" Belle is almost in a full on run to keep up with Sophie's long strides.

"Soph, I ca, can't answ, answer you when, you're walking so fast." They climb into Sophie's Jaguar and Belle pants loudly.

"You are so unfit! Now do you know the result?"

"I am not unfit, I just can't walk as fast as you, wee legs, remember?"

Sophie huffs as she starts her car, taking a second to appreciate the purr of the engine. "but to answer your question, no I don't know the result of the investigation, why would the boss tell me? And by text? No. I just wanted you to know it had concluded and I guessed it would come up in the court. Now are you going to put your foot down so we can both be put out our misery." Sophie didn't have to be asked twice to make her press down on the accelerator.

****

Sophie sits in front of a rather stern looking woman from Professional Standards, trying not to show how nervous she is. She knows the complaint is a made-up story of a desperate man, but would Professional Standards see it that way? She hoped so.

Trying to take her mind from what the stern woman was reading, Sophie starts to study the woman in front of her. Her hair is pinned up, coiffed to perfection, her makeup is light and natural looking. Her pale blue fitted dress was perfectly tailored and brought out the colour of her eyes.

She holds herself in a rigid manner, her every move deliberate and calculated. Sophie estimates the officer's age to be mid-fifties, so understands that her fight to get up the ranks in her career would have been slightly harder than her own, and that is why she is the way she is, like Sophie she would have had to have worked twice as hard as her male counterparts. She also understands that a year ago her own body language would've been that stiff and strained, but now she feels much more relaxed and it happened after she met Ross.

She has tried to fight against it, listened to her long-held belief that she isn't good enough, and couldn't, wouldn't rely on another man. But she has started to think about it all. Could she be stronger with Ross in her life? Not because he was a man and she should have a man in her life, but because she is happy with him, she trusts him, he was there for her even after she pushed him away, twice. Plus he loves her. Loves her for her. And if she is completely honest with herself, she loves him more than she ever thought any person could love another.

The Professional Standards officer clears her throat bringing Sophie back from her musings with a massive smile on her face and a lightness in her heart that she has never felt before, or ever thought would be possible to feel.

"Miss Pearsons, I have the findings here of the complaint that was filed against you." Sophie nods, her heart trying to beat its way out of its home behind her ribs. "Now we made this complaint our first priority due to it being connected to an ongoing court case."

Sophie nods again, then catches herself, she doesn't want to look like a nodding imbecile. "Thank you, I appreciate the promptness of the result." She smiles at the officer, hoping it comes across as sincere and not sarcastic, which is her default smile.

Dynamic Entry

"So as a part of our investigation into the complaint, we looked at your original investigation into Mr. Hamilton as well as the current one, and his connection to Mr. Crossan. We also looked at all your findings along with interviewing your colleagues and senior officers. Now I have to say, not all of them had nice things to say about your attitude towards men sometimes, but they did all say they did not believe the accusations, and they all sang your praises for your dedication to the job, even mentioning that it was to the detriment of your relationships." The officer takes a breath, "I'm going to forgo the full speech and get to the result Miss Pearsons, if that is alright with you?" Sophie shakes her head, muttering noises for the senior officer to continue. "We have dismissed the complaint as a complete fabrication. A story made up by a crook to save his own skin. You are cleared, and are free to go back to full duties, effective immediately." Joy radiates itself through every pore in Sophie's body.

She hadn't thought she had been worried about the result but judging by the relief sweeping over her and the grin on her face, she guesses she was.

"Thank you, Ma'am." Sophie goes to stand but the officer continues to talk, but in a more informal tone so she sits again. "Sophie, if I may, I know it's out of line of me to say this, but... please don't let the job interfere with your life and relationships. Don't end up with the job being your only relationship."

Sophie stares at the woman, surmising that she was being given advice from a lifetime of experience. "No Ma'am, and thank you, for everything." The officer nods at Sophie, dismissing her in a way that would normally get her hackles raised, but she is too busy processing everything that has been said for her brain to demand the eye roll it normally would.

Leaving the meeting her first priority is to find Belle and her DI. She enters their main office and starts to walk towards the office at the back of the room, feeling every set of eyes follow her, as she knew would happen.

She steps up to her DI's open door and he looks up from the paperwork he was reading with a twinkle in his eyes. "Well?"

A grin breaks out of Sophie's face that she can't fight, so much for playing it cool she thinks. "They have deemed it the crock of shit that it is. I am cleared to go back to full duties effective immediately." The DI moves from his desk, shaking Sophie's hand before pulling her into a backslapping man hug, bringing on a giggle and an eye roll from her.

"I knew it! Fantastic news." Sophie steps back feeling the sting of tears at the back of her eyes.

She fights them, she may have accepted how much she loves Ross; all the mushy feelings that come along with that, and the fact that the job is not going to be the be all and end all in her life, but she will not turn into a cry baby in the office.

She looks around the office to see every one of her colleagues standing on their feet applauding and cheering her, with Belle moving towards her, arms outstretched to embrace her. Those tears are getting harder to fight she thinks.

CHAPTER FORTY-FIVE

Sean brings over the last of the pints to their usual table, sitting down with a slurp of his own pint.

"So that's it all done with now? Professional Standards worked out it was all crap?"

Sophie places her pint down, the light feeling in her chest continuing. "The complaint yes, the court case, no. That is still ongoing."

Belle is almost bouncing in her seat. "Oh my god, you should've seen everyone in the office when Sophie came back in to tell the boss the result. They all sat silent as she spoke to him and then they were all on their feet cheering and clapping, like a standing ovation. She got a standing ovation in the office. Then they all came up and hugged her, telling her how they never believed the accusations for a second and how much of an amazing police officer she is, and that if wasn't for her we wouldn't have had two, yes two, massive arrests and they are all confident that they will be converted into convictions." Belle is almost out of breath after her monologue.

Ross places his arm around Sophie's shoulders and pulls her into his side, placing a kiss on her forehead as he smiles.

"I'm guessing you hated every second of those long moments of being hugged?" Belle bounces more as she answers for Sophie.

"Oh she did, but she accepted them all with a smile. Even the weird new guy that sits in the corner."

Sophie snorts a laugh. "It was surreal, if I'm being honest. I didn't think half the people in the office liked me and I as sure as hell didn't think the new guy even knew my name!"

Belle bounces more. "Of course they like you. They might be a bit frightened of you, but we get asked to go for drinks after work all the time, well I mean they ask me if we want to go for drinks, and I've just gave up asking you if you want to go as you give me that look that you're giving me right now."

Sophie smooths out her frown, then returns it. "Well don't think that just because I let them all shake my hand or hug me, that means I'm going to be more social with them. I may be happier, but I have not gone soft!" All three of her now family beam at her, as Belle sniffles and wipes her eyes. Sophie rolls hers. "I'm going to put some music on," She turns to Sean, "make sure your girlfriend has control of her emotions and of herself for that matter for me coming back please." Her sarcastic tone is more tongue in cheek and everyone at the table knows it. Sean gives her a salute with his best military 'yes ma'am!' as answer. Sophie laughs as she walks towards the juke box situated on the back wall of the bar.

Seconds later she feels arms snake around her waist and she doesn't flinch or feel self-conscious, or even annoyed at the public display of affection from Ross; even the fact that she knew it was Ross without looking didn't even freak her out the way it would have once upon a time.

"You're happy and you're admitting it?" He places his lips to her neck, and she leans her head to the side, giving him better access to the spot on her neck that makes her shiver.

Normally it was only in the privacy of them being alone did Sophie ever let him nuzzle like this. Something had changed in Sophie and she thought that it was for the better.

She turns in his arms. "I am happy, and I'm not afraid of it! Or afraid of us being an us because you Mr. Andrews, I do believe you have performed a dynamic entry into my heart." She goes onto her tiptoes and places a kiss on her lips. "Now pick some tunes before it's bedtime." She turns back to the jukebox and wiggles her hips against his, teasing him with what bedtime would consist off.

"We are an us again?" She leans her neck to the side again.

"If you want it too?" She holds her breath.

"Oh hell yes Miss Pearsons." She blows out the breath. They were together and she wasn't running away.

****

Sophie sits in the witness box the next day wishing the lawyers would hurry up with their questions, it was already midday and not much had moved on.

Eventually the sheriff dismisses the lawyers from his bench to sit back at their respected tables, then his booming voice brings everyone to attention.

"Normally I wouldn't allow an officer of the law to be questioned in this manner, as it has been pointed out, it is not Miss Pearsons career that is on trial here, but on this occasion I am going to allow it as I think it is pertinent to this case. So if you will counsellor it is your witness." He nods to the defence lawyer and Sophie knows what's coming, but with her head held high and steel in her spine she gives him a smile.

"So Miss Pearsons, yesterday I put it to you that everything my client was found with in Mr. Hamilton's place of business was actually yours and Mr. Hamilton's stock and so my client, Mr. Crossan, is entirely innocent." Sophie continues to smile all whilst reverting to digging her nails into the palm of her hand, only this time it's not in anger but because she is trying her damnedest not to laugh or roll her eyes out loud.

"Yes, well, your client did put in a formal complaint regarding this matter to my superiors who have, as you know, finished a detailed and thorough investigation and have concluded that the story is a complete fabrication. Oh and I have also been cleared to return to full duties, as of yesterday afternoon, you know, just for the record." The lawyer opens his mouth to talk, but Sophie continues, not giving him a chance. "And I'm sure under the Freedom of Information Act Scotland Two Thousand and Two, you could request the report. There was nothing left uninvestigated or swept under any carpet, Sir!" She smiles at the lawyer again, a sickly-sweet smile to give the sarcastic 'sir' it's intended sting.

The lawyer snaps his mouth shut. There is no come back to Sophie's words. He raises his hand to waist height, palms up in a 'that's all' gesture and turns to the sheriff.

"I have no more questions Sheriff." He sits back down with a tight smile to his client in the dock, who is at that moment glaring at the lawyer with undisguised hatred.

The sheriff thanks Sophie for her time, then dismisses her from the witness stand. With a respectful nod and a small smile, she thanks the sheriff and leaves, blowing all the air from her lungs once she is free from the courtroom.

This was a ritual she had developed over the years of giving evidence. To Sophie, she was ridding herself of the stale air of the courtroom and the whole case in general.

She leaves the building and heads towards the Tango Café, a coffee shop next door to the court that had been there since the building opened in the early 60s and the décor looks like it had never been changed in all those years, to wait on Belle as was their routine if they were giving evidence on the same day.

She settles into a booth with her milky tea and feels at peace. She may still have Jason's trial to endure, but with all the evidence they gathered, it should be an open and shut case and without her name, job, or reputation being called into disrepute.

CHAPTER FORTY-SIX

Grotty's trial continues with each witness putting another nail in his figurative coffin. Each time he catches the eye of one of the jurors he can see their contempt staring back at him. Each minute is longer than the last, and with each passing day Grotty feels more agitation, which in turn brings more feelings of anger towards Jason and that bitch policewoman Sophie.

If it wasn't for Jason being so desperate in his need to get Sophie in his bed, he wouldn't have taken his eye off the ball so much. Grotty wouldn't be in this position and he would be in the middle of implementing the rest of his original plan to take Jason's business from him, one contact and contract at a time until he had nothing left.

Now all he wants to do is take Jason's life, then the business will be his for the taking, even if he has to run it from behind bars. He is a man of means and has the contacts to run everything both inside and outside Barlinnie Prison.

A pull on his arm from the prisoner security officer sitting beside him brings Grotty back from his plans and musings. He looks around the court to find they reason for the rather rude interruption and sees the sheriff being brought back onto the bench.

Grotty stands with a lopsided grin. Everyone is waiting on him, even the sheriff, just what he likes. Once the sheriff is settled back into his seat he starts to speak directly to Grotty.

Dynamic Entry

"Well, Mr. Crossan, now that I have your attention, your case has brought about a first in my courtroom more than once, and if we could get on with things, I have a lunch to get." The sheriff turns his head from Grotty to face the jury and directs his next words at the foreperson. "Has the jury reached a verdict on all charges?" Grotty listens with a smug smile on his lips.

No matter the outcome he has plans, but as each guilty verdict comes through, he realises some of his plans will need to go onto a back burner for a few months until he can get through whatever crappy, limited sentence the sheriff can give him. "Mr. Crossan, that is certainly a list of crimes, so I think for justice to be served properly I will pass your sentencing up to High Court as nothing I can give you will ever be enough. Take him down." Now that was something he wasn't expecting.

Being tried in the kangaroo court is one thing, but to be sentenced in High Court, a real court, that could turn out so much worse than he was expecting.

Grotty realises he is going to have to make new plans, ones that gets him out from behind the bars of Her Majesty's Barlinnie Prison which is exactly where he was headed back to.

****

Every morning Jason wheels himself to the 'social area' of the prison after breakfast for an hour before heading back to his cell.

His thoughts that he wouldn't be sent back to prison had dwindled whilst he was in hospital. He had argued with the doctor's that there was something seriously wrong with his heart, he, Jason Hamilton, would not take something so weak as a panic attack, but they insisted that there was no sign of any issues in his ECG

326

and no sign of a heart attack. After that they unceremoniously handed him over to the prisoner transport guards with a handful of leaflets on panic attacks and stress management, and so here he is, behind bars in Her Majesty's Prison Barlinnie again.

The way it was looking these steel walls would be his home for the foreseeable future if he was found guilty once his trial got underway again. He had convinced himself that they would at least make him do any sentence in a hospital, he had even thought that if he plead guilty he would get a reduced sentence, he'd spend his days in hospital where there would be very little security and so be able to continue running his business whilst serving his time. But as he sits looking at the greyness around him, he realises that that is not an option. No, his only option is to hope for an easy jury or that Sophie hadn't found out everything about his business, but he highly doubted the latter.

He had stupidly taken her into his inner circle, and then tried to incriminate her with disposing of a corpse. Anger bubbles in his chest as he remembers everything he showed her, all the evidence he had handed her, and he still never got to have her body under his. With his anger getting the better of him Jason pushes himself off towards the gym to lift some weights.

The gym and weights are going to be a godsend to him if he is sent down for any length of time.

Not looking where is going, he knocks into another inmate's legs as he passes them.

"Haw! Watch where yir fuckin' goin' dipshit!"

Jason slows and turns his chair around in one fluid movement until he is facing the offending inmate. "Or what? You gonna start a fight with the guy in the wheelchair? Well? I didn't think so." Jason pushes himself away again, making people dodge him as he goes.

Dynamic Entry

The inmate stands staring at the receding figure of Jason as he mutters how 'that idiot needs to be taken down a peg or two, wheelchair or no wheelchair' then stalks off back to his cell.

Once in the gym, Jason makes his way over to the weights. It's the only thing he can use in the gym, but thankfully they were his main love when he trained daily, so he didn't feel like he was missing out on as much as he could be.

He picks out the weights he needs, placing them in his lap and wheels himself over to the mirror to watch himself do his reps. Even in the chair he likes the way his muscles bunch and ripple, plus the burn reminds him that no matter what he is, alive, and he will survive.

****

Grotty makes his way back into the prison still in a bit of a daze from the outcome of his trial. Once the complaint was dismissed, he knew they would find him guilty. He knew the complaint was a long shot, but the sentencing going to high court, that was a shock, and a shock that has him worried.

His lawyer did explain that it may not be as bad as he fears, but he couldn't shake the sick feeling in his stomach about it all.

Getting settled into his cell he lies on his bunk bed trying to get his thoughts in order before he needs to face people at dinner time, but his cell mate has different ideas as he charges in.

"Right, that pal ye yours needs taken down full stop. Chair or nae fuckin' chair. So whit you gonna do about it?" Grotty squeezes his eyes shut, he doesn't want to deal with Jason or anything connected to him at that moment in time, but like his cellmate was saying, Jason did need taken down from the pedestal he had put himself on, Grotty just didn't know how he was going to do it, yet.

"He's no friend of mine. I may have worked for him, but I never fuckin' liked him, but to answer your question. I don't know what I'm going to do about him, though I will deal with him, just give me time." And wasn't he going to have loads of that now.

CHAPTER FORTY-SEVEN

The day of the presentation has arrived, and Sophie's stomach is doing somersaults, not because of the award for bravery, but because her two worlds were colliding again. She was about to introduce Ross, her boyfriend, to all her colleagues, the people whose lives she was protecting when she was undercover and lying to Ross.

This was the first time in her whole career that her job life and her personal life were going to mingle and become one. Her thoughts go back to her life being like her father's. Two separate lives being led by one person, but now she realises that her life is completely different, she has a personal life to share with someone and a career life that is part of that, and if she is being honest with herself, she is the happiest she has ever been.

Ross walks into Sophie's living room and sees her standing staring at herself in the mirror like she is trying to solve all of the world's problems by herself, and then she smiles. Her shoulders relax and she smiles. A real smile, one that lights up her full face and makes her stunning silver blue eyes sparkle. His breath hitches in his throat at the sight of her. She was stunning looking in her dress uniform, but when she smiles her natural, full, uninhibited smile she is breathtaking. He clears his throat, not wanting to startle he.

"You look gorgeous, and smart, and I am so unbelievably proud of you." He walks towards her as he speaks and wraps his arms around her waist, leaning in for a kiss.

"I was only doing my job, and I didn't do it very well or you wouldn't have gotten shot in the first place." Guilt still eats at her that she put Ross in Jason's sights, but Ross isn't for letting her keep her guilt.

"Hey, we've discussed this. Me getting shot was not your fault. You tried to keep Jason from me and Sean. You saved Sean's business from being fleeced of thousands of pounds in the protection racket, which in turn probably saved Sean from going to prison for assault or worse, and then you jumped in front of a bullet to save me. The whole situation is not your fault, it was the crazy gun toting, gangster man's fault, so, enough of that. Go accept your award and be amazing doing it." He kisses her lightly, but deepens it, pouring his every feeling for her into it, but she pulls away.

"Behave, I don't want my make-up smudged and I certainly don't want this bun to fall out. It takes me the best part of half an hour to get it all pinned up, plus there will be plenty of time for that afterwards." She quickly gives him another chaste kiss, then turns to grab her handbag.

Ross lets out a huff. "Fine, but promise me I can unpin your hair and take your uniform off."

She blushes, normally a statement like that would have her angry, but coming from Ross it makes her heart beat faster and a smile curl at her lips. "Maybe," She winks at him coyly. "Now move or we'll be late and you won't get to see me accept anything." Giving her a quick salute Ross lifts his cashmere overcoat and walks from the house, closing over the door behind him and climbs into Sophie's Jaguar.

"You want me to drive?" He asks with his tongue firmly in his cheek.

"Nope!" Her word is short and clipped, but not meant in a hurtful way.

"Am I ever going to drive your car?"

Sophie looks over at her boyfriend and smiles, a sweet, loving smile. "Em, let me think, eh, no. I wouldn't be holding my breath if I was you." She laughs feeling free and happy for the first time in her life.

Walking into the room where the ceremony was being held, she directs Ross to a seat at the end of the row market reserved. Ross looks at her, a concerned look crossing his features.

"This is reserved." Sophie nods.

"Yes for colleagues and family." She gives him a kiss. "I'll be walking in on ceremony so stay here and I'll get you when it's all over."

****

The word 'family' hits Ross in his chest although he tries to hide the force of it. He is so proud at how far Sophie has come in her trust in him that he has become her family.

He bites the inside of his cheek to keep his emotions in check, he didn't want to show his girlfriend up by not being muscularly and blubbering all over the place. Again, he can hear his ex-girlfriend scream how weak he is, but he pushes it away. He is safe in the knowledge that Sophie loves him for him, and his body is perfect exactly as it is.

"Hey," Sophie brings him from his memories, "thank you for being here." He smiles, cupping her face in his hands.

"I wouldn't miss it." He kisses her quickly. "Now go do what you need to do and I'll be right here waiting on you."

Fiona Morgan

****

Sophie marches down the space between the chairs with the other officers being awarded that day. She had refused to accept her commendation if Ross wasn't getting one, but her boss and Belle convinced her that that would not look good on her record, plus her DI promised her he would move heaven and earth to get Ross the recognition he deserves.

So with that in mind she stands in her suffocatingly starched uniform and listens to the waffling that the higher ranks love to do in these situations.

The ceremony continues until everyone has received their awards except Sophie. The brass that is talking attracts her attention when they ask her DI to step up to say a few words, something that is unheard of at ceremonies.

"I know this is not normal," her DI starts "but I couldn't let this occasion pass by without saying a few words about Detective Constable Sophie Pearsons." He stops to clear his throat before continuing, "Sophie is one of the most hardworking, thorough investigators I have ever had the pleasure of working with. She is first in the office in the morning, and last out at night. There has been many times I have woken her at her desk as once a case gets a hold of her there is nothing stopping her from bringing it to a close, which is why I use the term 'working with' even though I am her superior. I know Sophie is more than competent to do her job, investigate every side of the case and bring it to its close with arrests and convictions, even sometimes to the detriment of her own personal life, which is why I see her as an equal and not a subordinate."

He takes another breath and Sophie is sure she sees him flick his thumb under his eye as to remove a tear.

"Then she went far above and beyond the call of duty, as she always does, but this time it nearly cost her her new relationship as well as her life, and that is why it is an honour to be presenting Sophie with this award for Bravery and Meritorious Conduct." He focuses his attention onto Sophie before talking again. "But, Sophie, can I remind you that the Armed Response Unit are trained to do dynamic entries with bulletproof vests, so please don't jump in front of a bullet again, I don't think my heart can take it." A laugh goes up from around the room and Sophie can feel a blush creep over her face, although she isn't sure if it's from embarrassment or annoyance, even if there is a touch of pride in there too.

Not only was she getting recognised for her dedication to the job, but also as an equal in the force. "So without further ado I present Detective Constable Sophie Pearsons with the Bravery and Meritorious Award." A cheer goes up in the room and emotion clogs in her throat, a feeling she still can't get used to, but not feeling so weak for feeling it.

Sophie walks over and accepts her award to more applause and cheering. She turns to get her photograph taken and catches Ross smiling at her as he surreptitiously tries to wipe his eyes.

Her own eyes pool as a rush of love for her boyfriend washes over her. He may have made her feel her feelings, but they have made her stronger, as does he.

After all the photographs have been taken, her DI stands again and asks for quiet in the room.

"Our presentations aren't quite over, I am led to believe that the next recipient of our bravery award is aware that he is about to be presented, but I have my doubts." Sophie bends her head, her face flaming with guilt. "Anyway, it is my proud honour to present this award for bravery to someone who risked their life to save a shop full of other people, including at that time an unborn baby, from an extremely dangerous man who was brandishing a gun. He tried to trade his life for all of theirs and received a gunshot wound for it. So could Ross Andrews please step forward." Sophie has been watching Ross' face throughout the DI's speech and saw every emotion pass over his features.

Her tears are flowing and no amount of dabbing with her fingers is keeping up with them. Thank goodness for waterproof mascara, she thinks.

****

Ross walks to the front of the room in a daze and shakes hands with everyone there then accepts his award. He looks quickly at Sophie and his heart swells, even though she blindsided him, again. Only this time he couldn't be angry at her for this, and now he understood why she was so adamant that he bought a new suit for the day.

He snorts out a laugh at the memory and turns to get his own photos taken. The ceremony ends and as everyone makes their way from the room, Ross remains standing stunned at his award, Sophie makes her way towards him looking sheepish, he smiles at her, letting her know he isn't angry.

He desperately wants to take her in his arms and kiss her senseless, but he knows that it is probably not the time or place and not something Sophie would be comfortable with. It is her work and all her colleagues are milling about, as are her bosses. He stands even more stunned when she wraps her arms around his neck and pulls his lips down to hers.

****

The wolf whistle that comes from Belle makes Sophie break the kiss. She was so proud of Ross and then so happy that he wasn't angry with her that she couldn't help herself.

"Sorry." She grins with a twinkle in her eyes, that may still be the remnants of tears.

"Don't ever be sorry for kissing me like that." Ross smiles back.

"Belle and I are going to change then we are all going for a meal."

Ross scrunches his eyebrows. "All? Change? I thought I was taking off-"

"Aye, all!" She cuts him off before he can finish his sentence. "Sean is behind you; he came to see you get your award."

Ross whips round and sees his best friend standing with a grin the size of the river Clyde on his face. "Did everyone know about this but me?"

Sophie shrugs innocently. "Maybe. I wanted it to be a surprise, and I wasn't accepting mine if you didn't receive yours."

"You put my name forward?"

She nods, emotion yet again catching in her throat. "I love you so much. After everything you still put others first." She shrugs again.

"You went through lots and deserve the award just as much as anyone, more even as it's not your job. Now I'm going to get changed for our night out," she steps closer to him hold the lapels of the well-fitting black suit she convinced him to buy, "if you want, I will get back into the uniform later." She drops another kiss on his stunned lips and walks from the room.

CHAPTER FORTY-EIGHT

"Right Grotty, he's at the gym again, driving into people, clippin' ankles like it's a fuckin' game. I mean I know he's in a wheelchair and it's a lot to come to terms with being paralysed and then ending up in the slammer, but come oan tae fuck, it's no oor fault. Someone has tae put a stop tae it. He needs told it's no oan, or even just taken out all the gither." The last bit is muttered under the inmate's breath, though Grotty hears it and takes his words on board.

"Okay fine, I'll go and talk to him, see what I can do."

Grotty storms from his cell and heads towards the gym. Annoyance Is turning to anger which turns to rage as soon as Grotty's gaze finds Jason sitting by the mirror pumping weights like he was on the outside, posing in a private gym instead of in Barlinnie Prison after ruining Grotty's plans to take over his side of the Glasgow underworld.

"Jason!" Grotty growls loudly, "What the fuck d'you think you're playing at?"

Jason places the dumbbell in his lap and turns his chair round to face the man who he trusted with his business and who screwed him over. He's been waiting on an opportunity just like this. A quick look around tells Jason that the gym in is quiet, enough. "Now Grotty, whatever do you mean? I'm not playing at anything. I am however trying to work out what you thought you were playing at by transferring all my deals over to yourself, eh? Trying to steal my business whilst I'm lying on my back in a hospital bed, paralysed?" He pushes himself over further to Grotty. "So tell me Grotty, what were you playing at?" His voice was steely cold and dangerous sounding, but Grotty wasn't frightened of Jason, he never was.

"Well it wasn't like you could control your business even when you were able bodied and free, never mind disabled and banged up. If it wasn't for you thinking with your dick, neither of us would be in here. So, now that you can't think with that, or use it for that matter, you want to stop with blaming everyone in here. Stop with using your chair as a battering ram."

"Or what? I'm still your boss Grotty. I never stopped being that just because I'm in this contraption and behind these bars."

Grotty leans down, holding one arm of the chair to growl into Jason's ear. "You're no fuckin' boss of mine. You're a fuckup. You were a fuckup the first time I met you when you first got to Glasgow to escape your death in South Africa and you're still a fuckup. One word from me to the polis and they'll have you back on a flight home where you can rot in hell in their jail, and if there is justice in this world, your old friends will get a hold of you and finish the job that that idiot you gave a gun to started."

Jason lifts the dumbbell in his lap and swings it until it connects with Grotty's temple. He's thankful that he's kept up with his upper body strength as every ounce of that strength is put into his swing. It connects with Grotty's head with a satisfying crunch, a splattering of blood and a grunt of finality from Grotty as he falls towards Jason sitting in his chair. As Grotty falls, the momentum of his swing tips them both over until Jason and his chair lands beside Grotty's prone body.

Within seconds five different inmates, who had been hovering around the gym watching things unfold, descend on Jason. They drag him from his chair until he is lying just as prone as Grotty's dead body and then they start raining down kicks and punches on his body, all aimed precisely above his waist, all over his back and torso. There is no point kicking a paralysed man in the legs.

A minute later the gym is flooded with prison guards, all pulling the riled-up prisoners off of the completely still body of Jason, and radioing for medics. Two dead looking bodies is not good news for either the inmates, who are still fighting to get back to give Jason one last kick, or the staff who will undoubtedly all be dragged into an investigation for not only a fight breaking out on their shift, but a fight that has ended up in at least one dead body on their hands.

Jason wakes lying flat on his back, again. He quickly realises he's in hospital, and he assumes it's the Royal Infirmary as that is the closest one to the prison, plus the room isn't quite as shiny and new looking as the Queen Elizabeth University Hospital.

His next thought was 'not again' as the feeling of déjà vu slips through his system. He tries to move his arms – nothing. Fear and ice replace the blood flowing through his veins, he has felt this nothingness before with the paralysis in his legs, and now his arms.

He stops trying to move and concentrates, just like he did the last time he was in hospital, only this time he is trying to feel any sensation in his upper body and limbs. He senses nothing, feels nothing.

Lifting his head as much as he can, he strains his eyes to look at his fingers as he tries to wiggle them, twitch them, anything, but there's nothing. They lie there, motionless and useless. In fact, his whole body remains motionless. A laugh bubbles from his chest, which quickly turns into a cackle, a manic cackle of madness.

He has spent every day of his adult life building his body to be the strongest it could be. He treated it with respect, only giving it a boost with steroids to help it be the temple he was proud of, but for what? To get shot and then take a beating that breaks his body so badly that it stops working. Just stops being able to do anything.

His laughing brings on tears. They run down the side of his face and neck pooling in his ears and there is nothing he can do about it as a female nurse walks into the room to check his obs. He curses.

"Now Mr. Hamilton, no language like that." She steps to the side of the bed. "Are you okay?" Without another word she takes a tissue and starts to wipe away his tears.

"I'm fine! I was laughing."

"So I heard," The nurse goes about her job checking Jason's vitals and talking to him in a kind and quiet manner, "now, doctor will be around soon to check on you." She turns to leave.

"Could I get some water?" His voice is raspy from overuse with his manic laughing. She turns back to him with sympathy in her eyes.

"I'm sorry Mr. Hamilton, you have a nothing-by-mouth order from doctor and a nasogastric feeding tube running from your nose to your stomach. Doctor will explain everything when she comes around." She gives him a tight smile then walks away, leaving him with the knowledge that his body is so badly broken he has to be fed through a tube.

****

Jason wakes for the second day in hospital and can feel his dark mood has darkened more. The doctor did her rounds the day before to explain that the new injuries he sustained during his beating had indeed compounded the original injury to his spine, so much so it had brought on complete paralysis from his neck down.

She then went on to say that they couldn't say for sure if the paralysis would be permanent due to the amount of swelling on and around his spine from the amount and the force of the blows he'd received, so until all the swelling reduces it is a waiting and hoping game.

Hope he did not have, at that moment in time he felt completely hopeless and helpless. He had had the same feelings the last time, but it was a hundredfold this time as he can move literally nothing except his head and even that was awkward with the feeding tube.

Two police officers enter his room and lean slightly over the bed so Jason can see them.

"Mr. Hamilton, I am Detective Constable Ben Loughran and this is Detective Constable Sian Young, we're here to ask you a few questions about the incident you were involved in, in Her Majesty's Prison Barlinnie. Jason makes a noise at the back of his throat which causes him to cough, the officers stand awkwardly looking at each other until he stops and catches his breath again.

"What's there to talk about, all they arseholes in the jail tried to kill me and as it is, they've paralysed me. I want them charged with attempted murder, injury to the impairment of life, assault and a hate crime."

Ben and Sian give each other a look of disbelief. "Everyone involved is being questioned, Mr. Hamilton, and arrests will be made once we have a clearer picture of the situation." Sian talks, but Jason only grunts at her.

She continues. "So, sir, if you could talk us through the events of the incident in question, in your own words."

Jason spends the next hour telling the officers his sob story of the discrimination against his disability and the bullying by every prisoner in his wing.

He explains how it all stemmed from Grotty and his jealousy and spite of Jason's business and the fact they were both imprisoned. He went on to make it abundantly clear that Grotty had blamed him for his own arrest and how laughable that excuse was. That was the only time either officer agreed with anything Jason had said.

"Okay, Mr. Hamilton, I think that covers the attack on yourself. We will get your statement typed up and get it back to you to sign, eh —" Radio cackle cuts off Ben from having to correct his faux pas. He looks towards Sian who replies to the cackle and walks to the other side of the room. After a minute she turns around and nods to Ben.

Ben turns to Jason.

"Mr. Hamilton, I am arresting you for the murder of Robert Crossan.," Jason looks between the two officers.

"Who the fuck is Robert Crossan?"

The officers share another eye roll. "Grotty, Jason. You are getting arrested for murdering Grotty." A manic laugh comes from Jason's chest. He can't believe how his life in Scotland has turned exactly into the nightmare he escaped from in South Africa, only this time there is no escape.

CHAPTER FORTY-NINE

5 Months Later

Sophie and Ross both wake up in his bedroom and he pulls her into him, kissing the side of her neck and bare shoulder.

"So one year today since we met. It's been a quick year don't you think?" Sophie turns in his arms to face him.

"I don't know about quick, eventful for sure."

Ross gives a snort. "That is very true. So what do you want to do tonight?"

"Tonight? I've got court today to give evidence against Jason, but, I mean, are we using today as our date, our, this is the day we got together date, after, everything."

Ross brushes her hair from her face. "Do you not want to celebrate us meeting?"

"I do, I just feel that when we got back together was more binding, for us."

Ross screws his features into confusion. "Binding?"

Sophie laughs, "Aye, I was definitely me and —" He kisses her to stop her talking more.

"You were always you in the relationship, regardless of what stupid, hurtful things I said, I knew deep down you were always you."

"I was, though looking back I was still closed off to the thought of love and a serious relationship, even though I was getting better at it. Now though, I'm open to it all."

Ross' heartbeat skips at her words. "All?"

He queries, she nods, her emotions shining through her eyes.

"Okay, well in that case I think we can celebrate tonight for us meeting each other and the date we got back together we can celebrate our together anniversary," he says.

Sophie gives another laugh as happiness bubbles inside her. "Okay, we will celebrate both, and with any luck we can celebrate the end of my involvement in anything Jason Hamilton related tonight." Ross kisses her deeply, taking the name away from her lips.

"Even better," he says. "What time do you need to leave? I think we should bind this binding fully." He nips at her bottom lip as he pulls her on top of him."

She playfully slaps his chest at his joking use of her words. "Not for a bit, and I can take my tea in with me in my travel cup." She leans down and kisses him soundly.

****

Belle sits in the café across from the court waiting on Sophie. She wondered why they had to go through the rigmarole of trying Jason when the evidence against him was stacked so high, plus now he had another murder charge to face, bringing his total to five. Why couldn't they just keep him locked up for the rest of his natural life?

But as a police officer, she knows that that's not how the justice system works, that everyone is innocent until proven guilty, and everyone is entitled to a fair and just trial. She just wished they would hurry up with the guilty part so they could all put this case to bed once and for all, leaving them free to get on with their lives again, and other cases. She was getting bored with this one.

Fiona Morgan

****

Sophie enters the café and smiles at the older woman behind the counter.

"My usual please Jean, but best make it a massive pot of tea please, we've a lot of talking to do." She smiles at the older woman who smiles and nods back at her.

"Nae bother hen, coming right over."

"How did it go?" Belle doesn't wait until Sophie has sat down before asking, "was he there? I'm raging they decided they didn't need me. I've been hiding out in here all morning telling the boss you'd need someone with you when you got out."

Sophie's eyes widen. "Don't throw me under the bus, just 'cause you canny be arsed going back to work. Did the boss actually believe you? That I'd need you, or anyone for that matter?"

Belle snorts out a laugh. "No, of course not. No, his words were, and I quote, 'aye right! Sophie may have mellowed in her private life, but no in her professional one.' I agreed with him and he let me wait about for you as long as I did some digging online for another case, but never mind that, you dodged every other question. So out with the rest of it." Jean places Sophie's order down to her with a warm smile and discreetly moves away.

Sophie nods her thanks for her food then turns back to Belle. "Very well. Yes, it was weird, very weird giving evidence without the accused glaring at you, but it was also a bit freeing. The defence lawyer was still trying to be as hard on some of the points, but others I got the feeling he was paying it lip service. Though to be fair, he must know the odds are stacked so high against his client and not having Jason glare at him from the dock was probably taking the heat off of him a bit. In fact, not having him there is probably a blessing for both sides. I mean, you know what that stare is like."

"Aye I do, though that's about all he can do now. There's no power behind that stare anymore. Not after the boys in the Bar L got through with him. I would say karma, but I don't know if I'm allowed to say that, professionally I mean."

Sophie laughs. "I'll not tell anyone, but I agree, and he won't be going free any time soon either this time, between this trial and the other murder trial. I think for sure we did our jobs right this time."

"You did your job right the last time, the case going to hell in a handbasket and him not getting a jail term is not your responsibility, but, hell yes, we absolutely did do our job right. Cheers!" They clink their chipped mugs together, sloshing their contents and laughing. "I hear you and lover boy have a big date night planned?" Belle comically wiggles her eyebrows. "I don't know about big date night, but yes, we are going out. You and Sean want to double?"

Belle shakes her head furiously. "Oh no. This night is all yours. A year since youse first met and your first date, plus your involvement in this crappy case coming to an end, all in the one day? No, me and my man will leave it to you both. We are having a stay in date night, you and yours go and enjoy yourself. You are off tomorrow, aren't you?" The women drain their cups and stand, leaving their payment on the chipped yellow Formica table.

"I am from this second on holiday for one week. We both are actually." Belle stops dead in her tracks, dramatising her actions of feeling Sophie's forehead.

"Be still my beating heart. You, Sophie Pearsons, have taken annual leave without threat of job loss? Wonders will never cease."

Sophie slaps her hand away. "Shut up! But yes, I — we, have taken the week off together."

Belle grabs her best friend into a bear hug. "That man has been the best thing for you. I love this new you."

Sophie hugs her back. "Me too."

CHAPTER FIFTY

Ross looks in the mirror in his room and blows out his cheeks. He is sure he is more nervous getting ready for this date than he was on that first night he was meeting Sophie.

He looks behind him at his bed and lets out a laugh. His clothes are strewn over the covers just like the last time, only this time he can also see evidence of Sophie in his room. A hairbrush sitting on the chest of drawers, her moisturiser on the bedside table on her side of the bed.

He also has memories of her in his bed, of seeing her sleep, completely relaxed and at peace. He smiles as his heart swells with how much love he has for her and how grateful he is that they have made it through everything and are back together, forever.

Having decided on black jeans and a dark purple shirt, Ross gives himself one last appraising look in the mirror, then leaves his bedroom and the mess of a bed. He promises himself he will tidy it all tomorrow; tonight he has a room booked at Blythswood Square Hotel for the night and he had told Sophie to pack an overnight bag and give it to him the night before, so once he checks them in, and sorts the room he would meet her and get their 'first day of meeting' anniversary started.

****

Sophie takes a look at her new dress. It's a dress she would never normally wear, but after an impulse buy and some convincing from Belle she is feeling a million dollars in the tight fighting black mini dress.

She has finished with the case that nearly cost her everything, including her life and the life of the man she loves, and she was apparently having an overnight stay in a hotel room with that very man, so she intends to enjoy every second of this night.

She walks into The Pub and heads turn. It's a warm enough night that she can forego a jacket. She fights the instinct to pull her dress down and walks to the bar knowing she is looking good with her hair styled in her natural curls, another first for her.

Sean growls at the two young workmen sitting at the bar whose eyes are popping from their heads as Sophie walks towards them. They turn their heads away only to look back immediately to watch her again. Sean walks from behind the bar and greets her with a hug.

"You look amazing! Curls and everything, wow! You want your usual or something more ladylike?" He laughs as he dodges the half-hearted punch she throws at him with a growl. He pours her a pint of lager and she thanks him sweetly. The workmen still stare, but she ignores them, nothing is going to break this good mood.

"Belle in yet?" Sean shakes his head in a 'no' gesture, "Okay, well I'll sit in my usual spot to wait. It's more ladylike up there." She sticks her tongue out at Sean and laughs as she walks away, her red pointed stilettos clicking on the wooden floor.

One of the workmen lifts his pint and goes to follow but Sean whistles on him.

"I wouldn't if I was you. One, she's like my sister, two, she's in a relationship with my best friend and three, well, she'd rip your balls off and hand them back to you with a smile and take your pint as payment. Take my advice, sit your arse back down and enjoy your night with your balls intact." Sophie hears what Sean says and chuckles to herself as she sits to watch for her date arriving.

She has spent years worrying that falling in love would make her too soft and vulnerable, but here she is in love and still being described as a ball buster. She hasn't lost herself. Life is good she thinks to herself.

****

Ross walks into the bar, his eyes going directly to Sophie's table and his heart skips a beat as his breath hitches. It takes him a second, but eventually he forces his feet to move towards the table. Sophie smiles up at him as he approaches her, her silver blue eyes glittering with love and happiness, her smile; her real smile, lighting up her face. She is here, waiting on him, looking stunning, smiling at him like he is the only person in this world and all with her honey blonde natural curls bouncing around her shoulders.

"You look, your hair. You are...will you marry me?" Oh hell, the words he had wanted kept in until the end of the night were out. He couldn't have stopped them even if he tried.

Sophie stares at Ross uncertainty painted all over her face.

"I'm sorry, what?"

His heart sinks, but he pushes on. "I didn't mean to ask like this, I have a full night planned and a room at Blythswood —"

Sophie laughs, throwing her head back and belly laughs. Ross throws a look to Sean who is staring at the scene unfolding without knowing what is going on.

"Sophie why are you laughing? Is that a no? Is marrying me that funny?" Old insecurities fight to take over his thoughts, but he pushes them away.

Sophie composes herself and pulls Ross into the seat next to her, holding onto his hands.

"No I'm not laughing at you, or us, or your proposal, if that is what you did actually ask. I'm laughing because you are taking me to Blythswood Square. That is where most of that horrid case was based. Sorry, I shouldn't laugh, it's just a funny coincidence, and maybe a sign that I can make good memories in a place that I thought would only remind me evil."

"So?"

"So, you gonna ask me properly?" Ross swallows as he pulls Sophie onto her feet and places a light kiss on the tip of her nose before dropping to one knee without letting go of her hands.

"Sophie Pearsons, I love you with all my heart and soul. We have been through more in this first year than most couples go through in — well, ever, and we are still here, still together. So will you make this night the best night ever by saying you will be my wife. Be with me for the rest of our lives, Sophie will you marry me?"

****

Belle walks through the door and sees Sean staring up at Sophie's table, she turns her head to take in the scene of Ross on one knee gazing up at Sophie. She holds her breath knowing this could go one of two ways. A shout leaves her throat as she sees Sophie nod her head followed by Ross grabbing her in a bear hug and twirling them both around. Belle rushes to the bar and Sean.

Dynamic Entry

"What's happening? Did what I think happen actually happen?"

Sean takes his girlfriend into his arms and smiles at her. "I have no idea baby, but I would think so." He turns to the workmen, "See, I told you." They grumble at him to shut up.

****

Ross brings out a velvet pouch from his pocket and empties the contents into his palm.

"I was going to leave this in the hotel room, I'm glad I never now." He holds out an emerald cut one carat diamond ring, set in platinum, brilliant cut diamonds set around the rectangle centre one sparkle under the bar spot lights.

"Ross it's gorgeous, it's perfect." She kisses him soundly after he places it on her finger. "And it's a perfect fit."

He nods and laughs. "Of course it is. This is my job, remember? Now let's put that pair out of their misery." They both look down to their friends who are continuing to stare at them with hope written all over their faces. The celebrations start with cuddles and back slapping before Sophie and Ross head out for their date and overnight stay.

Hours after leaving The Pub, Sophie and Ross climb into bed for the first time as an engaged couple. Ross pulls her close and kisses her.

"You really said yes, after a botched-up proposal you still said yes."

She laughs, feeling the effects of the alcohol she had imbibed that night, but knew she was speaking the truth. "I did, I absolutely did. I never thought I would, but I did. It was the curls that did it wasn't it?"

Ross laughs. "It sure was." He kisses her again, deepening it until they are lost in each other.

EPILOGUE

Jason lies in his hospital bed, alone. It's been one year since the beating that put him back in hospital. All the swelling and bruising had reduced, yet still he has no feeling in his body.

He feels nothing except a pounding in his head when wakes after one of his nightmares. His dreams are always about him being paralysed from the neck down, only he wakes up and the nightmare continues, which is why he refuses to move from his hospital bed. What's the point?

He had plans to keep his business going, to keep his control in the underworld, to even get his revenge on Sophie, but after being sentenced to four life sentences in prison for the four murders, plus ten years for the drugs, guns, and the protection racket plus the charge of murder of Grotty hanging over his head, he doesn't see a point in trying to keep his business going.

It didn't help that no one from his circle had come to visit him. They have all distanced themselves from him to save their own skin. Anger floods him that he can still feel, but where before he would react, lash out, go to the gym and lift weights until it burned, now he can do nothing but scream. Even that is hard, uncomfortable and even sore due to the feeding tube. He is useless.

Fear slithers in after the anger. Fear that after if he is ever permitted parole from his jail terms he will be extradited back to South Africa where his sad and sorry life really will be ended. No, he thinks, it's best to stay in this hospital bed getting sustenance. In here he is warm and getting all the medical care to make him comfortable and maybe one day even better. He lets out a bitter laugh. Who'd have thought being in a hospital as a quadriplegic would be his best life choice, but there it is.

The burly male nurse from his first visit to hospital enters the room, flexing his muscles and smiling.

"Good morning Jason, time to get you washed and your catheter changed, plus I'll check your feeding tube whilst I'm here. So, how are you feeling today then?" The nurse smiles again then starts to attend to his patient. Jason closes his eyes ignoring the nurse as he tends to him, gritting his teeth with shame until the nurse and his muscles leave.

****

Sophie opens the door to welcome her best friends into her new house—that is, her and Ross' new house. It was a house she never thought they'd get after a few stalled attempts to get the missives signed and the sale finalised, but here they are a proper house. A semi-detached in a nice area of Swinton on the outskirts of Glasgow, bought jointly, another thing she never thought she'd do, that list was still growing.

"Hello! But why are you knocking, just come in." She admonishes them.

Belle grabs her into a hug. "Happy housewarming! We didn't know if we would be interrupting anything." Belle wiggles her eyebrows in her comical 'I'm not implying anything' way.

Dynamic Entry

Sean rolls his eyes at his girlfriend and hugs Sophie. "Next time we'll just come in, but seeing as this is a first, we wanted to be invited." They hand Sophie a bag with wine and beers inside then make their way through to the as-yet undecorated living room.

Ross greets their guests, then takes them on the grand tour of the house as Sophie pours them all drinks and places snacks out. Once everyone is seated and drinks in hand, Belle looks around again and sniffles, wiping her cheeks. Sophie looks at her with worry.

"What's wrong Belle, are you not happy for us?" Worry sets itself in Sophie's stomach as her friend laughs and cries at the same time.

"No, I'm ecstatic for you. I just can't believe it's real. You, Sophie Pearsons, happy, in love, living with the man; god help you Ross, that you're engaged too. I mean I never thought this would happen. I can't believe how far you've come since you came back up from Northumbria and I had to tell you to calm the hell down on all the guys in the office."

Sophie throws crisps at her friend, laughing at the memory. "Excuse me, but I wasn't that bad!" Belle, Sean and Ross all give her pointed looks, "Fine, I was a bit prickly with the male of our species, but not anymore — well, at least not with these two."

Sean speaks. "So this is it for youse then. New house, engagement and —," Ross and Sophie smile at each other.

"And a wedding." Sophie nods at Ross' words. Belle dives at Sophie embracing her in a tear covered hug.

"Oh my god, oh my god, oh my god! That is brilliant. When, have you set a date? Oh a dress, have you thought about dresses? Flowers —" Sean pulls his girlfriend from their pinned down friend as Ross answers the questions and bringing Sophie onto his knee.

"Yes. It's going to be a quiet affair in Cyprus on October the twenty fourth. Do youse two have passports?" Belle and Sean stare at each other then back at their friends nodding. Sophie smiles.

"Will you be my bridesmaid and witness, Belle?"

"And you my best man and witness, Sean?"

"YES!" They both answer at the same time.

The four friends stand and hug, celebrating their next   step   in   life.

Fiona Morgan

ABOUT THE AUTHOR

In addition to Dynamic Entry, Fiona Morgan is the author of thriller romance novels Free and What's Mine. She began writing as a way to fight depression. She enjoys writing about strong female characters who find their inner strength. In her day job, she works as a British Sign Language Facilitator and a Deafblind Guide Communicator, having learned BSL after the birth of her second daughter. She lives in Airdrie, a small town near Glasgow, Scotland, with her husband and two daughters. Her ambition is to be a full-time author, writing and attending writing festivals and book signings

Made in the USA
Middletown, DE
18 August 2019